1930

1930

ALSO BY M. L. GARDNER

The 1929 Series

The Evening Star (A Prequel Novella)

1929: Book One

Elizabeth's Heart: Book Two

1930: Book Three

Drifter: Book Four

Purgatory Cove: Book Five (A Novella)

1931: Book Six

~

Short Stories from 1929

A Homespun Christmas (A Novella)

~

A 1929 Serial

Purling Road: Season One

Purling Road: Season Two

Purling Road: Season Three

~

Other Works

The Unraveling of Us (Contemporary Fiction)

The Rebellion: Eris: Book One (Dystopian Fiction)

Frugal Eating in the New Depression (Cookbook)

BOOK THREE OF THE 1929 SERIES

1930

M. L. GARDNER

Content Editing: RMJ Editing & Manuscript Service, RogenaMitchell.com
Cover Design: Monica Haynes, TheThatchery.com

❀ Created with Vellum

JUNE 29, 1930

"Tell me one more time, Caleb. About the explosions."

With the memorial service for their best friend behind them, Jonathan turned his attention to the explosion. He hadn't yet said so out loud, but he didn't believe it was an accident. However, he couldn't think of anyone in town who would be capable of murder. If someone wanted them out of the way for the sake of easing competition, it would have been easier to sink the boats in the wee hours of the morning than to rig delicate explosives.

"I've told you everything," Caleb said and sighed. "A dozen times now." He lay back on the length of a hay bale and stared at the rafters.

"I know. But I need to hear it again. Something's not right."

Caleb rolled his head and narrowed his glassy eyes. "We just buried a box in place of our best friend. I'd say something's not right today."

Jonathan sat down. He held out his hand for the dark amber bottle, yet another illegal gift of sympathy from an anonymous friend. Caleb handed it to him reluctantly.

He took a gulp, and it burned.

"Not bad for bathtub hooch. Sheriff Vincent again?"

"No, he hasn't caught any runners in the last few days. I think he looks the other way to tell you the truth. No, this was from someone who didn't want their name known."

"Caleb, I need every detail you can give me. I just don't think this was an accident."

"What?"

"Think about it, Caleb. The other two boats wouldn't start. You *had* to take the Ava-Maura. If it were just an explosion, I don't know... I might be able to pass it off as very bad luck." He shook his head. "You said there was a second explosion."

Caleb sat up and took the bottle back from Jonathan.

"Are you sure there isn't anything you forgot?"

"No. I told you everything. Some parts were hazy. With the wind and the rain...it all happened so fast."

They were both quiet for a long time. Intermittent noises from the pigs at the other end of the barn and the goat wandering freely filled the empty space between them.

"It should have been me," Caleb said, breaking the silence.

"Don't say that, Caleb," Jonathan ordered. "You have a wife and twin babies to think about. You've just inherited this farm, and you have your mom to take care of."

"So it's better that it was him? Because he only had a wife and an unborn baby? One he'll never get to see? At least, I got to see mine." He gathered up his bottle and moved deeper into the barn.

Jonathan followed him to the dark corner where he preferred to hide. "No, it's not better. I just don't think you should do this to yourself."

Caleb shrugged, avoiding Jonathan's eyes.

"Hello?" Jonathan Sr. called into the barn from the side door.

"Back here, Dad." Jonathan took a step out into the light.

"Oh, there you are. Your mother and I are going. Everyone is starting to scatter, and we want to see Aryl's family home. Michael and Kathleen are feeling a bit smothered I think with all the well-intended sympathy."

"I'll be along in a few hours."

Jonathan Sr. took a step and hugged his son tightly.

"I'm so sorry, Jon. I know how close you two were." Jonathan ended the hug abruptly as he felt a bit smothered himself.

"Thank you. Say goodbye to Michael and Kathleen for me. I would, but ah—" He turned to Caleb, who sat slumped on a hay bale. "I need to keep an eye on him."

"I'm sure they'll understand. And Jon, if you need to talk—" He looked at Jonathan's face awkwardly. "I'm here."

"Thanks." Jonathan nodded and lumbered back to Caleb, pushing him up from his slumping position.

"Why don't we get you in the house? It's getting dark." He put his hand out and Caleb waved it away.

"I want to stay out here awhile longer. Till everyone's gone," he mumbled.

Jonathan knew he intended to drink himself to sleep here as he had for the last three nights.

"Caleb."

He looked up at Jonathan with a stone face.

"Do you have any idea how relieved Arianna was to see you? She was a wreck waiting to find out...genuinely terrified. If anyone had any question about her love for you, it was put to rest that night. You should be with her and your children."

"Why aren't you with Ava and Jean?" he asked with a slur. "Reveling in the comforts of your family." He stared at Jonathan, almost daring him to answer.

"Because." He blew out a hard breath. "Because I'm out here with you. And...I'll admit it's hard to look at Claire. The last thing I want is for her to see me holding my wife and son...an intact family."

"The doctor sedated her pretty heavily," Arianna said from the doorway. "She won't be coming downstairs tonight."

Jonathan turned and acknowledged with a nod.

"Why don't you let me talk to him," she said quietly. He nodded and rose, brushing bits of hay off his black slacks.

"I'll be inside for a while if you need me," he whispered as he walked by.

· · ·

3

ARIANNA SAT down beside Caleb and reached for the bottle between his knees. He grabbed it away instinctively.

"Calm down. I just want a sip," she said. "I'll give it back." She took a swallow and grimaced.

"Homemade," she said with a growl. He nodded and looked her over as she handed it back to him.

"You're so beautiful."

"You're drunk."

"That may be, but you're still beautiful."

She looked at him. He could tell she wasn't going to let him distract her with compliments. She wasn't that person anymore.

"You can't blame yourself, Caleb."

His smile dropped as he looked away quickly. "I don't."

She put her hand on the neck of the bottle keeping him from lifting it again and stared at him. His eyes flickered between her hand and her stare, and he began to squirm under her piercing blue eyes. He shifted uncomfortably and tried to look anywhere else as her watch relentlessly bore through the denial, the sturdy exterior, and the alcohol. He sighed in frustration as she put the bottle aside and sat on his lap, making it nearly impossible to look away.

"Caleb." She turned his head to look at her. "No one blames you. No one hates you for being the one that lived. You shouldn't either."

"You don't think Claire does? She doesn't look at me. She wishes it was me at the bottom of the ocean."

"She does not," Arianna snapped at him. "Don't you say that."

"It's true," he said and reached for the bottle while trying not to spill Arianna off his lap. "And I can't say as I blame her."

She jerked his face back to look at her. "Just stop it, you hear me? Stop it. I'm not going to let you kill yourself with guilt. It's not your fault."

"What is it then? Dumb luck?" He pulled his chin from her hand and placed the bottle in his lap between them.

"Fate," Arianna said. "It was fate. And you had no control over it."

"I don't believe in fate."

"Oh, really? So you don't believe it was fate that the one weekend

4

Jean stayed with us was the weekend the kitchen caught fire, and he was there to save Samuel's life? There was a reason Jean was here, and there is a reason you were the one to survive."

He leaned his head back on the barn wall and sighed. "What's the reason then?" he asked and closed his eyes when he felt them start to sting.

"I don't know, Caleb," she said in a softer tone. "I don't know why you lived, and I don't know why Jean was there to save our son, but... there's a reason." She put her hands on the sides of his head, tangling her fingers in thick auburn hair, putting her forehead on his. "I'm just so glad you were the one to get out of that car. I was so scared. I don't know what I'd do without you."

His mind flashed through a thousand memories behind his closed eyes and, as if reading his mind, she repeated his words back to him. The same words he'd used during their late night conversation almost a year ago.

Her voice was sincere when she made him a promise. "I'm not going anywhere, and neither are you. I'll help you through this, Caleb. And I'll love you no matter what."

His eyes popped open. "How did you know what I was thinking?"

"What were you thinking?" she asked, sitting back to look at him more clearly.

"Nothing," he said, still staring at her. "Show me."

She looked at him, confused.

"Show me how much you love me, despite how awful I feel."

She smiled, remembering now a time when she had asked the same of him. She removed his loose tie from his neck and moved the bottle from between them, setting it aside. Without taking her eyes from his, she slowly unbuttoned his white dress shirt and he closed his eyes and let her take him far away from the sadness of the day.

~

INSIDE, Jonathan found Maura and Ava sitting in the darkened living

5

room talking quietly. Jean lay curled up on the couch with his head in Ava's lap, her hand on his head.

"How are you, Mr. Jonathan?" Maura asked in a hushed voice.

"I'm very tired," he said and sat on the arm of the couch. "We'd better get him home."

Ava nodded and looked anxiously at Maura. "Where will you be staying tonight?"

"Well, the doctor said Miss Claire would be asleep until morning, and Shannon and Patrick are resting in the next room over if she needs something. I thought I might sleep the night at yer house—if we can come back early, that is. I need to see to it that she eats."

Jonathan nodded. "I'm going to need to talk to Patrick and Caleb early. We can come back just after dawn."

Caleb's mother walked in, weary from the day, and handed a set of keys to Jonathan. "Since your father already left, you can use the truck to get home. We won't need it tonight."

"Thank you, Ethel." He tucked them in his pocket and leaned down to pick up Jean, who stirred and whimpered before settling on Jonathan's shoulder. He cradled him with one arm and held the other out to Ava. "Let's go home."

JONATHAN LAY restless on the couch. He had given his bed spot to Maura, knowing that Ava would want to spend every possible moment with her that she could. He smiled as he heard their whispering as the rest of the house fell silent.

"Tell me about Jean." Maura poked her in the arm. "I've not been able to take proper stock through the tears and the sadness, but it seems to me things are a might bit better than yer last letter led me to believe," she whispered.

"Oh, they were awful." Ava cast her eyes down in the dark. "I was awful," she said quietly.

"I don't think ye have the power to be awful, Miss Ava."

"Oh, but I was. I was cold to Jean and mean to Jon. It was a horrible time. But things are better now."

"T'was quite a shock, I'm sure."

"Oh, you have no idea," she whispered, recalling her first glimpse of Elyse and Jonathan's illegitimate son. "I was devastated. I had just told him about our baby just minutes before."

"But things are better now?"

"They are. He really is a sweet boy. He's so worried about people liking him. That's his biggest worry in this world. I see more of Jonathan in him every day, and I love to sit and watch them together."

"Is that what changed your feelings toward Jean? Watching Mr. Jonathan as he comes to love him?"

"No," Ava answered honestly. "It was Elyse's letter to me."

"Her letter? I'd not known the two of ye were pen pals. How awkward." Maura smirked.

"Oh, no. When she died, there was a trunk of Jean's things delivered. There was a letter to me that Jonathan held back until he thought I might be willing to read it." She paused, recalling the ugly fight that ensued after he'd produced the letter.

"What did she say?" Maura lovingly pried.

"She tried to set things right. She..." Ava hesitated, feeling as if at least some of what Elyse had said in her letters should remain between them. She felt gratitude and a bit of compassion for this woman who had the decency to reach from beyond the grave to give comfort and reassurance.

"She told me things about Jean and some about her life before and after Jonathan. She did reassure me that nothing had happened between her and Jonathan on that last trip to Paris. I don't know how she knew I would be worried or that I would even know about it."

"A woman always knows," Maura interrupted in a whisper.

"I suppose. And it helped. Watching what Jean went through after she died, it reminded me a lot of when my own parents died."

Maura patted her arm, and Ava knew she didn't need to go on.

"I'm truly glad it all worked out." Maura frowned in the dark. "Under this roof, anyhow. I am very worried about Miss Claire. And Mr. Jonathan, for that matter. Such a tragic loss," she said with a sigh.

JONATHAN TRIED to tune out the whispers that echoed down the stairs and concentrated on Caleb's telling and retelling of the afternoon the Ava-Maura went down. He had talked to all the men in the search party that moored their boats near his, and they couldn't recall anything out of the ordinary. They hadn't seen anything...heard anything. His thoughts turned then to the business that was losing money every day they were unable to work.

They would have to repair the two remaining boats as quickly as possible and train Patrick before more money could be made. They would have to work longer and harder than ever before as Jonathan decided that all profits would be split four ways, with a share going to Claire and her baby for as long as they needed it. He knew the others wouldn't object. They would want that if it were their wife.

He thought about Patrick, grateful he had agreed to come and thankful for his vast knowledge and skills. He would fill a void in a physical sense, a working sense. But he would never be able to fill the empty spot that Aryl had left. The one they noticed but didn't speak of when he and Caleb sat on the bench against the back of the house, passing a whiskey bottle back and forth after each day of their fruitless search. And he hoped Patrick wouldn't try. He wanted Patrick to be a friend and a coworker. But he could never replace Aryl.

He changed his train of thought as his eyes misted, going back to the safer subject of boat repairs and business plans.

JUNE 30, 1930

Jonathan, Ava, and Maura arrived at the farm just after seven. Jean ran ahead to join Aislin, who was busy throwing handfuls of feed at the chickens. They knocked on the wooden frame of the screen door, but it went unheard over the commotion inside.

Samuel screamed in Ethel's arms as she tried to soothe him and stir a large pot of oatmeal on the stove. Shannon walked the floor with Roan, who also wailed, upset at Samuel's crying. Arianna sat trapped in the rocking chair with a blanket over her shoulder, nursing Savrene with her eyes squeezed shut. She looked like she was about to scream as well.

Jonathan took in the scene and said a silent prayer that Ava wasn't carrying twins.

"Where's Caleb?" he asked.

Her eyes popped open, and Jonathan took a step back seeing the depth of frustration in them. "When I woke up, he was gone. I think he's in the barn again," she said curtly. She peeked under the blanket and shifted Savrene.

"Ethel!" she barked. "Bring me the other one."

Jonathan backed out of the room slowly and slipped out to the barn.

He found Caleb slumped over on a hay bale with the goat lovingly snuggled up to his leg, head in his lap. He sighed and dropped his head in frustration. The goat grunted and stood, bumping Caleb and knocking an empty bottle out of his hand. Jonathan watched it roll off the hay bale and onto the dirt floor. He nudged Caleb's leg with his toe and called his name, but he didn't stir. Deciding what to do next, he casually walked over to the door of the barn. Seeing the old milk cow Hannah and patting her rump as he passed, he took the wooden bucket from its peg on the wall. He stood patiently at the well, filling it with ice-cold water, and walked the full bucket back to where Caleb slept.

"No. Let me do it," Arianna said from behind. He turned with a slight grin and handed her the bucket. She moved in close and dumped it over his head. He came up coughing and sputtering, seeing Arianna standing with her hand on her hip, glaring at him. She turned without a word and walked back to the house. Caleb saw Jonathan and avoided his eyes.

"I told you I needed to talk to you this morning, Caleb. We have some decisions to make."

"Yeah, I know, I know. Sorry," he mumbled as he found his way to standing.

"Go get cleaned up. Patrick and I will wait for you at the table."

Caleb nodded and stumbled off.

"And hurry up!" Jonathan barked over his shoulder.

CALEB SHOOK off as much as he could and entered the kitchen without speaking to anyone. He made his way up the stairs with a throbbing headache. He stopped briefly in front of Claire's door. She was sitting in the chair, staring out the window as Maura spoon-fed her oatmeal. He sighed heavily and walked on to his own room to change.

"ONE MORE BITE FOR NOW, Miss Claire," Maura insisted. Claire opened her mouth but needed to be reminded to chew and swallow. She sat with a vacant expression. With slumped shoulders, her hands lay limp in her lap.

"Let's go for a walk after breakfast," Maura suggested. "Or maybe for a drive. We could go into town for a bit." After a few more bites of oatmeal and one-sided conversation, Maura stood, looking down at her pitifully. "I'll be right back, dear," she said, patting her hand.

She went downstairs and sat at the kitchen table. "She's lost in her grief, poor thing," Maura said, pouring a cup of coffee. "I didn't want to leave before she was past this." She sighed, rubbing her tired eyes.

"How long can you stay?" Ava asked.

"Two more days at most."

"Who knows when she'll come around," Jonathan said.

"Might need a bit of pushing." Shannon eyed him and Maura. They stared at each other for a moment, and Maura gave a small nod.

"Do you want help then?" Shannon asked. Maura shook her head.

"Not now. I'll call for you if I need you," she said with a heavy sigh, knowing what she must do but not looking forward to it. She stood and looked at everyone. "No matter what ye hear, unless I call for ye, leave us be, Miss Claire and me... Agreed?"

Ava looked concerned, and Shannon took her hand. "It'll be fine," she said.

Jonathan's eyes went around the table before settling on Maura. He trusted her completely, and even though he had no idea what she was planning, he nodded his agreement.

Maura took a large mug of coffee and retreated to Claire's room for what was certain to be a long day.

❧

CALEB WAS CLEANED up and presentable at the dining table with Jonathan and Patrick when Claire let out a sobbing wail from upstairs. He winced as if it caused him physical pain. Ava poked her head inside the back door and looked around and up.

"It's all right," Jonathan told her. She stared at his deep blue eyes for a long moment, and then returned to the yard, joining Arianna and Shannon where they worked in the garden.

A second, ragged sob echoed from the stairwell, and Caleb looked at Jonathan with begging eyes.

"Can we please leave?" he whispered. Jonathan nodded and led the group out to his father's old car. He stopped along the way to hug Ava.

"We're going to go look over the boats and get some work done. We'll talk there. Caleb can't stand to hear Claire." He glanced at the house where Claire could be heard from the open window. She nodded and hugged him a second time. "You're not going out, are you?"

"Not today." He kissed her forehead and waved to Jean before driving away.

~

"I THINK I can have them both fixed in a few days' time," Patrick said, wiping his hands on his pants. "There's a few wires cut on the Ahna-Joy. Shouldn't be too hard a job. The engine on the Lisa-Lynn, well, it looks like there were some hoses ripped off. But I'm confident I can make the repairs if ye get me the parts."

"Thank you, Patrick. That's really good news." He looked closer and saw Patrick touching his stomach. He belched and grimaced, reaching for the railing.

"Are you all right?"

"Just feel queasy. Not used to raw milk, I guess. It'll pass," he said. Jonathan shot Caleb a look of concern.

"Tell me, Patrick, were you sick on the ship when you came to America?" he asked curiously.

"Aye. Had the stomach flu somethin' fierce. They almost didn't want to let me in. I stayed in quarantine on the Island till it passed."

"Did Shannon get the stomach flu as well?" Jonathan asked.

"No. why?"

Jonathan looked at Caleb and almost laughed. He wouldn't—*couldn't* begin to worry if their all too important third man was going to suffer from seasickness. Time would tell, he supposed.

"I'll go get the parts. Patrick, if you could make a list of what you'll need to get the third boat running, please? It will be a much bigger job.

It's barely floating." He nodded toward the neglected old sloop Aryl's uncle had only used for storage the last few years. Patrick jumped down to the pier looking a bit green.

Jonathan walked over to Caleb, who stood staring out at the ocean with a blank expression.

"I need to know now, Caleb. Are you going to be able to go back out there? No one will think less of you if you can't, you know."

"I'll be fine," Caleb said, not taking his eyes off the horizon. "Besides, what choice do I have?"

"What about the farm?"

He answered him with a shrug. "It's not enough. I have to find a way to do both."

"Patrick is here now. He'll be a big help," Jonathan offered. "And I'll do what I can."

Caleb, who looked indifferent, continued to gaze out across the water. When Jonathan started to speak again, he turned, jumped down to the pier, and walked away.

~

"SOMEONE IS HERE to see you, sir."

Victor looked up from his souvenir newspaper, the smile lingering on his face.

"Who is it? I'm rather busy."

"It's the detective, sir."

Victor took one last look at the headline of the small town newspaper.

Captain of the Ava-Maura lost at sea, presumed dead.

He set it aside carefully, walked to the door rumpling his shirt and coat and mussing his hair. Just before rounding the corner, he gave his eyes a hard rub.

"Mr. Drayton. I am sorry to disturb you. I'm afraid one of our officers found something in an alley not too far from here. I'm going to need you to identify some items."

"What items?" Victor's low, distraught voice cracked slightly with a look of apprehension. The detective opened a small box and pulled out Ruth's handbag. His lip quivered, and his eyes narrowed in a perfect theatrical performance of grief. He opened it and pulled out Ruth's wallet.

"This was hers," he said quietly flipping through the contents. "This is all you found?" He looked up at the detective. "Maybe she's all right. Maybe she just dropped this, and she's still...somewhere."

The detective then pulled out of the box a woman's shoe, soaked through with blood.

"We found this next to the handbag," the officer said apologetically.

Victor's show was grand. Shaking with fake tears, leading the detective to believe he was on the verge of a full-blown breakdown.

"This was hers as well?" the officer asked.

Victor nodded as a few more phony tears fell.

"I'm sorry, Mr. Drayton."

He nodded as he cradled the shoe caked with dried blood.

"We'll be in touch if we find anything else." He took the shoe and handbag from Victor, placing them back in the evidence box, and turned to let himself out.

As soon as the door latched, Victor smiled as he straightened his posture, wiped his face, and smoothed his hair.

"Grayson," he called with a jovial tone as he tucked his shirt in. "Get my tails ready. I'll be going out tonight."

~

"SHERIFF, I'm glad I caught you." Jonathan walked into the small office and sat down across the desk from Vincent.

"Jonathan. How can I help you?" He set aside a small stack of papers and looked Jonathan over with a critical eye.

"I need to talk to you about something. The Ava-Maura. What if it wasn't an accident?"

Vincent stared at him, twisting the end of his mustache. "Why would you think it wasn't an accident?"

"I don't know exactly. I've talked to Caleb several times. He's mentioned there was a second explosion. Someone meant to do this."

"I've interviewed Caleb as well, and unfortunately, we can't be sure of either of those things. He admits to everything being very confusing, and his memory is hazy at best. Your other two boats, well, I've closed that investigation. Some of the other fishermen reported seeing some kids playing around the pier around sunset a few days before. Chalked it up to vandalism."

"No." Jonathan shook his head in frustration. "That's not what they told me. It wasn't vandalism. Someone meant to disable the other boats so we'd be forced to take the Ava-Maura."

Vincent leaned back with a look of sympathy. "Jon, I wish I could help. Bring me something solid, and I'll take a look at it, but until then, I'm sorry." He sighed. "I've seen this more times than I care to count. A boat is lost, and folks tend to lose themselves in the details instead of facing the grief."

Jonathan glared at him in frustration. "I'm not avoiding grief. I know this wasn't an accident," he insisted. "I just don't know who...or why."

"Then bring me something to work with, and I'll do everything in my power to help." He leaned under his desk, pulled out a bag, handing it to Jonathan. "Here. Dispose of this properly for me, would you? Took it from a runner last night. I'm ah,"—He looked at the few papers on his desk— "extremely busy." Jonathan didn't need to look in the bag to know what was inside.

"Thanks," he mumbled and looked back up at Vincent, who had resumed his mustache twisting.

"Still trying to grow that thing out?"

"Yep. Been workin' on my quick draw, too." He grinned. Jonathan glanced over at his small bookshelf full of books on the old west and Wild Bill.

"I hear they're looking for lawmen out in Montana."

Vincent laughed. "I'd love that, Jon. Getting Elle to move out there... that's another thing entirely."

Jonathan gave a sympathetic shrug and just as he was at the door, Vincent spoke.

"I mean it, Jon. Bring me something to work with, and I'll look into it."

"Thank you." Jonathan held the bag. "Do something else for me in the meantime. Don't hand off any more charitable gifts to Caleb, all right? He's leaning on it too much."

"Sorry to hear that. Let me know if I can be of any help."

Jonathan nodded his goodbye and tucked the bag away in his father's car before walking down Main Street to the hardware store.

CLAIRE LAY CURLED on her side, her head on Maura's lap, with swollen eyes that refused to produce more tears.

"One of my favorite memories of Mr. Aryl was at my home last Christmas. He was lying just like this on yer lap. He was so tired, and I remember him drifting off to sleep as Tarin sang. He looked so peaceful."

Claire's face crumpled with the memory, but her eyes remained dry.

"Miss Ava told me about the time he got the men to dress up as women for Halloween." Maura laughed lightly. "I only wish I could have seen that."

"He was always doing things to make people laugh," Claire whispered her first words in days.

Maura looked down at her. "What do you remember, love?" she asked.

She sniffled and sighed deeply before slowly recounting memories. One led into another, and she went on for almost twenty minutes. As her memories slowed, she pulled herself upright and leaned against the wrought iron headboard next to Maura, holding her hand. Desperate sadness had replaced the vacancy in her eyes, and her posture was empty, but no longer lost.

Maura, having pushed Claire past her catatonic state of shock by talking of Aryl, saying his name repeatedly, and recounting memories, decided to take it a step further. She looked down, holding Claire's hand in hers as she spoke.

"Do you know what I miss the most about Patrick?"

"Shannon's Patrick?" Claire asked with a scratchy voice.

"No, love. My Patrick. Before Ian. Before I left Ireland."

Claire stared at her as if she were still catatonic.

"Aye, I was married before Ian," Maura volunteered. "We were very young and only married a year before he died. But what I miss the most is his laugh. It would fill a room, and even the saddest sap would have no choice but to smile once Patrick started laughin'. Your Aryl reminded me very much of my Patrick. Not in looks, mind you. They couldn't be more opposite. But in mannerism...very much like Patrick." She trailed off with a faint smile.

"Maura, I had no idea," Claire whispered.

"I know. I never wanted to speak of it. The only one who knows is Ian. And had I not been carrying Patrick's babe when I married him, he'd not of known either. It's something I prefer to tuck away safe, just for me."

"So Scottie is..."

"He is Patrick's." Maura smiled. "All I have left of him. You'd never be able to tell, though. Ian loves him so." She turned to Claire. "I know what you're going through, Miss Claire," she said with conviction. "I've walked this road myself, and I can tell ye that it will get easier...with time. But you've got to start makin' the motions of living and getting ready for the baby. Ye don't have the luxury of a year in mournin' as other widows do."

Claire broke down in tears again with a look of helpless anguish. Maura let the wave of despair pass before pressing on.

"If there is one place you had to choose to feel close to your Aryl, where would it be."

Claire hesitated to speak.

"Where, Miss Claire?" Maura lovingly poked her in the thigh.

"The lighthouse," she whispered.

Maura moved off the bed and stood with her hand held out to Claire. "Let's go then."

· · ·

17

ETHEL WAS SURPRISED to see Claire beside Maura as they came down the stairs into the kitchen, and even more surprised when Maura asked to borrow the farm truck.

Maura drove slowly through town in no particular direction for a half hour. Claire leaned her head on the door frame with closed eyes, letting the afternoon sun warm her face and the wind whip her hair in all directions for a long time. Then she raised her head and began to give Maura directions toward the ocean. She pointed for her to make a right onto a long dirt road that led to a small lot. Maura parked the car, and Claire sat staring at the base of the lighthouse for several moments. It was only slightly easier than looking out toward the open ocean where her love was lost.

Maura quietly exited the car and opened Claire's door, motioning for her to get out. She did so sluggishly and kept her head down, holding Maura's hand tightly as they walked the sandy ruts and jagged rocks.

"I have to leave soon, Miss Claire. But I don't want to do so till I know ye can take care of yerself. My heart hurts for ye, with me having to push ye the way I did. But you've a babe to think of, and I can't have ye starin' out the window, helpless."

Claire sniffled and nodded, eyes still down.

"I met Ian only one month after Patrick had died. I was already startin' to show. He was a friend of me brother who had just moved from Dublin. My brother brought him over for dinner one evening, and in private, told me that Ian had taken a likin' to me. Ye know what I did?" She stopped walking and looked at Claire.

"What?" she whispered.

"I punched him. Then I chased him out of the house with a stick of firewood. I thought he was an ignorant pig to even broach the subject with my Patrick only gone a month."

Claire nodded her agreement.

"Ian, however, saw somethin' in me beyond the grief, and he came by almost every day and tried to talk to me. Most times, I just threw things at him and yelled for him to go away and never come back." She paused, smiling at her memories.

"I didn't count on him being just as stubborn as me, though, and he continued to come. When I got tired of throwin' things at him, he just sat in the front room, quiet and still as a statue, only moving to help himself to tea or bring firewood in from the yard. About two weeks later, he walked through the door as if it were his own and poured a cup of tea. He sat at the table across from me and thanked me for not throwin' anythin' at him. Then he asked me to tell him about Patrick. I fell apart, of course, cryin' and blubberin'. He continued to ask me questions about him and wouldn't let up until I gave him an answer, just like I did to you this morning."

Claire looked at her, suddenly understanding. Last night, it had been impossible to think Aryl's name. But this afternoon, desensitized by saying it repeatedly, she had managed it twice. As if reading her mind, Maura hugged her.

"And one day, you'll say his name, and speak of him to your babe, with no tears. A smile even, for the memories."

Claire couldn't, at the moment, comprehend that idea, but trusted Maura and hoped it were true.

"And feeling him?" She looked out at the ocean that began to glint gold with the setting sun. "Does that go away?"

"That's why I brought you here, Miss Claire. So you could feel him. But yes, to an extent, that feeling does fade," she said.

"It's not just here. I feel him everywhere. I can't accept that he's gone." Her face twisted again with a fresh round of tears.

"It will fade," Maura repeated. Claire didn't know if she wanted it to, although it was most painful, the feeling that he was still close.

THEY WALKED several feet out into the sand and sat next to each other. Maura stayed quiet as Claire went through several emotions, starting the process of settling her grief. The sun had just begun to dip into the horizon, and Maura's stomach growled loudly. She laughed, slightly embarrassed. It reminded her, however, of the next thing she wanted to address with Claire.

She turned and took her hand again when she spoke. Ian had done that when he was talking her through her grief. He was easy to tune out, and she would retreat to the safety of the small, deadened place inside her mind. When he touched her, she was forced to come and stay in the moment. And to hear him.

"I'm going to prepare a schedule for ye, Miss Claire," she announced. "I know a lot of folks will be around, to check on ye, do for ye and spend time, but there will be times when ye will need to look to a piece of paper to tell ye what to do, and when."

"Did Ian do that for you?"

"Yes, love. And it helped. And when yer done here, we're going to go to yer house," Maura said firmly against Claire's look of apprehension. "It'll be all right, love," she reassured.

MAURA WAITED PATIENTLY for Claire to get the courage to walk into her home where surely Aryl's ghost would be the strongest. She did eventually pull at the car door handle and walk slowly to the front door. She hesitated and looked at Maura, puzzled.

"Do you hear that?" she asked.

"Hear what, love?"

"That sound. It sounds like..." She looked all around her feet and scanned the porch. Her eyes went to the bushes that lined the front of the house when she heard it again. She stepped off the porch and began digging through the bushes, getting closer to the soft, desperate noise.

"Oh! Look!" she cried as she reached deep into the bushes and pulled out a very new tabby kitten, soaked to the bone and so thin you could see its skeleton. Maura instinctively shrunk back, having a lifelong, deep aversion to cats. She opened her mouth to tell Claire to throw the foul beast back where she found it when Claire looked up with wide eyes, hugging the tiny kitten to her chest.

"He must be hungry." She cuddled the kitten closer, balancing it carefully while opening her door. Walking through her front room, she didn't take her eyes off the kitten as she wrapped it in a towel.

Maura set aside her hatred of the evil fiend for the moment, noting that this wretched creature and its pathetic appearance had gotten Claire over the threshold of her door without incident.

"Perhaps some warm milk?" Maura suggested. *Or some boiling oil*, she thought to herself. Claire set the bundled kitten on the table and looked through her icebox for milk. What little was there was curdled, and she dumped it down the sink, holding her nose. The kitten watched her intently from the table and let out several soft mews—to each Claire would turn and look at it. She opened a can of tuna, dumped it on a saucer, and found a shallow bowl for water.

"This is about all I have, little fella," she said as she sat down at the table and unwrapped the kitten, leading him to the food. He ate ferociously, hardly pausing to chew.

"I wonder where he came from?" she asked aloud as she stroked its tiny head with one finger.

Maura held back her preferred response of *from hell* and tried to see the creature as something for Claire to care for. Something to provide distraction and companionship in the difficult days that lay ahead.

Claire stopped petting the kitten, her eyes fixed across the table on Aryl's coffee mug, still sitting on the table where he'd left it.

Maura watched and almost saw it, too. The faintest image of Aryl in one of the last places Claire had seen him. Sitting there with one hand on his mug, the other folded in front of him, smiling at Claire. In her vision, she saw him push his long brown curls off his forehead, as he had done a thousand times, his brown eyes crinkling with his laugh. His smile faded and his image dissolved, taking the light and warmth of the room with it.

A few moments later, Maura held her hand out to Claire and walked her through the house, room by room. Maura carried a basket, and Claire pointed to certain items she wanted her to remove. His razor and comb from the bathroom, a few pieces of clothing that lay about the bedroom, but not the ones hanging in the closet. She added a few random items that seem to hurt more than comfort, and Maura carried the basket to the shed in the backyard. Back in the kitchen, she glanced at the mug on the table with eyebrows raised in question.

21

"Leave it," Claire whispered. Maura nodded and turned to the icebox, cleaning it of food that had gone bad. Claire sat down, and the kitten wobbled over to her, mewing. She scooped it up with a smile that didn't touch her eyes.

Maura made a simple dinner of meat and cheese and made Claire promise that every time she went to feed the kitten, she would eat herself. She promised she would and excused herself to change for bed.

～

ONCE INSIDE THE BATHROOM, it hit her again. A massive wave of overwhelming grief. It crushed her to the floor, where she rocked herself, sobbing.

Maura had made up a bed for Claire on the couch when finally emerged. Her face was swollen and reddened. She looked at the couch gratefully. Maura had known she couldn't sleep in her own bed alone. Not yet. Tucking her in childlike, Maura turned on the radio to drown out the deafening silence. She then leaned over on the loveseat across from Claire for some much-needed rest.

JULY 3, 1930

Three days later, Patrick saw Maura safely to the station for the evening train. He had eagerly volunteered, seeing that even Jonathan was too upset at her departure to make the drive. They talked of Ireland on the way to the train station, discovering a few acquaintances they had in common.

As the boarding call was made, Patrick turned to Maura. After a moment's hesitation, he stepped forward and hugged her.

"Yer husband may clobber me for being so forward, Maura, but that's all right. You've been a Godsend, ye have, and I don't see how any of 'em would have made it through this without ye."

"Well, they would have," she said, shrugging off her usefulness as she usually did. "Keep an eye on them, Patrick, aye? And let me know right away if things aren't going as they should."

He nodded. "I promise. Safe journey, Maura," he said and helped her up three steps onto the train. She didn't look back.

Sitting by the window, she turned her body out of view from the older gentleman, who sat wheezing beside her, and cried silently as the train jerked to a start and carried her, every moment further and further, away from her second family.

She had wanted to make it home, safe behind closed doors to cry in Ian's understanding arms, but it bubbled up and over, and there was no stopping it. Dabbing at her eyes, cursing her weakness under her breath, she only grew more upset as the scenery began to change dramatically the further the train steamed from Rockport. Her shoulders shook with each silent sob she tried to hide.

After a good amount of time, she turned forward, wiping red eyes, and took a deep breath, determined to stave off any further crying jags until she reached home. Reaching into her bag with a heavy sigh, she pulled out her flask and shot the old wheezer next to her a formidable stare, silencing him before tilting it up. She drained it in three gulps and stared at the empty flask, disappointed that she hadn't had the fore-thought to fill it before she left. Replacing it in her bag, she sat back and folded her hands over her stomach, trying to think of anything but the sadness of the last few days.

SOMETIME LATER, she was pulled from her safe daydreaming by a very faint clinking noise coming from somewhere behind her. She stood, smoothing her skirts, and squeezed by her seat companion, who sat with his head back, snoring unattractively. She walked down the narrow aisle slowly, looking for the source of the noise. The distinct clinking grew louder toward the back, and her eyes rested on a small girl, roughly nine or ten. She stared out the window absentmindedly with a thick carpetbag tucked half under the seat between her swinging feet. From the carpet bag came the clink.

"Excuse me," Maura said softly as she slipped into the seat next to the girl. "My name is Maura. What's yours?"

The little girl looked hesitant, but then, glancing over Maura and thinking her accent quite funny, she grinned as she pushed her long brown hair from her face.

"Luella," she said shyly.

"Nice to meet you, Luella." Maura smiled and looked around. "Are you traveling alone, child?"

Luella shook her head. "My mother is in the next car back."

"Ah," Maura said. "Well, Luella, I have a bit of a problem you might be able to help me with."

Luella stared up at her, confused. Maura slipped her flask out of her pocket long enough for the girl to get a peek and slipped it back in.

"I'm in need of a refill, dear," she said quietly, glancing at the bag at the girl's feet. Luella stared at her with well-trained blankness.

"Look," Maura said, adjusting in her seat. "I know what's in yer bag. And I fairly know what ye intend to do with it once ye get to where yer goin'. I know it's illegal, and I don't care any about that. What I'd like to do is buy one of those clinking bottles from ye. Name yer price," she said with her hand on her change purse. The little girl looked nervously at the bag and back at Maura. She leaned over, and Maura met her half way.

"*How'd you know?*" she whispered. Maura came up laughing.

"I'm Irish, love. And there are two things I know well. How to swear in three different languages, and the clink of a bottle from a mile away." The little girl giggled and nodded, agreeing to the sale. "Let me grab my bag," Maura said.

She returned a moment later and set her bag close to Luella's bag. The girl swiftly pulled one bottle from her bag and slipped it into Maura's. Maura silently handed her payment. Luella's eyes bulged.

"Thanks, lady!" she whispered loudly. Maura couldn't spare the money, but feeling the sadness would have hurt worse.

Maura smiled. "No, thank you, dear." She patted the girl on the head and stood, bag in hand, looking down on the child with a smile.

"Safe journey, Luella."

Maura made her way to an empty seat at the front, and not bothering to refill the flask, took her whiskey straight from the bottle.

~

IAN WAS at the train station waiting over an hour for Maura to return.

25

He smiled in relief when the deafening train whistle blew, signaling his love was home. He knew he must share her, being the kind of woman that she was to folks, but that didn't mean he had to like it.

She slowly and unsteadily held onto the rail with both hands, navigating her way down the stairs, and stood, swaying numbly, staring ahead, and knowing Ian would find her and take her home.

She had felt him before she saw him, warm strong arms wrapping around her waist and pulling her close. She sighed, and all the tension began to drain from her weary body. He stood back after a moment and grinned down at her.

"Ye smell like a brewery," he chuckled, looking over her splotchy complexion and bloodshot eyes. "I know it was hard on ye," he said quietly. She looked up at him, knowing he knew the extent of her pain and it was enough. With an arm around her waist, half-walking, half-holding her up, he turned her away from the train. "Let's get ye home, and you'll tell me all about it."

"Mr. Drayton, someone is here to see you."

Victor looked up from his desk to his receptionist and past her shoulder to the tall, dark figure behind her.

"Send him in," he said with a wave. A broad smile spread across his face as Bomani stepped into the room, and the receptionist closed the door after him.

"Sit down, please," Victor said politely.

White teeth gleamed against his dark olive skin. "Are you sure it's a good idea to meet so soon?" Bomani asked as he neatly folded one leg over the other. He did little to hide his irritation.

"Well, that depends on how well you hid the body," Victor said casually as he sat back in his chair, bringing his hands together in front of him at the fingertips.

"She won't be found," Bomani said quietly.

"That's good." Victor's black eyes were dancing as his lips curled into a smile. "I am curious, what *did* you do with her?"

Bomani glared at him. "What do you take me for?"

Victor shrugged innocently. "I was just wondering."

Bomani shook his head tightly and leaned forward for emphasis.

"You honestly think I would tell you? That kind of information would give you all you needed to keep me at your call forever."

"You're not as stupid as you look," Victor said flatly. "Fine. Don't give me the gory details." He waved his hand and reached into the side drawer of his desk. He pulled out a few bills and tossed them on the desk between them. "I have another job for you."

"What job?" he asked with a sigh. His eyes were fixed on the cash he desperately needed. His resolve to refuse another job was beginning to weaken.

"I need you to fire some squatters." He pushed a paper across the desk with the address written on it. "Everything is in order. Make it look like some vagrants got careless," he said coldly.

Bomani looked hesitantly at the cash. "Why don't you just have them thrown out and rent to someone who can pay?" Bomani asked with an innocence that startled Victor. Contributing to Victor's silent, gaping mouth was the fact that this hired thug, who was overpaid in his opinion, was talking back to him. Disrespecting and questioning him.

"Bomani." He leaned forward, his temper flaring instantly. "I am a thinker. A businessman. You are a doer. A street man. You set things on fire, you kill people, you steal, and you rough people up. Simple tasks really, and when I pay you to perform one of these tasks, I expect you to do them with no questions asked."

Bomani's eyes narrowed, glaring at the man he hated more every minute he was forced to sit in his presence.

A big worm. Bomani thought to himself. *He reminds me of a big white worm with cold black eyes. Not man enough to be a snake, though he tries. Just a big, slimy, scheming worm.* Bomani swiped the money and the address off the desk with a nod and a huff. He bit his tongue knowing if he said anything at all, he would say too much.

"Now, don't go and pout, Bomani," Victor said patronizingly. "I'll tell you why I'm doing this. I'll give you some very credible and very damning information if you return the favor and tell me where you disposed of Ruth's body."

Bomani shook his head tightly, his dark eyes mirroring every ounce of Victor's stubbornness. "It'll take more than your motives for killing innocent people."

"They aren't innocent. They owe me money," Victor scoffed indignantly. "What else then. What do you want?" He put his hand in his desk drawer with a smile, knowing everybody has a price.

Bomani stood for a moment as debate raged inside his mind. Finally, he held up two fingers. Victor drummed the fingers of his free hand on the desk in contemplation, then reached deep into the drawer pulling out a small stack of bills. He counted out two hundred dollars in twenties and stuffed the remaining cash deep into the drawer.

"Where," he demanded while reluctantly handing over the money.

"Victor Drayton, *you* are a sick man." Bomani shook his head as he stuffed the money into the inside pocket of his coat. "The city dump," he said quietly, looking at the floor.

Victor shot out of his chair with owlish eyes. "Are you mad?" he screamed. "Do you know how many bodies they find at the dump?"

"Relax," Bomani chuckled, hardly phased by Victor's threatening stance. "They find whole bodies at the dump. Not parts. Tiny parts. Birds and bugs will have taken care of her by now."

Victor sat down slowly, struggling to regain composure. "Well, that's good then," he said running one hand over his white blond hair, smoothing it back down to one side. The wild patches of color began to drain from his face, and he nodded. "As long as you're sure."

"Positive. She won't be found," Bomani reassured.

"How did you do it? Kill her, I mean. Strangling? Stabbing? Strangle then stab? There was a lot of blood. Her shoe was caked, but I assumed you didn't shoot her. That would draw too much attention..." He trailed off, eyebrows up, waiting expectantly.

"Even you don't have that kind of money, Victor." He stood and left.

BOMANI WALKED several blocks at a furious pace, slowing as his anger subsided. He stopped in front of a small, unmarked church on a busy street corner. *Protestant? Baptist?* He decided it didn't matter and began walking again. The setting sun beat on his back and small trickles of sweat rolled down his neck into his shirt. He took his light black coat off and folded it over his arm, discreetly transferring his money to his front pants pocket. His mind shifted to his work for the night, and he decided he would do it early. He stopped at a small family run grocery, poorly lit with a heavy musty smell. He gathered basic foods in his arms, stacking and cradling it all until he could hold no more. He paid for the groceries and set out again.

Two blocks away, he pushed open the aging door of a small brick tenement and jogged up two flights of stairs. He rapped hard and put his lips to the seam of the door. "Mama, it's me, open up." He waited several moments, shifting the box of groceries and heard her distinct shuffle, the heavy clinking of three locks, and the door opened a crack.

"Is that my Bo-bo," her old voice squeaked.

"Yes, Mama. It's me."

She opened the door enough to let him in and quickly closed it, flipping the many locks. She turned to hug him, and he had to bend far over to embrace her shrinking frame.

"I brought you groceries," he said, setting the box on the kitchen counter of the two-room apartment. She petted his face briefly and motioned for him to sit at the table.

"I'll make some tea."

The chair creaked loudly as he settled his large frame into it, and he prayed it wouldn't break. He stared intently at the small bunch of dying flowers that sat in a chipped vase. He didn't notice when she sat across from him and silently poured two cups of tea. Reaching out, he plucked a few of the brittle petals and leaves, crumbling them between his fingers in a neat pile. *I'll bring her fresh ones next time.* Fixated on the flowers, he jumped when she spoke.

"What's wrong, Bomani?" she asked, suddenly very lucid and perceptive. He looked from her to the cup of steaming tea and sugared it heavily.

"I'm just tired, Mama." He sighed as he thought of all the things that had begun to tax his soul. He was tired of this life. Of murder and theft. Of fire and destruction. He had grown weary of sitting across expensive mahogany desks from men like Victor Drayton. Men no less evil than himself; they only had the means to pay someone else to dirty their hands. He remembered clearly the night that Victor asked him to kill his wife, Ruth. He never said *kill*, however. *Get rid of my problem*, were the words he used, but the meaning was clear. Of all the horrendous, evil, and despicable tasks that he had been paid to do, never had someone asked him to murder their spouse.

In Victor's parlor behind tightly locked doors, Bomani gave the last lesson in the handling and placement of explosives. Victor looked up, black eyes shining, drunk with anticipation as he fondled the explosives.

He'll be lucky if he doesn't blow himself up before he ever gets to where he's going, Bomani had thought to himself, half-hoping.

"I'll be out of town next week," Victor spoke in a low voice and nodded to the parlor doors. "Why don't you get rid of my little problem for me while I'm gone?" Bomani stared at him, waiting for him to laugh and slap his knee with the joke. But Victor wasn't joking.

"You can tell her that I have sent for her, and you'll take her to the train station. Don't let the staff see you leave, though. You can use whatever method you prefer. I don't care. I just don't want her found. Maybe leave a shoe or something so I can collect the insurance money within a reasonable time."

Bomani had kept a clean face throughout the conversation. Necessarily unreadable. His mind was reeling, and a dozen thoughts raced about and collided with one another. And quite suddenly, he formed a plan. He nodded his head to Victor in agreement and held up five fingers. Victor's eyebrows shot up, and he gawked. "Five hundred?" he squealed. Victor shook his head, walked over to his safe, and paused. "Highway robbery," he mumbled. "I could do it myself for free."

"You'd get caught," Bomani said, hoping Victor knew the truth in this and didn't change his mind to save money. It was two nights later that Bomani led Ruth away from her house, never to return.

The third time she called his name, his mother fairly shouted.

"Bomani!"

He snapped his head up and grinned sheepishly.

"Sorry, Mama," he said, resuming his tea stirring.

"You need rest," she said, laying an aged hand on his. "You talk to your boss. He'll give you time off. You get some rest, all right?" Her smile revealed a few missing teeth and her small eyes all but disappeared under the layers of wrinkles when her cheeks puffed up.

"All right, Mama. I'll talk to him." The way he made his living had always remained hidden from his mother. He led her to believe he was a shipbuilder.

He forced a smile as he listened for almost an hour as she recounted the last two days in detail only fascinating to the elderly. She seemed well enough, and Bomani began to forget, as he often did during these visits that she, in fact, was growing more demented with every passing week. He only heard every other sentence as he weighed his limited options heavily. He jerked back into the now quickly when she looked at him, her eyes shining in an absent way.

"Your father stopped by today. He was so sad he missed you."

He stiffened in his chair, and his smile faded.

"You shouldn't have stayed out with your friends so long, Bo. But don't worry. He'll be back a few days. He said to tell you to be a good boy and study hard." She looked up at him suddenly as if she had forgotten something. "Did you have a good day at school?" She rose without waiting for an answer. "Here. Let me get you some bread and jam," she said as she shuffled to the kitchen.

Bomani closed his eyes and sighed deeply. She had slipped twenty years in the past, and he knew from experience she would stay there for a while. It was her favorite time. His father would visit regularly, and it was like Christmas when he did. He would bring presents and tell stories. His mother would light up in a way that only unconditional love can illuminate a soul and, for those few hours, they were happy. The small, sparse apartment felt complete. But the visits always ended too soon, and his mother would cry while his father apologized with a gentle tone. He could remember the torment in his father's eyes, and Bomani knew he loved them, but he had to go. His mother told him that he must go away on business often. The neighbor told him his father had another family.

〜

JEAN SLOWLY EXTENDED a finger and pushed Jonathan's plate an inch closer to him. Jonathan looked up from his deep thought.

"You should eat, Dadee," he said softly. A faint smile touched Jonathan's lips, and he nodded as he glanced at Ava across the table from him.

"He's right, you know. You've hardly eaten anything today." Ava had begun to worry. He ate little and slept poorly. She didn't expect him to have bounced back to his old self barely two weeks after losing his best friend but hoped for faint signs that the worst was over. He seemed preoccupied much of the time, distant in his sorrow, and only seemed to come to life when he saw the worry on Ava's face, and she feared he would sink back into the dark depression that almost claimed his life after the stock market crash the previous year.

He picked at his food, taking microscopic bites so it would appear that he was eating more than he really was. He had no appetite for reasons beyond the heartache. The heat hung in the kitchen like a damp wool cloak, and there was little relief from it. The house seemed to bake in the early July sun, and by evening, it was nearly unbearable. Jean and Jon, having identical thick, black hair, seemed to suffer worse than Ava did with her shorter, dirty blonde hair, pinned loosely off her neck.

Ava watched the two, noticing damp hair at the temples and a matching ring of sweat around the collars of their thin cotton shirts.

"When's this heat wave going to let up?" Jonathan grumbled, using his napkin to dab his forehead.

"Christmas," Ava said sarcastically. "Why don't we go outside after the sun dips down and dump water on each other?" Jean threw her an excited look and began wiggling in his seat.

"Please, Dadee? Please?"

"All right," Jon said, managing a smile.

〜

JEAN STOOD IN HIS UNDERPANTS, wriggling in anticipation as Jonathan

33

walked up to him with a bucket full of water. He raised it over Jean's head and waited a few seconds, causing Jean to squeal while dancing on tiptoes. Finally, he dumped it, drenching Jean, who started giggling.

"Again! Again!" he yelled.

After dousing each other repeatedly with the cold well water as the sun set, they lay on the grass, the earth still warm from the July sun, and watched the stars as they appeared in the night sky, one by one.

"There's the North Star." Jonathan pointed out to Jean. "And there's the Little Dipper...and the Big Dipper."

"Like you and me," Jean said with a grin.

"Oh, I'm a big dip, am I?" he growled and tickled Jean halfheartedly, still too overheated to exert much energy.

They all lay quiet for several moments as night fell. Ava had lost the cheerful feeling of the giggling water fight as she remembered what Jonathan had told her the day before.

"Are you still going out tomorrow?" she asked quietly. Jean's head craned up and over, turning his attention from the songs of the crickets to Ava's nervous voice.

"Yes. We have to get back to work. And we have to get Patrick trained." He snorted and huffed. "Well, we have to find out if Patrick *can* be trained. He gets mighty queasy just working on the boat when it's moored."

"What will you do if he can't?"

Jean's eyes followed the conversation intently.

"I have no idea." He sighed.

JULY 11, 1930

Claire woke slowly. The antique couch caused stiffness throughout her whole body. She blinked twice before reality filled her consciousness. Sadness was heavy and suffocating, and she longed for those first few seconds before anything registered. The reality, painful memories, and sorrow, none of it existed in that precious time.

The kitten stirred and stretched long with a wide yawn, nearly rolling off her stomach where it preferred to sleep. Claire scooped him up and snuggled him close under her chin.

"I guess I better get you something to eat," she said with a sigh. The last few mornings, she found less and less reason to function. Maura's schedule helped...when she followed it.

She pulled her robe tight and placed the kitten in her pocket. He was perfectly happy to nestle there, occasionally poking his head out to mew.

Opening the icebox, she remembered she was out of milk. And tuna. The evening before she had promised the kitten she would get dressed and go shopping, but she completely lacked the desire or will to do so now that morning had come. She dug around the small cupboard for anything that might be suitable to feed a small, malnourished kitten.

The sound of an engine sputtering to a stop pulled her from her futile searching. She walked to the living room window and pulled the curtains back a peek, hoping it wasn't anyone who wanted to stay long. She saw a long, lanky man with golden blond hair unfold himself out of the front cab of a ramshackle delivery truck. 'Gordon's Dairy' was hand painted on the side of the red box on the back, faded from years of weathering. Walking to the rear, he opened the wooden doors and pulled out a small crate. Claire noticed water dripping from under the truck and small puddles quickly accumulated around the tires. He turned toward the house, and she dropped the curtain. She listened, heard the thud of the crate on the porch, and opened the door, unsure of what she would say. He had turned by then, making his way back down the walk with long strides.

"I didn't order that," Claire blurted out awkwardly. The man turned slowly and removed his hat with a polite smile.

"I'm aware, ma'am." He returned his hat and turned toward his truck.

"I can't pay for this," she called after him. He half turned this time, the polite smile returning.

"I'm aware of that, too, ma'am," he said and pulled out of his back pocket a folded piece of paper. "I've been instructed to send the weekly bill to a..." He scanned the paper for the name. "A Jonathan Garrett."

"Weekly bill?"

"Yes, ma'am. I'm to deliver twice a week to this address and send the bill to him."

Claire stared at him blankly, and when the silence became awkward, he tipped his hat once more. "If you don't mind, ma'am, I need to make all my deliveries before the ice melts."

Claire watched him climb into the truck, coax it to life, and sputter away down the road. She blinked twice as if waking from a confused daze, and looked down at the three quarts of milk in the crate. The kitten poked out from the deep pocket and mewed loudly. She petted the small head before bending to pick up the box.

"I guess breakfast is served."

Besides the milk, Claire unloaded onto the counter a half-pound of cheese, a pound of butter, and a pint of cream. She poured into a saucer a layer of thick cream and set it on the kitchen table. Her new pet clawed and mewed to get out of the pocket, and Claire almost smiled as he ran with an awkward wobble to get to the cream. Sitting down roughly as if exhausted from the day already, she settled back in the wooden chair and watched as the kitten lapped furiously.

"You need a name." She touched its small head with her finger. "What should I call you?" She stared at the kitten as if waiting for an answer and firmly concentrating on it, rather than the empty space across the table.

A light film of moldy scum grew on the surface of the remaining coffee in Aryl's mug. She could see it in her peripheral vision but refused to look at it directly. Instead, she cut a few pieces of cheese and a slice of stale bread, keeping her eyes safely on the kitten. She nibbled on it, not from her own hunger, but from Maura's orders. She glanced at a list tacked on the plaster wall next to the table and sighed. Her life seemed to be defined by lists.

Next to the list was a calendar on which Jonathan had inserted the names of friends designated to visit each day. Usually, they came at lunch and would make dinner before they left.

She felt like an invalid.

"Maybe I won't answer the door today," she said to the kitten. "Maybe we'll just take a nap and let them knock." She sighed, looking back at the list. It was Ava's day. She would be persistent, and if she didn't pretend to be better, she would tell Jonathan, who would tell Maura. She rolled her eyes, frustration being the only other feeling she could identify. She was mostly numb, sometimes sad and now, this new emotional addition was growing frustration at the doting of those who loved her.

The kitten made a small squeak and wobbled toward her, its little belly stretched round from fullness. His little eyes drooped sleepily, and he mewed to be picked up.

"Oh, to heck with them," she said. "Let's go take a nap."

~

AVA'S KNOCKING JERKED Claire from a dreamless sleep, and she looked around in confusion for a moment. She rose reluctantly as Ava called through the door.

"Claire! It's Ava. Open the door, honey."

She stumbled to the door clutching the kitten and not bothering with her robe. She opened the door, squinting into the bright light.

"Ava," she said, rubbing her eyes. "Maybe we could reschedule. I was just lying down."

Ava opened her mouth to protest, but Claire quickly continued. "I've been working a lot around here today, and I'm just tuckered out." She finished with a yawn.

Ava held up a small casserole. "Just let me put this in the icebox then," she said.

Ava stepped into the crypt-like living room. The air was stale and the room in disarray. The kitchen was no better, with dishes piled in the sink, and a larger pile of food dishes stacked on the counter spoilt from the summer heat.

"Claire," Ava turned with her hand on her hip. "You've been working around here?"

Claire dropped her eyes with a pout and snuggled the kitten close under her chin.

"It's like a cave," Ava grumbled as she threw open the heavy living room drapes. Claire turned her head, squinting at the brilliant rays of light that filled the room. Millions of dust particles floated through the streaks of sunshine, and Ava sighed again. She threw open the windows and the front door.

"No!" Claire said with panic. "Kitten will get out!"

"He won't get out, Claire. You never put him down," she said as she set to work tidying the living room. She looked at Claire often with a feeling of mingled sympathy and frustration that only the best of friends can feel.

"I miss him so much," Claire said quietly. She stood at the threshold of the front door, peering out.

"I know you do, Claire," Ava said. "I wish there was something I could do to make it better."

"Maura said it would get better. I'm just waiting for that." She cast her eyes down at the kitten nuzzled close, sleeping against her chest. "She told me to keep busy. Follow the lists and keep busy and one day, it won't hurt so badly." Her voice broke, and Ava's eyes misted.

She walked to Claire, putting her arm around her. Claire cried quietly for Aryl... and Ava for her.

"Look at us," Ava said a moment later, wiping her eyes. "Standing in the doorway crying. We must be quite the sight."

In fact, an older woman out for an afternoon stroll had stopped, gawking at the two of them. Ava waved with a big smile. The woman turned quickly, whispering to her silver-haired companion.

"Let her talk," Ava said, turning Claire around.

They walked into the kitchen, and Ava began chopping a few shriveled, barely usable lemons that Arianna had dropped off a few days before.

"What are you going to name yours?" Claire asked nodding to Ava's small swell below her apron.

"I'm not sure," she said. "Depends on what it is. We hadn't talked about it much."

"How's Jon?"

Ava nodded slowly while mixing sugar into the glass pitcher, planning her words carefully.

"He's all right, I guess." She poured two glasses full. "He's sad. He...he thinks there's something else to this. He tortures himself with trying to find out what."

Claire looked at Aryl's coffee mug across the table. It blurred as tears filled her eyes. "Tell him to stop. There's nothing else. He's gone."

Jonathan came in later than usual, having taken a trip into town to send the secret telegram. He was lighter this evening, his greeting smile to Ava touching his eyes.

"How are you?" he asked as he hugged her.

"Fine," she said, pulling back to look at him. "You?"

"Good," he said as he let her slip out of his arms. She wore her dresses looser around the middle, but he could easily make out the shape of the bulge beneath.

She stood at the sink peeling carrots, stopping intermittently to stretch her neck side to side.

Jonathan put his hands on her shoulders. As he began to massage deeply, she dropped her arms into the sink with a groan.

"That's wonderful," she said.

"I'm sorry I've been so distracted lately. I know I haven't taken very good care of you." He frowned.

"You've done just fine."

"It shouldn't matter," he said, moving one hand to her neck, working out tired muscles. "Nothing should matter but you." His other hand patted her belly. "And him. Or her. I'm going to do better, I promise." He kissed her head and went to sit at the table, his own back aching.

"So Patrick worked out well?"

"Not at all. He's out."

She turned quickly, shocked.

"But your good mood! I thought surely he must have worked out."

Jonathan interrupted her with a headshake and popped a toothpick in his mouth, chewing on it.

"He laid on the deck moaning like he was dying the whole time," he said.

"Well, what are you going to do?" She turned back to the sink and her pile of carrot peelings.

"I've got a few ideas," he said with a hint of excitement in his voice.

"Like what?" she asked worriedly. With only two men working, but the income being split three ways, she worried increasingly about money. They had adapted, made do, and improvised, but she worried about things that couldn't be avoided. Jean would need new shoes this fall. He was outgrowing his and went barefoot most of the summer now, squeezing his feet into them only to leave the house.

She hadn't bought much for the baby and didn't have any fabric to make any clothes. She pushed the thought away, relying on the fact she had a few months left to prepare for the baby, and then remembered Arianna's offer to use the clothes her babies had outgrown. But Jean would need winter clothes, a good coat, and thick pants. She sighed loudly with worry.

"It will be fine, Ava," Jon said patiently. "I promise it will be fine."

She nodded without looking back at him. Jean bounded into the room and jumped onto Jonathan's lap.

"Dadee, you're home," he said with a smile.

"I am. What did you do today?" He took a good look at him. "Looks like you got a haircut." He rubbed Jean's newly shorn head.

"And looks like you need one," Jean teased, pulling a lock of thick black hair over Jonathan's ear.

"Oh, a wise guy, huh?" He tickled Jean briefly. He curled up into a tight ball in Jonathan's lap, giggling. Jean stretched his arms around Jonathan's neck when the wiggly fingers stopped.

"Ava cut it for me," he said softly, glancing at her with a little grin.

41

She turned briefly, returning the smile.

"Did you thank her?" Jonathan whispered.

Jean nodded. "I did." He looked at Ava and, straining his lips to Jonathan's ear. *"She said I didn't need to thank her. She said that's what moms do,"* he whispered.

Jonathan smiled down at him and pulled his head over to rest on his chest. "It is," he said quietly.

"We picked carrots," Jean said returning his voice to normal. "We're going to have them for dinner tonight," he said.

"Jean is quite the helper in the garden," Ava said as she worked. "He picked several baskets of berries. We're having cobbler for dessert."

"Mmm, that sounds good." Jonathan smiled.

"You two go get washed up. Dinner will be ready soon."

Jean slid off Jonathan's lap and tore out of the room.

"No running in the house!" Ava called. His stomps stopped abruptly, replaced by softer footsteps and a giggle.

J onathan stopped at Claire's house, hesitating before he knocked. The house was silent, and he dreaded the overwhelming sense of sadness he felt pulsing from inside.

Finally, he knocked, and several moments later, Claire peered out into the bright light of the late afternoon.

"Jonathan." She left the door open and turned away, returning to the couch with the kitten.

"Claire, I need to talk to you." He sat in the chair facing the couch, noticing the house in complete disarray and sour smells coming from all directions.

She stared at him with no particular expression, and Jonathan couldn't help but feel she was still angry with him for not setting out right away to look for Aryl.

"Patrick isn't going to be able to work on the boats. He has seasickness pretty bad, so Caleb's back on the Lisa-Lynn with me while Patrick is taking care of the chores at the farm and fixing the other boat."

She nodded and pet the kitten.

"I want to ask Maura and Ian to come to Rockport. I think Ian would be the perfect person to—" He couldn't say *to replace Aryl,* so he left it at that. "The reason I'm here is that they are going to need a place to stay. I was wondering if they could live with you until they get settled."

Claire's eyes shifted, and she took a moment to answer. She, like any one of them, would do anything for Maura, but she knew what this would mean. She would be forced to wake up every day and *live*. She couldn't sleep the day away on the couch with the kitten and pretend, as she did too often, that Aryl was just away on an extended trip—that he would be home any moment.

She sighed deeply and nodded, refusing to both deny Maura or to meet Jonathan's eyes.

"I'm going to telegram them today then, and tell them it's settled. And another thing. We've decided to continue to split the money, the same as before. You don't have to worry about anything."

"You can't do that, Jon. Everyone else won't be able to survive."

"Let me worry about that. If we can get Ian here, and we all work together, it'll be tight, but it'll be okay."

She gave another small nod and Jonathan adjusted in his seat.

"How are you, Claire?" he asked quietly. The ticking of the clock filled the room, and it took Jonathan back to the moments just after the crash, just after telling Ava. His whole world ripped away from him, having no idea what he would do next. He shuddered, pushed away the memories, and waited for an answer. Claire shrugged one shoulder limply, keeping her eyes on her kitten.

"What can I do?" he asked. Her face twisted, and a few tears spilled onto her cheeks.

"There's nothing."

"How have you been feeling? With the baby, I mean."

She shrugged again. "All right."

"Has the dairyman been making regular deliveries?"

She had yet to acknowledge the arrangement Jonathan made, nor thank him, though thanks were the last thing Jonathan wanted.

"He has." Tension was thick in the room, and Jonathan thought desperately for something to say.

"Claire, I want to help. If there's anything else I can do—"

"You can leave, Jon."

He recoiled slightly as her words slapped him.

"It's hard to look at you."

He blinked and opened his mouth to say something, closed it, then opened it again.

"Because I didn't go after him," he said quietly.

"Because you were his best friend. I can't look at you without seeing him… thinking of him."

"Claire, you have to know that going after him that night wouldn't have…it wouldn't have changed anything. It would have done nothing but get us killed as well." She didn't deny or acknowledge as he stood up, making for the door, frustrated. He turned slowly to face her.

"I know he saved me, Claire. I know I owe my life to him. And I'm sorry—" He stopped as his voice broke. He blinked hard and started again. "I'm sorry there was nothing I could do. If there were any chance, I wouldn't have hesitated for one second. *Not one second*, Claire, to try to find him." He yanked the door open and paused in the doorway.

"I asked him once if he would take care of Ava if anything ever happened to me. He said yes, and even though he didn't ask me, I promised I would do the same. I intend to make good on that promise, Claire."

She kept her eyes on the kitten, hiding her tears. He stared out the open door for a long moment. "I loved him, too. He was like my brother, Claire. It almost kills me some nights, twenty years of memories flashing through my mind, and there's nothing I can do to stop them. There's not a day goes by that I don't think about him. I miss him, too, you know? We all miss him."

"No one misses him more than me!" she yelled suddenly, tossing the kitten aside on the couch cushion and standing clumsily. "Get out!" She pointed with her command, tears streaming down her face. "I don't feel sorry for you, Jon. You were his friend, but I was his *wife*." She put both hands on her stomach. "No one misses him more than me," she whispered.

He left without another word, closing the door behind him.

Claire fell into a sobbing heap on the couch, and the kitten crawled over her limp legs, nudging her cheek with its wet nose.

45

. . .

JONATHAN DROVE FOR A LONG TIME, wandering aimlessly around Rockport. Coughing in an effort to choke back emotion, his stone-set face only occasionally fractured giving way to a few tears that he angrily wiped away. He swerved and pulled over, beating the steering wheel with his fist several times, growling. With gasping breaths, he gripped it with tightly closed eyes and tried to make sense of it all. Opening his eyes, he saw a flock of birds take to flight from a tree, and his eyes remained fixed on the large billowy white clouds behind them. Not being overly religious, he found himself believing in God now, if only to have someone to be mad at and to ask why. He stared at the sky as it slowly turned orange and pink and repeatedly asked, *Why?*

Hearing no answer, he started the car again and began driving to Caleb's place.

~

CALEB SAT DEEP in the shadows of the barn with his new best friends, goat and bathtub hooch, one at each side. Not even dinner yet and Caleb was numb with a weathered, glassy-eyed expression Jonathan was becoming accustomed to seeing. He didn't acknowledge Jonathan as he lumbered in and sat on the other side of the goat with a heavy sigh. He reached for the bottle, and Caleb gave it up without protest.

"I just came from Claire's," he said after a long drink. Caleb's eyes flickered, and he nodded.

"How is she?" he asked quietly.

"No better, no worse. House stinks like something di— like she hasn't cleaned for a while."

"I'll tell Ahna. Maybe she and Ava can go help her out a little more."

"She's mad at me."

Caleb's head swung around, and he gawked at him.

"She holds me responsible, I think. Because it was my boat and because I didn't go after him, didn't bring him home."

46

Caleb stiffened. "Funny, I figured she hated me because I let him drown."

"You didn't let him drown, Caleb."

Caleb rolled his head back to face forward and studied the shadows the sun cast through the open door of the barn.

"I did let him drown. I should have gotten to him. I should have held onto him, given him something to hold onto till someone got to us. It's my fault he's dead. It's my fault Claire hates you. It's my—"

"Goddammit, Caleb!" Jonathan roared and scrambled to his feet, glaring down at Caleb. "Stop feeling sorry for yourself!"

"*Me* stop feeling sorry for myself! What about you? Coming over here whining because Claire hates you for not going after him. There was no way you could have saved him, but me...I was there! I could have. And should have!"

"I swear to God, I'm gonna knock you senseless if you don't stop this."

"Stop what? Grieving? Are you the only one allowed to grieve, Jon?" Caleb crawled to his feet and stood to face Jonathan with the barn swirling around him. "Are you the only one allowed to feel anything? Me and Claire need to just get it together—is that it? Claire should be cleaning and making dinner for a husband that will never come home, and I should go out with you every day and not remember! Not think about the fact that our best friend is out there somewhere, rotting in the ocean below us!"

Jonathan balled his fist and popped Caleb on the jaw before he saw it coming, sending Caleb sprawling back into the hay. The goat, who had been watching the exchange with interest, shrieked and ran for cover. Caleb shook his head, clearing his vision and rose clumsily to his feet. Jonathan instantly had a look of apology about him as Caleb took two steps toward him.

"Caleb, I'm—"

Caleb returned the punch, his drunken aim slightly off, his fist landing on the side of Jonathan's head. He took a surprised stumble back. Caleb paused to grab his bottle from the hay bale, took a long drink, and started rolling up his sleeves.

"We're not doing this, Caleb," Jonathan said, holding his hands up.

"The hell we're not," Caleb said and lunged at Jonathan. He plowed into him, and the two hit the ground with a thud.

They proceeded to roll around the dirt floor of the barn, cursing and beating each other senseless. They broke after several minutes, lying on their backs, panting and gasping. They both reveled in a long overdue release of tension, and neither had the sense yet to feel guilty that it was at the expense of the other's face.

Jonathan rolled and sat up, brushing off his arms and legs and touching the small trickle of blood from the corner of his mouth. He struggled to stand as Caleb raised a wobbling finger.

"I'm not done with you yet," he slurred.

"Yes, you are." Jonathan sat on a hay bale with his elbows on his knees, hanging his head down.

Caleb joined him a few moments later, taking the bottle from the floor before sitting a safe distance away.

Jonathan stared at him after he caught his breath, a realization dawning on him that he had refused to acknowledge before.

"It was supposed to be me."

"Now, you just chewed me out for feeling sorry for myself. Don't start that."

"No, Caleb. I'm not feeling sorry for myself. I don't know why I didn't realize it before. Both boats were disabled, and you were forced to take the Ava-Maura. I was supposed to be on my own boat. Disabling the other two made it impossible for me not to be. I was supposed to die that day."

Caleb stared at him, eyes swollen.

"I think someone wanted me dead," Jonathan said. "And it didn't matter who was with me."

"Who would want you dead? Everybody loves you. Jonathan the hero. Jonathan the organizer and fearless leader," Caleb slurred with resentment. "I think you're being paranoid."

"No, I'm not, Caleb. It all makes sense now. *It's so obvious,*" he whispered. He left Caleb in the barn with the goat and a fat lip and drove straight to the sheriff's office in town.

JULY 19, 1930

"**M**aura, stop pacing," Ian called out. She shot him an irritated look.

"Well, what am I to do, Ian? We'll not last long with no income, breadlines or no," she huffed.

"I'll go out again tomorrow. I'll find somethin'." He tried to be reassuring, but he knew the reality of it. In the last few weeks, he had found day work only three times, and worked on the auto of a wealthy man for under the table wages, all just enough to keep the roof over their head. The savings to bring Maura's mother was gone, most of it used to send Maura's crotchety old aunt back to Ireland. Maura hesitated using the last of their precious savings, but Ian offered to starve and risk arrest selling homemade hooch just to be rid of the foul woman. The house was peaceful now with just them, Scottie, and Tarin. She worked part time at a small sewing factory and gave every cent to Maura to help the family survive. That was about what they were doing now. Surviving. And dreaming of running away.

"Even if we wanted to, we haven't the money to go back," Ian said.

"I know," Maura stared out the window at lines of dingy laundry strung between her building and the next. "An' I'm not sayin' we should. Though I miss it terribly."

"We'll visit," Ian offered. She glanced at him with a condescending look. "We will. Mark my words, Maura. I will see ye back to Ireland one day. I promise you that." She turned back to the window with a long sigh.

A hard knock caused Maura to sigh again. "That'd be them to cut the electric," she said despondently.

Ian opened the door to a small boy, red-faced from the heat, holding out a folded piece of paper. Ian took it, dug in his pocket for a penny, and gave it to the lad. He opened the telegram, blinked hard, and read it again.

"What will that be? A bill?" Maura asked, sitting roughly on the couch.

"No, not a bill," he said softly. "Maura love, we need to talk." He sat beside her on the couch and took her hands, squeezing them hard.

"I do believe our prayers have been answered," he said, excitement spreading over his face.

TWO DAYS LATER, Ava was dancing around the living room when Jonathan walked in.

"Jon! Jon, look. Look at this telegram. It's from Maura. She says they'll be here the end of the week. What does that mean? Why is she coming? She said they'd have three trunks, why would they have three trunks, Jonathan? Three trunks for a visit?" She shoved the telegram at him, and he read it as she waited impatiently.

He looked up with a grin. "I didn't want to say anything, just in case."

"Just in case of what? What does it mean? Is she coming for another visit?"

"No," he paused, and her smile fell.

"But the telegram said . . ."

"She's moving here. Her and Ian, Tarin and Scottie." Ava's eyes popped wide, and she yelped, throwing her arms around Jonathan's neck. "He's going to be our third man," he croaked over the pressure of her hug.

"Really? You're not joking?"

He laughed, hugging her tightly. "No, I'm not joking," he said. He was overly happy as well. He missed his Maura. He knew that somehow, she would help to ease the sting of Aryl's loss and return them all to a normal life... or as normal as one could hope. He read the telegram over Ava's shoulder again and smiled.

Never been seasick.

Yes, Maura would be there for them all. *Claire especially,* he thought. *Help her heal and prepare for her baby. Her presence would ease his mind and bring happiness to Ava. And maybe, just maybe, she could get through to Caleb.* He closed his eyes with his silent prayer.

THE NEXT DAY, Jonathan and Caleb took the Ahna-Joy out leaving Patrick to do the chores on the farm. Neither of them spoke of the fight in the barn, though they eyed each other's lingering bruises with a modest look of victory and the slightest tinges of guilt.

"Ian's coming," Jonathan said abruptly, breaking the silence. Caleb paused then nodded. His pace picked up a little after that, and even though he and Jonathan didn't speak another word the rest of the day, they worked well together.

It was a good haul. Even with modest prices and splitting the money three ways, at the end of the day, they walked away with enough to get through one more day of life.

JULY 26, 1930

Maura and Ian stepped off the train just after noon the following Saturday. Jonathan used Caleb's Runabout to bring them to Claire's house.

The door was unlocked, and Maura stepped in and looked around, her lips pursed in disapproval. The house was silent and pent up. Acrid smells floated from the kitchen, stale ones from the rest of the house. Taking a brief walk-through as Jonathan and Ian brought in the trunks, Tarin lingered in the doorway with Scottie by her side. Maura walked from living room to bathroom, finding it neglected but empty. She tried one of the bedroom doors, and it swung open. A cold, musty scent met her nose. The second bedroom door, Claire's, was locked, and Maura knocked on it insistently.

"Claire, love, it's Maura. We're here."

After a long silence, the door creaked, and Claire's bloodshot, puffy eye peeked out of the slightest crack.

"I'm glad you made it safely. You can set yourselves up in the spare bedroom and make yourselves at home." The door creaked closed, and Maura put her hand to it.

"Won't you come out and have a cup of tea with us? Mr. Jonathan is here."

Claire's eye flashed. "No, thank you. I have a headache. I'd just like to lie down for a while."

MAURA SET TO WORK, insisting the house be cleaned before she put their things away while Jonathan went to fetch Ava and Jean, who were squirming with excitement and disappointed they couldn't go to the train station.

Maura and Tarin began in the kitchen, and Ian set to work in the yard. He walked around, taking it in. It was a patch of a yard, maybe twenty by twenty feet in the front, double that in the back. A dirt drive that ran the length of the house was neglected, potholed, and overgrown with weeds. He mentally roped off a section of the backyard for a garden and smiled, thinking how happy it would make Maura to have it. Short decorative bushes and flowers lined the house; the bushes dehydrated to death and the flowers wilted. The little white house could use a washing, and a few of the shingles on the roof needed to be tacked. A home didn't fall into this much disrepair in the short amount of time since Aryl had passed, and it warned him of the time consuming hard work ahead of him on the boats. *Best get to it then.* He knew it wasn't his, but he reveled in having something to care for. He dropped to his knees along the front of the house, pulling handfuls of weeds and small bushes that had little chance of reviving.

JONATHAN RETURNED WITH AVA, Jean, and all of their cleaning supplies. Ava jumped out of the truck and burst through the door, throwing her arms around Maura.

"You're really here!" She hugged her, swaying side to side, refusing to let go.

"Aye, I'm here. And just in time by the looks of it."

Ava grinned so widely her cheeks hurt, and finally, Maura wrenched her arms from her neck and made her way to Jonathan. He stood in the doorway, watching with relief what was visible in his stature.

She leaned close and whispered in his ear. "I'll be needin' to talk to you later, just the two of us. Make some time and have a drink ready, aye?"

Ava, Maura, and Tarin began cleaning the kitchen, listening to Maura's animated recounting of the last few weeks. Claire sat on the floor inside her room, leaning her head on the door. She listened to the commotion below but was unable to come out and face anyone.

Jonathan stepped into the kitchen, interrupting the cleaning party and feminine chatter.

"Ian and I are going to get Caleb and Arianna. We'll be back shortly." He spotted Ava and frowned. She was on her hands and knees in the corner of the kitchen working on the stained tile where the garbage can once sat. He walked over and reached for her hand, pulling her up.

"You're in no condition to be working this hard," he scowled.

"Jon, I'm fine, I—"

"Maura, is there something else that Ava can do?" Jonathan asked, ignoring Ava's protest. Maura put Ava to wiping down cupboards and Jonathan kissed her cheek. "I'll be back shortly."

When Jonathan returned, Aislin joined Scottie and Jean in the backyard while Arianna toted the babies inside to an eruption of ohs and ahs, a happier reunion than the last. Caleb stayed outside making small talk with Ian. He lifted his goat from the back of the Runabout and led him by his rope to a stake Jonathan had driven in the middle of the front yard. He began munching away at the overgrown yard, and Jonathan smiled. It had been his idea to bring the goat, initially to get Caleb to leave the barn, and also to help Ian get control of the wildly neglected yard.

Ian nodded his approval with a smile. Caleb frowned, avoiding looking directly at the house. He shoved his hands in his pockets and scuffed the ground with his shoe. He was the physical picture of uncomfortable and awkward.

"You don't have to go inside," Jonathan said in a low voice while handing him a pair of pruning shears. "We'll just stay out here, all right? There's plenty of work to do."

Caleb nodded in appreciation and found a small crabapple tree at the edge of the front yard to work on. He glanced along the side yard, into the back, and could see the three children squatting down looking intently at something. His breath caught, and he stared for a moment at the three heads bunched together, the dark curly hair of Aislin, Scotties dark auburn hair, closely shorn, and Jean's jet-black locks. He took a ragged sigh and pushed aside childhood memories that he wasn't prepared to deal with.

THE CLATTER, chatter, and laughter coming from the house made the men smile from time to time. They were so concentrated from the women's voices echoing from the house, they didn't hear the clunky dairy truck until it was in the driveway, sputtering to a stop.

Jonathan waved and rose from the dirt, walking over to meet him.

"Gordon, how are you?"

"Doing all right. And you?"

"Fair enough. There's someone I want you to meet." He nodded toward the house, and Gordon followed with a small crate of dairy goods in hand.

Inside the house, the smell of cleanser was slowly winning over the sour, and Gordon looked around in slight confusion at the commotion. Jonathan pulled him along into the kitchen.

"Maura, there's someone I like you to meet."

Maura pulled her head from inside the oven and wiped her hands.

"This is Gordon. He's the local dairy, and he'll be making deliveries here regularly." He turned to Gordon before Maura could make a polite acquaintance. "I'm going to need you to double that order. Maura and her family will be living here with Claire for a time."

He nodded happily and held his hand out. "Very nice to meet you, Maura."

She had smiled automatically, but then as she did a quick appraisal of him, smiled wider as she stood. "Mr. Gordon. How very nice to meet you."

"Oh, no. Just Gordon is fine."

"Trust me." Jonathan leaned in close to Gordon's ear. "Let her call you whatever she wants." He grinned.

"This is my niece, Tarin." She stepped out of the way to reveal Tarin standing by the sink, eyes glazed over, and her mouth hanging half slack. She began a sentence, but it cut off unintelligibly as she looked down embarrassed.

"Very nice to meet you, Tarin. What a lovely name."

She smiled, her cheeks flushed red and looked up just in time to catch his eyes move swiftly up and down in his own appraisal. Suddenly lightheaded and mute, she held the counter for a moment until the dizziness passed, with a nervous, unsteady grin.

AT FIVE O'CLOCK, Jonathan announced he would be heading over to fetch Shannon and Patrick, who had been left at the farm to finish the chores for the day and prepare dinner for the gathering. He was glad this was the last trip he'd have to make.

Jonathan drove slowly back to the farm. He enjoyed any gathering that Maura was at the helm, but he was still getting used to the different feel of it. It was full, but not complete. No one had said Aryl's name, but he was very much there. The ghost in the room that no one would speak of.

SHANNON LOADED several loaves of bread in the back of the truck along with a massive pot of stew and a large cake with the thinnest layer of boiled frosting on top. Patrick looked tired from his day of work but brought a few tools to help with the repairs and a few extra chairs from the barn to accommodate everyone at Claire's house. He climbed in the truck with Shannon squeezed in the middle of the cab.

"The cow's stopped givin'," he said with a hint of worry and frustration.

Jonathan glanced at him sidelong and raised an eyebrow.

"You mean milk?"

"No. Well-meanin' advice." Patrick shot him a tired look. "Aye, milk."

"I don't know anything about cows, Pat."

"Well, you should know enough that all they give is milk."

"What's to be done about it? Can we breed her again? Or is it time for old Hannah to go to that big pasture in the sky?"

"I have to talk to Caleb. See what he wants to have done about it." He scrubbed his face with a tired hand and sighed. "So Maura and Ian are settling in then?"

"Well, I don't know about settling. They're both working. Got the whole lot of us working, too."

Patrick laughed. "Sounds like them. Give me a fat piece of bread and a cup of coffee when I get there, and I'll be ready to put in another day's work."

IT WAS a loud gathering with standing room only spilling from the kitchen into the living room. Maura passed out mugs of stew and slices of bread, shouting out the next round of cleaning and repairs to be done before everyone called it a night.

Children ran underfoot from room to room with shrieks and giggles, and Ava smiled leaning against the wall next to Jonathan, wrapping her arms around herself, just above the small swell of her stomach.

At Maura's unarguable insistence, Gordon had returned after finishing his deliveries to eat with them. He stood in the corner, apart from the commotion of strangers. She handed him food with a cunning smile and from the corner of his eye, saw Ian's hard glare of warning.

Catching Tarin relatively alone, Maura passed her own word of warning.

"I've seen how ye been lookin' at Mr. Gordon."

"Auntie, I—"

"The only meat you need to be eyein' is the meat in yer bowl, young lady. Yer only seventeen and besides—" She cast a glance back at Gordon. "I've got plans for the man."

"What plans could you have for him, Auntie? Yer married!"

"Not for me, ye silly girl. For Claire." Maura's smile dropped when the room fell silent, reduced to a cough or throat clearing here and there, and the clink of silverware on dishes.

Claire stood at the bottom of the stairs.

"Don't stop on my account."

She had showered, dressed, and even styled her hair, and was wearing a light, sleeveless summer dress. Only the darkness under her eyes and a few wrinkles from lingering puffiness gave away the hardships of the last month.

The room reluctantly came back to life and Maura's eyes went from her to Caleb, who stayed by the open front door, staring at the floor, picking at his food.

It was Jonathan who noticed Gordon, frozen in place, looking rather love-struck, staring at Claire. Seeing her not in a state of sour dishevelment for the first time had a tremendous effect on him, and it showed. Jonathan glanced at Maura, nodded discreetly to Gordon, and raised his eyebrows in question. Maura made lightning fast glances all around and smiled, nodding back to Jonathan with a wink.

LATER THAT EVENING, as Maura readied for bed, she could feel Ian's stare on her back.

"Do ye have something on yer mind, Ian?" she asked, not attempting to hide her smirk.

"Well, since you asked." He sat on the bed and bent to aggressively unlace his boots. "I'm not entirely likin' the way ye were cozying up to yer new friend, Gordon."

"Honestly, Ian. I was just tryin' to make the man feel welcome."

"Well, I saw the way he was lookin' at ye in response to that welcome."

Maura laughed, and Ian's face flashed with anger.

"Ian, calm yerself. I have an idea for Mr. Gordon, is all. Maybe at first he thought I was being overly nice for other reasons, but he knows I'm married."

"Aye, he does. I was sure to let him know when you were in the kitchen."

"Ian!" She whirled around. "What did you say to him? You'd better not ha' scared him off or so help me God!"

"Calm yerself, Maura," he mocked. "I introduced myself as yer husband, is all."

She glared at him, waiting for the rest of the story. He sighed and pulled off his socks with a sheepish grin. "An' I may have said a few words to the effect of you bein' the love of my life and being willing to kill a man—"

"Ian!"

"I didn't word it *just* like that. I think it was more my grip when I shook his hand that said what I needed to say."

Maura closed her eyes and breathed through her nose to the count of ten, trying to ease her temper before she gave in to the urge of throwing Ian through the window.

"Ian. Mr. Gordon is a widower. Did ye know that? And did ye also happen to catch the way he stared at Claire when she came downstairs? Cupid's arrow didn't just strike him—it beat him over the head much like I would like to do to you right now. Now if you've gone and scared the man off when I've got plans for him to see Miss Claire,"—she stopped and leveled her voice—"then I'm going to have to pummel you even more senseless than you already are."

His look of amusement at her rant faded slightly, and he crossed the room to her, putting his hands on her shoulders.

"Maura, ye know I'm just a jealous fool. I know you've no interest in wee Gordon, and I know ye mean well. Ye see a widow and a widower in the same room and want to play matchmaker, see everyone happy again, but don't ye think it's a bit too soon?"

"I'm just laying the groundwork. We're having Mr. Gordon over for dinner next week. I'll just get him and Miss Claire talking."

He laughed lightly and took her hands in his, turning them over, examining them.

"What?"

He ran his fingers over hers, reddened from strong lye soap and bleach, scraped in places, burned in one, and brought them up to his mouth, kissing them each in turn.

"Ye started workin' the minute ye stepped off the train."

She wouldn't admit it, but she was tired to the core.

"Come to bed and let me rub yer back."

"I wanted to make a few lists first, and I need to check on Miss Claire."

"Maura. Yer notes and yer broken people and yer never-ending line of loving charities will all be there in the morning. Come to bed."

She peeled off her gown and lay on her stomach with Ian settling in beside her. He lifted the covers to steal a peek at her backside in the moonlight, and she swatted at him. He laughed and lay on his side, holding his head up with one hand and running a strong hand over her back with the other. He massaged her shoulders one at a time and then made a kneading motion with his knuckles down her spine. He heard her sigh and relax, sinking deeper into the mattress, her muscles gone slack.

"How's that then?" he whispered as he worked.

"Wonderful," she said, her voice muffled in the pillow.

"I just can't help but wonder if it might be too soon. For Claire, I mean."

"It wasn't too soon fer me. In fact, it worked out quite nicely." She turned her head towards him.

"She's not you," he said softly.

"She's strong enough," Maura answered. "She's got loving support from all sides...it'll work out fine."

"And what if it's too soon for Gordon? Does he even know she's expecting? Love struck as he might be, it might change things, you know."

"It didn't change anything for you," she said sleepily.

"He isn't me."

"We'll just do our best, all right, Ian?"

"We? So now yer pullin' me into yer little matchmaking business, are ye?"

She gave a tired, heavy giggle. "Ye know you'll help me because ye love me," she said with certainty.

He laughed, knowing he was caught. "Aye, that I do, Maura. That I do."

He ran his hand over her skin in such a relaxing way she began to drift off to sleep. Before she could, he put his lips to the back of her neck.

"Do you know yet?" he asked in a whisper before planting a small, neat row of pecks over her ear and down her cheek.

"No. If I did, I would have told you."

"Should you go to a doctor? He might could tell you for certain."

"Why would I pay a doctor to tell me what I can find out for free if I just wait a while longer? Besides, I'm only two weeks late."

"Would you be happy?" he asked. She was quiet, thinking deeply before answering.

"I think I would."

"You think?"

"It's a lot to consider, another babe is. Would you be happy?"

He couldn't help but smile and didn't hesitate. "I would."

Jonathan picked Maura up just after lunch, a smuggled bottle of whiskey under the seat. They drove several miles north, ending up on a sandy pullout near the ocean. He walked around to open her door and, with whisky bottle in hand, led the way down to a massive chunk of driftwood. It might look something like a date to someone who didn't know any better.

"Ava wasn't happy that I was coming to see you alone today," he said with a laugh. The sound was drowned out by a large flock of seagulls, squawking loudly overhead. It was hot, and she kicked off her shoes, digging her feet in the sand until she found the cool layer underneath.

Jonathan didn't waste any time getting to the point. "I'm worried about Caleb," he said. "He drinks every day. All day. When he isn't working on the boat with me, he spends his time in the barn. Drinking. With the goat. Patrick takes care of most of the farm business, and Arianna and Shannon have their hands full with the babies and the house. Caleb is just…lost."

"I was worried about that," she said and held her hand out for the bottle parked at Jonathan's side. "That he would blame himself for Aryl's death and hate himself for surviving."

"I don't understand that. I would be so grateful to come home to Ava, so happy to be alive—"

"You were not there, Mr. Jonathan. You have no idea how you would feel had you been through all that."

He lowered his head at her reprimand.

"You and Caleb are very different people. Opposite ends of the spectrum, really. And I have worried for some time that your friendship would suffer without Aryl there to balance the two of you out and help you meet in the middle."

A small pain shot through Jonathan's heart. *Aryl was always in the middle.*

"That doesn't mean that you can't help him through this."

"I have no idea how, Maura. I was hoping you could try to..."

"Aye, I know what ye hoped for. And I'll do my best. But he still needs a man friend to confide in."

JULY 30, 1930

Just before dinner, Vincent knocked on the door. Jonathan Sr. answered it and welcomed him in.

"I'm here to see Jon Jr.," he said as he stepped inside and removed his hat. Jonathan came into the living room followed closely by Ava.

"Is everything all right?" she asked nervously.

"Everything is fine, ma'am." He turned to Jonathan. "I looked into that lead like you asked me to."

Jonathan's eyes flickered to Ava, and he motioned for Vincent to move out onto the porch to talk. Closing the door behind him, they walked a few paces out into the yard.

"What did you find out?"

"Well, I can tell you that Victor Drayton wasn't here in Rockport the day of the explosion."

"How do you know?"

"Well, I spoke to the police department in New York City. They were very familiar with Mr. Drayton and most helpful in providing what information they could. Apparently, they are able to confirm his whereabouts because right about the same time that your boat exploded, his wife was abducted and murdered."

Jonathan's eyes were wide with shock. "Ruth is dead?" he asked.

"The police are calling it a homicide. They never found a body, but they found enough to declare her dead."

Jonathan grimaced. "Where was Victor when Ruth was killed?"

"Mr. Drayton has produced a stamped ticket to and from Florida and a ticket agent who identified him as boarding the train the day before both events."

"You don't think it's strange that he was out of town when Ruth was killed, and my boat blew up?"

"Well, actually I do. And so do the police in New York. But there isn't much anyone can do with an alibi as solid as a punched ticket and a witness."

"A witness on this end or in Florida?"

"In New York."

"How easy would it be to get on the train, walk a few cars back, and get off again?"

"Well, apparently the police in New York think this stinks to high heaven. They tend to think that if Mr. Drayton didn't kill his wife himself, then he may have hired someone to do it for him—which will be even harder to prove. But they were interested to hear from me. The detective did some looking into the train schedules and got back with me about an hour ago. I wasn't going to say anything, but..."

Jonathan shifted his weight impatiently. "But what?"

"There was another train leaving within ten minutes of Mr. Drayton's. Bound for Boston."

"Do you think he was on that train instead?"

"Impossible to say. They have him under surveillance, though. They smell foul play, at least with his wife." Vincent shrugged.

"I appreciate you looking into it," Jonathan said.

"I'm sorry this probably doesn't help ease your mind."

"Actually, in a way, it does. At least I know he's being watched."

Feeling watched himself, he turned to see Ava in the window, arms crossed tightly.

"Well, I better get back in there and explain," he said, running his hand through his hair with a sigh. "Thank you for looking into this. I know you're busy."

"Well, actually, I've got a bit of help now. The new deputy just arrived. It was somewhat of a surprise, but after that big bust last month—"

"What big bust? I knew about the string of robberies, but you caught that guy, right?"

"Well, no. But they stopped kind of suddenly none the less. But it was pokin' around trying to get to the bottom of those robberies that lead me to a good-sized operation right here in Rockport. Right under our noses."

"Runners?"

"Not just bathtub gin, Jon. Opiates. Coming in by rail and boat. So, to keep that sort of thing at bay, they sent me another deputy."

"They sent him? That's not the usual procedure, is it?"

"No, but I guess this is extenuating circumstances. Gotta keep this sort of thing under control. In any case, his name is Marvin. If you see him around, be sure and give him a welcome, will you?"

"Sure thing. Thanks, Vincent."

He lumbered back into the house absorbing the news of Ruth's death and not looking forward to filling Ava in on his suspicions.

Her eyes were pinned on him, and he nodded toward the couch. "Sit. I'll explain everything. Mom, Dad, you better come in here, too."

His parents, Margaret and Jonathan Sr., walked in quietly and sat across from them.

"You are all aware that I haven't been convinced that what happened to Aryl was an accident. I asked the sheriff to look into a possible lead, and that's what he was here to talk to me about."

"What lead, son?" Jonathan Sr. asked.

He took Ava's hand and held it on his lap. "I think that this might have been personal. I think it was supposed to be me, and—"

Ava gasped with wide eyes. He decided to stop beating around the bush.

"I asked Sheriff Vincent to find out what he could about Victor. I think he might have had something to do with this."

66

Ava froze, staring at him. "Did he?" she whispered.

"We're not sure. He's provided proof he was somewhere else when it happened and when Ruth..."

"When Ruth what?" Ava asked. Jonathan didn't realize until that moment that news of her death had had any effect on him, and he felt twinges of grief. He had known her, after all. They had spent a good amount together and even though he didn't love her, he had cared for her.

"Ruth is dead," he said quietly.

"How?"

He shrugged one shoulder lightly. "They aren't sure. She disappeared, and they found some of her things. The police in New York are treating it as a homicide."

"Do they suspect Victor?"

He nodded.

"Do they think he had anything to do with the explosions on the boat?"

"They don't know. If he had any involvement, he covered his tracks well." He looked over at Ava, who had held herself together much better than Jonathan had expected.

"He's being watched. He won't be able to get anywhere near here without the police knowing about it."

She sat holding on to his hand, looking unconvinced.

Jonathan Sr. nodded for Jonathan to follow him upstairs.

Walking to his bedroom closet, he dug around in the back and pulled out a wooden box. He set it on the bed and opened the lid, revealing two handguns. He picked one up and made sure it was loaded before handing it to Jonathan.

"I know this Victor character is being watched, but I'd feel better if these were kept handy."

Jonathan took a step back. "I don't know, Dad. With Jean around and all, I don't know if that's a good idea."

"Jonathan." His father took a few steps toward him and spoke low in his ear. "If this guy wanted you dead, as soon as he finds out that you aren't, he'll be back." Mirroring dark blue eyes stared insistently, and he pressed the gun into Jonathan's hand. He took it reluctantly with a heavy sigh.

"Teach Jean," he said and left the room.

Jonathan slipped the gun under the mattress before returning downstairs.

JULY 31, 1930

Maura fussed about the kitchen, mumbling to herself and occasionally yelling for Ian to fetch something.

"You'd think it was Christmas dinner the way yer runnin' about, Maura."

"Hush up, Ian and grab me that platter out the cabinet. It's on the top shelf."

He held it out to her, then jerked it back with raised eyebrows and puckered lips. Maura was less than amused. She gave him a quick peck and yanked the platter from him with a hard glare. The platter slipped from her hand as she spun around and landed on the floor with a great crash, sending shards of white ceramic in all directions.

Maura sucked in her breath and let it out with a long stream of language that made Ian shrink back out of the kitchen. When she finished, he poked his head in delicately.

"Can I help ye clean it up?"

She opened her eyes, holding the broom out to him and turned back to the stove.

"What's the big occasion?" Claire asked as she gingerly stepped over bits of the broken platter.

"We're havin' Gordon over fer dinner," Maura said simply.

Claire glanced over the homemade bread, colorful salad, and savory casserole that used precious rationed meat.

"And why is that a big deal?"

"It just is, my dear. Now go clean up and put on a nice dress. An' it wouldn't hurt to put a curl to yer hair and find some lipstick."

Claire raised her eyebrows at Maura. "And just *why* would I need to do that on a plain old boring Thursday night?" she asked.

"Because Mr. Gordon is a clean, educated man. You don't want him getting the wrong idea of us, now do you?"

"What in heaven's name does his being clean and educated have to do with my appearance?" Claire asked.

Maura spun around exasperated and pointed toward the stairs.

"Go!" she yelled. Claire huffed at her and narrowed her eyes, but went, slamming the bathroom door behind her.

"Stubborn girl," Maura commented under her breath.

"Are ye sure ye aren't pushin' things just a little too quickly, Maura?"

"Don't start wi' me, Ian. Help me find another platter."

~

WHEN GORDON RANG the doorbell at six o'clock, Maura scrubbed her face of irritation and put on a smile. Ian shook his hand very tightly and stepped a little too close in order to make one final statement with his eyes regarding his Maura.

Gordon had nodded a masculine understanding before he glanced around the room, Ian assumed, looking for Claire.

"She'll be down shortly," he said with a slight grin. Maura pulled him past Ian by the elbow, pushing a cold glass of lemonade in his hands and organizing him in a chair in the living room.

"Claire, we have company!" Maura yelled in the direction of the stairs. A stomp and a door slam were her answer. Maura excused herself to Gordon and headed up the stairs.

Ian sat across from Gordon and grappled uncomfortably for conversation. They talked of mundane and polite things for a few minutes before Gordon spoke freely.

"I've no interest in Maura," he said suddenly. "In case that's what you were thinking."

Ian smiled and sat back. He didn't truly see Gordon as a threat upon his territory. He was mild mannered and gentle, calm and lighthearted.

"It had crossed my mind. But that's good to know. Sometimes folks —men folks, in particular, tend to take her kindness the wrong way."

Gordon relaxed a little and eased back into the seat. "Don't take *this* the wrong way, but I don't think that I could handle one like her," he said with a smile.

"She's one to be reckoned with, that's fer sure. But she always keeps things interesting."

"I have to tell you, Ian, I debated even coming tonight, but curiosity got the best of me." Ian's eyes questioned as Gordon smiled knowingly. "Do you want to tell me what plans the woman has for me?"

Ian returned his amused smile. "I guess I should give ye fair warning. Though she'd kill me if she knew."

"I won't say a word," Gordon promised.

"Well, I think she has it in mind to play matchmaker."

"Ah. I see. And who does she want to match me with?" he asked with an entertained grin.

"Claire."

Gordon's face straightened, and he adjusted in his seat. Ian sensed his sudden apprehension.

"Who else?" he asked.

"Well, honestly, I thought maybe she had me in mind for her niece, Tarin. And she's a nice girl and all—don't get me wrong. She's beautiful. But, well…she's a bit young."

"So does that make it better or worse then? Knowing it's Claire she's trying to match you with and not Tarin."

"I'm not sure." He sat stiff, more nervous than uncomfortable.

"There are some things you should know, Gordon, just so it's fair on ye because Maura won't say a word about it up front." He nodded for Ian to continue. "Claire is a widow. Her husband died at sea not even two months ago."

Gordon's eyes flashed up to Ian. "I knew she was a widow, even

71

before Jonathan Garrett told me when he set up her deliveries. I'd heard. She can't be anywhere near ready!"

"An' she wi' child."

Gordon froze, staring at the floor in front of him.

"Maura tells me you're a widower."

Gordon nodded. "Yes, but it's been two years since..."

"I think Maura sees kindred spirits and an understanding of the loss. She sees ye bein' good for each other in that way."

"Well, there's that."

"But the child changes things, doesn't it?"

Gordon took a long time to answer. Finally, he shrugged. "Not for reasons you think," he said and looked toward the base of the stairs where he had last seen Claire.

CLAIRE WAS defensive and quiet at dinner, having been nearly physically dragged downstairs. Maura had placed her and Gordon beside each other with Tarin and Scottie across from them while she and Ian sat at the heads of the table.

Tarin glanced at Gordon frequently with admiration, looking away flushed and embarrassed when his eyes met hers. Maura kicked her under the table and gave her a growling scowl.

Maura had to work harder on keeping the conversation going than she had worked on dinner, and her exasperation was becoming obvious.

"So, Gordon, tell us about yer milk business," Ian said. A grateful Maura smiled at him.

"Well, it's a family business. It was my grandfather's and then my father's before it was passed on to me. Small operation, but it pays the bills."

"Do ye run it alone then?"

"My wife helped before she..." He stopped and cleared his throat, noticing Claire sitting very still, staring at her food. "Before she died."

Claire shifted uncomfortably before shooting a look of hatred at Maura.

"She died in childbirth. Two years ago," he offered.

"I'm so sorry for yer loss," Maura said. "Ye don't have to talk about it if ye don't want to."

"No, it's fine. It was hard at first, but...well, time heals. Every day gets just a bit easier," he said and glanced at Claire, who kept her head down and remained silent. "Took a few months to really start to think about living again. I didn't do much in the time before that but grieve. I think I started to get sick of it—crying and being angry all the time. One day, I left my house and walked for several hours along the beach. I realized I loved and hated, being alone. I discovered that what had gotten to me the most, I think, what was driving me insane was the loneliness. I was really tired of that, and yet, all I wanted was to be left alone. That took a few more months to work through. I forced myself to go to friends' houses and invite people over to mine. Even though I wanted to crawl out of my skin the whole time until they left." He laughed, and it broke the silent spell that had come over the table. Even Scottie had stopped eating as he listened intently to Gordon talk. "It's easier now," he assured and smiled over at Ian, in order to take a side-glance at Claire. A tear slipped off her nose onto the blue tablecloth.

"I'm sorry, I didn't mean to upset you," Gordon said softly.

She shook her head, tossed her napkin from her lap, and excused herself with choked words no one could understand.

All was quiet for several moments as they listened to Claire's footsteps on the stairs. Her door closed with a hollow thud, and Gordon let out the breath he had been holding.

"I'm sorry. I think I ruined dinner."

"Not in the least," Maura said with a congested sniffle. Looking as if she had been actively fighting tears, she smiled and patted Gordon's hand. "She needed to hear your story," she said. "She needs to know she isn't alone." She reached over to pick up stray bits of food Scottie had spread as she talked. "I think ye should wait a week an' then ask her to an evenin' out," she said matter of factly. With one hard nod of her head, she smiled. "Yes, I think that'll do just fine."

GORDON WALKED through the door of his home. It was quiet and cold, and he quickly turned on the radio to fill the empty space. He sat down in a chair by the hearth with a heavy sigh. Feeling as if he had, in fact, ruined dinner, he scolded himself for sharing so much of his life's story with Claire, whose wound was still so fresh. He very much wanted to ask her to dinner, as Maura had suggested—ordered, really—but didn't know if he would have the courage now. He glanced at a picture of his late wife on the side table. She stared back at him with a soft, gentle smile and kind eyes.

"It feels like I'm stepping out on you," he told the picture with a gruff laugh. "Feels like I'm doin' something wrong." He shrugged helplessly, heavy with guilt. "God, this is really hard, Marjorie." The picture didn't answer, but he stared at it regardless, waiting. A soft voice came from somewhere deep inside his mind.

If it were the other way around?

"Would I want you to live your days alone…if it were me who died? No. I wouldn't. I'd want you to be happy. To have someone to care for you. I'd like to think you'd want that for me, too." He took the picture frame in his hands and held it out in front of him. "She'd understand. Claire, I mean," he said to his wife's image. "She's lost her man, and she'd understand that a part of me still loves you. And I always will," he whispered.

Bomani left Victor's office for what he told himself was the last time. He hadn't told Victor that, of course; only taken money to do another job. He walked through the degenerate streets as night fell, anxiety twisting his stomach into knots. He couldn't firebomb these squatters. The insurance company was already getting suspicious of Victor, who had received compensation for three firebombed apartments in the last two months. He found the building and climbed the stairs to the apartment. He took a deep breath and told himself this was the last one.

With a hard kick, the door splintered, hanging off one hinge. A woman screamed from inside, and two men scrambled from the living room into the bedroom. The apartment was sparsely furnished, smelled of urine and something boiled in a pot on the stove. The woman scooped up a small child from the corner and screamed again.

"Time to go," Bomani told them. "You're being evicted."

The woman started babbling with a hard accent, waving her free hand around, pointing to the door. He heard rustling in the bedroom and backed up two steps toward the door with his hand on the pistol tucked in his waistband.

Suddenly, one of the men emerged from the bedroom with a shot-gun. He recklessly aimed and fired. The plaster above Bomani's head shattered and rained down on him. Grabbing his pistol, he dropped to a crouch and aimed, hitting the man square in the middle of the forehead. The woman started screaming again as she ran past Bomani and out the door.

Bomani heard glass shatter in the bedroom. He got to the doorway just in time to see the other man disappear onto the fire escape. Bomani made no move to chase after him. He turned slowly, his eyes drawn to the dead man in the living room. He'd landed on his back, arms and legs splayed messily. His head lay to the side in a halo of blood. Open vacant eyes stared past Bomani.

"You are the last," he told the dead man. "I swear. You are the last."

He walked to the broken bedroom window and jumped out onto the fire escape.

HIS OWN NEIGHBORHOOD was only slightly better than the one he had just left. He pushed open the thick glass door leading to a dank staircase. His was one of only two apartments over the small medical clinic that served the poor.

The stairs stank of dirt and mildew, the walls holed and stained, and he didn't touch the handrail as his boots stomped wearily up the stairs.

He walked in and was relieved to see his woman standing by the stove, cooking what smelled like pasta.

"You're late," she said, glancing at the clock.

"I know. Sorry." He sat down in a tattered but clean armchair and bent to unlace his boots.

"What kept you?" She turned around impatiently and waited for an answer.

"I had one last job to do," he mumbled quietly.

"One last job. I thought you promised no more. You promised me, Bomani."

"I know. I'm sorry. We need the money. No more. I promise. I'll find a real job."

He sounded sincere enough, and she sighed heavily turning back to the stove.

She startled when he put his hands on her shoulders, having not heard him cross the room.

"I'll feel a whole lot better when I know you aren't doing dangerous jobs for that monster."

"We almost have enough to leave," he said softly and moved to her side. He ran a large hand slowly up and down her back. "I can't wait to take you away from all this."

"And I can't wait to leave, Bomani, but it's not worth your life. And your eternal soul."

He stiffened and avoided her eyes. "From this day on, I won't do anything that will compromise my immortal soul. I promise."

"What about what you did today?" She held up her hand to silence him before he could speak. "I don't want to know what it was," she said quickly.

"I'll go to confession tomorrow," he said and glanced at the gold cross that hung around her neck. Being of Egyptian decent, he wasn't Catholic. In fact, personally, he held no particular religion at all and didn't believe confession would save his soul from the atrocious acts he had committed, but it made her feel better, so he went. Sometimes it made him feel better too, but only in the way of unloading some of his burdens and have someone tell him it would be all right if he did this and said that. Deep in his heart, he felt it was too late for him.

JONATHAN CARRIED three lobster pots off the boat and dropped them down onto the pier.

"We'll need to fix these, Ian. There's some cracked slats on the bottom."

Ian nodded and went back to offloading the day's catch. He had the same hard learning curve that they all had in the beginning, and he looked tired for it.

"You're doing well, Ian," Jonathan said as he went back to inspecting pots. They were a good team, despite Ian's novice and had pulled in a respectable catch, which was good with prices falling the way they had been of late. Jonathan spent most of the day preoccupied with numbers. Would it be better to always go out together, the three of them? They seemed to accomplish more. But if they could bring on one more man and split up in teams of two, it might be best financially.

Caleb had worked quietly through the day, his throbbing head keeping him from much conversation. He was used to it, for the most part, working with a violent hangover, and they had grown accustomed to his silence.

"Seasick as I get, I can still help scrape pots, if ye need it."

Jonathan looked up to see Patrick standing safely on solid ground.

"Have at it," Jonathan said with a smile.

"Tomorrow." He grinned. "I'm here to talk to Caleb."

Jonathan turned to see Caleb working steadily stacking pots.

"Caleb! Patrick needs to talk to you. Why don't you take a break?"

Caleb narrowed his eyes. "Could you not yell, please? My head is splitting."

Jonathan turned back to Patrick. "Everything okay?"

"Not really, Jon. I came here to talk to Caleb because tryin' to catch him at home sober is damn near impossible."

Jonathan scrubbed his hand over his face and sighed heavily.

"There are decisions to make about the farm and it not bein' my land and all, I need to consult him."

Jonathan turned to the boat and yelled again. "Hey, Caleb. Pat needs to talk to you."

Caleb stopped, grumbled under his breath, and jumped to the pier.

He stood in front of Patrick with his arms crossed and huffed impatiently.

"There's some decisions to make about the farm, Caleb. I've been trying to talk to you in the evening, but you're...indisposed."

"You mean I'm drunk."

"Yeah, that, too."

"Well, then, what is it? What's so important?"

"Well, for one, Hannah's stopped givin'. I need to know what ye want to do 'bout that."

"Shoot her."

"Caleb, we might could breed her again—"

"Then fine. Breed her again. Why'd you ask me if you already knew what to do?"

"Because it's *your* farm, Caleb." His words were laced with resentment and the two locked eyes, each stubbornly refusing to look away first.

"We still need to buy another milk cow till the calf is weaned," Caleb said. "Did you think about that?"

Jonathan stepped up, sensing the tension between the men. "I could ask Gordon. He runs that dairy, after all. I'd bet he has a milk cow he'd be willing to sell."

Caleb nodded at Patrick. "Yeah. Do that." He turned back to the boat.

"Excuse me?" Patrick took a few steps toward Caleb. Jonathan and Ian watched nervously. "Am I yer bitch then? Ye jest wave yer hand and order me what to do on yer land, like I'm a feckin' slave? Let's not forget, Caleb, ye asked me here. Ye asked for my help."

Caleb ignored him and stepped back onto the boat. Patrick took several aggressive steps, and Jonathan moved into his path.

"Let me talk to him, Pat. I'll set him straight."

Patrick's temper was flared, and he shifted restlessly. "Why don't ye do that, Jon. Because I'm not goin' to be treated like shite by that drunken arse. I'll just put me family back on a train to New York. That's what I'll do!"

"Nobody wants you to do that, Pat. Just calm down. Let me talk to him."

Patrick relented with a nod and turned away, cursing under his breath. When he was out of earshot, Jonathan glanced at Caleb.

"Hey, asshole. I gotta talk to you."

"Well, that's not what I'm used be being called, though it has happened on occasion," a voice behind Jonathan said with a laugh. He

79

spun around to see a man, short with thick glasses and plump rounded shoulders. Hardly the picture of authority, despite the badge on his uniform.

"Marvin's the name," he said, sticking out his hand. "New deputy for Sheriff Vincent."

"Right, he mentioned you. Nice to meet you. How are you settling in?"

"Pretty good. Me and the wife bought a house in Pigeon Cove. Cute little place. Helluva lot different than the city, I can tell you that."

"You don't have to tell us," Jonathan said with a smile. "This is Ian and Caleb." Both men stopped and nodded, but only Ian walked over to shake his hand.

"Caleb, come meet the new deputy," Jonathan called.

"I'm kind of busy," he called back, not looking up. Jonathan turned back to Marvin.

"He doesn't mean to be rude. He's sort of going through a rough time right now," he confided. Marvin raised his eyebrows, curious without directly asking.

"He and his wife have little ones at home, twins a few months old. And, well, I don't know how much Vincent told you, but we just lost our best friend."

"He mentioned it. Is there still an open investigation?" he asked, pushing his glasses further up the bridge of his nose.

"No, Vincent closed it. It's a long story. I guess what the report says and what I think are two different things."

"Maybe you could stop by sometime, have a cup of coffee and fill me in on that. The wife would love to meet you. She's anxious to make friends here."

"I'll talk to Ava. I'm sure she'd like to come."

Marvin wrote down his address on a scrap receipt and handed it to Jonathan.

"And you, too... Ian, was it? You're welcome anytime."

"Appreciate it, Marvin," Ian said and shook his hand again.

They watched him walk back to his car, a little unsteady on the rocks and sand.

"He sure looks like the runt o' the litter, don't he?" Ian laughed.

"Well, I guess you don't have to be menacing to uphold the law." Jonathan grinned.

"Well, that's good. Because I think Claire's wee kitten looks more menacing than he does."

AUGUST 7, 1930

Patrick was quiet, sitting in the old chair that belonged to Hubert, Caleb's late father, staring at the open window across the room. It was a muggy night. Sweat clung to them like an extra layer of clothes. The oppressive, damp heat always set Patrick in a foul mood, and he caught himself biting his tongue with Shannon and Aislin all night.

He sighed heavily and rubbed a hand over his face—more redistributing the sweat, rather than wiping it off. Shannon eyed him with concern over the edge of the book as she continued to read to Aislin on the sofa.

After the book, she settled her daughter on a makeshift pallet under an open window next to her infant brother, Roan, and covered her lightly with a thin sheet.

"Codladh Sámh," she whispered and kissed her forehead.

"I don't know how anyone could sleep well in this heat," Patrick grumbled and wiped his face with his arm.

Shannon walked behind him and put her hands on his head, massaging his scalp lightly through messy wet patches of hair.

"What's on yer mind, Pat," she asked, her voice tired but patient.

"A lot. I need to talk to Caleb again," he said. Shannon could detect the slightest hint of irritation in his voice.

"Isn't he upstairs with Arianna and the babes?"

He shook his head. "No. He's in the barn."

"Why not go talk to him then?"

"You know why, Shannon. He's likely drunk," he said flatly.

"Maybe I can help," she said as she walked around the chair and knelt in front of him. "What seems to be the problem?"

"There are several, Shannon. I'm not sure how to move forward with certain things...this isn't really my land. It's not my farm. I have ideas that might help, but I can't do anything without talking to Caleb. And every time I go to talk to him, he's fallen over stupid wi' drink." He sighed and rested his head on the high back of the chair. "It makes me angry, Shan. I'd kill to have what has been handed to him, and he doesn't care a thing about it. I'm left to do the work but not able to make any decisions that might help this place give a bit more." He was raising his voice in frustration, and Shannon glanced at the sleeping children and back at him. "I'm sorry. I'm just upset, is all." His eyes floated around the living room. "I wish this was all mine. Do ye have any idea how hard I'd work, day and night, to give ye a place like this to call your own?"

She smiled and took his hand. "I know, Pat."

"Ye deserve a place like this. Grander than this even."

"An' we'll have it one day, Patrick. We're workin' too hard not to."

"I wish that was all it took. Hard work."

"What else then?"

"A bit o' luck wouldn't hurt, that's fer sure."

She looked away, paralyzed to help him feel like an adequate provider.

He leaned forward and gave her a long, hard kiss on top of her head. Then he stood, swung his leg over where she knelt before him and walked out to the barn to confront Caleb.

◠

HE WAS SITTING in the corner at a makeshift desk with a barrel for a seat. Spread before him were pictures, dozens of pictures taken over the last few years. He laughed under his breath, not knowing Patrick was standing near and took a long drink.

"I remember that day," Caleb whispered, holding up a picture of all three couples on an African safari.

Patrick cleared his throat. Caleb startled and turned, a surprised expression turning to one that mingled blankness and irritation.

"I need a word, Caleb."

"Sure." He turned around on the barrel to face Patrick, wedging his bottle between his legs, his shoulders slouched, eyes swollen and tired, as he wobbled slightly. He was working on drunk, but not quite there.

"I'd like to talk to ye about a transaction. I'd like to buy a bit of this land from you. The bit with the cabin there on the back of the property."

Caleb straightened in surprise. "What do you want to do with that?"

"I want to finally make a place of our own. I don't have enough money to buy outright, but I could put a small down and make payments quarterly. We could draw up papers and you hold the deed until it's paid for."

Caleb nodded. "You know that cabin hasn't been lived in for decades."

Patrick nodded. "I'll do the work it takes to make it decent. But it's the acre or two surrounding it that I'm most interested in."

Caleb thought about it for a moment, debating in long, slow, slurred thoughts. His father had said he could never sell the place. But he didn't say he couldn't sell part of it.

"Sure, why not." He threw his hands up and smiled.

"Good. Thank you. I'll draft an agreement and have you sign it, aye?"

"Aye, Aye, Captain," he said with a smirk. He waved him away and went back to his bottle and pictures.

Patrick plucked a lantern off its peg by the barn door on his way out. He struck a match on a rock and lit it, lowering the wick to adjust the light. He marched off in the darkness toward the far back of the property.

It was a good ten-minute walk when the cabin came into view.

There was a small spot for a garden next to the south side, its short fence destroyed and the plot grown over with weeds and vines. An outhouse sat to the right, and in the distance, he could see what might have been an animal shelter of some kind. There were covered stalls with the beginnings of walls appearing to be abandoned mid-construction.

The cabin itself was old. The roof sagged heavily on one side, and the windows were long since broken out. He pushed open the heavy wooden door, and its old iron hinges groaned.

It took a moment for his eyes to adjust. After a few moments, he was able to survey the place. It wasn't large, but it was large enough. A room only twenty by fifteen, he guessed. And, he could add onto the back for a bedroom for the children. A large fireplace had doubled for heat and cooking, and an old cast iron stew pot lay on its side on the hearth, red with oxidation. He picked it up and set it upright. A few pieces of broken furniture littered the floor, and other than a wooden hutch that sat against the wall leaning at a dangerous degree, the room was empty. It had an earthy, tangy smell to it, and he was grateful it didn't smell of mildew or rot. He wondered if they had housed animals here at some time.

He walked slowly around the circumference of the room, inspecting the chinking, floor, and roof as best he could.

He smiled to himself after he'd finished his inspection. He would draw up the papers tonight, and begin the work needed tomorrow after the farm's chores were done.

Arianna sat in a chair in the kitchen holding a picture she had ripped from a magazine.

"I just can't take this heat anymore," she grumbled, holding out a pair of scissors to Ethel. "Cut it all off."

Ethel stood behind her, somewhat hesitant. "Well, now, Ahna, I've only ever cut men's hair...I don't know how to do the latest styles."

Arianna glanced at the picture. "Well, that's basically what I want. Just leave me enough to do a decent finger wave. Just do it like the picture here."

Her hair had grown significantly since the twins were born and now resembled a bob that nearly touched her shoulders.

Ethel grabbed the bulk of her hair in the back and cut straight across, right at the nape of the neck. She dropped the handful of hair on the floor and began to snip and clip all over her head, frequently glancing at the picture Arianna held.

"I want to look fresh for our dinner with Marvin and his wife tonight. First impressions are important, you know."

Ethel suddenly gasped. She froze, staring at the back of Arianna's head.

"What's wrong?"

"I just...nipped my finger, is all," she said, staring at the closely shorn patch of hair in the back where the scissors had slipped. "Ah, almost done," she said with the slightest tremor in her voice, trying to arrange other bits of hair to cover the hole. A few more snips and she stepped back.

"All done."

Arianna sprang up and went to the mirror over the fireplace. Ethel held her breath.

"Oh, it's lovely!" she said as she touched the top and sides. It's so short all over with just enough to wave! It feels so good to have it off my neck!"

Ethel stared at the spot she had clipped too short and groaned under her breath. It was horribly obvious, despite her attempts to disguise it.

"I'm going to find Caleb," she said turning away from the mirror. "Then I'll feed the babies before I go. Thank you again for watching them. It will be so nice to get out for a bit."

"You're welcome, dear."

Arianna gave her a passing peck on the cheek and headed out to the barn.

CALEB WORKED IN THE LOFT, pitching hay down onto the floor below.

"It's almost time to get ready." She used a sweet, light voice, looking forward to the first social outing in a long time.

"Okay. Let me finish up here and I'll be in." He threw another forkful of hay over and squinted down at her.

"Did you do something different to your hair?"

"Yes." She grinned. "Your mother cut it for me."

"It's nice," he said.

She twirled around like a ballerina, and when she looked at him again, his face had fallen, eyebrows raised.

"What?" she asked, touching her hair self-consciously.

"Oh, nothing, I'm just not used to seeing you with such short hair."

"Don't be silly, Caleb. I used to wear it like this all the time." She smiled and gave a quick wave, bouncing back toward the house.

"Not *quite* like that," he whispered as she left.

❧

JONATHAN AND AVA pulled up to the farm in his father's old relic of an automobile, and it sputtered to a violent stop. Jean jumped out, heading toward the house. His bare feet sent up small plumes of dust as he ran. Aislin met him at the door with a big hug, and they both scampered inside to find the babies.

Jonathan opened Ava's door and offered his hand to help her out, the picture of male chivalry. She stepped out of the car and directly into a hug, nuzzling her face in his neck, deeply inhaling the cologne he wore.

They broke, hearing the screen door slam as Arianna stepped out.

"We could run, you know." He grinned devilishly and kissed her quickly. "My parents aren't home. We'd have the whole house to ourselves," he whispered.

She watched his lips as he spoke and a slow, sinful grin spread across her own face as she considered the possibilities. With morning sickness over and her hormones in full swing, she found that hardly a day went by that she didn't think about all the possibilities and took almost every opportunity that presented itself for them to be together. She took a weak-kneed step back.

"Hold that thought until after dinner, okay?"

"You're right," he said, standing straighter. "We finally get an adults night out. We should enjoy it...first."

They turned toward the house with his arm around her waist.

"You look beautiful, by the way."

"Thank you." She blushed. She wore one of his mother's dresses, a light pink dress of thin material with a low scoop neck and room for her belly, now five months gone with their child. Her light brown hair was swept up in simple elegance and held with plain pins.

Jonathan reached over and touched a small piece of hair that had fallen out of place.

"It's getting darker," he said.

"It is?" she asked with a hint of panic.

"Yes. But I like it. Darker blonde suits you."

Arianna smiled as they stepped onto the porch.

"Oh, aren't you just so excited to have an evening out?"

Ava smiled back and started to speak when Arianna twirled around, opened the screen door, and went inside ahead of them.

"Arianna, your hair—"

She twirled back around again, touching the tight black finger waves. "Isn't it lovely? Mother Ethel did it for me this afternoon. It feels so good to have all that hair off my neck. You should let her do yours, too!"

"Ah, I'm all right," Ava said as she struggled to keep a straight face. Arianna disappeared into the living room just as Caleb came down the stairs. He looked clean and sharp with a fresh haircut of his own, minus the bald spot.

"Are you almost ready, Ahna?" he called.

"Yes." She rushed back into the kitchen and past Caleb to the stairs. "I almost forgot to change my dress. Give me just a second."

Jean waved to Jonathan from the living room where he sat holding one of the babies.

"You be good, mind Ethel, and help with the babies," Jonathan called to him.

He nodded and smiled, rocking Samuel in his arms.

"Shannon and Patrick aren't coming?" Ava whispered to Jonathan.

"No. It's a double date," he said with a wink. "Patrick is working late on the cabin, and Shannon offered to help Ethel with all these kids."

Arianna came downstairs in a white sleeveless dress with small delicate black embroidery along the neck and waist and pronounced herself ready to leave.

The air was light with excitement and romance, anticipating the evening ahead, as Jonathan sputtered down the long dirt drive with Caleb and Arianna in the backseat.

A few moments later, they pulled up to a house that didn't quite match Marvin's description of a 'small, cute house'. It was a grand square house made of gray stone with clean white shutters. Jonathan checked the address and looked back to the house.

89

"I guess this is it," he said as he turned off the engine and got out.

As they walked up the cobbled path, Arianna eyed the house with a cocked eyebrow. "A deputy's pay buys you all this, huh?"

Jonathan knocked on the door with Ava by his side, Caleb and Arianna standing behind. A tall, beautiful woman with long black hair and exquisite olive skin opened the door.

"Oh, I'm sorry. I'm looking for Marvin's house." He glanced at the house numbers by the door and back down to the paper as he took a step back.

"You have the right house," she said with a smile. "Marvin is my husband. Please, come in. We are expecting you." She spoke with an Italian accent. As she stepped aside to welcome her guests, they all filed in and followed her into in a lavishly decorated living room.

"I'm Donatella." She put a limp hand out to Jonathan, palm down. He took it and gave it a quick, impersonal shake.

"Nice to meet you. I'm Jonathan. This is my wife, Ava."

Donatella nodded to her with a smile, and her eyes traveled down to her stomach.

"When are you due?" she asked.

"December," Ava said with a flush of the cheeks.

"That long? Should be quite a healthy baby. Congratulations." She laughed, Ava didn't. Jonathan shifted uncomfortably and glanced at Ava. Donatella turned her attention to Caleb, and Jonathan leaned to whisper.

"Ignore her. You're not that big at all."

Ava nodded tightly, blinking away the sting of the insult.

She held her hand out to Caleb in the same fashion, and Caleb took it and kissed it quickly.

"Ah, now *this* is a man who knows his manners," she said.

"I'm Caleb." He had let go of her hand but continued to stare in a way that Arianna thought a little too admiring. She elbowed him in the side and cleared her throat.

"Oh, right. This is my wife."

Arianna stared at the side of his head and poked him in the ribs again.

"Her name is Arianna."

She smiled tightly and turned to Donatella, who was visibly sizing her up, comparing their striking features.

"Very nice to meet you. Mind if I call you Anna?"

"Yes, actually. Only my close friends call me Ahna."

"Well, that does sound fancier, doesn't it?"

"You can call me Arianna," she said with a fake smile as she did her own inventory of Marvin's arrestingly beautiful wife.

"This might have been a mistake," Jonathan whispered to Ava with a nervous grin.

"Jon, Caleb, nice to see you." Marvin appeared in the arch of the dining room and waved them in.

"Dinner is ready. Please, come eat."

They found themselves seated at a long table where Donatella fussed over every detail until everyone and everything were arranged perfectly.

"I've made a wonderful dish that is a favorite of my family back in Italy," she announced as a woman who was obviously her maid brought in plates of steaming food, placing one in front of each guest. She returned with slices of bread, side salads, and several other exotic smelling, colorful side dishes. She bobbed a curtsy to Donatella and left the room.

"My cousin," Marvin explained quickly. "Her husband is out of work. So she works part time for us," he explained. "We try to help out family when we can."

"That's nice of you," Jonathan said.

"Has everyone been introduced?" Marvin asked cordially as he shook a napkin out, placing it in his lap. Jonathan handled the introduction of the wives to Marvin.

Everyone nodded with a polite smile, making curious glances from Marvin's gawky, unassuming stature to his wife, who sat rather elegantly at the other end of the table.

He struggled to keep the conversation going and resorted to telling stories of his heroic acts as a policeman in New York City.

"From policeman to deputy...how do you make that transition?" Jonathan asked.

Marvin laughed with an awkward smile. "Depends on who you know," he said with a wink. "Donatella here wanted a quieter life, and it just timed perfectly with the opening here."

"Well, it is definitely slower here," Arianna said. "Nothing like New York." She rattled off a list of social clubs and restaurants they used to frequent in their old life. Donatella looked unimpressed. She picked up an elegant fan, spread it wide, and began fanning herself.

"The humidity is awful," she complained. "Takes my hairdresser hours to tame my hair with how frizzy it gets." She turned to Arianna. "Who does your hair?"

Arianna shifted uncomfortably. "I have a woman who does a fabulous job. I just went to see her, actually."

"What woman? I thought my mom cut your hair?"

Arianna's jaw set, and she turned slowly toward Caleb. "No, dear, the woman who *normally* does my hair. Your mother gave me a quick trim this morning, is all. My gal was booked. She's very popular," she said with a flick of her wrist and took a dainty bite of salad.

Donatella grinned and turned to Ava. "What about you? Do you have a good hairdresser to recommend?"

Ava wiped her mouth and shook her head. "I do my own."

Jonathan glanced across the table. Caleb was being rather obvious in his appreciation of Donatella. Jonathan had looked, as any man with eyes would have, but he kept his glances brief, and more importantly, discreet, simply appreciating the view and nothing more. Caleb, however, was doing little to be discreet and looked nearly daydreaming. And Arianna had started to notice.

"Caleb, darling. Tell Marvin and Donatella about our babies," she said, staring pointedly at Donatella. "We have twins." She smiled before Donatella could speak and ran a hand from her throat down the bodice of her dress. "I know it doesn't look like it, does it?" she said vainly. Ava snorted a muted laugh in her water glass, not for Arianna's act, but for the fact that she had a large piece of salad stuck between her teeth.

Caleb appeared awkward as he rattled off a few things about the babies—their names, ages, and cute things they were starting to do.

Jonathan and Ava sat quietly across from them, eating their dinner, praying the hissing would die down.

Marvin interrupted the escalating feminine war with talk of the town and his new boss, Vincent. He prodded Jonathan for information about the locals and broached the subject of the boat accident, but Jonathan shot him a look with a nod to Caleb, deferring the conversation.

Arianna, distracted by the obvious exchange of glances between Caleb and Donatella, was watching Caleb out of the corner of her eye as she ate. A glob of spaghetti slipped off her fork, down the front of her dress and landed in her lap. She gasped and grabbed for her napkin, smearing the sauce in messy streaks down her white dress. She looked up, horrified and frozen to Ava, who had already begun to stand.

"Where is your bathroom, Donatella?" she asked, motioning for Arianna to get up.

"Second door down the hall. Extra towels are under the sink." She offered no more help than this as her lips quivered, fighting a laugh.

The second the bathroom door closed behind them, Arianna began growling. "I have never *in my life* met someone so *rude!*"

Ava wet some hand towels and began trying to clean the mess off Arianna's dress.

"Did you see the way she's flirting with Caleb? She's looking at Jon, too, you know. I saw her." She stood there, tapping her foot, breathing through her nose like a bull getting ready to charge. "If she thinks she can flirt with my husband right in front of me, she's got another thing coming! I mean, granted, my husband is ten times more handsome than that mole she's married to. That's what he looks like! A mole!" She growled a few more unintelligible things and Ava hushed her while trying in vain to clean her dress.

"It looks like she's enjoying getting you riled up," Ava said, frowning at the dress. She stood up and held her hand out. "Take it off."

"Who *does that?* I mean, honestly. Saying and doing things just to cause a stir." She pulled the dress over her head and handed it to Ava, who stared at her for a long moment.

"I can think of someone who likes to do and say things that cause a stir."

Arianna narrowed her eyes and gave a snort. "I always had a good reason. And I never did it to intentionally hurt someone."

"Oh, I wouldn't say that. There was—"

"Okay, there was Ruth. But she deserved it."

"And there was Sarah. And the woman at the club in London and that poor gal at the—"

"I get your point."

"Let's just try to get through this dinner, all right? We never have to come back here."

"As if I would ever darken her doorstep again. She was practically calling you a swollen heifer as soon as you crossed her threshold!" Arianna slipped on her dress, the stains reduced to large red and pink patches. "Lovely."

Ava put her fingers to her lips and opened the door.

Arianna sat down with as much grace as she could muster.

"Donna, why don't you loan Arianna one of your dresses?" Marvin suggested. She seemed to debate it for a moment before she rose quietly and left the room.

"She feels bad, honestly, she does," Marvin said. "Sometimes she rubs folks the wrong way. She just blurts things out sometimes, and if she feels—" he lowered his voice to a whisper, "threatened in any way, she tends to be a little nasty."

Arianna moved her hand to flip hair that wasn't there anymore. "A little nasty?" she echoed.

Caleb nudged her under the table.

"What?"

"Don't be rude to our hosts, Ahna."

"Me? Rude? What the hell!"

He nudged her again, and she turned, growling. "Don't you nudge me, Caleb! I saw you looking at her breasts."

Jonathan choked on an olive and Ava came up, patting him on the back. He spit and coughed into a napkin while Arianna covered her face with her hand.

"Here, this might work," Donatella said, holding out a folded dress, with a polite smile.

Arianna threw her napkin on her cold food and took it with a terse, "Thank you.'"

The dining room was awkwardly silent with only the occasional throat clearing or clink of silverware.

She returned moments later, still wearing her stained dress, still looking like a bull ready to charge, holding the dress out to Donatella.

"If it's all the same, I'd like to wear my own dress. We'll be leaving shortly anyway." She shot a pointed glare at Caleb.

"Didn't you like it?" Donatella asked. "I could find something in another color."

"No, it's fine."

"But you can't just sit there in that wet dress. I'll find another color."

Arianna closed her eyes and growled through her teeth, "It doesn't *fit.*"

"Oh." Donatella struggled against a smile. "I could ask Marvin's cousin. She might have something...bigger."

Her nostrils flared. "No, thank you."

Donatella rose from her seat with the dress and walked behind Arianna's chair. She stopped, tilting her head with a grin and poked a finger at the near bald spot at the back of her head.

"I'll ask my beautician if there are any creams to help that balding you have there."

Arianna's eyes came up slowly. "What balding?"

"Oh, it's just really thin, is all. Not *quite* bald." She walked away with a snide grin, and Arianna turned her rabid eyes on Caleb.

"*Caleb. Do I have a bald spot on my head?*"

He shifted uncomfortably in his chair. "I was going to tell you."

"You were *going* to tell me? WHEN?" She slammed her fist down on the table so hard the silverware jumped.

"Arianna, please. it's not that bad," Caleb pleaded.

"Not. That. Bad? I' m sitting here with a bald spot, stains all over my dress and—"

"Psst. Arianna." Ava bared her teeth and picked at the front.

Arianna slowly and gracefully ran her tongue over her teeth dislodging a large piece of lettuce.

"Were you going to tell me about *that*, Caleb?"

"Stop making such a big deal over everything. You're embarrassing yourself and everyone else. It isn't that bad," he said, glancing at her.

"Not that bad?" She was trembling with rage as she reached out and grabbed a handful of spaghetti off her plate. She slowly and deliberately smeared it down the front of Caleb's shirt. He watched incredulously as she then took her napkin and dabbed at it.

"It's not that bad," she whispered.

"Christ." Jonathan's head swung over to Marvin. "I'm so sorry. I thought we left the kids at home."

"It's all right. Let's just all calm down and have some dessert, eh?"

As Caleb began to wipe his shirt, a loud mewing from the doorway grabbed everyone's attention. An orange tabby cat, just past being a kitten, sauntered in and circled Marvin's legs under the table in a figure eight pattern, mewing urgently.

Arianna gasped as small wet spots on her bodice grew larger as her milk let down.

"IT'S TIME TO LEAVE!" Arianna bellowed, shoved her chair back, and started for the door.

Caleb nodded to Marvin, apologized, and followed her out.

JONATHAN TOOK a deep breath before starting the car. He glanced over at Ava, and they exchanged a frustrated look. Everyone was silent, Caleb and Arianna staring in opposite directions in the backseat. Arianna's entire posture was wound up tight, ready to explode like a firework. Caleb pulled a flask out of his back pocket and took a deep drink.

"Oh, fabulous," she said glancing at him. "Don't even wait until we get home. I sure hope you were planning on sleeping in the barn because there's no way I'm sleeping in the same room after the way you acted."

"The way I acted? You acted like a spoiled little brat putting on airs! You didn't even try to be polite or make friends!"

Jonathan pulled quickly into the road with a squeal of tires.

"Make friends! MAKE FRIENDS! As if I would even consider counting that snide bitch as one of my friends!" She snatched up her handbag and started hitting Caleb about the head and shoulders.

"You... couldn't... stop... looking... at... her... long... enough... to.... tell... me... I... had..." Jonathan reached back, grabbed the assaulting handbag and threw it in the floorboard at Ava's feet.

Arianna's head snapped from Jonathan back to Caleb. "She was flirting with you *right in front of me,* and you didn't do anything about it!"

"How's it feel, Ahna?" he grumbled under his breath.

"What?"

He swung his head around and glared at her. "For years I watched you parade around barely clothed and never sober, while every man in the room ogled you. And now you lose your mind when a beautiful woman pays the least bit of attention to me." He took another drink and turned away from her.

"She wasn't *that* beautiful."

"Actually, she was."

With that, Arianna flew across the seat at him like a feral cat, hissing and cursing.

Jonathan swerved to the side of the road, skidded to a stop, and turned around in the seat.

"Get out!"

They froze, hands at odd angles on each other's face and throat, and stared at him.

"Get *the hell* out of my car. Now."

Caleb removed Arianna's hand from his throat. "Sorry, Jon. We just—"

"Get...out."

Caleb nodded and exited the door quietly. Arianna watched him in disbelief before her eyes snapped back to Jonathan.

"You, too."

"Honestly, Jon. You don't expect us to walk!"

He threw open his door and then hers, grabbed her by the arm, and pulled her out. She yelped in disbelief and stumbled back, landing on her rear in the dirt. Jonathan slammed his own door again and sped off in a plume of dust and gravel, tossing her handbag out the window.

"Well, great. This is just great, Caleb. We're stranded."

"Don't look at me. This is your fault."

"My fault! You inconsiderate ass! This whole ordeal wouldn't even be happening if you had just taken up for me in the first place!"

"Shit."

"What?"

"I left my flask in the back seat."

Her eyes flashed, and she growled again, picking up a handful of pebbles, hurling them at him.

AUGUST 20, 1930

Gordon sat in his truck, debating whether today should be the day he asks Claire out to dinner. He had rehearsed a half dozen different ways to ask her, ranging from horribly romantic to extremely aloof, and couldn't decide between them. He rubbed his eyes hard with his fists for a moment and slapped his cheeks.

With a check of his hair and breath, he stepped out of the truck. Opening the back doors of the truck, he pulled out Claire's crate and as he turned, the living room window curtain fell quickly.

Getting to the porch, he set the crate down and noticed the empty milk bottles missing. He grinned to himself, finding a good excuse to knock on the door. Claire opened it a moment later with a fresh face and clean hair. Gordon stumbled on his words right from the start.

"They're missing... the milk... I mean the bottles. Do you have... I brought the order." He pointed down to the crate full of fresh dairy.

"Step inside, Gordon, and I'll get them straight away," Maura yelled from somewhere deep in the house. Claire stepped aside, and they stood awkwardly, staring in different directions while Maura banged around the kitchen.

"Hot outside."

"It is," Claire said, glancing at the window.

"Fall's coming."

"Eventually."

"It will be nice to have some cooler weather. Easier to breathe. And to work."

"It will." Claire nodded and folded her arms, staring at the ground between them.

"Listen, Claire. I know it really is too soon, but I was wondering if you'd—"

"Here's the empty milk bottles, Mr. Gordon. They're washed but not boiled, I'm sorry."

Gordon gave a laugh of mingled frustration and relief at being interrupted.

"It's all right, Maura. Sterilizing the bottles is part of the service."

Maura glanced at each one of them and bit her lip when she realized what she had interrupted. She thought quickly on how to remedy it.

"Mr. Gordon, you don't look so well." She moved in front of him and inspected his face closely.

"I'm fine, Maura. Just a bit hot out, is all."

"No. No, I do believe ye look very poorly indeed. Yer face is flushed, and yer eyes are bloodshot and swollen!"

"Are they?"

"Aye. How many more deliveries do ye have to make yet?"

"Eight or nine."

"Well, I worry about ye drivin' around alone in such a state. What if ye were to pass out?" She winked at him.

"Well, not much I can do, Maura. Have to make the deliveries."

"Claire. Why don't ye go with Mr. Gordon."

Gordon's eyes flew open. "Why, she can't lift the crates!"

"No, but she can drive the truck. I don't think it wise for ye to be behind the wheel on the verge of passin' out from the heat."

"I wouldn't want to trouble you, Claire. But I guess I could use the help if you're willing."

She hesitated, looking at Gordon. "But I've only ever driven that one time."

"Well, it's not that hard. Consider this your second lesson. We can just go real slow until you're comfortable." He looked up with a smile, speaking of much more than driving.

She agreed silently and pulled her eyes from his. "I guess I better get my sweater."

"It's ninety-five degrees out!" Maura cried.

"Oh. Well, I should grab my purse." She wandered off distractedly.

A few moments later, Claire pulled out, the truck jerking and weaving down the road.

"You're doing great," Gordon lied, gripping the door handle with white knuckles and praying all the milk hadn't toppled over. "I really appreciate you doing this for me. I've known folks who have passed out from the heat. You're a lifesaver. A guardian angel, even."

He bit his lip at the reference to an angel, reminding himself to think a sentence through several times before speaking it.

"And this is only your second time?"

"Yes."

"Right here—this white house on the right is the next stop."

She pulled up slowly and carefully. One tire rolled up onto the curb.

"I'll be right back." He stepped out, made his delivery, gathered the empty bottles and containers, and slid back into the seat.

"Great. Only eight more."

She nodded and pulled back out, the truck giving a hard jolt when it came off the curb. Finding an even speed she was comfortable with, somewhere around ten miles per hour, she visibly relaxed and unlocked her elbows, settling into the seat. Gordon was quiet and calm, looking out over the scenery, but inside his mind, he was screaming at himself to find conversation.

"Sure is hot."

She glanced over at him, then back to the road. "I'm afraid I'm no good at talking. I'm sorry."

"You do fine at talking. I'm no good at sparking conversation."

They rode in awkward silence a few minutes more. Suddenly, they both spoke at the same time.

"How many cows do you have?" "How long have you been painting?"

They both laughed awkwardly.

"Ladies first."

"I was just wondering how many cows you have to tend to. It must be an awfully hard job to do alone."

"I have a lot of cows, but I do have help. I've got a few hired hands... Maura said you love to paint."

"I do."

"What do you paint?"

She visibly tensed and took a deep breath. "I've always painted..." Her eyes threatened tears, and the road became blurry. "I'm looking for something new to paint these days."

"I have cows."

She glanced at him sidelong. "We established that. That's where you get the milk."

He laughed. "Yes, but what I meant was, if you were looking for something new to paint, I have lots of cows. You could choose any one you wanted. They stay real still and you could—oh! The next delivery was right there." He pointed as they sailed past the house.

The truck skidded to a stop, and when Gordon pulled his head up from his lap, he laughed.

"I can back up—"

"No, no, I'll just walk it. Stay right here."

~

A FEW MOMENTS LATER, he returned, mopping his brow with his handkerchief.

"As I was saying, I wouldn't mind at all if you wanted to come out to the dairy. Paint cows and pastures and...things."

She didn't answer but started out again at a slow, steady pace.

"I could make some coffee. Or, no. It's too hot for coffee. I can make lemonade. You could come out and we could—you could paint the lemons, even."

She stared at him with a cocked eyebrow.

"Oh, you know, I'm sure you've seen the paintings of bowls of fruit and vegetables and all that... that's what I meant. If you like that kind of thing."

He shut his mouth, mentally cursing his awkwardness. Finally, still staring out the window, he sighed heavily.

"I'm sorry. I must sound like an idiot."

"You're not an idiot."

"What I'm trying to say, in a really awkward, stupid kind of way, is that I would love it if you would come out to my place and paint my cows. Or my pasture. Or whatever you want. And I'll make lemonade."

She smiled briefly, but he could see she was shrouded in sadness, and it visibly weighed her down.

"I'll think about it," she said quietly.

He instructed her to take a few more turns and made a few more deliveries. He stayed on the safe topics of his customers and insignificant tidbits of information about each one.

Walking back from the last delivery, the idea came to him as he passed the wooden panels of the enclosed delivery truck with its faded and peeling paint.

He slid back into the seat, smiled, and smacked the dashboard.

"I'd like to hire you to paint my truck," he blurted out. "The paint is old, and I need a fresh job done on it. What do you think?"

HE DROPPED Claire off at her house and spoke to her from inside the truck. "So I'll come by tomorrow, and we'll discuss a design for the side and a price, all right?"

She nodded, smiling faintly and turned to the house.

"Thanks again for driving me around today!" he called out after her. "You did great."

She waved as she disappeared into the house.

"So, how was yer second driving lesson?" Maura asked with dancing, curious eyes.

"It was fine. I didn't wreck, at least."

"That's always good. Did you and Mr. Gordon have a nice time?"

"He was working."

"Well, that doesn't mean you can't have a nice time of it. Did ye have good conversation, at least?"

"He wants to hire me to paint his truck."

"Well, now. That sounds interesting."

"It's charity." She huffed and poured a tall glass of lemonade. "The paint on the side isn't that bad. He's doing it because he feels sorry for me."

"Well, I doubt that. I think he sees an artist that could do a good job at a fair price, and he has the need of your services. Don't read so much into it, Miss Claire."

"So, I shouldn't assume that he wants to spend time with me? Or that you are playing the most obvious matchmaker?"

"Well, would that be such a terrible thing? Mr. Gordon is a nice man."

"He is a nice man. But does he know?" She looked down at her stomach.

"Aye, he does." Ian stepped around the corner and leaned against the wall. Maura's head spun around, and she pinned him with a disbelieving glare.

"Ian! You told him!"

"Maura. T'was only fair. I know ye want to make the match, but tis best to be honest. And now we know he wants to spend time wi' Claire, knowing everything."

Claire grew increasingly uncomfortable being talked about while she stood in plain sight.

"I don't need you to play matchmaker, Maura." She stood with a huff, and Maura grabbed her hand.

"Love. I'm going to be straight with ye, all right. I understand you're still grieving Aryl. You will be for years. But that babe is growing every day and is going to need a father. *You* are going to need a husband. I know it seems impossible to think of right now. But, if it's a good match, and ye could at least be happy, ye should give Mr. Gordon a chance. I know it's not what your heart wants to hear, Miss Claire, but that's the reality of it. These are hard times, and you'll likely not make it alone."

Claire wanted to deny it, but deep down, she knew Maura was right. She had a working husband and yet her clothes were bordering threadbare, many times hand repaired, and her cheeks showed the thinness of eating just enough.

"He's mighty fond of ye. I can see it in his eyes. He looks at ye much the way Ian looked at me when I came out of my deep sadness enough to notice it."

Claire shook her head with closed eyes, feeling scared, uncertain, and traitorous to the memory of Aryl.

"I just don't know, Maura."

"Just…don't close yourself off, love. Go over and paint his truck."

"And his cows. He offered me to paint his cows."

"Well, paint the cows. And the fields and the barn and whatever else strikes your heart."

She nodded without meeting Maura's eyes and gave her hand a squeeze.

"I'll try," she whispered. "For the baby."

THE NEXT EVENING, just as the brutal sun had dipped below the tips of the trees providing welcoming relief, Gordon knocked on the door. Despite the heat, he arrived crisp and clean in a thin linen shirt, his wet hair combed back.

He smelled of light cologne as he walked by, and Maura smiled a tight smile, looking much like a mad scientist whose experiment was going terribly well.

He was seated at the table with a glass of lemonade and a slice of eggless cake drizzled with lemon frosting.

"Lemons are on the menu, Mr. Gordon. They're cheap and plentiful at the market. We split a lemon herb fish with lemon rice this evening. Tomorrow we'll have a lemon cucumber salad for supper with lemon pie for desert, should you feel like stopping by."

"Thank you, Maura."

"Claire will be down shortly." She smiled and set an identical snack and a drink for Claire right next to Gordon and left the room. He moved the plate and glass across the table, giving her the space he knew she needed and improving his view.

She entered the kitchen nervously with a sketchpad tucked under her arm and sat down.

Getting right down to business, she pulled out the pencil from her hair.

"So what type of new design were you thinking of?"

CALEB SETTLED down at his makeshift desk in the barn with his bottle, goat, and pictures. He'd begun a collage in an old frame, arranging and rearranging the pictures, studying each one before he placed it. When he thought he had them just right and was ready to lay the glass, he'd see something out of line and that made him scoop up all the pictures and start over again. Over and over, he arranged and scooped, getting quite drunk in the process, until he scooped the pictures one last time and hurled them out to rain down on the barn floor. He choked back tears with hard swallows from his bottle and stared out through the small, dirty window.

Tonight the kitchen light burned brightly, and he saw Arianna's figure moving about inside. The twins would be asleep by now. He was foggy minded, but he thought he might have promised her he'd help bathe them tonight and tuck them in. A few more drinks and he could convince himself that he hadn't.

"I hope I'm not interrupting anything."

Caleb swung around and nearly fell off the barrel at the sound of Marvin's voice.

"No, come in," he said and struggled to stand.

Marvin had taken a few steps before he noticed the pictures scattered on the ground. He stooped to pick them up.

"Please, leave it. I'll get them later. Just don't step on any."

"Pictures of your friend?"

"Pictures of all of us. We had a hell of a life, you know? Before the crash...a hell of a life."

"You had money?"

"We all did. More than we knew what to do with. Parties and dinners, trips to Paris and London, nice clothes and servants...Maura was Jonathan's maid, did you know that?" He narrowed glassy eyes at Marvin.

"No, I didn't. I haven't had the chance to meet Maura." Marvin walked carefully between pictures, catching glimpses of them in fantastic finery in luxurious places.

"When we lost everything, she stuck around when no one else did. Pull up a barrel," he offered.

"Tell me more about your life before," Marvin said, having to heave his small frame up on the makeshift stool.

Caleb shook his head. "I will apologize for my wife's behavior at dinner, Deputy."

"Call me Marvin."

"Well, Marvin, my wife can be a bit overwhelming at times. I'm sorry she got out of hand."

Marvin's serious expression softened into a smile. "Actually, I haven't been that entertained since I went to a comedy show in Boston. And my wife can be a bit catty, as well. She was just as much to blame. Arianna is a beautiful woman. She was just jealous. Don't give it another thought."

Caleb smiled and took another drink.

"Speaking of that, I have something for you. Vincent told me to bring this out to you. Caught a small time runner the other night." He held out two bottles of whiskey.

Caleb eyed it with restraint but held his hand out. "Thank you."

"Listen, I've been trying to get ahold of Jon but can't manage it. He's busy, you know?"

"He is. What do you want to get ahold of him about?"

"Well, I'm worried, is all. Vincent told me that Jon is convinced that what happened to your friend was done on purpose. He'll never come to terms with what happened if he's chasing an illusion...trust me, I should know."

"How would you know?" The barn began to bulge and sway around Marvin's head. The goat's noises seemed distant as Caleb became blissfully numb.

"I lost my brother in the Great War, you see. Everyone in our family was shocked, but then grieved and eventually, returned to their lives. But not me. I insisted he had only gone missing and became obsessed with the idea. For months, I believed he was alive because, after all, there hadn't been a body found. But they did, eventually, and sent home what was left of my brother. I had to face it then and wished I had from the start. It would have been easier to get on with it, rather than dragging it out."

"But you'll never find Aryl's body."

"No, but Vincent mentioned foul play, and if I can rule that out, then Jon will have no choice but to face the grief. I understand the sheriff is too busy to chase down leads to nowhere. I have some free time and connections. I could look into it. I just can't seem to get a minute with him. I thought you might tell me what Jon thinks happened."

With a long sigh, Caleb began. "He thinks it was supposed to be him. He thinks Victor Drayton somehow came here, damaged the boats, rigged the Ava-Maura in order to kill him, and got out before sun up."

"Victor is an acquaintance of his?"

"I wouldn't say acquaintance. They go way back with nothing but trouble. Jonathan was smarter in the apprenticeship, and quicker to jump on opportunities and a hell of a lot more charming. He stole Ava right out from under Victor's arm."

"I guess that would give him reason to hate Jonathan. Sounds humiliating. How did that play out?"

Caleb drank, scowled. "That's a whole other story."

"Right. So, Vincent checked into Victor's whereabouts when the accident happened, I'm sure."

"He did. And he has a punched train ticket heading south."

"And that wasn't enough to convince Jonathan that Victor had nothing to do with it?"

"Just the opposite. He's more convinced than ever. Seems too convenient that he would be on a trip in the opposite direction when this happened. I don't know if any of this helps you at all."

"It does, and I'll do what I can. What about the night of the accident—"

Caleb's face hardened. "You'll have to read the police report. I won't relive it again."

AUGUST 26, 1930

Claire sat bolt upright at the first light of dawn. Shaking and sweating from a nightmare, she tried to slow her breathing and reestablish the world around her. For all the nightmares she'd had, she often found it was easier to get past it by going over it in her mind. But she didn't want to go over this one. She moved the kitten, who was snuggled close by her side, and she swung her legs over the side of the bed and walked quickly to the bathroom. Splashing cold water on her face and willing the dream away, her hands shook with the realness of what she saw and felt. Small segments forced their way to the front of her mind.

She was eating dinner with Gordon, and suddenly, a flash of lightning blinded, followed by a swallowing darkness. The front door swung open slowly. Aryl stood at the threshold, soaked to the bone. Seaweed clung to his shoulders and legs, and water dripped from his hair running in small streams down his face. He stared at Gordon with a dark hate, leveled a gun, and fired. Then Maura. Then Ian. They all three lay in a bloody heap with blank, lifeless eyes. Then, swinging his head slowly toward Claire, he smiled. "I would have never given up on you."

Her dream ended with the next flash of light from the gun, aimed directly at her.

There was no going back to sleep. She dressed, still shaken from the nightmare, and went downstairs.

Ian had left for work, Maura, Tarin, and Scottie still asleep. She started a pot of coffee, making it weak for the sake of extending their supply, and leaned against the counter, holding her head.

This morning, she had arrangements to paint Gordon's truck. She tried to tell herself this was just business. She was earning money. Five dollars is what he insisted on paying. She could buy things for the baby with that money. She couldn't go on forever living on charity. Maybe, if she could get back into the swing of it, she could paint...something, and set up a stand near town to sell her work. It was just business, but no doubt, the guilt of being the slightest bit interested in Gordon—even just for practicalities sake, brought on her nightmare. And she couldn't get Aryl's livid expression out of her mind.

She set out mid-morning, not having said a word to Maura or anyone about her dream. The kitten, which she had named Kitten for lack of any better ideas, followed her. Walking slowly, she swung her basket of paints and brushes at her side and tried to enjoy the cool morning air. Kitten looked up at her every now and then, as if wondering if she knew where she was going. She told herself she wasn't procrastinating, but saving her energy for the baby's sake and walking slowly for her furry little friend. Her thoughts darted from one thing to the next, wondering if Gordon would mind if the cat had come with her, and thinking she might be looking forward to painting again.

She was still sorting out the business of feeling, distinguishing what emotions to let in as the numb wore off. Painting would be relaxing for her, as it always had, so long as she didn't paint anything regarding oceans, lighthouses, boats, or sea life. A dairy farm, she supposed, was safe enough. She turned up the dirt road and saw the large red barn in the distance. Split rail fences lined the long drive, leading to a good-sized white house, built and painted in simplicity. Several cows bellowed in the pastures on both sides and began lazily making their way over to investigate the visitor. Kitten ran ahead as if recognizing

Gordon, who stood on his porch. When she caught up, he was holding it and welcomed her inside for a moment before she set to work.

~

JONATHAN UNROLLED a map on the hood of his car and felt a nauseatingly strong feeling of déjà vu as he assigned search areas to friends and neighbors. The sun was setting, and the last of the heat stung his back through his thin cotton shirt. It had already been a long day working, and he was tired and sunburnt. This search was on land, not on the sea, and it wasn't for Aryl but for his wife, Claire, who hadn't yet returned home. By dinner, Maura became alarmed and sent Ian to Gordon's to fetch her. Gordon said she had left a few hours earlier, and no one along the path home had seen her. Maura sent for Jonathan and an emergency search began.

Sheriff Vincent looked over his shoulder, nodding with approval as Jonathan sent each person with an assigned area. Ava clung to his other side, nervously chewing on her nails.

Caleb stepped up to be given an area to search, and Jonathan considered him up and down with uncertainty.

"Can you drive?"

He smelled of whisky, as he did on any given night, but didn't seem unable to function.

"I'm fine." He seemed particularly antsy—angry even. Even in the absence of slurred speech, Jonathan was hesitant to put him behind the wheel of an automobile.

"I'm going to be searching downtown. Why don't you come and help me?"

"Why don't you give me a real area to search? I don't need to be babysat."

"I'm not babysitting you, Caleb." He sighed impatiently. "There is a lot of area to cover in town. Lots of shops to duck in and out of. I genuinely need help."

"Why can't she help you?" Caleb gave a hard nod toward Ava.

"Because she is going to go home."

"What—? Hold on, Jon, I want to help!"

"You can help by going home. I'll let you know as soon as we find her." He gave her a quick kiss and led her by the arm to the car. "Ian will take you home."

"But Jon!"

"Ava." His tone and look made it clear that this was not open for negotiation in any way. She sat down in the car with one hand on her stomach and slammed the door as hard as she could.

"C'mon, Caleb. Let's take your truck. I'll drive."

IT WAS A TENSE, quiet ride and for Jonathan, it felt like it was taking forever. Only a sliver of the sun remained, and Jonathan wondered what would really be accomplished when all the small businesses that dotted the downtown area would be closed soon. He'd go door to door all night long if he had to...till he found someone who had seen her.

"Why'd you make Ava stay home?"

"She's tired. She's pale and isn't eating right. This pregnancy has been nothing but stress and fear and...potatoes." He laughed without humor. "This baby is liable to be born a nervous wreck."

"But she's going to worry at home."

"I know. But I'm not going to drag her all over town."

Caleb shrugged indifferently and gazed out the window for the rest of the drive.

"No, can't say that I've seen her. You say she disappeared today?" The owner of the small hardware store shook his head. He returned her picture to Jonathan, removed his hat, and rubbed his skinny bald head.

"Earlier this afternoon. She left Gordon's dairy about two in the afternoon. I know the picture is small, but...could you take another look? Are you sure you haven't seen her?"

"Well, now, I'll take another gander." He adjusted his spectacles, squinted, and then shook his head. "Nope. Sorry."

"Will you let the sheriff know if you see or hear anything?"

"Certainly." He saw them out, and then locked his door, closing for the night.

They walked from shop to shop, then house to house, talking to everyone on the streets, too. After two hours, they turned back toward Caleb's truck, frustrated with a complete lack of progress.

The streets were near empty, most folks at home with family and most shops closed for the night. They stopped in front of an odd place with trinkets and charms in the window. Their eyes followed a scruffy black dog as it trotted across the street toward them, panting with its tongue lolling out one side of its mouth. It circled Jonathan twice, as if reuniting with an old friend, then rolled onto its back, legs splayed open. He leaned over and scratched its belly, causing one leg to shake madly.

"You need a dog for your farm, Caleb?"

"Nah. Why don't you take it home for Jean?"

"Can't have the extra mouth to feed," he said, saddened at the fact. Jean would love the fuzzy old beast.

"You're looking for the girl?" A woman's voice came from behind, scratchy and tired. Turning toward it, a woman dressed in colorful layered skirts, a mass of unruly black, wavy hair, and Indian feathers and charms around her neck stood with a wry smile. "She is not on land but mourns on the sea."

Jonathan blinked, glanced at Caleb and back at her, warily. "What are you talking about?"

She turned slowly toward Caleb, eyes narrow, swaying slightly as she studied him.

"You stand to lose everything. There will be a man...a strong, fearless man, you will be indebted to him...he will take everything...if you let him."

Jonathan pulled at Caleb's shirt. "C'mon. Let's go," he said quietly.

"Wait, Jon. What man, lady? What does he look like?"

"He has two faces. You will not see his true nature until he chooses to reveal it. Be wary of your friends," she whispered.

"Let's go, Caleb." He pulled at his arm, forcing him from his hypnotized stare at the gypsy.

"You come see me. I'll tell you more," she called out after him.

"Don't you dare waste money on that nut, Caleb."

He put Caleb in the truck, slammed the door, and walked around the side, angry at the distraction.

"*She mourns on the sea,*" Caleb repeated out loud. "What do you think she meant by that?"

"I have no idea." Jonathan rubbed his face with his hand, frustrated at the fruitless search.

"You think she knows something?"

"No, I think she was fishing. She's a scammer, Caleb."

"But she knew we were looking for a girl. And she said something about her mourning."

Jonathan gripped the steering wheel, trying to muster patience. "We've been walking around for a couple hours asking about a girl. And everyone knows who she is and that she's a widow. Trust me. She was fishing for a paying client."

Caleb settled back with a frown and stared at the darkening clouds on the horizon.

"Can we just check something?"

"Check what?"

"The marina."

Jonathan sighed long and hard. "I sent Vincent to check the marina. If she were there, he would have been back with her by now."

"Let's just go check again. Please?"

"Fine." He turned around and headed toward the water.

THE SUN WAS NEARLY GONE as they walked alongside each boat. Everything looked as it should. Nothing appeared disturbed, and there was no sign of Claire.

115

"Can we go now? There might be word waiting at home."

"Not just yet."

Caleb stepped onto Aryl's boat. He opened the door to the wheelhouse and looked back at Jonathan.

"She's here."

Jonathan moved to step onto the deck, but Caleb held his hand up.

"Let me."

He ducked in quietly and closed the door behind him. Claire lay sleeping on the floor with Aryl's thick wool sweater clutched in her arms.

With the sound of the door latching closed, she opened her eyes and stared at Caleb.

"We've all been looking for you."

She sat up slowly, holding the sweater close. "What time is it?"

"Almost nine."

She put her hand to her forehead. "I'm sorry. I must have fallen asleep."

Caleb sat on a stool, still unable to meet her eyes.

"Why did you come here? And why didn't you tell anyone?"

She focused on the sweater, picking at it. "I didn't know I was coming here...until I was here. As far as why?" Her eyes floated all around the wheelhouse. "I wanted to feel close to him."

Caleb nodded and cleared his throat.

"You scared us. Rumor has already started that Gordon is a serial killer." He attempted a laugh, but it had been so long he'd forgotten how.

"I didn't mean to start any trouble." She folded the sweater and reached past Caleb to place it next to the wheel.

He took her hand before she could pull away.

"I'm sorry, Claire," he whispered. "I'm so sorry."

Her throat began to close and her eyes stung.

"We both have to get on with life, you know? I'm just having a real hard time doing that."

"So am I." Claire pulled her hand away and clasped them in front of her. "I know what I need to do but can't seem to accept it."

He nodded slowly. "I don't know when I'm going to have the chance or the nerve to talk to you again. So I'm just going to say it and get it over with. I'm taking Arianna and the babies to the city. Boston most likely. I've been thinking a lot about it during the day and I just can't—"

"I wish I could run away," she interrupted.

He looked at her for the first time. "I'm not running away. It's just…"

"I don't hate you, Caleb. Arianna told me you thought that when she came to help me a few weeks ago. I don't, really."

"I still think it's better if we leave."

"Does anyone else know?"

"No."

"Maybe you ought to talk to Jon."

He shrugged. "He's outside. We'd probably better not keep him waiting. Everyone's worried about you."

Neither made a motion to leave.

"Maura has this idea to match me with Gordon."

"Is that what you want?"

"I don't know. Kitten seems to like him. He followed me to Gordon's today and refused to come home with me. I guess he lives there now."

"Don't let yourself be pushed into marrying someone you don't love. Unless you do."

"Of course, I don't. I've only barely met the man. And I couldn't ever love again. Being with Gordon would only be for practicalities sake."

"Is that fair to him?"

"He's a widower. I think he knows what I'm going through. At his house today, I saw he still has pictures of his wife up."

"How long's it been?"

"Two years."

"Maybe you should give yourself more time. It's only been a season. Don't commit the rest of your life to something when you don't know if it'll make you happy."

"But the baby'll be here before I know it." She looked at him in a way that broke his heart. "I don't want to be alone when it comes."

"You won't be alone. You have all of us." He stood and stepped toward her. "You have me."

"But you're leaving for Boston, remember?"

117

He sighed, lowered his head, and crossed his arms. "How about we make a deal. You don't marry anyone before this baby comes, and I won't take my family to Boston until after you have it."

"You'd do that for me?"

"I'd do anything, Claire. Anything and everything and it still wouldn't be enough."

"All right. I won't get married before I'm ready. If you're sure."

"I'm sure." He took her hand and led her out the door and onto the pier.

Caleb came to a screeching halt in front of Jonathan's house. Arianna jumped out and ran to the door.

Ava ended her furious knocking, swinging the door open wide.

"What's wrong?"

"Has Jean left yet?"

"No, why?"

Arianna held out a blue lump. "This is for his first day of school. I promised him I would make it and just barely finished it last night." It was a thick wool knitted sweater. "It'll keep him warm until you can get him a coat."

Ava tilted her head. "Thank you, Arianna. So much. I'm sure he'll love it." She stepped inside, fanning herself.

"He might not need it right away. Seems like summer doesn't want to end."

"He'll need it eventually, don't worry." She turned and called Jean downstairs.

His eyes lit up the way they always did when he saw Arianna, and he ran to hug her.

"Look what Arianna made you, Jean. Special for your first day of school." She held up the sweater, noticing one side was a little longer than the other, and the buttons were slightly out of line with the button holes. She suppressed a grin.

"I love it! Thank you," he said, reaching out for it. He wriggled into it, and despite the slight defects, it fit perfectly.

"It might be too hot today, little man, but I wanted you to have it on your first day." Arianna was still getting used to her usefulness as a homemaker and stood proudly.

"Merci," he said with a flattering little smile. She kissed his cheek just as Caleb called for her.

"Hold on, Mr. Impatient!" she called back. "You have a good day," she said, kneeling down to straighten the sweater. "Learn a lot and don't let anyone pick on you. If they do, you let me know."

He grinned. "Ava already told me that," he said, looking up and taking her hand.

"Come to my house later and tell the babies and me all about your first day." She stood, gave a quick wave, and darted out to the road.

Jean turned to Ava, already starting to sweat under the heavy wool.

He stared at her with a wide-eyed innocence. "Why does she love me so much? I'm not her bebe."

"Because you are very lovable, Jean."

SEPTEMBER 5, 1930

Maura sat at the table with her hands flat in front of her, fingers spread wide. She stared intently, studying the bones and veins of her feminine but sturdy tools. These hands had worked hard for as long as her twenty-seven years could remember. They had loved and soothed, healed and disciplined, cooked and cleaned, setting a frantic pace with only minor thought to direct them and their purpose. Everyone around her depended on these hands. She turned them over, studying the palms. Slightly callused with long fingers and a prominently branched love line. And yet, she had thought so little about her hands over the years, these instruments of work. She ticked off a mental list of all the things these hands had done, weaving and spinning, knitting and sewing, and she envisioned each project, from start to completion.

Concentrating on her hands was safe. Whatever she touched, be it material or loved one, she shielded and repaired. Only these hands, she thought with resentment, failed *her*. They failed to save the child she had just announced to her friends and family, and the steadfast hands that everyone depended on, now lay limp on the table before her. Useless.

She glanced at the clock. Ian would be home soon. She had no dinner prepared—none in mind, either. She had wasted her day, and she chastised herself silently. For the most of the day, she'd spent staring, helpless.

That morning, after Ian had left for work, she rose with the morning sun and bathed—her mind racing through her list of loving obligations. Caleb and Claire were her priorities. She had sewing to do for Jean. There were gardening and baking, and Jonathan had requested some time to talk to her.

It was a rare, quiet day, with Tarin and Scottie off at Arianna's farm, and Claire spending the day with Gordon on his deliveries.

She smiled at the day before her, quiet and productive as she set one foot on the commode to dry her leg with a towel stiff from line drying. After a stabbing pain she pretended to ignore, she felt it. A slow, warm trickle from between her legs. She hesitated to look, floating in denial for a few precious moments, insisting to her emotional mind that she had only peed. But she did look down, eventually, and stared blankly at the small pool of blood forming around the arch of her foot. With a deep shuddering breath, she returned to the bath and cried.

After cleaning herself and forming a makeshift pad, she sat at the kitchen table and reviewed her hands. And here she still sat, when Ian came home.

She heard the door but made no move to welcome him. Still tucked away safely in her own mind with the deliberate scrutiny of her hands, she heard the door close and his solid footsteps nearing the kitchen. He stopped short when he saw her and stared a moment at the back of her bent head. He knew nothing short of catastrophe would cause Maura to sit so still, so quiet. He moved toward her, slowly. He had seen this look before, forlorn and lost, desperately trying to stay above the pain.

"What is it, love?" he whispered. Not quite catatonic, but not ready to leave her safe place either, she gave the smallest shake of her head, eyes glued to her hands.

He took one of them slowly and gave it a small squeeze. "Talk to me, Maura."

He smelled of salt water and hard work.

"How was fishing?" she whispered.

"Fine. Tell me what's wrong. Is Scottie okay? Tarin?"

She nodded.

"Where are they?"

"Out."

He bounced one leg under the table, partially from impatience and partially from the urgent need to pee.

He postponed it as long as he could, sitting with her for nearly ten minutes in silence, giving her time to share what had her so eerily calm.

"I'm sorry, love. I really have to use the bathroom."

She gave a small nod again and resumed counting the minuscule veins on the back of her hand. Eighteen that she could see, small and delicate blue, one pulsed ever so slightly. She heard the door to the bathroom close and then open again quickly. The next second, he was behind her, arms around her chest and his head resting on hers.

"Oh, Maura," he whispered. "I'm so sorry." She stiffened in his arms, and he tightened his grip. "Does anyone else know?"

"No."

"You've been alone with this all day?" he asked incredulously.

Small nod. He reprimanded himself for not staying home. He'd had the feeling as he dressed for work, a pressing need to stay with her. He stared at her a long while as she slept in the early morning hours, trying to make sense of the strong urge, but having no viable reason, he went.

"When did it start?"

"This morning after my bath." Her mind being fully pulled away from her hands, she gave a hard shake and began to cry. He cried with her for only the third time in their marriage. The first, when she married him, the second when Scottie was born, as much for him and the fact that she had lived through the difficult birth, and now for her, and a little one they would never know.

After a few moments, he scooped her up carefully and carried her upstairs. He walked slowly, thinking with each step. Feeling the fragile bones of her ribs under one arm, he wondered if the cause of it was her thinness. She hadn't eaten a proper diet in months. Maybe she worked too hard. She moved a large piece of furniture that he should have been here to move. He stopped short at their bedroom door—maybe it was him. If something was wrong with him that caused...he pushed the

123

thought away and opened the door. He set her on the bed and knelt down in front of her.

"What can I do?" he asked helplessly. There was so much blood in the bathroom despite her efforts to clean it up. There wasn't much more to be done but to see that she rested and healed. She shook her head and pushed herself back on the bed, pulling her knees up to her chest and resting her head on them. He moved beside her with a hand moving slowly over her back and sat quietly as the sun slowly set.

~

THEY HEARD Tarin and Scottie return just after dark. He mumbled something about returning and left the room quietly.

He instructed Tarin to make something for Scottie to eat and to bring something up to her aunt in a little bit. He wasn't ready to tell her what was wrong exactly but told her that Maura was feeling very poorly and not to disturb her. Then he set to cleaning the bathroom before either of them could see the mess.

He drained the bathtub, its water tinted dark red, and he knelt on the floor with a rag and a small bucket of bleach water. He could smell the tang of fresh blood and felt a twisting pain in his chest as he cleaned.

He tried to work quickly and quietly but wasn't quite finished when Tarin appeared in the doorway.

"Uncle," she whispered. "What's happened?" Her eyes grazed over the wet floor and red water in the bucket.

"Your auntie...she lost the babe." He dropped his eyes and cleared his throat.

"Oh, no," she said quietly and glanced back at Maura's closed door. "Is she all right? Should I go see her?"

"Not just yet. Give her a bit of time, aye? And don't say anything to Scottie just yet."

She turned and went silently.

He finished the last of the mopping and returned downstairs. Tarin had warmed up leftovers and was just pulling biscuits from the oven.

Ian put two on a plate, smearing them with butter and honey and started up the stairs to bring them to Maura.

"What's wrong with Mam?" Scottie whispered to Tarin as he left.

Maura was curled up, just as he had left her sitting on the bed, hugging her knees. He sat as carefully as he could and held out the plate to her. She waved it away.

"Ye need to eat something," he said quietly. She ignored him, staring over her knees, studying, this time, her toes.

After sitting in what was, for him, uncomfortable silence, he heard a knock at the door downstairs and was grateful for the reason to move. He wanted to be near Maura, but more than that, he wanted to fix her hurt, and that was something he was incapable of right now. He knew she should cry more. Tears would cleanse, but she had only cried briefly and then had resumed her blank stare.

IAN OPENED the door to Jonathan, who stood smiling. His deep blue eyes danced excitedly as if he knew some wonderful secret.

"Hey, Ian. I'm here to see Maura." He stepped around Ian and inside, stopping just over the threshold and suddenly sensing the unnatural quiet of the house. His eyes turned sharply on Ian.

"What's wrong?" It was then he noticed the deep, dark look shadowing Ian's face.

Ian scrubbed his face with his hand and sighed. "I'm afraid that Maura's lost the pregnancy," he said with a quiet finality that told Jonathan this was not fear, but a fact.

His face dropped into solemn seriousness.

"Where is she?"

Ian nodded toward the ceiling. "Our room, resting."

"When did it happen?"

"Started this morning."

"Has the doctor seen her yet?"

"No, I hadn't called him." He looked down, slightly ashamed. "Ye see, back home, this is something a couple would just get through unless there were complications. The cost of a doctor in these times..." He trailed off, embarrassed. For if it weren't for the lack of money, he would not hesitate to have a doctor look at her, complication or no.

Jonathan took a deep breath and made for the stairs. It was then he smelled the sharp scent of bleach, and an alarm went off in his head. Bleach meant blood.

"Go get the doctor. I'll pay for it." He took the steps two at a time and knocked on Maura's door but didn't wait to be called in.

It swung open wide, and he stood in the doorway. He hadn't known what to expect, but it took him with a bit of shock to see her curled up, hugging her knees in the center of the large bed. She appeared small and fragile, almost childlike. His mental image of her, strong and brash, fearless and fearsome, crumbled.

She didn't acknowledge him, seeming deep in thought.

"Maura," he breathed. He moved slowly to the edge of the bed, looking down on her auburn hair. "Can I sit with you?" She gave a small nod, and he sat carefully. The bed shivered, the springs giving a tiny squeak of protest. Sitting close, but not touching, he reached an arm around her shoulders and rested it there. He smelled it coming from her, the salty stench of fresh blood.

"Toes are the funniest looking things," she said quietly, wiggling them wide. "They aren't quite fingers, but they have knuckles like them...stubby, strange little things, they are." Jonathan glanced at her feet as she studied them.

There was nothing to say, nothing to ask. They just sat and stared at her toes, studying together every detail.

He hated himself for being mute in her time of need. She had done so much for him, for all of them, and now, when she needed those words and actions returned, he was stupid and helpless. Feeling self-conscious, he forced himself to say something. Anything.

"Maura, I'm so sorry," he whispered. He wasn't sure if she heard him until a moment later when she slowly let her head fall to the side, resting it on his shoulder with a deep exhale. She went limp against him. He tightened his arm, holding her close, and sat with her for the longest, most quiet hour of his life.

THE DOOR OPENED SLOWLY, and Jonathan looked with only his eyes to see Ian step in. An elderly, pudgy doctor stood behind him in his black suit, a black bag at his side.

"Maura, love, the doctor would like to take a look at ye." He was concerned—for not only her but also knowing she'd be angry at the expense.

She sat up with tired eyes. Strands of auburn hair hung in her face, and she simply brushed them away as she pulled from Jonathan's side. He gave her a kiss on the top of the head.

"We'll wait downstairs."

THE COFFEE HAD JUST FINISHED brewing, and Ian was pouring mugs when the doctor made his way downstairs with short, panting side steps. His hips having lost their full range of motion after age seventy, he grunted with each stair.

Jonathan and Ian met him at the landing.

"She'll be okay?" Ian asked. The old doctor nodded.

"She will. It was a clean loss, and she seems to be dealing with it well. I told her to stay in bed for a week and to take it easy for a month after that."

Jonathan dug in his pocket for payment while Ian anxiously shifted from foot to foot.

"Tell me, Doctor...is there any way to know why? I mean, this was our first together, ye see, and I'm afraid it might be me...a problem with me. I don't want to put her through this again."

"I highly doubt it was you. Sometimes these things just happen. There's no way to know why. Try to get everything back to normal as quickly as possible, and you can start trying again in a few months if you'd like. I'll come back in a week or so to check on her. Come get me if she spikes a fever, all right?" Ian nodded and opened the door.

Jonathan sat on the couch with his coffee and stared at the floor in front of him.

"I'll take care of letting folks know." Jonathan sighed. "I'll also organize some people to come help out until Maura's feeling better."

"Not Ava, if it's all the same, Jon. That might be a bit too hard on Maura just yet."

Jonathan nodded. "There's no helping Claire being here, but I was actually thinking of some of the older ones."

"Oh?"

"Aryl's mother."

Ian nodded slowly.

"I haven't seen much of them since Aryl died, but I know Kathleen. When she finds out, I know she will volunteer to help."

"Their loss is similar enough to be of a comfort. But different enough not to stir old wounds. You think?"

"I do. I'll stop by tomorrow." He stood and put a hand on Ian's shoulder. "I'm really sorry, Ian. Why don't you take a few days off and be with Maura."

"I'd like to. But I don't have the funds to do that."

"I'll cover your lost wages."

"No offense, Jon, but yer shellin' money like yer still livin' yer old life. I don't want you hurtin' yourself or the business for the charity. With everything that's happened in the last few months, what little savings the business had, it has to be close to gone."

"I'll work it out," he said and saw himself to the door.

SEPTEMBER 7, 1930

Caleb took a deep breath, bracing for the rant. Downing the last gulp of whiskey, he turned to face Arianna, to apologize again and go through the heated exchange they'd had at least twice a week.

"I was just headed inside, honey," he said with a huff as he turned.

"Well, then, I'm glad I caught you, sweetheart." Marvin removed his hat with a grin.

"Oh, Marvin. I thought you were my wife," Caleb said with relief as Marvin motioned for permission to sit down.

"What brings you out here?" Caleb sat back down a little too quickly and swooned, batting his eyes.

"Well, a few things. First, a gift." He pulled a whiskey bottle from behind his back. "Second, just to chat and third, I need a small favor."

Caleb reached for the bottles. "Well, let's chat."

"How've you been?"

Caleb gave a sloppy shrug and looked away.

"Still having a hard time?"

Caleb tilted up the bottle.

"Listen, I know how you feel. I lost a buddy in the war. Harder than hell to walk around, wishing your best friend was by your side."

"I thought you said it was your brother."

Marvin shoved a hand through his hair. "Yes. Brother. Buddy, same thing, you know?"

"He was my best friend," Caleb whispered. "More than that even. Jonathan...Jonathan's everyone's damn hero. Always has all the answers. But me and him alone...we're not so good." He shook his head slowly. "Aryl was the balance between us. From the first day we starting running together as boys, he was the balance." He drank again.

"I've tried talking to Jon, but he's closed himself off. Won't talk about it."

"He won't. And he doesn't like me talking about it either. Says I'm feeling sorry for myself."

"You're not."

"It's just not fair."

"It's not."

"I'd trade places with him if I could."

"I know you would."

There was a long silence, and Caleb willingly handed Marvin the bottle. He took a drink and handed it back.

"Don't listen so much to Jon. He talks about it plenty."

"Oh yeah? To who?"

"Vincent. He's been in his office several times trying to get him to look further into it."

"Oh. You mean Victor," Caleb scoffed.

"And you don't think he did it?"

Caleb raised his head, his face ragged. "Does it matter?"

After a long moment, Marvin shook his head. "I suppose it doesn't." He looked all around. "Nice spot you've got here."

"Yeah, 'bout the only place I can get any peace."

"No one else comes in here?"

"No. Well, Arianna comes to yell at me a couple times a week."

"Maybe you can help me out."

"How so?"

"Well, the store room at the office is getting full. Been catching a lot of runners lately. I was hoping to find a spot to keep stuff in until we can get around to destroying it."

"You mean hooch?"

Marvin smiled. "Yeah, hooch. Bathtub gin, moonshine, homemade brandy. The whole gamut. You wouldn't believe the amount."

He saw Caleb's eyes widen with interest. "Of course, times are hard, the sheriff's office couldn't pay you for storage space, you know, with cash." He smiled and winked.

"I think I could make some room."

"And we'd need you to keep it strictly confidential. I wouldn't want it to get out that it's being kept here. You'd find yourself with more friends than you ever knew you had!"

"No, no. I'd keep it quiet. How about right back here?" Caleb rose and walked unsteadily to the back of the barn. He opened the gate to an empty horse stall.

"This would be great. Appreciate it, Caleb. I really do."

"Not a problem." He wobbled back to his seat. "Say, I'd love to have you over for dinner sometime. Think we can get the women together without a cat fight breaking out?"

Marvin laughed. "I doubt it. We'd better stick to a poker night with just the guys."

"Yeah, that might be better."

"I'll just go get a few boxes and put them in the back, okay?"

"Okay. And Marvin...thanks. For talking."

"Anytime, Caleb."

SEPTEMBER 10, 1930

Jonathan's car sputtered and died alongside the curb in front of Aryl's parent's house. He took a long, deep breath as he reconsidered. He hadn't been to visit Kathleen and Michael since the memorial, and the longer he waited to go see them, the harder it was to actually do it. He always found an excuse to not go. Deep down, the excuse was it would hurt. It would be hard on all of them. He saw traces of his best friend in their face and mannerisms, and they saw the empty spot where Aryl always stood next to Jonathan growing up. Getting into trouble, having a grand time and causing general childish mayhem. Even Claire had told him it was hard to look at him. He wondered if Kathleen and Michael would turn him away, as well. For Maura, he had to at least try.

He knocked on the door and thought about running. Something he and Aryl used to do for fun as kids. That spurred flashing memories and misty eyes, and just as he was about to abandon his plan, Michael opened the door.

"Jonathan, hello!" He smiled, looking a lot older than the last time they had seen each other.

"Hello, Michael."

"Come in, please. Can I get you some lemonade?"

"That would be great, thank you." He stood awkwardly in the living room. Not sure what to do with his hands, he tucked them behind his back and looked around, somewhat surprised. Kathleen had always kept a spotless house. But today, it was neglected. On the fireplace mantle, a few pictures of Aryl were clustered and mingled with several well-used candles. Jonathan blinked hard and moved his eyes quickly. Michael returned with two glasses and a smile.

"I'll have to apologize. It's not too sweet. Running low on sugar lately."

"No, that's fine." He took a sip and tried to find somewhere safe to set his eyes.

"Haven't seen you in a while, Jon. How've you been?"

"I've been fair."

"And Ava's doing well?"

"She is. Once she got past the early sickness, she's done all right."

Michael's eyes dropped, and he gave an apprehensive smile and spoke quietly.

"And how's Claire?"

"She's all right, I suppose. I haven't visited with her in a while. Last time I did, she sent me away."

Michael nodded. "We had a similar issue."

"She won't see you?"

He shook his head. "No. Not after the last time Kathleen went over there to bring some of Aryl's baby things."

"I guess that would be hard."

"It wasn't so much the visit or the clothes. It was the things Kathleen said to her. I guess it got very heated and didn't end well."

He nodded for Jonathan to follow him through the kitchen and into the backyard. They sat on the swing, safely shaded from the overbearing summer sun.

"I'm really glad you came over, Jon. I've needed someone to talk to about this, and you might just know what to do."

He crossed his arms and leaned back, wondering if this was the same quiet frustration that Maura felt when folks ran to her, one after the other, with their problems.

133

"What's the trouble?"

"Well, it's Kathleen. She's not been right lately. Of course, Aryl's death was hard on all of us, and I don't think we'll ever get over it. The first few weeks Kathleen did everything you'd expect a grieving person to do. We were in town one day, and she stopped in this little shop...the kind that sells potions and fortunes, all lit up with candles. It's run by some gypsy. Anyway, she stepped in and paid for a fortune. I waited outside thinking it all hogwash, but I hoped this woman would tell her something that would help her get over the loss."

"What happened?"

"Well, when she came out, she was very quiet. Very deep in thought. But she seemed to be at peace. I figured this gypsy lady told her Aryl was at peace on the other side, said he loved her, all the typical stuff. But later that night, she lit the candles around Aryl's pictures and sat me down. She said she had something very serious to tell me. She didn't seem herself at all. It was really kind of strange, Jonathan. It's like my Kathleen walked into that shop, but a different woman walked out."

"How is she different?"

"She's never been one for superstition, charms, and chants and all that mess. But she goes to see this woman a few times a week. Financially, it's bleeding us dry. It's why we can't afford sugar. I know I should put a stop to it, but it seems to be the only thing keeping her from going into that dark, sad place again. The biggest problem...what I need to figure out how to prepare for, is when she realizes that all this is bull pucky. Smoke and mirrors and all that."

"What's smoke and mirrors?"

"Well, in all seriousness, she told me...well, this gypsy has her believing that Aryl is alive, Jonathan."

The words slammed into Jonathan's chest like a punch, and he dropped his head.

"And this is what she told Claire the last time she saw her?"

"Not only that. When Claire told her about Gordon, that she was considering seeing him more regularly for the baby's sake, Kathleen got really upset saying that she was making a huge mistake, that Aryl would be angry when he got home and found another man in his bed, raising his child."

"Oh, boy."

"It was ugly. Claire threw her out and forbade us to ever come back. And with our first grandchild on the way, too."

"Where is Kathleen now?"

Michael tossed him a look that told him exactly where she was and took another sip of his bitter lemon water.

"When will she be home?"

He shrugged and sighed.

"Well, I have something I need her to do. It might take her mind off this gypsy nonsense."

"Wonderful. What is it?"

"Well, Maura miscarried this morning."

"I'm so sorry to hear that, Jon."

"She's going to need some help for the next few weeks. With Ava expecting, I thought it would be a little insensitive to have her go over and help. So I was going to enlist some of the other women."

"I'm sure Kathleen would love to help out. And who knows. It might help bring her around.

"Well, I can come back tomorrow and talk to her about it."

Just then, Kathleen's voice echoed from the house.

"Michael! I'm home!"

She stuck her head out the back door, saw Jonathan, and waved with a big smile. She didn't look deranged or too terribly detached from reality, besides an aura of overwhelming happiness that seemed to radiate from her. But Jonathan did notice a rather large ugly rock charm hanging around her neck.

"Oh, good! I needed to talk to you!" She hurried over and wedged herself in between them on the swing.

Before Jonathan could get to asking her how she was, and for the favor of looking after Maura, Kathleen turned and took his hand in both of hers. "I have some exciting news, Jonathan." Her eyes were alive and shining with joy that went deep down to her soul. "Aryl is *alive*."

~

JONATHAN WALKED in and sat down at the table with Ava and Jean, who were just finishing dinner. He nodded and whispered thank you when Ava handed him a plate of potato casserole and green beans.

Ava gave him a few minutes to eat and take a long drink of cold tea before asking the obvious.

"What's wrong?" *If I only had a dime for every time I have asked that,* she thought wearily.

"Well, a lot, actually. Maura's going to need someone to help her out for the next couple of weeks. She's lost, well..." He glanced at Jean wanting to be discreet and gave a pointed nod at Ava's growing stomach. "She's going to need a little help. And I don't think it should be you, for sensitivities sake."

She half stood out of her chair, as if ready to bolt out the door and to Maura's side.

"Oh, Jon! You don't mean—"

He gave her a sharp glance.

"Jean, if you're done, why don't you go turn on your radio show."

He nodded and wiped his mouth, placing his napkin on his cleaned plate, and slid off the chair.

When he was gone, Jonathan spoke freely.

"I know you want to rush over there. But she needs to rest and heal, and I don't think that anyone expecting should go over there for a bit." He read her apprehension and felt her need to be of support to Maura. "I know how you feel, Ava. But I think she needs some space right now. Let Ian and she have some time."

"Who will help her then?"

"Well, I thought maybe Kathleen and my mother. Some of the older ones. I think this needs the delicate wisdom that only they have."

Ava opened her mouth to protest. What was needed right now were friends that knew Maura to the core. Those who loved her fiercely and wanted to protect her. She closed it, however, knowing that Jonathan was most likely right.

He omitted details of Kathleen's sudden obsession with the gypsy and the belief that Aryl was alive. It would hurt to recount it…to say the words. A small part of him wanted to believe her, despite her lack of any proof beyond that of a small town fortune teller trying to string money out of a desperate woman. But still, it was tempting. He found refuge for just a moment, closing his eyes and indulging in her delusion. *Aryl's alive.* Her words echoed in his mind, stirring a ridiculous hope and a selfish longing for it to be true. He raised his head, cleared his throat, taking a firm grasp on reality and stopped the illusion before it had a chance to spiral out of control.

SEPTEMBER 20, 1930

Kathleen, Margaret, ETHEL, and June all descended upon Jonathan like a small army. He was in the garage with his head stuffed under the hood of an abused truck his father had acquired. He was taking pointers, learning basic mechanics from his self-taught father. He didn't enjoy it, but he was determined to master it.

Jonathan Sr. saw the women approaching and stood up, wiping black grease from his hands.

"I sincerely hope they're here to talk to you and not me," he snickered.

"What do you mean?" Jonathan poked his head out to the side and saw them with decided looks on their faces and a steady march.

"Jonathan! We need to talk to you."

"I don't know what you did, son, but...I'll be inside."

"Thanks a lot."

He stood and met them as they all came to a halt at the same time.

"We need to talk to you, Jonathan. It's about Maura," Ethel said.

The slightly entertained look on his face dropped, and seriousness took its place.

"Is she all right?"

"Well, yes. Mostly. She's moving about, eating and such. She's thin and pale and weak, but the worst of it is over," Kathleen said.

"That's good to hear."

"She's not up for visitors, though," June said.

"Well, that's not abnormal."

"Yes, it is," June countered.

"I'm sorry, I'm not following."

"Jonathan. You enlisted our help to get Maura through this and back on her feet," Kathleen reminded. "Physically and mentally."

"Yes, I did."

"Then trust us when we say that we are worried about her."

"It's not that I don't trust you, it's just—"

"There's something missing in Maura," Margaret said, using a gentler tone. "Physically she is fine, but emotionally, this has changed her, and I'm worried that if we don't do something soon, it may change her for good."

Jonathan blew out his breath and folded his arms. He wanted to argue that something like this would change a person. That she shouldn't be expected to receive visitors and act like nothing happened. Realizing he was drastically outnumbered, however, he chose his words carefully.

"What do you ladies propose we do, then?"

"She needs something more than we can give her, Jonathan. We can clean her kitchen and make food and small talk with her. Tell her jokes and distract her best we can. But it's not enough," Margaret said. "She needs something stronger, more powerful to pull her past this."

"And what would that be?" Jonathan asked, rubbing his eyes and digging for patience.

"Her mother," they all said in unison.

~

THE NEXT DAY, Jonathan brought it up in the midst of casual conversation with Ian. They stood in line with the other fishermen waiting for their catch to be weighed. At the suggestion, Ian went a little pale.

"Are ye sure ye want to do that, Jon?"

"The others seem to think Maura needs her. That she can help her get back to herself. I've heard stories, but you know her mother. I want to know what you think. Because if we send for her, it's going to take every cent we have. As much as I love Maura, it's not a decision to be taken lightly."

"No, I understand. Can we manage to put the business and our families in such a predicament?"

Jonathan took a deep breath and shrugged. "If I can do something to help Maura, I want to try. I don't know if she ever shared it with you, but she saved my life. I owe a lot to her."

"No, she never mentioned. What happened?"

Jonathan shook his head, closing that part of the conversation. "I just need to know what you think about bringing her mother over. Do you think she can help Maura?"

"Aye. Most likely. She's a strong, stubborn woman. God help ye if you cross her, but she's full of hard love and won't hesitate to set a person straight."

Jonathan smiled, remembering Maura's words on Christmas Eve, the night he almost ended his life. She'd handed him an heirloom cross and said, *Mr. Jonathan, if ye don't take it, I'll have me mother on the next boat from Ireland, and trust me—I'm a mild-mannered angel compared to that woman.*

"It would take a Maura to save a Maura, wouldn't it, Ian? I'll go to the others tonight, and we'll try to pull together the funds. Don't say anything to her, all right? I don't know how soon we can do it, and I want it to be a surprise."

"I'd like to say I've something to contribute, Jon, but after we buy Scottie shoes, and even if Maura makes his winter coat this year, we'll barely have enough to survive the winter. And that's not counting another mouth to feed if her mam does come."

"No, let us do this for you."

Ian nodded with a grateful and somewhat relieved smile. "Thank you, Jon."

. . .

LATER THAT AFTERNOON, Jonathan took a mason jar from the cupboard and began the collection. He opened the trunk in his and Ava's bedroom, digging around until he found a small canvas bag with their life savings. He explained everything to Ava as he dug around, counted out change, and did some math in his head. Jean clung to Ava's side, listening to Jonathan recount Maura's hurt and need.

"I don't know that we can come up with enough money right off but...we'll do the best we can," he said with a sigh.

Jean turned and left the room. Ava's eyes followed him and then returned them to Jonathan with a smile.

"I think it's a wonderful idea, Jon. How can I help?"

"Well, I'm going to everyone that knows Maura and asking them to help. Maybe you could organize something with the women...a bake sale or something. All the proceeds can go toward the effort."

"I'll get right on it. I'll bet we could put some flyers up in town and hold it out on Caleb's property. Maybe a rummage sale, too."

"Good thinking. I'll leave the planning to you." He held up the jar. "I'll be back in a few hours. And I'll telegram her mother while I'm out."

"Wait, please." Jean's small voice came from the doorway. He stood with one hand behind his back. "I want to help, too."

"Well, now, Jean, I appreciate that, but I think you should stay here and help Ava." Jonathan knelt down in front of him, balancing the jar on his knee.

"I don't want to go with you. Here." He pulled his hand from behind his back and dropped three pennies in the jar. "I was saving them for a present for the new bebe."

Jonathan stared at the three shiny pennies among the quarters in the bottom of the jar for a long moment.

"Thank you, Jean," he whispered. "Every little bit helps."

Ava took a deep breath as her eyes misted at the generosity of such a small child, who had lost so much, yet gave so freely.

E veryone gathered early at Caleb's farm. Patrick, Arianna, and Shannon had worked hard to begin gathering in the garden, and Ethel was preparing for a massive canning.

Jean and Aislin were in charge of collecting strawberries, and for every two they picked, they ate one.

"Will Maura be here today?" Shannon asked.

"I'm not sure. I've invited her." Jonathan lifted a crate of mason jars from the backseat. "I think Kathleen will talk her into coming."

Claire's eyes flickered at the mention of Aryl's mother, and she clung to Ava's arm.

"I've talked to her," Jonathan said. "I've asked her not to mention anything upsetting."

"Thank you."

Ava craned her head, looking for Kathleen and Michael's car. Jonathan took her arm.

"Let's get inside. They'll be along."

They heard a sputtering and Ava turned with a smile. It dropped when she saw it was only Gordon's milk truck. She narrowed her eyes with a presumptuous nod.

"I didn't know he would be here."

"He said he might stop by to help." Claire looked toward the house and back to the truck. "I'll catch up."

~

"You made it," Claire said.

"Are you glad?"

"Every pair of hands makes the job easier."

He smiled. "I meant are you glad to see me."

"I think everyone will be."

He nodded slowly, patiently.

"I brought some jars I found in the barn. Thought you could use them."

"I could, thank you."

"I've been meaning to ask you something. I hate to be so forward, but did you have a good time last Friday?"

"I did. Thank you."

"I know the 'firsts' are hard. First date, first holiday, first anything. I wouldn't have been upset if you said you hadn't enjoyed it."

"It was a wonderful dinner and the picture was fine. The comedy was a good choice."

"I thought a lot about it."

"I can tell. And I appreciate it."

Gordon squinted past her at the car coming up the lane. "How's Maura been?"

"Not herself. She's moving and doing but the fire's gone."

"It's hard to imagine that."

"It is. She didn't even grill me for details after our outing."

"How's the collection coming to bring her mother?"

"We're about half way there. We were thinking of arranging a bake sale after harvest to raise the rest of the money."

"Sounds fun. I'll donate ten quarts of milk. You have to have milk with cookies and cakes."

"Thank you, Gordon. That's really sweet." She gave a slight smile.

"I can't wait to see what it really looks like."

"What?"

"Your smile. A big, honest, true smile. I'll bet it's beautiful."

She sighed deeply and fidgeted her fingers.

"Gordon, glad you could make it." Jonathan came up beside Claire and shook his hand.

"Jon, how can I help?"

"Oh, there's an army of women in the kitchen...I'd avoid that, but Patrick knows what's going on as far as bringing in the produce. If you find him, he'll direct you."

Jonathan's eyes flickered to Claire and back to Gordon.

"I have to run into town, I'll be back in an hour or so."

"What for?" Claire asked.

"I just need to pick something up. But Ava's asking for you. She's in the kitchen."

VICTOR DRAYTON SAT DOWN and glanced around the restaurant. It was a grand one that he and Ruth used to frequent often. He ordered a drink and sat back, sweeping the restaurant with his eyes.

"Where are you, you little bastard," he whispered. For a moment, he worried he'd misread the meeting place. He pulled the letter out of his jacket pocket and nodded. He was in the right place. He lit a cigarette.

"Sorry I'm late. Thank you for meeting with me."

Victor kept a solid expression.

"Did I have a choice?"

His companion smiled. "Not really." Looking at his cigarette, he held out his hand. "I forgot mine, do you mind?"

Victor reluctantly held out his case and tossed a match across the linen tablecloth.

"Why don't we just get down to business? I'm not one for small talk."

"Can't I order a drink first?"

Victor waved the waiter over with strained patience.

"You enjoy keeping me waiting."

"I'll have scotch, please. And the French onion soup...charcuterie for a starter, roasted rack of lamb, and let's finish with Crème Brulee."

"Very good, sir." The waiter nodded and turned to Victor. "And for you?"

"Nothing." He kept his eyes pinned across the table as the waiter left. "You have expensive taste."

"Is there any other kind to have when you're not paying the bill?" He smiled.

"Why don't we get down to the business of your letter?"

"Right." He tapped his cigarette and took another drink.

"My patience wears thin," Victor warned.

"Then perhaps you'd better dig deeper, Victor. Because I have a lot to say."

Victor stubbed out his cigarette and ground his teeth. "Then perhaps you'd better get on saying it."

"You do spoil my anticipation."

Victor stared. One eye twitched.

"I'd like to know how I know you."

"You don't. But I know you. And I know people who know you."

Victor laughed. "You have a beef with me for...let me guess. Did I sleep with your wife? Impregnate your daughter? Shift you on a business deal? You look too middle class to have lived in one of my slums so doubtful I evicted your granny."

"Oh, I do enjoy a good game of cat and mouse. Surely you can appreciate that, Victor."

"Surely. But at some point, the game must get underway. I grow old waiting."

He smiled tightly as the waiter placed his drink.

"I saw you, Victor. That night in Rockport. At the marina. I saw you."

Victor went white and sat back slowly.

"I watched you cut the wires and spend a good amount of time messing with the engine of the Ava-Maura."

Victor held his gaze and swallowed hard. "Who are you?"

"Does it matter?"

After a long moment, Victor shook his head and regained his

145

posture. "I was in Florida when that happened. I've already been questioned and cleared by the police."

"Have you, now?"

"I have. So whatever your goal is, you've wasted your time." He made to stand.

"Take a look over there."

Victor turned his head and briefly met the eyes of a man staring at him over the top of a newspaper. He quickly flipped it up.

"You're being watched, Victor, by the police. Seems they don't quite believe your story about a sunny vacation in Florida. And it appears you've wasted your time and risked your neck for nothing. Because Jonathan Garrett is alive and well."

Victor's eyes flashed. "That's impossible! The newspaper said—"

"Newspapers have been known to make mistakes. And they made a big one when they interviewed that old fisherman that told them it was the captain of the Ava-Maura that went down. They rushed it to print without verifying anything. The other newspapers followed."

"But it did go down."

"It did. And took Aryl Sullivan with it. Nearly killed Caleb Jenkins. But Jonathan Garrett didn't go with them that day. You failed, Victor."

His body tremored, and he struggled to find something to say.

"What do you want?"

"What any blackmailer wants. Money."

"And if I go to the police for harassment? You have no proof but your own word."

Laughter rang out from across the table. With a heavy thud, something landed on the table. Victor looked at the badge, closed his eyes, and sighed.

"My name is Marvin. I'm a deputy in Rockport. All I may have is my word, Victor, but it'll hold a hell of a lot more weight than yours. Now, let's talk about what it's worth to you to make this go away."

MAURA STEPPED out of the car and straightened her clothes. Kathleen grabbed her hand—to keep her from running away, perhaps—and smiled.

"You'll be better for getting out a bit, Maura."

She shot her an irritated look and started up the stairs. The whole kitchen hushed as she stepped inside. It was just what she was dreading. The sympathetic looks, the careful glances, the hushed words when she wasn't looking. If anyone asked, *'How are you?'*, she'd send them through the roof, she was sure of it. She knew she was pale, her cheeks gaunt, and the dark circles around her eyes didn't make her look any younger. Her hair was flat and her lips dry. She'd tried in vain to make her appearance look better than she felt. The earthy smell of green beans grated on her nerves. The bright light streaming in the windows gave her a headache. She scanned the faces staring at her and grew more irritated by the second.

"I'm so glad you could make it." Ava stepped forward and gave her a hug. "There's a lot to do, so jump in wherever you want. Tarin is washing, Shannon is packing, Claire is putting on the lids, Arianna is running bushels from the porch, and Ethel and I are processing.

"Where's Jonathan?"

"He had to run into town. Patrick, Ian, and Caleb are out in the gardens gathering."

"Or in the barn, drinking," Arianna snorted.

The only available spot in the kitchen was at the table. Tin strainers filled to the brim with green beans waited to be snapped. She sat down and her thin fingers, quickly found a mindless rhythm, and soon, she was staring at the wood grain of the table while her hands worked.

Trying to tune out the conversation of the women, desperately trying to talk about anything other than children, she heard a scuffle on the porch. Patrick set down a heaping bushel of carrots, tipped his hat, and smiled at her before turning toward the garden. Maura went back to her green beans. The air was thick with caution and careful words— but nothing like the bustling chatter she had walked in on. It quickly became too much.

"Has anyone taken the men something to drink?" she asked.

"No, they get a drink with every few bushels they bring to the porch," Arianna said, setting the carrots out of the way in the pantry with a grunt. She sat down to help Maura while waiting for the next bushel. Maura saw no reason why she couldn't do both and stood up, excused herself and stepped out into the humidity. Taking a deep breath, and feeling as if she might drown for doing so, she headed up the hill to where the men worked.

Men may spend most of their married life daft, she thought, *but they sure knew when to keep their mouths shut when it came to delicate subjects. And they were good at the business of moving on and acting like nothing ever happened.* She glanced over at the barn and thought of Caleb. *Well, most of them are.* A small part of her wanted to go to him. She struggled for a moment, lowered her head, and walked on.

THE CLOTHES KATIE MALLORY wore were simple, yet she wore them with an air of staunch dignity. With no particular expression at all, she might appear angry, thoughtful, displeased, or content. All dependent on who was looking and what *they* thought she might perceive of them. It ran in the blood, this 'seeing into the soul' and Katie, like Maura, had a way of making you understand yourself or your particular problem without saying a word. Of course, words helped.

"Where's my Maura?"

The entire kitchen turned toward the harsh Irish accent standing in the doorway. The familial connection was undeniable. *This* was Maura's mother. With wide eyes and open mouths, the crowd of women in the kitchen stood beside themselves. It was only moments ago, amidst feverish water bath canning of an endless stream of green beans, that they made plans for the bake sale—and perhaps a rummage sale to bring Katie Mallory overseas. And now here she stood with Jonathan behind her holding a sheepish grin.

She seemed larger than life and the spitting image of all of Maura's terrifying tales. Ava stepped forward.

"You must be Maura's mother, Katie."

"I am. And you must be Ava."

She grinned at Jonathan over her shoulder. "How on earth did you know?"

"Maura's writings. That woman writes letters that take days to read. And she's a fair descriptor of her friends. You fit the image I had in my head exactly, dear."

"How on earth did you know to come?"

"How did you get here?"

"Have you been waiting long?"

"Jonathan, what's going on here?"

"Does Maura know you're here?"

Questions came from all directions in the kitchen. Katie shook her head and held up her hand. A gray lock fell from its place, and she swiped it back in order.

She looked at Kathleen. "I knew to come because Jonathan sent me a telegram a few weeks ago."

She looked at Arianna. "I came by ship, as most do when traveling from other countries." Arianna stiffened at the elementary tone Katie used.

She looked at Claire. "And I've not been waiting at all. In fact, Jonathan had to wait fifteen minutes for the train. It was a bit late."

Finally, she looked at Shannon. "And I'm glad to see it was kept secret...my coming, that is. You see—" she paused and looked all around, "do they not have tea in America? And I'm starving for a bite to eat."

She sat down gracefully as the kitchen burst into a flurry of activity.

～

"Now." Everyone gathered around the table to listen, forgetting altogether about the canning. She smiled as she stirred her tea. "As I was saying, when I got the telegram from Jonathan, I immediately sent a telegram back saying that I would be on a boat by the end of the week. I have a sixth sense about these things, you know, and I had been setting a bit of money aside for just such an occasion. I told him to keep it a secret, and he did." She gave him an approving glance and took a sip of tea. "Now, I've answered all of your questions. Would you please answer mine and tell me where my Maura is?"

"She's out in the back garden with Patrick," Ava said. "I'll take you to her."

~

MAURA STOOD, braced her hands on her back and stretched.

"Ye don't have to do this, Maura. If ye want to go back and join the women in the kitchen, I won't think any less of ye," Patrick said.

"No, Patrick. It feels good to move. Seems I've been sittin' and doin' nothin' forever." She wiped sweat from her forehead, closed her eyes, and blew out a long breath.

"You all right, Maura?" Patrick stood and took her arm.

"Just dizzy from the heat. I'm fine." She opened her eyes toward the direction of the house and squinted. She closed her eyes and opened them again, readjusting to the bright light.

"Jaysus sufferin' Christ!"

"What, Maura?"

"I'm seein' things, Patrick. I'm having an apparition of sorts!"

"What do ye see?" Patrick sidled up to her and followed her eyes.

"I swear I see me mother. Just there by the house. See!"

Patrick squinted. "I don't know what yer mother looks like, Maura."

"Oh, for the love of...either I'm dyin' or she is, Patrick! People only see their loved ones when they're dyin'! And she's coming towards me! She's comin' to say goodbye!"

"Now, hold on, Maura. I see two people as well. Don't get yourself worked up. Let's just go on down there and see who it is, all right?"

Her hand was shaking as Patrick took it, leading her out of the bountiful garden.

"I can't bear to walk toward me mother's ghost!"

She stopped and covered her face with her hands.

"'Tis not yer mother's ghost, Maura. Likely one of Ethel's friends come to help."

Maura shook her head fiercely from behind her hands.

After a moment, she heard the harsh Irish brogue calling her name. "Maura!" Maura yelped.

"Take yer hands from yer face, child. It's me."

Slowly, Maura lowered her hands, hardly believing her eyes.

"Mam?" She studied her carefully deciding that she was, in fact, alive.

"Aye. Come here." She held her arms open, and Maura walked into them, still disbelieving. She was taller than her mother was, only for Katie's aged back.

"How did you get here?"

Katie rolled her eyes. "Same way you did, ye simpleton. A big boat."

"But why?" She pulled back and stared at her. "Why did ye come?"

"Because ye need me."

THE HOUSE WAS alive with noise as a long day of canning came to a close. Maura had hardly said two words since returning to the house as Katie got on with the business of getting to know everyone. Patrick smiled over the crowd and decided now was as good a time as any to surprise Shannon. He tugged on her sleeve.

"Can I have a word with ye, Shan?"

"Of course, what's wrong?"

"Nothing's wrong. Just wanted to take a walk, is all."

"A walk? But I've got to get the babies down."

He nodded to Jonathan and he took Roan from Shannon's arms.

"He'll tend him while we're gone."

Confused, she took Patrick's hand.

"What on earth's goin' on, Pat? It'll be dark soon!"

"There's enough light for what I need to show ye."

They walked out into the warm night and started up the hill to the back of the property.

"I wish you'd tell me what this is all about."

"You'll see, soon enough."

They came to a clearing where a small, neat cabin sat bathed in the last of the sunlight.

"What's this?"

"I've been working on it in my free time. It was a dilapidated mess at first, but it cleaned up well. I worked out a deal with Caleb. This cabin and the acre that surrounds it. Got it for a fair price on contract. I gave him a little down, and we can make payments on the rest. We can't move in for a week yet. There're a few things left to do, but—" He took a deep breath. "It's ours, Shan."

She stared, dumbfounded.

"Do you like it?" He took her hand and led her closer. "I strung up some laundry lines on the side here and already marked off a spot for yer garden. I can work on a spot for chickens and a small barn, maybe." He watched her, waiting.

"Say somethin', Shan," he whispered.

"Ours, Patrick?"

"Ours."

She smiled as a tear slipped down her cheek. "This is what's been keeping you out till dark every night?"

He nodded and she scrunched up her face.

"And just the other night I yelled at ye fer being gone so much and not spending time with us. I'm so sorry, Pat."

"You didn't know."

"I should have known better." She wiped her eyes. "That if you were out and away, it was fer a good reason."

"Don't worry none about that. C'mon. Let me show ye the inside."

OCTOBER 5, 1930

T he pounding on the door jerked Bomani out of a light sleep. His eyes opened, and he laid stock still, listening.

Another round of intent knocking had him up on his feet, loaded gun at his side. He stood off to the side and asked who it was.

"It's Victor."

He motioned frantically for his woman to move, and she darted to the coat closet. He opened the door a crack.

"Why are you here?"

"Because I sent for you twice and you never came."

"I'm working for someone else now."

"Oh, really?"

"Really."

Victor stepped toward the door, placing a hand on it. Bomani cocked the gun. Victor's smile was strained and impatient.

"Going to kill me, Bomani?"

"Only if you're here to try to kill me."

He laughed. "Here to kill you? Bomani, if I wanted you dead, I'd have hired someone, and it would have been done last week." He laughed again harder. "You think I'd knock on your door if I came here to kill you? A murderer with manners!"

"Why did you knock on my door then?" He eyed him and the dimly lit hallway beyond.

Victor quit laughing suddenly. "I need to talk to you."

"About what?"

"Can I come in?"

"No."

"I don't feel comfortable talking about it through the door, Bomani."

"And I don't feel comfortable with you coming to my home."

"Then let me in so no one sees me," Victor said slowly.

Bomani sighed and opened the door.

Before he knew what was happening, Victor was pinned with his face against the wall, his arm twisted behind his back, as Bomani checked his pockets. He stepped away and kept the gun in his hand.

"Not how I'm used to being received," Victor complained as he straightened his jacket.

"Get to the point and go." Bomani sat on the sofa with the gun dangling between his knees.

Victor sat down on the worn armchair and crossed his legs. "You aren't going to offer me a drink?"

"No, now get on with it."

He pointed at Bomani. "You, sir, are not a murderer with manners." He grinned.

Bomani wanted to deny that he was a murderer. But he couldn't. "I have manners with those who deserve it."

"*Fine.* I'll get to the point. I've just learned that my arch nemesis, the man I most despise on this earth, the man I *tried* to kill, is apparently still alive."

"I told you to let me do it."

"It wasn't my failing, Bomani. He just happened to not be on the boat that day. His worthless friend died in his place."

"And that brings you here why?"

"I need you to take care of it."

Bomani shook his head. "No way."

"I'm prepared to pay. Handsomely."

"No. I'm done. Not doing that kind of work anymore."

Victor looked amused. "Retiring, eh?"

"From that line of work, yes. I'm going honest."

"Well, that's unfortunate for me, now isn't it?"

"Plenty of men out there to help you, Victor."

"I see. Maybe you could recommend one?" He laughed.

"Any big guy in line for day work. Lots in the breadline, too. Even the best man will turn bad if he has a family to feed."

Victor narrowed his eyes. "But what would cause a bad man to go good? The same thing, perhaps?" His grin widened. "Do you have a family?" He stood and glanced around. Bomani rose quickly. "It's time to leave."

"Listen, Bo, you will do this job for me."

"No, I won't."

"You will. You see, it would be nothing for me to draw up the papers to show that you leased an apartment from me a few months ago. I have a man who's good with signatures. Nor would it be any effort to call the police and tell them you abandoned the apartment and left behind a strangled prostitute."

Bomani had the urge to kill him right then, right there. Only the fact that Victor was standing in front of the coat closet where his woman hid stopped him from shooting.

"When?"

"I knew you'd see things my way. I'll be in touch with the details." He smiled and let himself out.

Bomani locked the door and pressed his head against it. He hated being trapped like a rat in a cage. He would do this job for Victor, but it wouldn't be his last, he decided. Victor would be his last. He visualized killing him over and over... all the ways he could kill him. Bloody or clean... fast or slow... knife or gun... quietly or loudly... this life had damaged him to enjoy the possibilities as much as he did.

A muffled cry tore him from his fantasy. He opened the coat closet and pulled her to her feet. She was shaking.

"It's all right. He's gone."

He thought long and hard before speaking.

"I'm not going to do this for him, don't worry."

155

She nodded against his shoulder. "But he'll kill you if you don't. He'll kill both of us."

"No, he won't. We'll be gone. I'll make like I'm going to do the job for him. I'll go to Rockport, and I'll take you with me. We'll warn them. We'll tell them everything. And then we'll leave. We'll head west. Maybe California. I don't know where yet. We'll find a place and start a new life, okay?"

"And we'll be safe?"

He pulled back and steadied her face to look in her eyes. "I will do everything in my power to keep you safe, Ruth."

OCTOBER 7, 1930

"'T is an interesting bunch of friends ye have, Maura."

Katie smiled and sat across from Maura with a cup of tea. "But then, you've always run with the interestin' sort."

"What's that supposed to mean?"

"Just statin' a fact."

"Don't pick a fight, Mam. You've only been here three days, and I'd like to be happy to see ye awhile longer."

"I'm not pickin', Maura. Ye know, I came here to help ye, but I see I'm needed all over this barnacle covered town."

"Mam, I'm happy ye came. I am. But I don't need ye here. I'm sorry Jonathan went and gave ye the impression that I was lame and helpless. I'm not. I'm getting along just fine and so is everyone else, all things considered."

Katie pinched up her face and scoffed. "Sad, sorry lot of ye! A bit of hard times come, and everyone falls to pieces."

"That's not true. Mr. Jonathan is—"

"Jonathan is a fixer, not a healer. Aye, he's strong, and I can see the weight he's carryin'. It's as if he's responsible for half the town's welfare. He runs around putting out small fires as he sees the need. But he's powerless to help those near him that need it the most."

"If yer talking about Mr. Caleb, he'll come around in his own time."

"He's one, but not the only. Take his wife, for instance."

"There's nothing wrong with Miss Ava."

"There isn't?"

"No. She's come to love Jean and is happy to be havin' a babe of her own. She's probably been the steadiest of all of us through everything."

Katie ran her finger around the rim of her teacup. "Has she now?"

"Aye, she has. Just what are you getting at?"

"You know her that well?"

Maura's patience was wearing thin. "Aye. I do."

"Seems to me there's something else there. You say you know her, but it seems she doesn't even know herself. She's too quiet. Too reserved."

"That's just her nature."

"Hmm." Katie stared into her coffee cup. "And Caleb will come around, but it'll take a team of horses to pull him out of the hole he's dug himself into. And that Arianna." She laughed and took a sip of tea.

"Now, Miss Arianna has come a long way. You didn't know her back when she had money. Why, she's hardly the same person now."

"Perhaps not. But she wants to be."

"I'm beginning to think you made the long journey here to lose what's left of your mind and to torture me in the process." Maura picked up a piece of mail and began to fan herself against the mugginess.

"I overheard you talking to Claire this morning."

"You were listening, you mean."

Katie shrugged, unembarrassed. "I don't think you're steering her in the right direction, my dear."

"What other direction does she have? Mr. Gordon is a nice man. It's a good match. It's not dizzy romance and blinding love, but it could work if they let it."

"I think her heart should guide her to the one she should be with. It's not a match that will work."

Maura huffed and looked away.

"You should get some rest, Maura."

"I'm fine."

"After what you've been through, you should be in bed two months at least."

It was the first mention of the miscarriage and the real reason Katie Mallory had seen fit to cross the ocean.

Maura's eyes dropped down to her folded hands. "I'm fine, Mam. Really."

"I'll be the judge of that. Now off to bed with ye. Scoot!"

OCTOBER 10, 1930

Jonathan walked into the garage, catching a rare moment when his father was home. "Can I talk to you, Dad?"

"Sure, what's up?"

"You okay?"

"Fine. Why?"

"It's just that you and Mom haven't been around a lot lately. Ava's worried that it's too much having us here."

"That's nonsense."

"Where do you go when you guys leave?"

Jonathan Sr. grunted from under the car and stuck his hand out. "Can you hand me that screwdriver?"

"Sure."

"You know, Jean misses you, too. Where do you guys go every day?"

"Just out."

"Just out, where?"

Tossing the screwdriver out from under the hood he said, "Just out, Jonathan. Why does it matter?"

"It matters because we feel like we've driven you out of your own home. You guys get up early and leave and don't come back till almost

0007083659

bedtime. If us being here is a problem, you need to talk to me. I can make arrangements."

He stopped working and sighed heavily. "You don't need to make arrangements." Pulling his head out from under the hood, he wiped his blackened hands on a rag. "We just go out."

Jonathan rolled his eyes and shoved his hands in his pockets.

"Fine, Jon. We pack a lunch, and we just go...drive. Most of the days we end up at the beach. We walk and read and talk. We do what everyone else that has been financially ruined does. A whole lot of nothing."

"I just want to make sure you don't feel like you have to leave. This is your house. I haven't forgotten that we're guests and—"

"You're not guests, Jon. You're paying all the bills."

"Oh, so that's it." He nodded. "Okay, you paid all the bills while I was growing up, so consider this a returned favor."

"That isn't how it's supposed to work."

"But this is how it is working."

"I was stupid, and I didn't listen to you. I rammed all this financial education down your throat from the time you could crawl, and when it matters, when it really matters, I don't listen to you, and I go and lose every cent we have and—"

"And we'll get through it."

"Will we, Jon?"

He narrowed his eyes. "What are you getting at?"

"I just don't know if it's going to get better. Ever."

"It will get better. We've just got to ride out the storm, that's all. If we stick together, we'll make it."

Jonathan Sr. nodded slowly. "I hope so. I'm too old to live a life this hard."

"No, you're not. So what's wrong with old reliable?"

"Engine kept revving on the way home. I think I got it."

"Find any more junkers to fix and sell?"

"No. I think I've picked the town clean."

"So, go to Boston. Look there." After a hesitation, Jonathan dug in his pocket. "I have a little for gas if you—"

"I won't take your money. Not any more of it, anyway. But it's a good idea, son. Thanks. I better go clean up."

"Should we set the table for two more?"

"No, we're going over to some friend's house for dinner." He held his hands up. "Honest, we've had the plans for a week. But tomorrow maybe we can talk more about going to Boston. Maybe you could go with me."

"Sure. We'll make plans."

THAT NIGHT, Jonathan couldn't sleep. He couldn't get comfortable, and he couldn't cool off. He threw the sheet back and took a magazine from the bedside, using it to fan himself.

"You okay?" Ava asked.

"Yeah, just can't sleep. I didn't mean to wake you."

"You didn't." Ava rolled toward him. "We need a fan."

"We need a lot of things." He turned the magazine toward her and the breeze gave her bare arms goose bumps.

"Is that what's bothering you?"

"Yes, that and my father. I talked with him out in the garage tonight. He seems...broken. I think he's lost hope."

"How can we help?"

Jonathan shrugged and settled into his pillow. "Damn if I know."

"Should we move out?"

"You know we can't afford that. And neither can they. I'll talk to him again after I get home."

"You're going out tomorrow? There's talk of a storm moving in."

"I have to work, Ava."

"I know, but—"

"It'll be fine, baby, I promise."

She smiled. "It's been forever since you called me that."

"I'm sorry."

"It's also been forever since we... you know." She put her hand on his chest and blushed in the dark.

He rolled over and pulled her close but not quite touching. "I know. I'm sorry. This heat has been overbearing. It just zaps my energy. My...everything."

"Mine, too. Maybe this fall?" she asked, and he laughed.

"Anything below eighty degrees, I promise." She sighed as he began to fan her with the magazine. "I might fall asleep with you doing that."

"Then I'll keep doing it," he said and kissed her.

◦~◦

JONATHAN FINALLY CLOSED his eyes in the early hours of the morning. When they snapped open again, he hadn't moved.

"Someone's knocking, Jon," Ava said and rolled, pulling the sheet over her. She settled back in bed with a cool morning breeze drifting over her.

Jonathan put on his robe and went downstairs, rubbing his blood-shot eyes. He opened the door to find Vincent looking troubled. Instantly, he was alert.

"What? Victor?"

"No, Jon. Worse. Can I come in?"

He stepped aside and Vincent removed his hat.

"I've got some bad news."

Jonathan stiffened. "No, Vincent. I can't take any more bad news."

"I'm sorry, Jon. You're going to have to take this. Do you want to sit down?"

He took a deep breath. "No. What is it?"

"Your parents were in an accident last night. It looks like the gas stuck. They hit a wall at a high rate of speed. A passerby found them a few hours ago."

"Are they..."

"I'm afraid they didn't survive."

Jonathan stared at him dumbfounded. "*The gas stuck?*" he whispered. "But that can't be, Vincent. He fixed that. My dad fixed that."

"Jon, in case you're thinking it, we've checked it out pretty thoroughly. There's no evidence of foul play."

He took a moment, remembered how to breathe, and anger flashed across his face. "I'm not saying there was foul play! Do you think I'm so deranged that I think Victor messed with their car!"

Vincent watched him, unable to say anything of comfort.

Breathing heavily, he looked anywhere but Vincent. "I'm just saying...he fixed that. I saw him." The anger melted away, and he broke down in tears. *"He fixed that."*

∾

WORK STOPPED AGAIN. Fresh tears were spilt on suits and dresses of black. New wounds formed around the scars of the old ones as Jonathan Sr. and Margaret were laid to rest, next to each other in the yard of the old church the following Tuesday.

Against everyone's advice, Jonathan went back to work the next day.

OCTOBER 17, 1930

Claire opened the door just as Gordon set the milk bottles down and played it off as coincidence.

"Claire, hello. How are you?"

"I'm fine." She studied the ground intently.

"I'm glad to hear it."

She shuffled, trying to speak but words failed her. *"I'm sorry."*

"Don't be sorry."

She still didn't look up, and he turned to leave.

"Wait."

"Yes?"

"I needed to ask you something."

"Anything."

"How do you...um." She bit her lip and twisted her hands. "How do you deal with holidays?" She finished in a whisper. He could see she was on the verge of crying. "Halloween is coming, and I have these memories and I can't..." The tears won, and she turned her head. He took a few steps toward her.

"The firsts are hard. Remember when I told you that?"

She nodded.

"Well, the first year I just went somewhere else. Anywhere else that

165

didn't remind me of my wife. I spent Halloween night shivering on the beach. I spent Christmas with some friends who didn't celebrate it. We barbecued in the snow and listened to the radio and had some drinks. And Easter, I put up Christmas decorations. I don't know why. Just to confuse myself, I guess. It was hard, but I got through it. By the time the next set of holidays came around, it was a lot better."

She sniffled but didn't look up at him.

"Do you have any plans for Halloween?"

She shook her head.

"Are you worried about it?"

She nodded.

He thought for a moment. "Would you like to spend Easter dinner with me? Kids don't come out to my place, and I didn't grow any pumpkins this year. There's not a black cat to be seen for miles. And Kitten is still around. He'd be glad to see you."

She took a moment to think. "Easter?"

"Sure. We'll have ham."

With a hint of a smile, she nodded.

"I'll pick you up before sunset then?"

"Okay. Thank you."

"You're welcome. I better get back to work now. I'll talk to you soon, okay?"

"Okay."

He started down the walk and suddenly, turned around. He felt like he was pushing his luck, but it wouldn't hurt to ask. "Do you want me to come back later on tonight?"

"Would you?"

"Of course. I'll see you after work."

Claire closed the door and took a deep breath.

BOMANI WALKED into Victor's office. Normally, he was not a nervous man. But he was nervous today. Suddenly, he was afraid that Victor could see right through him. See through his plan to not only deceive him but also to rat him out and expose his plan. See through the fact that he not only harbored Ruth but had fallen in love with her, too.

Victor took several moments to look up from his desk. When he did, Bomani couldn't read his face. He hated it. Victor was usually easy to read. He was one dimensional like that. But not today.

"Never mind. Go away." He waved his hand and went back to his paperwork.

"What do you mean, go away?"

"I'm not sure what smaller words I can use, Bomani. Go. Away. I've decided not to use you."

He maintained his composure. "Found someone to do it cheaper?"

"You could say that." He slammed a file closed and stood. "I'm doing it myself."

Bomani laughed. "Got a death wish, do ya?"

"Don't laugh at me!" Victor roared. The room fell silent. "You good for nothing street thug. Don't you dare laugh at me. How hard is it to walk up to someone's door and put a bullet in their head? Any idiot can do it." He sneered down his nose at Bomani. "You're proof of that."

"You're right. It is easy enough. It's the getting away part that gets people tripped up." He winked.

"I've got that covered."

"Why? You've paid me to do a dozen dirty deeds for you, and now suddenly, you want the thrill? That's not like you, Victor."

"I can and will do this myself."

"You're confident."

"I am. You see, I just found out that Jonathan Garrett's parents were killed. He'll be distracted. I'll make it look like he did it himself."

"And you wouldn't have had anything to do with his parents?"

"No." He sounded disappointed.

"Just gonna hop on the train and head up there and do it yourself, are you?"

"Not exactly. I've got half the New York police department following me. I should have had you leave Ruth's body in the alley or just—" He waved his hand with irritation. "Killed her in the bedroom and left her for Grayson to find. Bastards still think I know where she is."

Bomani stiffened at the reference to Ruth and Victor caught it, studying him with scrutiny for a moment.

"I think you're making a mistake," Bomani said.

Victor laughed and shook his head. "Oh, no. I've thought of everything this time."

"You'll be going soon?"

"Yes." Victor smiled. "Soon as I throw the cops off my scent, that is. I'll have to hop trains for a bit."

Bomani stood and raised his hands. "Well, I won't waste any more of my time or yours."

"Close the door on your way out."

BOMANI WALKED CASUALLY the first two blocks. After crossing the street and narrowly missing being hit by a truck, he broke into a full run and didn't stop until he burst through his own door.

Ruth was almost packed. She stood in the living room holding two dresses, trying to decide which one to take.

"Let's go, *now.*"

"What's wrong?"

"He changed his mind. He's doing it himself. We don't have much time."

OCTOBER 21, 1930

Knocking on Claire's door was getting easier every day. The air was cooler, a welcome relief. It felt easier to go about the day's business and have the energy to call on Claire after work. He had found it was more successful to get right to the point with Claire. Not that he wasn't a romantic. He was a hopeless one and wanted to shower her with flowers and candy and window serenades. But what she needed right now were point blank questions that she could answer yes or no with not a lot of thought. At least, it usually worked that way.

She opened the door. "Hello, Gordon."

"I was wondering if you'd like to go for a drive. It's a lovely afternoon."

"Oh, I don't know, I was going to read to Maura."

"Don't tell me her mother still has her in bed."

"She does." Claire rolled her eyes. "It's driving Maura crazy, but trust me, it's better than going up against her mother. They've had some fights about it. Katie won't budge. Wants her in bed until further notice."

"Doesn't sound like Maura to put up with that."

Claire made a face. "You haven't had to deal with her mother. It's easier to lie down and give up."

Gordon laughed and so did she, surprising herself.

"Getting closer to that real laugh," he said. She looked down, shy and self-conscious.

"Is Katie here now?"

"No, she went out."

"Can I see Maura for a moment then?"

"Of course." She turned, and he resisted the urge to plant a kiss on the back of her neck. She led him upstairs.

"Mr. Gordon, how are you?"

"I'm good. And you?"

She looked around the small, clean room with frustration. "Apparently, I'm on bed rest."

"I see. But feeling better overall?"

"I feel fine. Did ye come all the way here to ask me that or were ye here to see Miss Claire."

"Well, I had been thinking about you." He gave her a most charming smile. "But to be honest, I had come to ask Claire if she'd go for a drive with me. It's a beautiful evening."

"That sounds lovely." Maura smiled up at Claire.

"But she told me she was reading to you tonight, and I wouldn't want to interfere with that, so I thought I'd come up and look in on you. Now that I have, I'll be on my way."

"Oh, now wait. There's no need for Miss Claire to stay here just to read to me. I'm perfectly capable of reading to myself. Or I'll just listen to the radio." She rolled her head toward Claire. "Go and have a good time."

"Are you sure? I promised—"

"I'm positive, dear. Go."

～

PATRICK CALLED into the barn from the door. No answer. He stepped inside and called for Caleb again. The place was in its usual state of disarray with a larger than normal collection of bottles overflowing a wooden crate.

He passed it, shaking his head. He called a few more times and only the goat answered him. Something shifted in the back of the barn, and the goat came bounding out of the last stall, bleating.

"What are ye up to, ye old goat?"

He opened the gate to the stall with a creak. Patrick's eyes widened.

"What the hell's going on here?" he mumbled. The gate flew from his hand and slammed shut.

"None of your business, that's what."

Patrick froze at the voice behind him. He recognized it, and it wasn't Caleb.

He turned slowly and found Marvin smiling tightly.

"What's going on here, Marvin?"

"I thought I answered that question. It's none of your business."

"Look, while Caleb is chronically indisposed in the bottom of a bottle, I help run things around here. I think I ought to know why there's a truckload of bootleg gin sittin' in this stall."

Marvin dropped his smile and stepped forward, pinning Patrick against the wall.

"Let me make something perfectly clear," he hissed. "You didn't see anything here today, got it? You didn't see a damn thing, and if you go saying anything to anyone about this, well, I just might have to bust your friend for being the biggest booze supplier north of New York."

Patrick stared, undeterred but silent. Had Marvin not been a lawman, he would have revisited his 'Irish Tornado' days of fighting for prize money on the boat to America. But, hard as it was, he had to remain still, fists clenched at his side. The last thing he could afford was to get thrown in jail. The only reason he had come into the barn was to tell Caleb that they were moving into the cabin today. He was growing more anxious to do so by the second.

Marvin gave him a few inches, still staring.

Patrick sidestepped and walked out of the barn, not looking back.

Marvin's eyes followed Patrick, and when the barn door slammed, he stepped into the stall, grumbling and cursing under his breath as he threw back the sheet that covered most of the stash. Although he was certain this was the first Patrick had seen of it, he did an inventory, anyway.

Wooden crates clinked as he moved them. Stacked like a pyramid, he removed several from the top. In the center, hidden from view, was what he wanted to protect the most. Carefully packaged bottles of elixir. Not the imitation stuff, either. The best cocaine and opiate tonics you could find. There were only a handful of regular buyers in Rockport, Pigeon Cove, and Gloucester. Folks tended to stick to the old habit of morphine to cure what ailed them. But the world was changing and that would, too, he assured himself. He had excess now, but soon, he wouldn't be able to keep up with demand as people sought stronger ways to ease the pain of hard times.

"Anyone in here?" Caleb yelled from the door.

"Yep. I'm back here," Marvin called as he quickly restacked the crates. He closed the door to the stall, flipped the latch, and stepped out into the light.

"Just picking some up. Thought I could fit more into my car, but I can't." He shrugged. "Guess I'll have to get it next time."

"Well, don't take all of it." Caleb grinned.

"I wouldn't dream of it."

THEY WERE silent as Gordon drove. Claire took in the scenery as he deliberately drove away from the ocean toward the countryside. The truck bounced along the dirt road, and Claire's body bounced with it. It was peaceful, and she closed her eyes often, smelling autumn in the air. She liked how Gordon was comfortable with silence now. He didn't feel the need to keep constant conversation. And when he did spark up a topic, it was easy to engage. But then, they only ever talked about easy things. The weather, the dairy business, her friends, which he hoped would soon become his.

Gordon began humming. Claire smiled as she felt the baby kick.

"It did it again," she said. "It always kicks when you hum."

Gordon smiled and began humming louder. The baby kicked harder.

"Either it doesn't like it or it loves it. I can't decide," she said as she shifted in her seat to get more comfortable. After a few minutes, she grunted.

"Actually, could you stop? It feels like it's rioting in there."

He slowed the truck and took a long look at her.

"How much longer?"

"February."

"Why do you call it an 'it'?"

She appeared lost for a moment. "I don't know what else to call it. I haven't thought of any names."

"Don't you ever wonder if it's a boy or a girl?"

"Sometimes."

"What do you think it is?"

"How should I know?"

"They say mothers can tell that kind of thing. They have this gut instinct as to what it's going to be."

She shrugged, as if clueless.

She had an instinct, but it was too painful to think about. Some distant, detached part of her told her it was a boy as if it were the most obvious thing in the world. She wanted it to be a boy. She wanted him to look just like Aryl, with big brown eyes and curly locks, and she wanted to name it after him, too. She didn't feel right calling it a 'she' when on some level, she knew better. But it hurt to say 'he.' Every time she had tried the word on for size in private, it evoked images of Aryl, and it was safer to stay away from his memory altogether. Something she found necessary while spending increasing amounts of time with Gordon, too.

"Can I ask you a question, Claire?"

She studied a pair of horses as they passed. "Sure."

"Is there anyone else you're interested in, er, seeing, that is?"

She laughed. The sound of it caused him to jolt, shocked and delighted at the sound. It was contagious, and he smiled.

"What's so funny?"

"You are."

173

"It's an honest question. You're a beautiful woman. Why wouldn't men be lined up at the door?"

"You know, it's funny because just the other day, I was wondering why I didn't have suitors for miles and then I remembered, oh, yes, I'm a pregnant widow." The genuine smile faded, replaced by a sad one. "That combination pretty much keeps anyone from knocking on the door."

He pulled off to the side of the road and turned off the engine. "That's not true. I'm knocking."

She felt a panic well up inside. Part of her had known this was coming. They couldn't go on forever spending time together, talking of nothing important, pretending they weren't wondering what it was all for. He didn't hold her hand when they were out, didn't kiss her good-night when he dropped her off, and anyone looking on would think they were brother and sister, or simply good friends. She knew it was on his mind—no man spent this much time and energy on a woman without thinking something might come of it—and hard as it was to deal with, it was on her mind lately, as well. Maybe it was that she was moving out of the hard grief and, thanks to Gordon, more into a state of living. Or trying to, anyway.

Maybe it was feeling the baby start to move. More and more, it was moving inside her. Nothing like the reality of a new life to force one to figure out what their next move was. Practical as reality could be, when Gordon reached over and took her hand, it was uncomfortable only four months after Aryl.

She pushed aside the thoughts and kept her hand in his.

"Will you be mine, Claire? Nothing would make me happier."

She hesitated, and he gave her hand a squeeze. *He must have had pointers from Maura,* she thought.

"Nothing has to start changing right away, Claire. I'm not going to... jump on you or anything. I know you need time, and frankly, so do I. You'd be the first woman since my wife died, and a part of me feels guilty."

"So that won't go away?" she whispered, staring at their clasped hands.

"It gets better. And who knows, maybe if we can manage to make a life together, it will."

She nodded slowly, deep in thought. She knew this wasn't just a guy asking a girl to be exclusive. This was a proposal to see if they were compatible, and that would lead to another proposal, eventually. If she accepted one, she knew the other would be soon. She debated for a moment if she could. *If she would*, under normal circumstances. Not pregnant. Not a widow. If she had always been single and they met on the beach or in the city, and it was just them, with no history, no dark clouds, no fear of the future. She looked up from her deep thought. His eyes were shining and his smile nervous. Hers, practical and resigned.

"I will, Gordon."

PATRICK STOMPED into the house and called for Shannon.

"Up here, Pat." He jogged up the stairs and found her packing their things.

"Good. Can ye hurry it up, Shan? I want to get out of here."

"What's the rush, Pat?"

"Damn deputy's up to no good, that's what. I want to get as far away from here as possible."

"What deputy? What no good?"

Patrick gave her a run-down of what had just transpired in the barn.

"Pat, ye have to tell Caleb! Ye do! He's got to know!"

"Drunken bastard doesn't even know what's going on with his own land. Even if I told him, he probably wouldn't care, loopy as he is most the time."

"Yes, but, if it were yer land, wouldn't ye want someone to tell ye if something was amiss?"

Patrick dropped his head and paced, shoving his hands in his pockets.

"Marvin told me that he'd have Caleb arrested if I said a word."

"Then you have to! Marvin obviously is takin' advantage of Caleb." She stood and stopped his pacing, putting her hands on his shoulders.

"Tell Caleb and have him make like he found it by mistake. No one needs to know that ye said a word. Then Caleb can destroy it, and Marvin won't have a leg to stand on."

Patrick stood with tightly clamped lips.

"I might could do it like that."

"You could. Now help me get some of this stuff downstairs. Can we use the truck to make one trip, do you think? Easier than carryin' it all by hand and it'll be dark soon."

"We can. I've got the keys to the truck."

On the short drive to the cabin, with all their worldly possessions piled behind them, they passed Caleb walking down from the upper field. Katie walked beside him.

Patrick slowed the truck. It looked like she was doing all the talking, and Patrick was grateful he wasn't on the receiving end of her words. Caleb walked with his hands shoved deep in his pockets, brow furrowed, staring at the ground.

"Movin' in today!" Patrick called as he passed. Caleb waved, but his expression didn't change.

"I'll not be talkin' to him today, Shan. Looks like he's getting an earful from Katie."

Shannon smiled. "Maybe it'll help him, poor thing."

Patrick shot her a look. "Well, it better. I've got my own wee bit of land to work now. And I have to squeeze every last ounce of profit from it. I won't have time to clean up all his messes. That reminds me. Arianna said we could have a few chickens and one of the roosters to get a flock started."

"That's sweet of her."

They pulled up to the cabin. "Home sweet home. Humble as it may be."

"It's wonderful, Pat. And we'll make it even more wonderful with some time and hard work."

They moved their things in as the full moon rose.

Arianna stopped short on the third to the last stair at the sight of Caleb. He sat at the table freshly bathed and clean shaven, waiting for her.

He half-stood as she passed and she afforded him only a grunt of acknowledgment.

"Can we talk?" he asked with eyes jointly hopeful and pitiful.

She went to the stove and put on a kettle of water.

"Please?" he begged, turning in the chair to look at her.

She was silent for a moment and spun around, irritation visible on her face.

"What? Did the goat have a hot date or something? Leave you all alone for the night?" She crossed her arms leaning against the stove with her lips pursed in a tight knot.

"No, it didn't have a date." He shook his head. "Goats don't date."

She stared at him blankly and shook her head.

"Jesus, I wasn't serious, Caleb," she huffed.

It was unseasonably warm with every door and window open, hoping for a breeze.

Suddenly, she laughed, and it surprised them both.

"What?" he asked cautiously.

"You thought I was serious..." She trailed off with her hand over her eyes. Her laugh was for that side of Caleb she loved. The serious and literal, yet sweet and naïve.

She dropped her hand and glared at him.

"Who's it gonna date, Caleb? The pig?"

He brought his shoulders up slowly. "I hadn't really thought about it," he said apologetically.

She laughed again despite herself. "I can't believe we're having this conversation."

She turned away, focusing on the teakettle.

"Why are you drinking tea on such a warm night?"

"What do you want, Caleb?" she asked, her voice annoyed yet slightly entertained. She turned slightly to hold up a teacup in question.

"No, thanks," he said quietly.

"Oh, that's right," she said, turning away again. "You don't drink anything that hasn't been sitting in a still for a week."

"It tastes better after at least two, I think," he said, and she laughed again, instantly angry for it.

"What do you want, Caleb?" she repeated.

"I just wanted to tell you I'm sorry."

"For what?"

"You know for what."

"Caleb, there are so many things you could possibly be sorry for— I'm just wondering which one you have in mind."

She walked past him, catching a whiff of cologne as she sat down across from him. A thick pillar candle sat between them, burning with a soft glow. Ethel had emptied all the oil lamps after the fire that killed her husband and destroyed her kitchen.

"I'm sorry for being gone so much," he said, avoiding her eyes.

She sighed, loud, long and slow, trying to muster patience.

"I know this has been hard on you, Caleb."

He nodded, eyes cast down, playing with his shirt's hem.

"But it's been hard on us, too. We need you. Me, and Samuel and Savrene. Whenever you're not working, you're in that barn with that goat."

"He's a nice goat—"

"Caleb, I'm in no mood," she said dangerously.

"I just wanted to hear you laugh again," he said, and her face melted slightly.

"Maura's mother got a hold of you, didn't she?"

He nodded with a grimace.

"What did she say?"

"Well, the babies." He glanced up at the ceiling. "I don't know if I should repeat most of it with the babies in the house."

The corner of her mouth twitched, and she took a sip of tea. "I can imagine," she said. "Did she make you talk to me tonight? Or was that your idea."

"My idea," he said softly.

"Well, I'm not going to pretend that I'm not mad as hell at you, Caleb. You've spent the better part of four months passed out in that barn, forgetting we even exist. Did you know that Samuel rolled over?"

His eyes darted up. "He did?"

She nodded. "And Savrene is trying. Next thing you know they'll be crawling, walking, talking, and you're going to miss all of it."

He scrubbed his face with his hand, but the frown remained.

"I'm sorry. I'll spend more time with them. And you," he added.

"I can count on one hand how many times you've slept in our bed. And even then, all you did was pass out and keep me up with your snoring."

"I'm sorry. I won't sleep in the barn anymore," he promised. "And I won't drink so much. I'm sober now," he said, holding his hand up in promise.

"Because you're out? Or because you want to be?"

"Because I'm trying to be."

She looked him over before moving her gaze to the darkness past the back door.

"Tell me what happened."

He rolled his eyes before closing them.

"You know what happened."

"Maura said it would help you if you talk about it."

179

Cricket songs filled the kitchen for several long moments while he deliberated.

"I feel bad for being the one who lived. I feel guilty for feeling *glad* that I lived. That I got to come home to you and the babies." He blew out his breath and cleared his throat. "And I miss him."

He took a moment to gather himself and to avoid tears before he continued. "Nothing is ever going to be the same," he said finally.

Having no idea what to say, she hoped that listening would be enough for now.

"It still stings like it was yesterday," he said.

A few whimpering cries echoed from the staircase, and they both turned to look. Samuel settled himself quickly, and Caleb went back to staring at his folded hands on the table.

"When I can stay busy, it's not so bad. But when I don't have anything to do, nothing else to think about, that's when it kills me. Guilt, anger, and relief. It's a hell of a combination," he said rubbing the back of his neck.

"It's going to take time, Caleb. A lot of time. But it'll get better."

"That's what they tell me," he said softly.

"But running away to that barn and drinking to oblivion isn't going to help you get past it. In fact, it's only prolonging it."

"That's what they tell me, too," he said, nodding slowly. They stared in opposite directions.

"Will you come to bed?" she asked, breaking a long silence where only heat filled the kitchen. He nodded, looking forward to sleeping on something other than hay.

"Will you come to bed with *me?*"

He picked up the slight change in her voice and looked up, her eyes confirming the tone. He raised his eyebrows in question. "You're not so mad at me then?"

"I've been lonely, Caleb." She shrugged, and a simple smile turned slightly devious. "And I didn't say you weren't going to have to work hard for my forgiveness," she said with one eyebrow cocked.

He grinned and it almost touched his eyes. "Well, ma'am, I reckon I'll have to give it everything I got," he said, donning a heavy accent from her native Georgia.

"You just do that then," she said quietly as she stood. He took her hand and led her to the stairs just as Samuel started wailing. Arianna growled in frustration.

"Let me get him," Caleb said and jogged ahead.

It took him five minutes to settle the baby, and when he returned to the bedroom, Arianna was just finishing undressing. He stopped and stared for a moment as she turned around.

"You look amazing," he said, frozen in place. Her long, lean figure had fully returned. The only evidence of childbirth were slightly widened hips that suited her well.

She walked over to him impatiently and started unbuttoning his shirt.

OCTOBER 24, 1930

Bomani and Ruth stepped off at the train station in Rockport.
"Do you know where he lives?"

"I do."

"Are we going to just walk up to his door, knock, and say, 'Hi, there.
We were just in the neighborhood and thought we'd stop by to say that
Victor is headed this way to kill you, and, oh, by the way, I'm alive. Have
a nice day!'"

Bomani smiled. "I'll handle it, Ruth. It will be short and sweet. We do
need to stop at one place first."

She stopped and put a hand on his arm. "And then we can leave?
Start a new life somewhere?"

"We will."

They started walking again. Ruth was frowning. "What if he realizes
you aren't in New York anymore?"

"He's too preoccupied with his plans. Besides, he needs to train hop
for a bit before he can head here. I think we can give them twenty-four
hours' notice."

"This is a cute town," Ruth said as they walked. "Not where I
pictured Jonathan ending up in life, but cute, nonetheless."

Bomani nodded but said nothing. He knew the past that she and

Jonathan shared and didn't feel directly threatened by it. After all, they'd only dated. She admitted to having loved him but used the word in past tense and was quite honest that he never returned the sentiment. He was a good, decent man, according to her, and after he had met Ava, no other woman existed. Still, it bothered him that she mentioned him as often as she did. He wondered if his urgency to help Jonathan was purely based on trying to turn a new leaf and be a decent human being, or because he knew Ruth would sleep better at night knowing Jonathan was safe, help her move on and to make a life with Bomani.

He'd told her he loved her a dozen times. A few more than that as she slept. She never said it back. When directly asked, she smiled prettily and said, "Of course I do." But it wasn't the same. Maybe when life settled down. Maybe when he could provide her with a comfortable life and that life fell into a blessedly predictable routine, she'd feel safe enough to say it.

They turned down a long street. He could smell the salty air and hear the call of the seagulls.

"Where are we stopping?"

"The sheriff's office."

They stepped inside and a short, pudgy receptionist looked up from her newspaper.

"Can I help you?"

"I need to speak with the sheriff."

"Reporting a crime?"

Bomani hesitated. "No."

"Then what's this regarding?"

Growing impatient, Bomani decided that it was only a matter of time before news spread all over this little town like a virus. He supposed it didn't matter if the receptionist was the first or the second to know. She'd know soon enough, and it would be all over.

"I've knowledge of intent to commit a crime. I'd just like to prevent it if I can. Could I speak with him, please?"

She perked up with interest. "Well, now, the sheriff is out on some business, but I can get a deputy for you. He can take a report."

"That's fine."

She rose and waddled to a back corner office, knocked briefly and poked her head inside. Bomani couldn't hear what she was saying, but she was whispering intently.

"Are you sure this is a good idea?" Ruth asked. "I thought we were going to keep things quiet. We're leaving a trail."

"It's fine. We'll go warn him and then head out of town. After we leave, I'll feel better if someone was keeping an eye on things." He looked at Ruth and smiled. "Who knows, maybe we'll get lucky, and they'll catch him and throw him in jail for a really long time."

"Jail is too good for him."

Bomani turned at someone clearing his throat. "Hi there. Name's Marvin. How can I help you?"

CALEB STOOD STARING at the stash in the stall, holding a small bottle. "He said it was only booze."

Patrick leaned against the rickety wall. "Looks like he lied."

"I can't have this here."

"No, ye can't. We could take it to the boat. Dump it in the ocean."

"No. This is the property of the Sheriff's Department."

"And my granny's the Queen of England."

"It is. He said it was. They didn't have room to hold it at the office. This is the overflow. He's been slowly destroying it."

"Funny, because it looks like the pile is growing."

Caleb put his hands on his head and sighed. "I need to talk to Jon."

"No, don't do that. I wasn't even supposed to tell you."

"Did Marvin threaten you?"

"No. He threatened *you*."

"This doesn't make sense."

"Trust me, Caleb. If you've ever trusted me on anything in the world, trust me on this. Just dump it in the ocean. Act like you don't know anything about it. Like someone found out and broke in and stole it. Else he'll be out for you and me both."

"He's a lawman, Patrick."

"Caleb, yer a hell of a lot nicer to be around when yer sober, but not much brighter. Him being a lawman doesn't make a damn bit of difference. Looks to me like he's got a side business going. If you'd open your eyes, you'd see it, too."

Caleb sighed and sat down on a crate, staring at the pile.

"Jon would know what to do."

Patrick removed his hat and slapped it across his hand. "Jon just buried his parents. His wife is pregnant, and his business is barely keeping food on the table. He has enough on his plate. This is *your* land. Be the man of it. I'm goin' home. I'll be at the cabin if ye need me."

JONATHAN AND AVA sat on the couch listening to the radio. The window was open, and the curtains moved with a cool breeze. The Indian summer had finally relented and was giving way to the start of autumn. Leaves seemed to turn brilliantly overnight and mornings were crisp. The mid-day sun was warm but tolerable, and just as the sun went down, it was the kind of perfect comfort that one dreamed about all through the hot summers and frigid winters.

Ava yawned and leaned her head over on Jonathan's shoulder.

"Do you think Jean will be okay?"

Pulled from his deep thoughts, he seemed startled. "What do you mean?"

"It might get chilly tonight."

Relieved, he smiled. "He'll be fine. I'll put an extra quilt over him before we go to bed if it will make you feel better."

She nodded and settled her head back on his shoulder. "What are you thinking about?"

"Everything."

"Impressive. I can only think of one thing at a time."

"So do I. Just very rapidly."

"Doesn't seem like you're thinking. Seems like you're troubled."

"Same difference anymore."

"Arianna is bringing some baby clothes by tomorrow."

"That's nice of her." His brow furrowed, remembering they didn't have much for the baby at all.

"Katie is throwing a diaper party."

"A what?"

"Where a bunch of us get together and visit and sew diapers."

"Ah. I'll be sure to organize a poker game during that time."

"You're not going to help sew?" she teased.

"Do you want the diapers to function? If so, I'd better not." She grinned as he pulled her close.

The knock interrupted a peaceful silence. Jonathan rose and opened the door. His face fell as he scrutinized the stranger.

"Are you Jonathan Garrett?"

"Yes, who are you?"

"My name is not important. I have an urgent message for you. Can I come in?"

"I think you'd better just tell me from where you're at."

"I'd really prefer to come inside. I don't feel comfortable standing out here."

"And I don't feel comfortable letting a perfect stranger into my house."

Bomani nodded. "I understand. You don't know me. But you do know her." He stepped aside, revealing Ruth and Jonathan's mouth fell open.

"What the hell is going on here? You're supposed to be dead!"

"It's nice to see you, too, Jon. Will you let us in? We do have something urgent to tell you."

Jonathan turned and saw Ava, who sat on the couch with a look of utter disbelief.

"Maybe we should talk outside. I don't want to upset her."

"It might not be safe outside," Bomani said. His eyes were desperate, and Jonathan quickly nodded them in.

Ava stood up with her hands on her hips and her mouth still hanging open as Ruth took off her jacket.

"Why is it that every time I am having a most relaxing evening with my husband, *you* show up?"

"I'm sorry to disturb you like this. But it is very important. Not good news, I'm afraid."

"Is it ever with you, Ruth?"

Jonathan put a hand on her shoulder. "Let's just hear what they have to say."

"If you have another child besides Jean, I swear to God—"

Ruth smiled. "She's gotten feisty."

"I'm learning pregnancy does that to women," Jonathan said with a hint of warning.

Ruth's eyes traveled down to Ava's stomach. "Congratulations. When are you due?"

"She's due in December. I'd really like to know what this is all about. Why did Vincent tell me you were dead and who is this you're with?"

She got right to the point. "I've been in hiding. Victor tried to have me killed for, I assume, insurance money. Maybe he was just tired of me and wanted to clear the air, maybe it's because I know his secrets. Or because I tried to warn you about him right before you left New York. I don't know."

"Who is this?"

"This is Bomani. He has been helping me stay out of sight. Victor still thinks I'm dead. And we are here because he just found out that you are *not*."

The hair on the back of Ava's neck stood on end, and she folded her arms tightly.

"Excuse me?"

"He thought it was you who died on the Ava-Maura last June. The newspaper got things mixed up in translation."

Bomani nodded. "And when he found out, he was livid. At first, he tried to hire out your murder. Then he changed his mind. He is intent on doing it himself. He knows where you live, and he's on his way here now."

Jonathan exploded into action, grabbing Ava and ushering her upstairs. "Get some things together for you and Jean. We're leaving."

"Where are we going?"

"Caleb's. No, Claire's. He doesn't know where Claire lives. Just go and hurry!"

She moved as fast as she could. She was off balance and the quicker her step, the more unsteady she became. Twisting her ankle on the last stair, she fell as she caught herself with her hands splayed out on the floor, and called for Jonathan. He came bounding up the stairs with Bomani and Ruth behind him.

"Are you okay?"

"My ankle," she hissed, trying, but unable to reach it. Jonathan lifted her up in one swoop and carried her down the hall, setting her on the bed.

"I don't mean to drop bad news and run, Jon, but if Victor finds out Bomani and I was here, we're as good as dead. We have to get out of town."

"Just wait!" he ordered. "I have more questions. Wait downstairs for me." He turned to Ava, lifting her leg to look at her ankle. "Can you turn it?"

"Barely." It was already beginning to swell.

"I think it's just sprained. I'll get Jean and our things. You sit here, and I'll come back for you."

"Jon, I'm sorry, we have to go," Ruth pleaded. It was clear they were not going to wait.

He spun around. "How long before he gets here?"

"Tomorrow, most likely."

"Why does he care if you were here?" He stared pointedly at Bomani. "Who are you to him?"

"I worked for him, for a time."

"Worked for him how?"

"He hired me to do jobs for him. Jobs he didn't want to do."

A flash of understanding crossed Jonathan's face, and he stood slowly. "Was it you that rigged the boats?" he asked. His voice was dangerously low.

"No. But I taught him how to do it."

"Bomani—" Ruth whispered.

"You *taught* him?"

"He could have learned from anyone, anywhere, Jon. It wasn't Bomani's fault. He didn't know why Victor wanted to know. He had no idea about any of this."

Jonathan hadn't taken his eyes from Bomani's. "You helped kill a good man. May God have mercy on your soul."

"I pray He does. Though I don't deserve it."

Ruth grabbed his arm. "We have to go, Bomani. We've done what we've come here to do. Our conscience is clear. I don't want to stay any longer."

Still staring at Jonathan, he said, "If he has more questions, we'll wait. I owe him at least that."

"Five minutes," Ruth said, and turned away. Bomani followed her downstairs.

Jonathan sat down in front of Ava and covered his face with his hands. "Jesus, when is this going to be over?"

She put her hands on his head. "Go get Jean and our things. Let's get to Claire's. We'll talk there and send someone to get Vincent."

He nodded and rose, grabbing a suitcase from the closet.

Jean sat next to Ava, rubbing his sleepy eyes. "Why are we going to Claire's?"

"Because she invited us for the night. Doesn't that sound like fun?"

"It does. Does she have her bebe yet?"

"No, not yet."

"Will Maura be there?"

"She will."

"Can I get my blanket to take with me?"

"Yes, go ahead."

He slid off the bed and padded out into the hallway. Jonathan packed what he thought they would need for three or four days. He darted out to the bathroom to get his razor and overheard Jean at the bottom of the stairs.

"Who are you?"

Like a shot, he was down the stairs, grabbing Jean by the arm.

"Dadee, why is the back door open?"

"Who were you talking to?"

"Him." Jean pointed and in the darkened corner of the living room stood Victor, gun in hand, a drunken smile on his face.

"Get upstairs now." He shoved Jean in the direction of the landing and stepped in front of him.

"Cute kid. Is that the bastard Elyse went on and on about? The reason she came to me when she needed help finding you?"

Jean stood quivering behind Jonathan's leg. "Elyse was my mommy," he said quietly.

"Get upstairs, now!" Jonathan yelled without taking his eyes off Victor.

"Kids these days. Don't listen to a damn word you say."

"Get out of my house."

"Soon." A slow smile spread across his face.

"Jon, what's going on?" Ava yelled from upstairs.

"Just stay upstairs!" he yelled back.

"That's good," Victor said. "Very good. Keep her up there. It'll be easier to take care of her and the kid when I'm done with you. Can't have any witnesses, you know. And the kid *did* see me."

"You're not going to lay a hand on them."

Victor raised the gun. "I wasn't going use my hands."

Jonathan picked up a vase from the side table and hurled it at Victor. He ducked and fired, missing Jonathan by a hair, shattering a hole in the plaster wall behind him. Ava screamed from upstairs. Victor looked up, and Jonathan took his moment, bolting across the living room and running headlong into Victor, knocking him to the ground. The gun fell out of his hand, landing with a thud on the hardwood floor. They both lunged for it and banged their heads. They rolled together, each having a hand on the gun. Jonathan used his free hand to punch Victor in the head. He let go of the gun and delivered a punch of his own, right to Jonathan's throat. He gasped and wheezed, his eyes watering and his hands instinctively going to his neck. Victor grabbed the gun and pointed it. Through his watery eyes, Jonathan could see the barrel right between his eyes. He threw himself to the side, missing yet another shot, and bringing Victor over on top of him.

"Well, if that's how you prefer it," he said, grinning. He put a forearm across Jonathan's throat and brought the gun down to his temple. Jonathan swung wildly through fading vision and had just enough time to stick a finger in Victor's eye before the world around him started to fade. Victor let out a growling scream as blood flowed out of the socket. Still intent, he shoved the barrel against Jonathan's skull. Neither of them noticed the movement at the door.

"Jon! MOVE!"

A shot fired and then everything was quiet. Both faces were splattered with blood. Both men were perfectly still.

Caleb ran in and rolled Victor off to the side. Jonathan's eyes were open. His body was limp.

He blinked. Then he gasped for breath.

"Oh, thank God. Thank God," Caleb whispered.

Marvin stood over them, the gun still in his hand. "Looks like I got here just in time."

❧

JONATHAN COULDN'T SHAKE the ringing in his ears. He rolled his head to the side and saw Victor lying on his back. One vacant eye stared back at him, and his head had an odd shape about it. It looked deflated.

"He closed his eyes, trying to sit up.

Caleb pulled him to his feet and helped to steady him.

They heard whimpering from above.

"Go to Ava," Jonathan said and pointed to the stairs. "Tell her I'm all right."

Caleb jogged up the stairs while Marvin disappeared into the kitchen. He closed the back door and began rummaging through drawers before returning to the living room.

He held out a towel. "You have blood on your face. And...bits."

"Bits?"

"Of Victor."

Jonathan felt a wave of nausea as Marvin began to clean his face for him. "You can't let Ava see you like this."

"Jon! You'd better get up here!"

Ava lay on her side at the top of the stairs, holding her stomach. Jean crouched down near her head, holding Jonathan's gun with both hands, looking scared.

"I heard the shots and tried to get to you." She looked down and covered her face with her hand, mortally embarrassed. "I think I wet myself."

JONATHAN PACED the small waiting area of the hospital. His disheveled and bloodied state caused passing nurses to eye him with curiosity and a few stopped to see if he were waiting to be seen. He sat down and hid his shaking hand in his hair.

"Talk to me, Caleb. About anything."

"Jean will be fine. I don't think he saw anything and Katie will take good care of him."

"I know."

"Oh, ah…she'll be okay. Ava, I mean. Don't worry."

"Not about Ava. Anything else. How did you know to come to my house?"

"I didn't. I came to talk to you about something. I needed your advice."

"Well, ask away. Distract me. Please."

He bounced his knee, looking back every moment or so at the door.

"Just a problem I have at the farm. I don't want to burden you with it right now. You've got enough to worry about with Ava."

He glanced over his shoulder again and wrung his hands. "It's too soon. She can't have it yet."

"Hey, that's what I thought with Arianna, and it all turned out fine."

"That's different. That was twins. They always come early. Thank God Marvin was there." He wiped his face and stood again. "Sorry, I can't sit still. I feel like I could run a marathon right now."

"You probably could. And I'm glad Marvin was there, too."

"What did you want to talk to me about? Give me something else to think about or I'll go mad."

"Fine. Well, see, not too long ago, Marvin asked if he could store some overflow hooch in the barn. I didn't think anything of it, and since I could pick a little off the top for free, I agreed."

Jonathan looked at him as if it were the first time he'd seen him.

"Are you sober right now?"

"Have been for two days."

"Damn, that's a record lately."

"Thanks. Anyway, so Patrick comes to me and tells me Marvin is storing much more than hooch in the barn."

"What else is he storing?"

"Opiate elixir, it looks like."

"Why would he store that at your place?"

"Damn if I know. But Patrick said Marvin would have me busted as if the stuff was mine if he told me. Well, he told me anyway. I'm not sure if I'm glad he did or not, but I thought you'd know what to do."

"Marvin said that? Marvin? The deputy?"

"Patrick thinks he's crooked. What do you think?"

"Nothing would surprise me anymore, Caleb. And there's a lot of money to be made in that stuff. But I'm sure Marvin has a good explanation. It's gotta be confiscated stuff. Why don't you talk to him? Even if it's on the up and up, tell him you want him to get rid of it. Tell him you're getting another horse and need the room or something."

"He'll know Patrick talked to me. I'm actually a little afraid of him, Jon." He looked down, ashamed.

"Then dump it in the damn ocean, that's what I'd do."

"That's exactly what Patrick said. But I can't do that."

"Why not?"

"Jonathan Garrett?"

"Right here." He moved quickly across the room. "I'm Jonathan. How is she?"

"The doctor can see you now."

He followed the nurse through the door and down a long hallway.

The doctor was in his office at his desk. He was older, thick in the middle with a balding head and round spectacles. He appeared troubled as he scanned a chart but put on a smile as he raised his head.

"Mr. Garrett, come in."

"How's Ava?"

"She's resting."

"Is she going to be okay? Is the baby ok?"

"She is going to be fine, I believe. As for the baby, time will tell. I'm afraid we aren't able to stop the labor."

"You mean she's having the baby now?"

"In the process of it, yes. It's early, as you know. Seven weeks early, and while I've seen a number of babies born and thrive at this point in gestation, it's always prudent for the parents to be aware that, well, to put it bluntly, anything can go wrong. The baby's lungs might not be mature enough to breathe on its own. The heart may not be strong enough, the kidneys and liver might not function properly, leading to jaundice and buildup of blood toxins. Then, there's always infection to worry about."

Jonathan nodded and swallowed hard. "If you had to put odds on it?"

"I can't do that. There's too much out of my control. I would never get a father's hopes up only to be wrong."

"But it could all be okay, right? It's early, and it'll be small, but it could be fine?"

"Anything is possible, Mr. Garrett." He tried to smile. He wanted to give Jonathan hope. Experience had taught him it was better to avoid giving a shred of false hope to a parent during a dangerous delivery. "But do you understand *all* of the possibilities?"

"I do."

"Let me assure you we will do everything we can. *I* will do everything I can."

"Thank you, Doctor. I'd like to see Ava now."

"I'm afraid she's been sent to the delivery ward and no visitors are allowed. She is being made comfortable. You can wait in the father's waiting room, and her nurse will give you updates."

"Wait! No! I have to be with her!"

The doctor stood with an amused smile. "In the delivery room? We don't allow fathers in the delivery room, Mr. Garrett."

"She wants me in there."

"We will take good care of her." He put a hand on his shoulder and turned him toward the door. "We will keep you informed," he said with finality.

BOMANI STOOD FACING AWAY from the few people gathered on the platform of the train station. He glanced at his watch. The eight o'clock train was running late. His nerves were wracked, and he tried to shake his anxious feeling, wanting to get out of this town as fast as possible. It had been too close a call. If they had just left a few minutes earlier when Ruth wanted to—he froze. If they had left a few minutes earlier, they would have run smack into Victor as he came up the sidewalk. He shuddered. It was only by staying those extra minutes and waiting downstairs that they narrowly avoided him. Huddled together in the middle of Jonathan's living room, they had seen the front door handle start turning, ever so slowly. They had run for the back door and left it wide open.

They'd heard the gunshots. Ruth wouldn't let him stop. They ran two blocks and hid in a broken down shed for over an hour. Then they heard it. An old lady going door to door. Rockport's very own town crier, telling everyone that someone broke into Jonathan's house and got shot. Bomani prayed nothing had gotten confused in translation.

They crawled out of the shed and came nose to nose with a shaggy black dog staring at them, his head cockeyed and curious.

"Good dog," Bomani said as he slowly stood. "That's a good boy, stay right there. We're not going to hurt you, and you don't hurt us, okay?"

He put his hand out for the dog to sniff. After a moment, the dog backed up. He gave a low 'woof' and went about his business, leaving the yard.

"Let's get to the train," Ruth said, pulling him along.

And here Bomani stood, waiting for Ruth to get out of the restroom

195

—seemed like she'd been in there forever—when he heard the train whistle in the distance. He walked over to the women's restroom and called to her from the door. A young woman gave him a distrustful look as she passed him.

"Excuse me, ma'am. My...wife is in there, and this is our train. Could you let her know, please?"

He stepped back affording her plenty of room to pass, and after a moment, she emerged from the restroom.

"There's no one in there."

"Are you sure?"

"Positive. It's empty."

Bomani scanned the platform. Folks had started to line up to board the train. He passed by them quickly, looking for Ruth. She had been right there, right by his side, and he watched her walk into the restroom. She couldn't have gone anywhere else. He walked around the small ticket office and scanned the lot in vain.

"Ruth!" He walked out onto the road toward town, still calling her name.

OCTOBER 25, 1930

"**M**r. Garrett?" A waif-like nurse with thin blonde hair touched his shoulder. "Wake up, Mr. Garrett."

He sat bolt upright in the chair. The first rays of dawn were peeking through the window.

"Is she okay?"

"I was just coming to let you know that things are progressing very slowly. You might want to go home and clean up. Change and get something to eat. You have plenty of time."

"I don't want to miss it. I want to be here."

"I understand, Mr. Garrett, but the doctor doesn't expect anything to happen until tonight at the earliest."

"Tonight?"

She nodded with a patient smile.

"Ava's doing all right?"

"She's doing fine, Mr. Garrett. Sleeping right now as a matter of fact. We're taking very good care of her. Now, you have to take care of yourself, okay?"

"I'll take him home," Caleb said and just as Jonathan started to protest, added, "and bring him right back."

His stomach growled, but he didn't feel hunger. His neck was pinched from spending the night in a steel chair, but he didn't feel the pain. He rose and walked toward the exit looking distracted and anguished.

"Take me by Maura's, would you, Caleb?"

~

KATIE HAD to all but nail the door shut to keep Maura in through the night.

"I need to go to him," Maura said.

"Ye need to rest," Katie replied, guiding her back down into bed.

"I don't need rest! I need to go to Jonathan!"

"Don't raise yer voice to me, child."

"I'm not a child! And I'm not sick! I've lost a babe, and I've had ample time to get over it! I don't need ye here anymore, Mam."

She threw the covers back and stood, defiantly. "What are ye going to do, Mam. Throw me back in bed and sit on me?"

"If I have to. You're not fit—"

"I'm perfectly fit!"

She was almost there, and Katie's smile was impossible to suppress as she turned around, fidgeting with the clothes in Maura's top drawer.

"I've got just about everything straight, and I don't need ye to go messing it up."

"What do you mean, you've gotten everything straight?"

Maura crossed her arms.

"Everything straight. With yer wee broken friends. I've been working my magic, making them see the light, so to speak, and things have worked out quite nicely."

"Worked out how? What have you done, Mam?"

"Well." She turned around, still smiling. "I've talked with Kathleen and gotten her to realize that Aryl isn't coming back. She's grieving hard, but she'll start eating again, eventually. It's better than letting her fly around on false hopes."

"You had no business doing that. Let the woman grieve how she sees fit! If it comforts her to believe it—"

"It's a silly notion that had to be set straight. Also, I've convinced Arianna that Caleb has gone worthless. She's asked him to leave, and he's agreed. He has plans to head to Boston, alone."

"You WHAT!"

"And yer friend, Claire, well, we've had a lot of time to talk with ye on bed rest, and she knows now that the only way she will ever be happy is if she allows herself to fall in love when she is ready, not when it's practical. She's rejected Gordon, and he didn't seem overly broken up about it. Proves it wasn't a good match." She drew herself up tall.

"Are you mad, woman? How dare ye come here and start messin' in other people's affairs like that!"

"I wasn't messin', Maura. I was helpin'."

"The hell ye were helping! Ye don't know these people! Ye don't know what's in their hearts or what's best for them!"

"Oh, and I suppose you do!"

"I do, thank ye very much! Much better than you, that's for sure!" She gripped her forehead. "How am I going to undo all the damage you've done," she grumbled.

Katie leveled her head and stared at Maura. "Ye can't."

Maura met her stare with an equally stubborn one. "Yes, I can."

"No. Not with you up here brooding on bed rest."

"Yer the one that's got me up here on bed rest!" she roared.

"You're not strong enough to help them."

"Yes, I am!" Without thinking, she grabbed the lamp and hurled it across the room. It exploded against the wall.

"Are ye angry, Maura?"

"Yes!" Maura seethed.

"Good! Tell me, how does that *feel?*"

Maura opened her mouth, but no words came. She stared at her mother in shock. Her heart was pounding, her face was flushed, and her lungs felt full of air for the first time in weeks. She felt the floor beneath her feet and her finger, which bent when she threw the lamp, throbbed. Her stomach was empty, and her bladder was full, and she wanted to laugh, cry, and scream all at the same time. She took a moment to gather herself and leveled her gaze at Katie.

"Ye never told Miss Arianna to kick Mr. Caleb out, did ye?"

Katie shook her head.

"And ye didn't speak to Kathleen?"

"No."

"And Miss Claire is still seein' Mr. Gordon, isn't she."

"She is." Katie's smile bordered smug. "I said those things because—"

Maura held up her hand. "I know why ye said it. So long as none of it was true...that's what's important."

"No, Maura." Katie walked over and put her hands on Maura's shoulders. "What's important is that you've come back to yourself." She glanced at the shattered lamp.

"I really thought you'd done those things. Kept me a prisoner in this bedroom just to ruin my friend's lives."

Katie kissed her on the cheek. "Don't doubt me, child."

She paused at the door and looked back at Maura. "Jonathan is downstairs. Don't keep him waiting, aye? He needs you. They all need you." She winked.

A FEW MOMENTS LATER, Maura emerged downstairs with her handbag tucked under her arm. Katie stood in the kitchen sipping a cup of tea, smirking. Jonathan stood holding Jean, talking to him in a low voice, his little arms wrapped around his neck, listening intently. He moved him to his hip when he saw Maura.

She smiled and hugged him tightly. "I've heard all about it. How is Ava?"

"In the hospital. They can't stop the labor. It'll be born tonight, the doctor thinks."

"And what I heard about Victor, is it true?"

"He's dead if that's what you heard."

She crossed herself. "I shouldn't be glad that someone has lost their life, but I'll have a hard time grievin' that one."

"I'm glad," Jonathan said. "And I'm not ashamed of it."

"You look a mess, and you haven't eaten." She eyed him up and down. "Let's be on our way to your house." She nodded firmly. "You can tell me more in the car."

Jonathan moved Jean back to where he could look him in the eyes. "I need you to stay here with Katie a bit longer, okay? I'm going to go back to Ava, and as soon as you have a new little brother or sister, I'll let you know."

"I want to go home," he whined.

"You can't go home just yet, Jean. Soon, I promise."

"Because the bad man is still there?"

"No, he's not. And he's never coming back."

He nodded with an apprehensive look as Jonathan set him down and he ran to Katie, clinging to her leg.

She ushered them out and when Caleb hesitated, she turned and held her hand out.

"Well, come on now!"

He just smiled.

"What is it, then?"

"You're back."

A look of relief washed over his face as a smile crept across hers, confirming. He took a large step forward, kissing her on the head before jogging ahead and opening her door.

THEY STOOD STARING at the pool of blood in Jonathan's living room.

"Go and get bathed. Me and Caleb will take care of this mess. And after, I'll make ye something to eat."

"Maura, I couldn't possibly—"

"You'll eat, or I'll shove it down your throat," she said calmly. "You've got a long wait for this son or daughter of yours, and you'll need to keep your strength up. Now go get cleaned up. Is that how you want to meet your child? Covered in blood and sweat and bits of that bastard?"

Jonathan turned toward the stairs.

Caleb stood, grinning at her. "It's so good to have you back, Maura. God, it's good."

Jonathan stopped and turned slowly. He managed a smile and a nod, acknowledging her return, before heading upstairs.

"Caleb, I'll need some rags and a bucket of hot water. And a scrub brush and some bleach, if you can find it."

He frowned at the grisly task. "Sure. I'll go look."

The blood was still shiny in the middle but starting to dry out around the edges. A spray of delicate dots fanned out in an arch, starting before and ending after the pool, and she knew she was staring at the last moment of someone's life. The last second, even.

It's for the best, a voice told her. *He was no good.*

She heard the water running in the bathroom above, glanced at the ceiling and back down at the blood. She put her hands on her stomach and took a deep, ragged breath.

It's for the best, the voice said again. She nodded. Not for the same reason, but whatever the reason, it's for the best. Perhaps it wasn't healthy. Perhaps harder times were coming, and it would be difficult to provide for a baby. Perhaps, the possibilities were endless. And though she was not to know why, maybe not ever, she acknowledged and accepted it with a deep, cleansing breath.

Caleb set the bucket on the floor. "I can do this, Maura."

"No, I'll do it. I need to," she said and took the rag from his hand.

JONATHAN ARRIVED BACK at the hospital clean, with something in his stomach but still holding a look of desperation. Everything happening was totally out of his control, and he hated it. He was forced to wait and pace and sigh and glance at his watch every three minutes with the other ragged looking fathers in the waiting room. How he wished that she was far enough along to have it at home. At least then, he could be by Ava's side.

Maura and Caleb stayed until the sun had set, and when the nurse told them there was no progress, the doctor hoped for something by morning, Jonathan insisted Maura and Caleb go home. They didn't want to, but he was adamant. He wanted to be alone.

He sat in a chair after they had left, resting his elbows on his knees, hanging his head down. The minutes passed painfully slow as he rocked, counting the seconds off to make them go faster.

Bomani walked the streets of Rockport long before the small town had woken up. He picked up his pace with the first rays of sunlight. Looping back to the train station where he hoped he'd find her but didn't, he began to feel frantic. He started asking around. Had anyone seen her? The ones who weren't too leery to talk to a rumpled, sleep deprived stranger told him they hadn't.

He hated himself for not arranging a plan in case they got separated. But Ruth should know not to go anywhere. She should know to stay at the train station where he would surely find her. She should know better! Unless...unless she was in trouble. Unless she couldn't get to him. The thought crossed his mind that Victor might not have been alone. After all, they hadn't stuck around to see exactly who came through the door. She could have been spirited away while he had his back turned.

He broke into a run towards the sheriff's office. Worried, hungry, and very tired, his legs didn't last long. He slowed to a fast walk, and it was then that he noticed someone behind him. Close behind him. He turned quickly, and a man following him came to an abrupt stop. A quick look around found them on a road sparsely populated. A few houses dotted, a corner business half a block away, a stray tabby nonchalantly crossed the street. The man was balding, short, with large eyes and an equally large smile.

"Relax, buddy." He mopped his forehead. "You haven't been easy to catch up with. Fit guy like you."

"Do I know you?" Bomani asked.

"I have a message from Ruth."

Bomani relaxed, blew out a breath, and stepped forward.

"Thank God. What is it?"

"I got it right here."

From under his jacket, the short man pulled out a gun and raised it.

"She said to tell you she loves you." He pulled the trigger.

The sound echoed through the street, and the cat sprinted off. The short man stepped over Bomani's body and walked away. Around the corner, he got into a waiting car, as if he didn't have a care in the world.

PATRICK WALKED UP THE HILL, past the back garden, toward his little cabin. There was a spring in his step, and he whistled. They had just enough supplies to get through winter, Shannon was happy in their new little home, and Caleb's problems were Caleb's problems. There was a great relief in being separated from them. Since Katie Mallory had set him straight, he'd been sober for a bit now and with any luck, he'd stay that way. Either way, shrugging as he walked, they weren't his problems anymore.

He heard a car behind him as it pulled up to the front of the farm-house. He heard Arianna talking but couldn't make out what she was saying. Then someone called his name. Patrick stopped and turned around. It was Marvin. He stood slightly hunched, looking small and meaningless, waved and smiled in front of Arianna. He pushed his glasses up his nose and started walking past the house and up the hill toward him.

He changed as he walked, out of eyesight from Arianna. He began walking straight and tall. Slowly took off his glasses and his friendly smile morphed into something ugly and angry.

He got right to the point.

"You talked to Caleb."

Patrick drew himself up tall. "Aye. Man had a right to know. What he does with it now is between you two." He turned to walk away, and Marvin grabbed his arm.

"You think it's that easy? After I specifically told you not to say a word, you go and squeal. You disobeyed my order, Patrick. Now, what am I supposed to do about that?"

"Ye can start by taking yer fecking hands off me. Else, lawman or no, I'll lay ye flat out."

Marvin held on for a few more seconds, pressing his luck before he let go. "I suppose you're one hell of a fighter."

"Yeah. I can be. So ye can throw your wee hissy fit and flash yer badge and have Caleb arrested for all I care. But know this, if ye do, I'll find ye, and I *will* rid this town of one crooked deputy. At the very least, they won't be able to recognize ye. That's a promise."

"Ah, be careful, Pat. Threatening a lawman could land you in jail."

"So could the thousands of dollars of opiates you've got stashed in that barn."

"Tell me, Pat, is it just the heritage that makes you hate authority, or does your friendship with Caleb have anything to do with you getting all ruffled up."

"Caleb's a good man, deep down. He's taken my family and me in. I've been madder than hell at him for his choices lately, but I won't see him busted for something he's not responsible for."

"Well, Patrick, in the last few seconds, I've had a revelation of sorts." He smiled, lopsided and devious. Patrick stared, wary.

"Let's say that you do something for me, and I won't hold my promise to have Caleb busted."

Patrick narrowed his eyes. "I won't do anything illegal."

"Well, for me, what's legal and what's not is in the eye of the beholder. And I am that beholder. After all, if a deputy were to tell you it was okay to do something, as a favor, it's kind of like a free pass, you know?"

"I figured it would be something underhanded. The answer is no. Whatever it is, I won't do it."

"Even if it means sending your friend down the river?"

Patrick stared at him. "Ye won't do that. And ye know how I know ye won't? Because ye need him. If ye didn't, you'd have yer stash somewhere else."

"You're right. And they say Irish are all temper and no brains." He laughed. "What I don't need, Patrick, are witnesses. Like you. Now, if you were willing to do something to be needed, like use those muscles on some guys who haven't paid, then we'd have more of a partnership, of sorts."

"I'd sooner die than be a dirty partner of yours."

"Stubbornness. Now that's a spot on typecast of your people."

"Ye go about your filthy business of muddlin' up people's brains with that stuff yer selling. But I won't have any part of it."

He turned and started to walk away. Marvin spoke with malice in his voice.

"That's a real pretty wife you've got there in that cabin. Cute wiggle she has when she's reaching up to hang clothes on the line."

Patrick froze and spoke through clenched teeth.

"Unless you want to see the full fury of hell—" He turned and looked Marvin in the eye. "I'd not mention my wife ever again."

Marvin just laughed. A loud, boisterous laugh that made Patrick want to choke him silent.

"I'll be watching, Patrick," he said as he turned and walked leisurely back to his car. "Should anything happen to my investment, we'll talk again."

"Jon." His head jerked up, and he saw Vincent standing in the doorway with his hat in his hand. "How are you?"

Not readily having an answer, he brought his shoulders up. He looked lost. He felt lost. Vincent motioned with his hat to sit down, and Jonathan invited him.

"How's Ava?"

"There's no word yet," Jonathan said. "They thought tonight, but…"

"I hope it all works out, Jon. I really do."

He nodded, bouncing one leg, twisting the arms of the metal chair under his palms.

"I know this isn't the best time. I've talked to Marvin and gotten his account of what happened. I'd like to get yours."

"Ah—" He blinked and rubbed his eyes, trying to clear his mind. "He showed up and tried to kill me. After Ruth and her friend showed up…I don't remember his name."

"Her friend? What did he look like?"

"Tall with dark hair. A little bit of an accent, I don't know, Egyptian, maybe?"

"Bomani?" Vincent asked.

"Yeah, that's it. He showed up and said Victor was on his way."

"How did he know?"

"Said he used to work for him."

"And you're sure this person was her friend? Boyfriend maybe?"

"Maybe, probably. I don't know. She seemed awfully protective of him."

"Okay." Vincent held his hat between his knees, twirling it slowly. "I'm just trying to put all the pieces together."

"What's to put together? Ruth and Bomani tried to warn me, Victor showed up, and now he's dead. And the whole damn thing caused Ava to go into labor. I'm glad he's dead. In fact, I've never been happier that someone is dead!" The other fathers glanced over at him.

"I'm not trying to upset you, Jon," Vincent said in a hushed voice. "In fact, I owe you an apology. You came to me months ago, and I didn't listen to you. I'm sorry."

Jonathan rolled his head around for a moment, stretching the tight muscles in his neck. He appreciated the apology, but it didn't change, nor did it help things now.

"Thanks, Vincent," he said. It wasn't his fault. He was angry at the situation, not the sheriff.

The nurse appeared at the door, and three expectant fathers popped their heads up anxiously. She didn't call Jonathan but another fitful soul waiting for news. He scurried away while the two remaining looked down in disappointment.

"Do you want me to stay with you?" Vincent asked.

"No, thank you. I'll be fine."

Vincent stood. "Can I get you some coffee? Bring anything back? A book or something?" He glanced at his watch. "Dinner?"

"No. I appreciate it, though."

He turned to leave, and Jonathan stopped him.

"Hey, wait. How'd you know the name of Ruth's friend?"

Vincent stepped closer and lowered his voice to nearly a whisper.

"He turned up dead on the sidewalk this morning."

If Jonathan hadn't been overwhelmed to the point of breaking already, this certainly pushed him dangerously close to the edge.

"Ruth showed up yesterday evening saying she'd been kidnapped, managed to escape, and ran straight to the sheriff's office. Marvin is giving her an escort back to New York now."

"Kidnapped?"

"I take it she didn't look under duress?"

"Not at all."

"Well, now you see what I mean by putting the pieces together. I'll let you know when I—"

"You know what Vincent? Don't. I don't want to know. It doesn't concern me anymore."

Vincent agreed with a reluctant shrug. After he had left, Jonathan scrubbed his face with his hand. He didn't want to know. Didn't care. The only thing he cared about was several rooms away, fighting for life with an unknown fate. The long wait, the little voices in the back of his head, the blasted ticking of the clock on the wall, it all reminded him of what was truly important, and he closed his heart to everything else. The whole world could burn, and he wouldn't give it a second glance. *Just let them be all right*, he pleaded.

JONATHAN NODDED off sometime after midnight. He jolted with the feeling of falling and grabbed the arms of the chair with a gasp.

Another father, who hadn't been there when Jonathan fell asleep, nodded his understanding, and repositioned his sweater as a makeshift pillow, leaning at an awfully uncomfortable angle. Jonathan stretched his leg out to avoid a cramp.

"I just keep telling myself it's not as bad as what they're going through in there," the man said with a smile.

Jonathan nodded.

"This is my sixth. You?"

"First. Well, second, but...long story."

The man didn't feel the need to ask questions. "After you have as many kids as I have, it gets easier. That is after you get them home, it's easier. This is never easy. The waiting."

Jonathan nodded again, stood and stretched, letting out a big yawn.

"The night shift nurses just brewed a pot of coffee. It's in the hall on a table to your left."

"Thank you." He opened the door and peeked out. All was silent. It seemed unnaturally bright. He'd always disliked hospitals. And this nerve-wracking waiting game didn't improve his opinion.

"Mr. Garrett?"

Jonathan turned around. "Right here."

"Would you come with me?"

A plump nurse with her hair pulled in a tight bun fluttered her hand and turned, walking quickly. Jonathan jogged to catch up. "Is she okay?"

"Right this way." She led him with a fast waddle down a series of hallways and through a number of doors. The last room was small, and the lights were off. The nurse flipped the switch, blinding them both. Jonathan blinked, shielding his eyes.

"She's right in there."

"Ava?" he asked, squinting.

"No, your daughter." The nurse turned him around by the shoulders and through a thick plate of glass stood a nurse holding a tiny bundle. He couldn't see a baby for all the blankets and took a step forward. The young nurse, clad in a gown, cap, and mask stepped forward as well, tilting the bundle so Jonathan could see the smallest face he'd ever dreamed possible.

"She's a strong one. It was a little concerning at first, she didn't want to breathe, but once she did, she let out a holler we nurses love to hear."

Jonathan stood with his mouth agape, staring. He could see thin wisps of hair peeking out from the edge of the bulky knit hat; it was light, like Ava's. Her little mouth was pursed, but she didn't frown like most babies he'd seen who looked rather inconvenienced at the process of being born. She slept peacefully.

"She's healthy?" he managed to whisper.

"She appears to be. Tiny, but healthy. Only four and a half pounds and seventeen inches long. She's breathing well, and she's even had a half ounce from the bottle."

"And Ava?" He turned to the nurse. "How is she?"

"Very tired. But doing well. It's late, but I can take you to her, just for a moment, if you'd like."

"Yes, please." He turned with the nurse to leave but didn't take his eyes off the baby until the last second.

Ava lay sleeping in the hospital bed as Jonathan approached. The room was dark with only a dim lamp at her bedside. It was odd to see her figure flat, with only the slightest rise and fall of her chest.

It was a large room with five other beds. Three beds were occupied besides Ava's, and those mothers slept soundly. Jonathan pulled the curtain surrounding Ava's bed closed. When he sat down, her eyes were open.

"Have you seen her?" Her voice was hoarse and weak.

"I did. She's so beautiful. Just like her mother."

Ava managed a weak smile.

"I'm so sorry I couldn't be there with you."

"I wanted you. I asked for you. They said it wasn't allowed."

"I know," he said with a frown. "I'll be there next time. I promise."

She grimaced with a smile. "I really don't want to think about next time right now. She may have been small, but that was really hard."

211

"I'm sure it was."

"I'm so tired," she whispered, closing her eyes.

"I'll go tell the others and let you sleep."

She lifted a weak hand to find his. "Don't stay gone too long."

"I'll be back first thing in the morning." He leaned over to give her a kiss.

"Bring Jean," she said just before she slipped off to sleep.

~

THE NEXT DAY, Ava was sitting up in bed when her visitors arrived. She had eaten, and her arms were restless to hold her new daughter.

Smoothing the blankets over her legs for the third time, she sighed heavily, growing impatient with the nurse who was supposed to be bringing her baby.

Jean's dark locks poked around the privacy curtain and she smiled.

"Are you hurting?" he whispered with nervous eyes. Jonathan rumpled his hair.

"I told you she was all right this morning," he said, stepping around Jean and producing a bouquet of flowers.

"Oh, they're beautiful, thank you." She knew better than to chastise him for spending precious money. An occasion like this justified flowers and, as she painfully readjusted in the bed, she'd earned them. He bent to give her a kiss.

"How do you feel today?"

"Like I've been hit by a truck. My ankle doesn't hurt so badly in comparison." She smiled. "Come sit by me, Jean."

Jonathan lifted him up and sat him carefully on the edge of the bed by Ava's legs. He took a long look at her stomach and all around the tiny, curtained cubicle.

"Where is the bebe?"

Ava opened her mouth to speak but stopped, her eyes darting to Jonathan. "Did you tell him?"

"No." He grinned. "I thought I'd let you do that."

"Ah. Well, the baby will be here in a few minutes." She craned her head to see past the curtain. "Or at least it had better be. That nurse is taking forever."

He wriggled with anticipation. "So, you are not going to tell me if I have a brother or a sister?"

"Nope. You have to wait."

"If I guess will you tell me?"

"No," Ava said. "But I do want to thank you."

His eyes popped wide. "Thank me? For what?"

She motioned him closer, and he moved cautiously.

"I know what happened the other day was very scary."

"When the bad man came," he whispered.

"Yes, when the bad man came. You were so brave. You stayed right by me, even after I fell."

He dropped his eyes down. "I went away one time."

"You did. But it was to get something to protect us with. I wanted to thank you for that, too."

He was upset, biting on his lip. "I didn't even know how to use it."

"But you knew to get it when we were in danger. And I could have used it if I needed to," Ava said.

He raised his head and faced Jonathan. "You aren't angry at me for getting it? You told me never to touch the gun."

"Well, not this time, no, I'm not angry at you. You did the right thing. But I do think it's time I teach you how to use it properly. Maybe we can go out into the woods sometime soon and start practicing."

Jean sat up a little straighter and beamed as the nurse pulled the curtain back. "Here you go. Sorry for the delay, dear. Delivery's really busy with that full moon tomorrow." She moved close to the bed and transferred the baby from her arms to Ava.

"Jean, meet your little sister." She pulled the blanket back from the baby's face, and Jean stared for a moment.

"It's not a doll?" he asked, amazed.

"She's not a doll. She's real. Just very tiny."

"Will you bring her home this tiny? Or will she have to grow up first?"

213

"She'll stay here a while longer, and I'll stay with her. When the doctor says we can come home, we will."

He moved his hand to touch her and stopped, his eyes darting up for permission.

"Go ahead," Ava said with a smile. He touched the small curled fist with the tip of his finger and stroked it a few times.

"She's so soft. What's her name?"

"Well," Ava said, "that's why I wanted Jon to bring you today. So we could all decide on a name together."

JEAN SAT in the front seat of the old truck, stretching upward to see the road ahead over the dashboard.

"You are really going to teach me to shoot?"

"I am."

"Is it hard?"

"Not if you know what you're doing."

"When can we go?"

"Well, I'm not sure. We have a lot to do before the baby comes home."

"I want to learn before the bebe comes home."

"Why?" Jonathan looked over at him curiously.

"She's so little. She is the sweetest thing I have ever seen, and I want to be able to protect her." He gazed out the window. Houses passed slowly, and he seemed to be inspecting each one. "In case the bad man comes back."

"Jean, I told you, the bad man isn't going to come back. I promise." It was a harsh reality, but he wanted to set Jean's mind at ease. "He's dead. He's not coming back. Ever."

"I missed school today."

"I know. It's a special occasion. I'll write you a note."

"I don't want to go back."

Jonathan glanced at him sidelong. "You have to go back, Jean."

"I won't."

"Jean, you—"

"I won't go back." He looked up at Jonathan with a stubbornness he'd never seen before.

Jonathan let out a deep breath, thinking before speaking. The kid had been through a lot. He'd had more than his fair share of death in the past few months, and he was so protective of those he loved. There was something different about him, just in the short time since he'd laid eyes on his new sister.

"We'll talk about it later, okay?"

Jean nodded. "Will you take me to Arianna's?"

"Sure. I was headed there anyway to give them the good news. Do you want to sleep there tonight instead of at Maura's?"

"Yes, please."

THEY PULLED up to the farmhouse and Arianna flew out onto the porch.

"Is everything okay? Did she have it yet?"

Jean jumped out of the car and ran to her, jumping up into her arms.

"Go ahead and tell her, Jean!" Jonathan called ahead.

He put his small hands on her cheeks and looked into her eyes. He started speaking rapidly in French and stopped, corrected himself and dropped back into English.

"It's a girl!" He beamed. "And she's the tiniest thing I've ever seen and the sweetest, too! She has a cry like a cricket!"

"A cricket?" Arianna laughed. "Oh, that's wonderful news, Jean! You're a big brother!" She hugged him tightly and looked at Jonathan over his shoulder. "Ava's all right?" she asked.

"She's fine."

Her face grew serious. "How small?"

"Four and a half pounds. Doctor thinks she's doing really well, all things considered."

Jean pulled back and grabbed her face again, demanding her attention. "Can I stay with you tonight? I want to tell you all about the bebe, and I need to practice with yours."

"Practice?"

"Yes," he said, growing serious himself. "I need to know how to change their diapers and bathe them and rock them to sleep. I have to know because I have a new little sister, and I need to help her."

"Don't you think your parents can handle that?"

He shook his head as if she were clueless. "They need my help, Auntie Arianna."

"I'm sure they do, my little man." She smiled and lowered him to the ground. "We'll get to work right away teaching you those things. Why don't you run into the house and see if Ethel has a bit of cake left."

He started up the steps and turned around. "After cake, can I run up and see Aislin?"

"You can. I'll go with you."

"Will you pick me up in the morning so I can go see my new little sister again?" he asked Jonathan.

"I will, I promise."

Scrambling up the steps, he called for Ethel.

"Caleb's in the barn if you want to tell him the good news yourself."

"In the barn?" he asked, one eyebrow cocked.

"Working." She smiled. "He's been sober for a whole week."

"I'm glad to hear that."

Just then, Caleb stepped out of the barn with a wave.

"You're an uncle again," Jonathan yelled across the yard.

Caleb smiled and walked a little faster. "Girl or boy?"

"Girl."

"Congratulations," he said with a handshake. "I'm glad it all turned out all right."

Arianna started up the steps. "I'll leave you boys to talk. I have work to do."

"Is lunch ready? I'm starving," Caleb said.

"It will be when you come in."

She disappeared into the house, and Jonathan turned to Caleb. "It's been a hell of a week," he said.

"Isn't that the truth?"

"Listen, I wanted to talk to you about what you mentioned to me in the waiting room when I asked you to distract me. That thing about

Marvin. I couldn't think clearly then, but now that Ava and the baby are safe, I wanted to know if you've figured out what's going on."

"Yeah. I had a talk with him. I told him I wasn't drinking anymore and having the stuff there was too much of a temptation. I asked him to move it somewhere else."

"What about the other stuff. Did you ask about that?

"No. Honestly, Jon, if it *is the* property of the sheriff's office and going to be destroyed, then everything's on the up and up. If it's not, and Marvin is crooked, I don't know if I want to open that can of worms."

Jonathan shifted his weight and crossed his arms. "Yeah, but don't you want to know what's really going on?"

Caleb glanced over at the house. "Would you get all confrontational with your wife and kids right here?"

Jonathan conceded with a shrug.

"Besides, trying to stay sober is a good enough reason to get him to move it. It doesn't have to get ugly, and it can just end right here."

"When is he moving it?"

"He says he's looking for another place now."

"All right. But if he starts to procrastinate—"

"Jon, I can handle it," Caleb interrupted. "Your being preoccupied with Ava gave me a chance to think things through. I'll deal with it."

"All right. If you're sure."

OCTOBER 31, 1930

All Hallows Eve looked and felt very similar to something out of a scary book. The Indian summer had come to a sudden and abrupt end. It was a dark, overcast day and the blustery winds held an icy streak that promised winter was near.

Piles of gathered leaves in yards were blown about, scattering along the sidewalk and carried on the wind, swirling in the street.

Claire watched as the last of the leaves were torn from the trees and hoped they didn't lose the lights. That might send Maura over the edge. She was already nervous and fitful on Halloween, being superstitious as she was. And it was the only time she voiced any displeasure at her going out to see Gordon.

"I don't understand why he can't come over here," she huffed. "I don't like ye going out on a day like this!"

"Oh, Maura. No ghosts are going to pop up and get me." She had grinned before a hard shiver ran up her back. The smile dropped. "Besides, it's not like I'm out there wandering alone."

"Aye. But spirits are. Yes, they are!" she insisted, seeing the look on Claire's face. "You don't believe, but I've seen. When I was a wee girl, my sister and me snuck out on All Hallows Eve, thinking our parents were full of shite. We had the life scared out of us, and

I knew then it was true. Never again will I go out on this evil day!"

"You and which sister, Maura?" Katie asked slowly. Maura closed her eyes and cringed, having forgotten her mother was in the next room and had the hearing of a hawk.

"Never you mind, Mam."

"What happened?" Claire asked.

Maura shook her head. "Another time," she whispered. "Just be careful, Miss Claire."

"If you'd like, I'll wake you when I get in and let you know I'm safe and sound."

"She'll be awake, you can be sure of it," Katie called from the next room. "Likely she'll be tellin' me the story of her and her sister sneaking out!" She snickered under her breath, and it gave Maura something other than Claire to worry about momentarily.

As she stepped into his living room, she felt the heat first. The furnace was working hard and between that and the wood stove blazing, it had to be ninety degrees. There was lawn furniture in the middle of the living room, and a lot of plants.

"Why do you keep your house so hot? And why is there a picnic table in the middle of your living room?"

"It's all part of the plan," he said with a grin. "It's Halloween. But you had your mind all set for Easter. Probably spent a good amount of time pushing away memories of the last few Easters, am I right?"

"Yes, actually."

"Well, actually, it's the Fourth of July. It's blazing hot, there is no relief, and you are as far as possible from both Easter and Halloween. I have cold drinks, a barbecue in the back and potato salad in the icebox."

She smiled. "I can't believe you went to all this trouble."

"Hardest part was hauling the sofa out of here by myself. But it was no trouble," he said as he put on a record. Soon the room was filled with "O, say can you see."

She couldn't help but laugh. His plan had worked. She was so thoroughly confused now that her mind was blank, her heart light.

She felt something brush against her leg. Kitten was circling her feet, staring up at her.

"Hi, sweetheart! Are you enjoying your new home?"

"All the land he could ever want to roam and all the cream he can drink. I'd say he likes it."

"Gordon, he's getting fat!" she said as she picked him up and cradled him. Kitten purred and rubbed each side of his face on hers.

"That would be the cream," Gordon said. "He's great company, actually. Keeps my feet warm at night."

"Every cat's dream. To be owned by a dairyman." She smiled wide. Gordon simply stared, seeing her true smile for the first time. "I'm glad to see him happy." She set him on the ground, and Kitten trotted over to Gordon, pawing at his pant leg, mewing. "And spoiled," she added.

"Are you hungry?"

"Famished," she said. "Can I help?"

"No, just have a seat at the picnic table. I'll be back in a minute."

When she sat down, Kitten followed her, jumped up on the table, and began bonking his head on her arm, demanding attention.

Dinner was simple—grilled hamburgers, potato salad, green salad, and lemonade. They talked casually as they ate.

"You really made all this?"

"Yes. I can cook, you know. It was rough at first, but I've gotten the hang of it. The potato salad isn't too spicy, is it? I don't want you to get heartburn."

Claire smiled. "I get heartburn from breathing air. But no, it's not too spicy. I'm impressed, Gordon. I would have never guessed you were so good in the kitchen."

Kitten had to be removed from the table at least a half dozen times, and Claire couldn't remember when she had been more relaxed.

When Gordon pulled out a small cake for dessert, decorated with red, white, and blue icing, she pointed a finger at him.

"Now, I know you didn't make *that*."

"No, I didn't. An older woman I deliver to made it for me."

"Ah. Did you tell her what it was for?"

He grinned, looking down. "I might have."

"So, the whole town knows about us now?"

"No, I wouldn't say that. I didn't give your name. And that old gal wouldn't say a word anyway. I've talked to her a lot over the years. She was a friend of my wife before she died."

"Oh." Claire looked down quietly.

"That's part of it, too, Claire. At least it was for me. Seemed to help."

"What's part of it?"

"Bringing them up when your mind is confused. It's Halloween, you still have bunnies on the mind, and we're eating patriotic cake."

"You mean talking about them?"

"Or just saying their name out loud. Once."

She appeared nervous and hesitant.

"I'll go first. Marjorie. There. That wasn't so hard."

Claire took a deep breath and looking into Gordon's eyes, said, "Aryl." She bit her lip, waiting for tears or the familiar pain that would rip through her chest. It was a small dull stab, simply reminding her she still had a heart.

"See," he said, reaching out and holding her hand across the table. "Everything's fine. And it'll get easier every time."

She smiled, shaky at first, but it melted into sincerity. "Thank you, Gordon. For all of this. For just…being you."

They finished their cake and Gordon offered seconds. She shook her head. "Oh, no. I couldn't."

"Because you're full? Or because you're self-conscious to eat in front of me."

"Obviously, I'm not self-conscious to eat in front of you, Gordon. I polished off that huge hamburger and had seconds of potato salad. I'm stuffed. I have less room for food as each day passes." She looked down at her stomach.

"Well, maybe if he moves you can eat a bit more." He started whistling.

"No, stop!" she yelled, laughing. "Please, don't. He gets so active when you do that."

221

Gordon sat back and smiled. "So it is a he."

She sat quietly for a moment and looked up at him. "I think so."

He jumped up so quickly it startled her. Switching to a new record, he turned it up loud and dashed to the closet, pulling out a bag.

"What on earth are you up to now?" she asked above the music.

He smiled with a wink and took her hand. Out in the backyard, he pulled a firework out of the bag and set it on the ground. He motioned for her to move. "I'll join you on the porch in a moment."

She moved, he lit the fuse and ran to meet her. They watched it shoot up and explode in the night sky, reflecting against the ominous clouds that threatened rain.

"This is going to terrify your neighbors," she said.

"Can't have Fourth of July without fireworks. And I don't really have neighbors out here. No one will notice."

He walked out to light another and returned to Claire just as it shot up. He slipped an arm around her waist as it exploded. She noticed, of course, but didn't say anything. The music was fast and upbeat. As far from romantic as music could get. But as she stood watching the last of the embers burn out in the sky, shivering at the cold nip in the air, and his warm arm around her, she felt the faint veil of romance enveloping them. She missed this. She missed it so much. He ran to light another, resumed his spot next her, returned his arm, this time pulling her slightly closer. Before she could think too heavily about Aryl, the firework went off. It was large and loud, shaking the windows and driving out any thought at all.

After the last sizzle and pop, he turned to her. Her heart began to beat loudly in her ears.

"I only have one more," he said apologetically.

"Well, let's see it," she said, slightly relieved he didn't move in for a kiss. She relaxed her shoulders, and he did lean in but stopped a fraction of an inch from her lips. She felt his breath and closed her eyes. When she opened them, he was walking out into the darkness to light the last firework. She pursed her lips, fighting a smile.

They watched it explode and stood together listening to the night sounds. The cows made several grunts of irritation. The cat was nowhere to be seen. A coyote or a wolf, Claire wasn't sure which, howled in the distance.

"We'd better get inside. I don't want you to catch a chill," Gordon said. He moved. She didn't.

"The firsts are hard," she said as he turned and faced her. "But, a minute ago, that didn't feel hard. I don't know why." She threw her hands up in frustration. "It should have. I can't handle carved pumpkins and Easter ham, but I could handle that. You kissing me," she said, looking down. "In case you were wondering."

He watched her patiently.

"You probably think I'm horrible that so soon after Aryl I could even think about enjoying—"

He grabbed her and kissed her, taking her by complete surprise. She stood stiffly at first but quickly relaxed. His lips were warm and soft, and she let him expertly get her through this first, enjoying it more than she wanted to admit. He was a gentleman with his hands, keeping them on her face, moving them to her waist and back to her face, not quite ready to end it. Aryl drifted into her mind, and she pushed the thoughts away purposefully, not wanting to let them ruin this.

He stopped gracefully, a little out of breath and smiled down at her. "That wasn't so bad, was it?" he whispered.

"Not at all," she said, keeping him close with her hands on his chest.

"Can I press my luck for another first?" Before she could answer or presume anything raucous, he stepped back and held out his hand. "A first dance?"

She took his hand with a smile and stepped back inside. "I'd love to."

NOVEMBER 1, 1930

Maura woke just after dawn. The bed was still warm where Ian slept, and she hugged his pillow for a moment; it was heavy with the smell of him. He'd been working himself hard lately, desperate to fill the pantry for winter and provide for them all the things they needed. He seemed tireless and lately, he and Jonathan both worked every day of the week.

Wrapping her robe tight, she went downstairs to find Katie sitting at the table sipping tea. Her carpet bag sat at her feet.

"Mornin', Maura."

"Mornin', Mam. What are ye doing with yer bag?"

"It's time fer me to go."

Maura sat down at the table, more than a little shocked and accepted the cup of tea Katie poured for her.

"Go, where, Mam."

"Home, dear. I catch the noon train, then the boat to take me home."

"But you've barely been here a month. I thought you'd stay through winter, at least?"

"Oh, I couldn't. What would yer sisters do without me?"

"They're grown women. I'm sure they've been managing just fine."

"I need to go home, Maura."

"Well, what about everyone else? Don't you want to say goodbye to them? Jon and Ava and Caleb…" She held her hands up in question. "Ye can't just go disappearin' one day without saying a proper goodbye."

"They are *your* friends, dear. I'm sure they won't be so broken up if I don't run around with hugs and fond farewells."

"But they like ye."

"And I like them all just fine. And I leave them in your strong, capable hands."

"I just think—"

"Maura, I came here fer one reason and one reason alone. That was to see ye back on your feet, body and spirit. Now that's done, and I must go home."

In Katie's mind, it was as simple as that, and there was no arguing.

Maura smiled. "I'll miss ye, Mam."

"And I'll miss you, too. But I'm sure you'll be writin' me those letters that give the postman a hernia and take me a week to read."

"Of course, I will."

"I look forward to it."

"How will you get to the train station?"

"I've called fer a car."

Maura's eyebrows went up in surprise. "Feelin' fancy, are we?"

She grinned. "Gordon, the dairyman, is taking me. I hope the ride doesn't reek of sour milk," she thought aloud.

She sipped and remembering something, set her teacup down.

"Can I ask one more thing of ye before I go, Maura dear?"

"Anything, Mam."

She pulled her flask from her carpet back. "Do ye have a wee bit to spare? I'd like to start the trip full up."

NOVEMBER 2, 1930

Maura, Kathleen, ETHEL, and June arrived early at Jonathan's house. They had scrub buckets filled with rags on their arms, and lots of gossip to pass the day as they worked. Their mission—to scrub the house top to bottom in anticipation of the new baby coming home.

No sooner had Jonathan opened the door, the gang of women pushed past him, cheerfully announcing their reason for coming and politely asking him to stay out of the way. He grinned, running his hands through his hair, helpless to stop them even if he wanted to. Still rubbing the sleep from his eyes, he sat at the table with fresh coffee and opened the paper.

Jean, hearing all the commotion downstairs, woke soon after and padded down to see what was going on. He watched as the women bustled around the house, blinking owlishly and swaying slightly. He hadn't rested well since the incident with Victor and slept with Jonathan while Ava was gone. He was a snuggler. Jonathan stretched his neck to each side to work out a kink. He wondered how someone so small could take up so much room, and he made a mental note to talk to him about returning to his own bed once Ava came home.

Jean drug his feet to the table and took a seat with a big yawn.

Before Jonathan could get up, Maura poured him a glass of milk and put jam on a piece of bread, setting it before him.

The women were bursting with energy. Jonathan and Jean were a picture of exhaustion.

Ethel and June, best friends for the better part of fifty years, chatted in the next room. Jonathan tuned them out, for the most part, busy with thoughts and worries of his own, like the hospital bill that was due, until June said, "Oh, it's so sad that Margaret isn't here to see her first grandchild."

Jonathan's first reaction was of irritation. Jean was Margaret's first grandchild. Yes, he was illegitimate, but he was still the first. The next feeling was a returning stab of grief.

Reading him, as she was so good at doing, Maura turned from the sink. "Have you dealt with it *properly*, Mr. Jonathan?"

He knew her meaning, and he didn't like the question. On more than one occasion, people had mentioned, both to his face and behind his back, how he wasn't dealing with his parents' death. That he had never *dealt* with it. He sipped his coffee and nodded without looking at her.

"Jean, why don't you run upstairs and get dressed."

Maura waited until after he was out of earshot. "I just worry, is all. I care about ye, just as ye care about me. There's been a lot happen in the last month, and I don't want it to all come crashing down on ye suddenly. Grieving them, that is."

"It won't, Maura. Thank you."

"It just seems to me—"

"I know people mean well. I know *you* mean well. And I know that because I haven't openly wept since the funeral or talked about them a lot, people think I'm not dealing with it. But I am. I have."

"Ye understand that it's just fer love that we wonder?"

"Yes, I do."

"Then will you share with me? So I can know and not worry?"

The house had grown quiet, and he knew they were all listening, as old ladies liked to do.

"One of the last things my father said to me was that he was too old to live a life this hard. He had lost faith that things were going to get better." Jonathan shrugged. "I can't say I blame him. There's not a lot on the horizon that looks promising. And, if I'm right, by the looks of things, life is going to get a lot harder, before it gets better. I miss him— don't get me wrong. Mom, too." He blinked hard and readjusted in his seat. "I guess I would feel guilty if I cried every day, wishing they were still here. It would be selfish to wish that. To have them struggling to survive with the rest of us when they're better off…there." He glanced up at the ceiling. "Peaceful and happy. No worries. No fears. It's hard for me. But it's better for them."

Maura blinked away a few growing tears. "That is a very Jonathan way of looking at it." She rose and walked over to him. "I can see now that ye have dealt with it, and I will call the dogs off ye at once," she said jokingly, planting a kiss on the top of his head.

"Thank you, Maura."

"You're welcome. Now, is there any chance ye can make yourself and Jean scarce for the rest of the day? We've a lot of work to do."

"Actually, yes. We're heading over to the hospital to see Ava. I think we might finally name the little girl today."

Maura shrugged. "Caleb took a month to name his."

"After that, we're going out into the woods to practice shooting."

"Oh, do try to get a deer!"

"Well, we're just practicing, is all."

"Well, if all you can get is a rabbit, I'll make a stew," Maura said.

"I'll see what we can do," Jonathan said smiling as he left the kitchen.

JONATHAN SET three tin cans on a log. He wanted to teach Jean with Caleb's rifle first, thinking it more practical. There would be lots of opportunity and need to hunt food. Not so much opportunity, he hoped, for shooting someone at close range. However, Jean insisted he learn the pistol first.

Jonathan taught him how to hold it, made him memorize the name of each part, and explained how it worked. He showed him how to handle it safely, and how to load and unload it.

"Yes, but when can I shoot?" Jean asked impatiently.

"All right," he said, handing him some cotton for his ears. He knelt down next to him. "Hold it with both hands. Steady, now...level it and aim. Blow out your breath, count to three and—"

POW!

The sound ricocheted through the woods. When Jonathan looked up, one of the cans were missing.

"I got it!" Jean yelled.

"You shouldn't have done that, Jean." He frowned. "You need to listen to me. If I'm going to let you do this, I have to be able to trust you."

"But," he pointed to the log, "I got it."

"Yes, I see that," he said with a sigh. "Beginner's luck," he added. It was impossible not to smile at Jean's elated expression.

"I will listen, Dadee, I promise. Can I do it again? Please?"

"All right. Do you want me to go through the steps again or do you remember."

"I remember," he said and raised the gun, closing one eye.

"Don't close your—"

POW!

The can flew off sharply to the left.

"I almost didn't get it because of your talking, Dadee."

Jean handled the gun as if he'd handled one all his life. He was comfortable and relaxed when he asked for permission to shoot the next can.

"Go ahead," Jonathan said, standing to give him a little room.

He fired and Jonathan couldn't help but be impressed.

"Three shots, three cans. And at a hundred feet, too. You might be a marksman in the making."

Jean looked up at him curiously. "If three cans with three shots don't make me one, what does?"

Jonathan laughed. "Let's see if you can do it again."

Jean set the gun on the ground while Jonathan searched for the cans. He found one but the other two were torn in half, and he had to improvise with other things from the ground. A split log standing on end and a discarded paint can were his new targets.

229

"How about you move back a little?" Jonathan asked as he returned.

"How far?"

"About fifty feet."

Jonathan carried the pistol, and when they stopped, he handed it to Jean, who took note of how he passed it.

He followed the steps and just before he blew out his breath, he looked up at Jonathan. "You don't think I can do it, do you?"

Before he could answer, Jean fired, sending the paint can flying back.

Jonathan's eyebrows went up. "Are you sure you've never done this before?" he asked.

"Never," he said and shot two more times quickly, adjusting the gun slightly between firings. The log stood empty of targets. He turned the pistol around and held it out to Jonathan, who stood staring at his son, not quite sure what to say.

"How...did you do that?" he asked, scratching his head.

"What do you mean? I just did what you told me to do." He smiled. "You are a good teacher."

"No, Jean, you are a good shot. Amazing."

"Can I learn the rifle now?" he asked casually as a frog hopped out from behind a rock, and Jean set off to catch it.

NOVEMBER 3, 1930

"Caleb. Just the man I wanted to see," Marvin said as Caleb stepped out onto the porch. "Can I have a word?"

Caleb glanced back into the kitchen and saw Arianna passing through to the living room with Samuel on her shoulder.

"Out there," Caleb said, gesturing to the yard.

They walked until they were out of earshot.

"Is this about getting the stuff out of the barn?"

"Yes, actually. I'm in one hell of a bind, Caleb. I can't find anywhere suitable with anyone I can trust. I need to keep it here a while longer."

"Marvin, I told you, I can't drink anymore. It's too damn tempting to have it there."

"Oh, come on now, Caleb. You're a strong man. You can resist it. You're doing great, and it's been here all this time. How about I make it worth your while." He reached into his pocket and pulled out some cash.

"I thought you said the sheriff's office couldn't afford to pay me."

"Desperate times. The office can spare it if it has to."

Caleb deliberated, glancing warily at Marvin.

"Name your price, Caleb. And I tell you what, I'll keep looking for another place and try to get it moved by the first of the year. All I need to know is what you want for the inconvenience until then." He smiled knowing Caleb couldn't resist the cash. No one could in times like these.

NOVEMBER 4, 1930

They stepped inside to a large gathering of people. Everyone was there, anxious to see the new one. Jonathan and Ava hadn't shared her name yet, wanting to wait until everyone was together.

Maura had cooked a big meal of simple food—baked beans, bread, potato salad and shortbread cookies. Jonathan's living room was bursting. The loud chatter switched to adoring whispers as Ava pulled the blanket back.

"Her name is Amy," Ava said.

"I call her Cricket. Because that's what her cry sounds like," Jean said, and everyone laughed. Ava sat down on the sofa, and he scrambled up to be next to her.

"Who is she named after?" Arianna asked.

"No one. She just...looked like an Amy." Ava smiled and lifted the baby up in offering for Arianna to hold.

"Oh, yes, please!" She took Amy carefully, and her mouth dropped open in surprise. "She's so light! Feels like there's hardly anything in my arms."

"She's almost five pounds," Jonathan said with pride. "She lost a little at first, but her appetite kicked in, and she's been gaining steadily."

Caleb peered over her shoulder, putting his arm around Arianna's waist. "Can you remember when ours were this small?"

"I don't think ours were ever this small," she said.

"Makes you want another, doesn't it?"

Arianna tossed a strained smile to Caleb and smiled at Maura. "Would you like a turn?"

She wiped her hands on her apron and held her arms out. "Of course." She didn't say anything as she cradled Amy, only watched her sleep. The others went about talking, serving plates of food, and making jokes. Suddenly, Maura spoke.

"There's nothing like a new life to bring folks back together."

She looked at several of them in turn.

"How long has it been since we've all been in the same room and smilin'?"

It had been a long time. Too long.

NOVEMBER 7, 1930

J onathan, CALEB, and Ian set out to sea with a brilliant sunrise lighting their path. Jonathan was glad they were there; glad he'd decided for them to go out together, always. Caleb worked more efficiently sober, and Ian always worked hard regardless. They were a good team. When one was unable to go out, the others picked up the slack. He marveled at the way it had come to work, seamless and steady. While he was waiting for his daughter to be born, work continued. While Ian took a few days off to be with Maura, work continued. When Caleb was too busy with autumn duties on the farm and needed to take a day, work continued.

Working this way was an insurance policy, of sorts, between friends. It was unofficial, unannounced and yet they all knew it was vital to everyone's survival. That and his decision to use the very last of the business's savings to purchase additional equipment had kept them alive. Things that allowed them to fish for things other than lobster ensuring they would always come home with something, no matter the season.

"Let's pull in a record catch, boys," Jonathan said as he steered out to sea. "I've got a little girl at home that needs pretty dresses." He smiled back at Caleb and Ian, who were readying the line of pots.

Jonathan sat at the table in his bathrobe, holding his coffee in one hand and Amy in the crook of his arm. He nodded off and caught his head with a jerk. Sitting up with a yawn, he adjusted the baby as she scrunched up and began to whimper. He bounced her lightly as he set his coffee down. The baby ate every hour and a half, and Jonathan and Ava were forced to take turns in six-hour shifts if either of them were to get any sleep at all.

Jean, who Jonathan was sure hadn't slept at all since Amy came home, woke at the tiniest sound she made. He rounded the corner into the kitchen.

"What's wrong with her?" he asked urgently.

"She's fine. Just hungry again."

"I'll hold her while you make a bottle," Jean said and climbed up on the couch with his arms out.

Jonathan gave him an amused smile. "You know, Jean, I don't know what we'd do without you."

His eyes popped with his smile. "Really?"

"Yes. How would I make a bottle while holding the baby? I'd have to wake Ava up, and she needs her rest. You're a big help."

He leaned over and put the baby in his arms. He was already an expert at holding babies and rocked gently as Amy began to fuss.

"*Shh, little crick-et. Shh, little crick-et.*" He sang to her as he moved.

Amy was too ravenous to calm, and her squeaks quickly escalated to sharp bursts of desperation. It didn't bother Jean.

"*Shh, little crick-et. Shh, little crick-et.*" He continued to sing softly over her cries. He waited patiently and calmly while Jonathan made a bottle of diluted condensed milk mixed with a little sugar. He dipped the nipple in boiling water and let it cool before attaching it.

Jean didn't hand over the baby but held his hand out for the bottle, instead.

"I can do it."

"Are you sure?"

He gave a nod and took the bottle. "Arianna taught me."

"Well, then, I'm sure you're an expert." Jonathan sat down beside him and watched him feed the baby. He was a natural. They enjoyed several quiet moments and Jonathan felt tempted to lay his head back and rest.

They heard Ava on the stairs, and she smiled as she sat down next to Jean.

"I have her. She's fine," Jean said quickly.

"I figured you did," she said. "I wasn't worried."

"You're supposed to be sleeping," Jonathan said, reaching behind Jean and touching her cheek.

"I heard Amy and woke up." She shrugged. "Couldn't go back to sleep."

Jonathan glanced at his watch. "Two more hours until your shift. Try to get some sleep if you can."

They yawned together and laughed.

"Oh, Jon, you look so tired. Let me take a turn early."

He ran his hand through his hair, making it stick wildly in all directions. He hadn't showered in two days, and his eyes were bloodshot and puffy. Dried spit up stained the shoulder of his robe. He deliberated, watching Amy grow groggy. Her eyes were half closed, rolling around in full-bellied bliss. A thin stream of milk escaped the side of her mouth and ran down her cheek. When he smiled up at Ava, he found her with her head back on the sofa, sleeping open mouthed. She had the ability that new mothers quickly acquired, to fall asleep at a second's notice. She let out a light snort, and Jean giggled. Jonathan didn't want to sleep. Not right now. He was content to simply sit and watch his sleepy family, nestled together on the couch.

He thought ahead to the coming holidays. They deserved so much more than he would be able to provide, even with the tiny miracle he'd received in the mail the day before. He'd been waiting for the amount due to the hospital. What he received was a statement from the hospital showing the bill as paid in full. It wasn't charity, the receptionist assured him when he went to the hospital to inquire about it. Someone had simply walked in and asked to pay the Garrett bill. Didn't leave his name. Just paid it and walked out. For the life of him, Jonathan couldn't figure out who would have done that. Who *could* have done that— produced sixty-five dollars without batting an eye? In any event, it was a relief, and he was grateful for it. He looked down at Jean, who was dabbing Amy's mouth with a burp cloth.

"Think you can get us a Thanksgiving turkey this year, Mr. Sharp-shooter?" he asked Jean.

"Of course, I can," he said smiling with confidence. "As long as you don't talk while I'm trying to shoot."

JANUARY 1, 1931

Caleb climbed into bed tired and more than a little tipsy. He'd taken a few bottles of brandy from Marvin's stash and hosted a small New Year's get together. He was thankful no one asked where he'd gotten it. It was well after one o'clock when everyone finally left, and the house was a disaster. Ethel insisted on cleaning up in the morning, and Arianna didn't argue. She was bone tired as she settled back into the pillow.

"Everyone looked good tonight," Caleb said.

"Mm-hmm."

"Amy's growing."

"She's still so tiny. Three months old and she's the size of a newborn," Arianna said.

"She smiled at me, you know. No one else. Just me."

"I know, I saw. It's just because you look goofy," Arianna said with a smirk.

"No, it's because I gave her a taste of my mom's boiled frosting."

"You did good tonight," she said, not speaking of the baby at all. Playing a good host, not over drinking, laughing even though his eyes clouded with sadness when he saw Claire with Gordon at her side. She knew gatherings were hard for him and likely would be for a long time.

She shivered and snuggled deeper into the blankets. "It's cold tonight."

"C'mere. I'll keep you warm. It's about all I can do," he warned with a smile in his voice as she rolled toward him. "I can't feel my lips and the room is spinning."

"That's fine. I'll wait and hope for better things."

He lay quiet for a moment. "Better things," he repeated softly. "Seems like things are getting better."

"Does it?" she asked. In her day-to-day life, things seemed to be moving along as best they could. She'd learned to steel herself against too much hope and just play the hand she was dealt as best she could.

"Sometimes, I think so," he said, taking a deep, relaxing breath. "Maura's feistiness is back in full swing, and my mom's found a lot of joy with her volunteer work. The twins are healthy. Shannon and Patrick are happy in the cabin. Jon and Ava look good, and since Victor died and Amy was born, they seem a lot happier. Fatherhood suits him. Claire seems happy with Gordon." He stopped abruptly. "I think," he paused again, and she raised her head.

"You think what?"

"I think he's good for her. And I think they'll end up getting married."

She lay her head back down on his shoulder. "I think you're right."

"We're all getting by. With enough to keep body and soul together, anyway."

"True." She rolled away from him and stretched.

"And there's nothing saying this year won't be the year everything starts to get better for good."

"Maybe." She wanted to warn him against too much false hope but didn't want to ruin his mood. He moved closer and draped his arm over her. Giving her hip a pat, he adjusted to get comfortable. "This old mattress," he grumbled. "I wish we could get a new one."

Arianna started to say there was no use wishing for things, when he rolled back, letting his hand glide past her hip and over her stomach. He stopped cold. Arianna didn't breathe.

"When were you going to tell me?" he asked. All traces of the light-hearted reminiscence of the evening gone.

"I was trying to find the right time," she said.

He moved his hand, feeling the small slope. If he hadn't had every inch of her body committed to memory, it might have gone unnoticed. It was a subtle change, but one she wouldn't have been able to hide much longer.

"There's not much to stop it from happening, Caleb. It'll be a wonder if we don't all end up with a dozen kids."

He sat up, pushed the covers away, and held his head in his hand. "We watch the calendar. What happened to that?"

"We didn't look at the calendar the night you sobered up and apologized to me."

He remembered now. Neither had given a thought to anything else besides remedying the lonely ache of the last few months. What had resulted from that night, aside from a rekindled marriage, was the coming of another mouth to feed. He sighed heavily with worry.

"Caleb, it'll be okay." She sat up next to him and pulled on his arm, taking his hand in her lap. "I didn't say anything sooner because I knew you'd worry."

"I wish you had. I'm still going to worry only I've got less time to prepare for it now."

"Not that much less time. July-ish. Plenty of time."

He nodded and growing cold, he lay back down and covered up.

"I'm actually happy about it. Imagine that," she said.

"You're happy because you don't feel the weight of it like I do. I'm responsible for making sure everyone has what they need."

"We're doing better than the others. We have the farm, and it's making all the difference in how we get by. I feel guilty sometimes, seeing how hard our friends struggle."

He remained deep in thought.

"I thought you wanted a lot of kids, Caleb." She didn't try to hide the disappointment in her voice.

"I did. I mean, I do. Just not like this. I wanted to give them a better life."

"Their life will be fine, Caleb. They have parents who love them, friends who will look out for them, a sturdy home, and a warm bed. They'll be fine. We'll make it."

He smiled as he touched her face. "Sometimes you are nothing like the woman I married." She smiled, knowing it to be a compliment. "You're right. We'll make it."

JANUARY 7, 1931

C aleb kept a close eye on the drive, and when he saw Marvin pulling in, he called to Arianna that he was going out to the barn. He arrived at the same time Marvin did and opened the door to the barn.

Marvin looked bothered; Caleb didn't ask why.

"I know you're looking for me to move the stuff, Caleb, but I'm having a real hard time with that."

"That's what I wanted to talk to you about. I decided you can keep it here. So long as the sheriff's office can keep paying rent."

Marvin's face lit up in a mix of surprise and delight.

"What changed your mind?"

"It doesn't matter. Do we have a deal?"

Marvin stuck his hand out. "We do."

"One more thing," Caleb said. "You can't come around so much anymore. Arianna asked me why you're coming by a couple times a week. It's becoming obvious."

"What did you tell her?"

"That you were checking on me. Making sure I stay sober."

Marvin laughed. "That's a good one. Did she buy it?"

"She did. But I don't like lying to my wife, Marvin. I need you to space out your visits. If she finds out there's booze in there, she's going to throw a fit. You won't have any choice but to move it then."

He walked to the back of the barn and peeked through the crack in the stall door. Everything seemed fine, and he began glancing around.

"Does this barn have a backdoor?"

"Yeah, over there." Caleb pointed with a hint of irritation.

He followed the wall and found a small door. A hatch, really, and pointed to it. "How about I come around back and bring it in through there?"

"That's fine. So long as no one sees you too often."

"Well, I'll do whatever I can do to help, Caleb."

The false friendship in his voice grated Caleb's nerves. That, and the fact that he knew he was in way over his head with Marvin.

JANUARY 11, 1931

Jonathan leaned against the wheelhouse of the boat, eyeing the horizon. He clenched his jaw and adjusted his stance to better withstand the rough sea. The sun shone, but off on the horizon, darkness lurked in bold thunderheads. He blew his breath out, and it swirled in a large plume of white.

"I don't think it's a good idea, Jon. Those clouds look bad," Caleb said.

"They're far off enough. We'd have time."

Caleb shook his head and took a wide-legged seat on a crate, swaying with the movement of the boat. "We always come home with something. It won't be the end of the world if we don't today."

"None of us have any room to breathe. We can't afford to go home empty handed. We need to go farther out."

"Look around, Jon! Everyone else is going in! Everyone else isn't being stupid!"

Jonathan's surprised expression made Ian laugh.

"What do you think?" Jonathan asked him.

Ian studied the horizon for a moment and said, "Flip a coin. I don't care. But if I had to say, I think we can make it back in time."

Jonathan looked at Caleb and smiled. "Two to one." He moved

behind the wheel and began to change direction.

Caleb glared at Ian. "This is a mistake."

THE BOAT WAS TOSSED HARDER and more frequently as they ventured into deeper water. There was no rain or snow, but the increasing winds threw white capped waves higher and higher up the sides of the boat, eventually spilling over the top. A thin layer of ice formed on the deck and railings. All three men huddled in the wheelhouse shivering and blowing into their cupped hands while Jonathan frequently glanced at a chart, deciding where to stop.

The boat was thrown sharply to the left. Crates and nets flew across the deck behind them. Jonathan nodded for them to go back and secure the equipment they couldn't afford to lose.

As they did, the winds grew so strong, Jonathan could barely steer the boat. He put up a good fight, but when he realized he was losing, he left the wheelhouse to tell Caleb and Ian they were turning back.

He yelled, but the winds whipped louder. Laying a hand on Caleb's shoulder made him jump, slip, and fall on the slick deck. Caleb landed on his back with a terrified look of shock. Jonathan reached down, grabbed his hand, and when he hoisted him to his feet again, he lost his balance as a strong wave slammed into the side of the boat. He felt himself as he fell backward, feeling the pressure of the deck railing against the back of his thighs. Felt himself going over the edge. Icy water swelled up eager to swallow him, and he saw himself as a small boy at Christmas, opening an abacus, his first day of school, his mother and father standing at his graduation, the first time he met Ava, the day they were married, he saw himself on his knees the moment he realized he'd lost everything, he saw Aryl's smiling face, teaching him knots, the way Jean stared at him curiously, the day they buried the box, Victor's sick expression and the first time he saw his baby daughter. He squeezed his eyes shut as Caleb's hand shot out and clutched the front of his coat. Suspended over angry waters, his arms flailed as the deck rails froze their impression into his calves. He glanced over his shoulder at the churning water below and let out a frightened gasp.

"I got you!" Caleb yelled. Ian rushed over and reached past Caleb, grabbing what he could of Jonathan, and they pulled him upright and onto the deck.

He slithered down into a heap, adrenaline racing through his veins. His fingers dug into the wooden deck. He pressed his forehead against it as the boat tossed him about. Caleb pulled him up and held onto him with both hands as he walked him to the wheelhouse.

He threw him inside. "I told you we shouldn't have come out here!"

"I know! I'm sorry!" Jonathan yelled over the ocean noise and though still shaken, moved to step in front of the wheel. Caleb shoved him out of the way, assuming command.

BACK AT THE MARINA, the men worked quickly and quietly, mooring the boat and preparing it in case the storm came inland.

When all was settled, Jonathan stepped onto the dock and started making his way to his car. Ian made quick feet to catch up; Jonathan was his ride.

"Aren't ye going to say anything to Caleb?"

"No. I'll let him cool off a bit first."

Ian glanced over his shoulder. "I think ye might want to prepare something to say now because it doesn't look like he's going to cool off anytime soon. Here he comes."

Caleb grabbed the back of Jonathan's coat and spun him around.

"That was a real stupid thing to do, Jonathan Garrett!"

"Oh!" Ian said, taking a step back. "He used your whole name."

"I know it was stupid! I said I know, and I said I was sorry!"

He turned to leave, but Caleb wouldn't let go.

"What else do you want to hear from me?" Jonathan yelled as snow began to fall. He knocked Caleb's hand away.

"I want to hear you say you were wrong. You made a bad decision, and you were wrong."

Ian turned to Jonathan, waiting. He squirmed uncomfortably, knocking snowflakes from the crease of his collar.

"You can't do it, can you? You can't say the words, *I was wrong.*"

"Of course, I can say it!"

"Then do it!"

"Fine!" he roared. "I was wrong!" He stood glaring at Caleb. "Anything else?" Jonathan asked, jerking his coat back properly on his shoulders.

"You could thank me for saving your life," Caleb said and turned to walk away.

Jonathan dropped his head and took a deep, regretful breath. "I am such an ass."

"Aye. Ye are," Ian agreed.

Caleb was just coaxing his old truck to life as Jonathan reached the driver's door. He grabbed it. "Wait."

Caleb huffed and looked away impatiently.

"I'm sorry. I would have gotten around to thanking you. You know I would have, Caleb, once the shock wore off."

Caleb stared at the steering wheel. His lips clamped shut, his face was flushed, the tips of his ears red.

"Thank you," Jonathan said quietly. "Thank you a thousand times for saving my life today. Ava thanks you, Jean thanks you, Amy thanks you—"

"No one needs to know," Caleb said, turning his head slightly. "Don't tell them."

"Why not? I want them to know what you did for me."

"They don't need to know because it'll make them worry. All of them, not just in your house. And, if you tell them what happened, you'll have to tell them you were wrong. And I know you don't want to do that."

"But I *was*…wrong."

"What?"

"I *said*, I was wrong."

"I know. I just wanted to hear it again."

Jonathan fought a smile and shoved Caleb's shoulder through the open window. "I'll see you tomorrow."

FEBRUARY 14, 1931

Claire felt like a frilly whale. Her dress was simple, or it had been this morning before Maura insisted she let her pretty it up, adding lace here, there and eventually, everywhere on the pale pink garment.

The whole town had turned out for the Valentine fundraiser dance. Anyone who couldn't afford to pay admission could bring a donation of food or fabric to the town's relief fund that had been established by the older women. The Valentine Dance was their idea, as voluntary donations had begun to dwindle.

Held in the community hall, some of the youth were just finishing putting up decorations under the command of Ethel and June when the first guests arrived. The first half of the evening was open to all ages to encourage everyone to attend, but the younger ones had a curfew of nine o'clock. It would be adults only after that.

Refreshments were donated and set out on a long table against the wall. Candles burned on every table next to dried flower arrangements in pink and red painted mason jars. Ethel and June had gone door to door for the better part of two weeks, not only letting people know about the upcoming dance, but also collecting all the dried flowers they could. They labeled them carefully so they could be returned to their owner afterward.

June had the idea to set up a room for the young ones in the back where teenagers and the very old could see to the small children to keep them out from underfoot. And since it was a dance, there had to be music. There had been no shortage of volunteers, but the older crew took their time choosing. What showed up was a dedicated group of twenty-somethings who played jazz worthy of the radio. They were eager, excited and didn't tire easily.

"You want to sit down?" Gordon asked Claire, who did tire easily and wouldn't be doing much dancing tonight.

"Yes. Why don't we get a big table for when the others get here?"

He showed no disappointment at not having Claire all to himself this night, though he was. He was still getting used to the way she and her friends were. Always around each other, talking about each other, including each other in every part of their lives as if they were one large family. It wasn't that he didn't like it—he found it fascinating, but it wasn't what he was used to. He was more of a solitary fellow, happy to tackle his social interactions while at work and leaving it at that. But loving Claire meant loving her friends, so he reminded himself that he had to try.

"Looks like Ethel and her friends thought of everything," Claire said as the music started to play. The hall was starting to fill up, and Claire waved to several people she hadn't seen in months. Everyone waved back with a smile before glancing at Gordon with curiosity. Whispers ensued.

"I guess we're announcing ourselves tonight," he said, reaching over to take her hand.

"I suppose we are. If they keep whispering, I'm going to make you stand up, announce it, and tell them all to settle down already."

"I'd be happy to. Just tell me when."

Arianna pulled out a chair, grinding it against the hardwood floor.

"Sorry we're late. Did we miss much? Who's all here?" she asked looking around. She wore a short black sleeveless dress, a remnant from her old life, layered in shag and sequins. Tall and thin, her bump wasn't so noticeable that she couldn't still pull off a deadly look, and she knew it. "Oh, look, there's Samantha. She was so rude to me at the grocery the other day. I don't know what's got her thinking she's so special."

"Not wasting any time, are we, Ahna," Caleb said with an entertained grin.

"Well, I'm only speaking the truth." She sat back with a catty smile. "By the way she's dressed, I can't tell if she's here to donate money or make some."

Gordon coughed with surprise while Claire grinned.

"You have to understand Arianna," Claire said, leaning close to Gordon. "Normally, she's fine. Sweet and caring, even. But, sometimes, when she gets in a social setting, she gets a bit..." Claire paused and smiled, "competitive."

"Competitive?"

"Yes."

"That's one word for it, I suppose."

"Is Miss Arianna causing trouble already?" Maura asked, slapping Arianna over the shoulder with her gloves. "I've got no bail money this time, girl, so mind yer manners." She and Ian took their seat.

Gordon's eyes bulged. "Bail money?" He locked eyes with Claire. "Is she serious?"

"Not...entirely."

Gordon tilted his head in Claire's direction. "Has she really been to jail?"

"A few times."

"For what? Anything serious?"

"Oh, no. Public intoxication and indecency, mainly. But that was almost always when we were overseas."

"Overseas?" Gordon looked horribly confused.

"She loved Paris and Paris certainly loved her. She's practically a legend there." She laughed with a few memories. "If you were to go to Paris right now and walk up to any policeman that's been there more than four years and say Arianna's name, they'd smile and break up laughing. I guarantee it. But trust me," Claire said as Arianna honed in on a new target and began hissing. "She's harmless."

251

Shannon and Patrick showed up, breathless and smiling, crowding in at the table.

Jonathan and Ava were the last to arrive. Amy had been hard to settle in the back room, and though Jean was invited out to sit with everyone and have a treat, he refused, insisting on staying with Amy.

They were short one chair, and after Jonathan had held the last one out for Ava, he found an extra and carried it back.

"Everyone looks so wonderful," Ava said as she settled in her seat, placing her handbag under her chair.

"Thank you," Caleb said with a flashy smile.

"I meant the women," Ava said.

"Yeah, that's why he thanked you," Jonathan said as he pushed a chair in next to Ava.

"Oh, it's like that, is it? Insulting me in front of my wife. Okay, buddy. I'll play," Caleb said and pointed a finger at Jonathan, grinning. "When you least expect it."

"Okay, fine," Jonathan said, holding his hands up in surrender. "I'll be nice. I don't want to get my ass kicked...by Arianna."

The whole table roared. Caleb sat back, nodding his head slowly, fighting a smile. "I'm keeping track, Jon, just so you know."

Jonathan laughed and shook his head in apology.

As everyone sat down with their plates, the music started up again, and they had to raise their voices to be heard.

"They're having a Charleston contest at nine. It's ten cents to enter, but the prize is two dollars," Arianna said, grinning confidently.

"Oh, that sounds like fun," Gordon said.

Claire shook her head. "No. Even if I could, there's no beating those two," she said, pointing to Arianna and Caleb.

"Are you guys going to enter?" Gordon asked Jonathan.

Jonathan laughed. "No way. I've lost to them enough times. I'll give someone else a turn."

By eight thirty, the hall was packed, and one by one, jackets and sweaters were peeled off from the warmth of so many bodies crowded together.

Arianna and Caleb sat down from a lively Foxtrot.

"Now, have a good Highland fling or Irish step and me and Ian could beat the pants off all of you."

"Oh, you should teach us!" Arianna said, a little winded.

"Oh, no. I'm not creating competition," Maura said. Arianna's face slowly went from gleeful to disturbed. It settled somewhere between a frown and a sneer. Her eyes were pinned over Maura's shoulder.

"Look what the mole dragged in," she seethed. Everyone turned toward the door. The crowd had parted, and Marvin stepped through, overdressed and looking around expectantly. By his side, and directly under Arianna's fierce glare, stood Donatella over decorated and standing in such a presumptuous way as if awaiting worship.

Caleb sank down in his seat. "Oh, shit."

"Arianna, ignore her," Ava ordered, sitting forward, trying to pull her eyes away. "We are all having a nice time, and we aren't going to let her ruin it."

Arianna was in some distant place, frothing and boiling. Ava's words went unheard.

"How are we going to keep her from causing a scene?" Ava asked Jonathan desperately.

He laughed. "Oh, just like old times," he said, rubbing his eyes.

Claire gave Gordon a pat on the arm. "I'd sit back and relax. The rest of the evening is shaping up to be very entertaining." She grinned and folded her hands on her stomach, waiting for the show to start.

Caleb snapped forward, speaking quietly. "You aren't going to even acknowledge her, Ahna. Understand? Don't you say a word to her. Do you hear me, Arianna?"

It was as if saying her name was a beacon. Donatella's eyes, previously scanning the crowd delicately, stopped on Arianna, narrowing and sharpening. Then she smiled.

"Let the games begin," Ian said.

Their eyes were locked, searing a path across the room. It was only when several people walked past, blocking her view that Arianna turned back.

"The nerve she has to show up here!" she seethed.

"It's open to the whole town, Arianna," Ava said.

"Still, it's not like she has any friends. I've asked around, you know. Peggy at the grocery told me. No one knows much about her. She stays holed up in that pretty little house of hers. She doesn't even do her shopping here. She's too good, apparently. She goes to Boston."

"Well, I don't know if any of you noticed," Jonathan interrupted, eager to change the subject, "but this is a dance and all we're doing is sitting around." Jonathan turned to Ava and held out a hand. "Darling?"

As they wandered off, Caleb put his hand on Arianna's and started to speak. She stopped him.

"No. I think they're out there."

"You're not going to let her ruin this night, are you?"

"I'm not *letting* her do anything."

"Then dance with me." He said it the way he would dare someone to do something. He knew she couldn't resist that.

"Fine. Just stay far away from them."

She kicked off her shoes, followed him to the dance floor, and let him lead. She tried to relax, but her eyes stayed on alert, scanning as they made slow circles. Caleb tapped her lower back.

"Relax," he whispered.

"I'm trying, Caleb."

"Try harder."

"You don't understand. That woman humiliated me. She went out of her way to be cruel and did everything she could to make me feel like she was better than me."

"No one tops my Ahna," he said with a grin.

"Exactly."

"No, that's what you're forgetting." He pulled her close with his hands firmly on her lower back. "*No one* tops my Ahna. So forget about her. She's nobody. Imagine how bad she must feel about herself to treat people like she does. And she gets all her happiness from your reaction. You don't want to make her happy, do you?"

Her face fell in horror. "No!"

"Then ignore her."

She reluctantly gave her silent agreement and put her cheek to his. Jonathan and Ava came into view amid the sea of swaying couples. He made a few eye and hand gestures to Caleb that roughly translated to 'Keep the feral cats apart.'

Caleb clamped his lips, resisting a laugh and gave a helpless shrug.

Arianna watched them from the corner of her eye. Jonathan and Ava were the picture of romance as they danced. Her head on his chest, her eyes closed, and his arms wrapped around her, they appeared to be all alone in this crowded room of people. Jonathan put his head on hers and pulled her a little closer.

"I wish I could be more like Ava."

"Why? You two are like night and day," Caleb said.

"I know. She's boring but she's happy," Arianna said with a sigh.

When the song ended, they announced it was time for the Charleston contest and asked everyone who wasn't participating to leave the floor. Arianna smiled and started rolling her ankles to stretch them, her neck bobbing like a prizefighter getting ready to box.

Jonathan gave Caleb a salute as he walked by. "Good luck."

"We don't need luck," Caleb called after him. Just then, they saw Marvin and Donatella walk onto the dance floor and take their position. Caleb's face grew serious as Arianna's smile dropped. His eyes locked onto hers, and he brought his shoulders up.

"Looks like we're gonna have to show 'em how it's done, baby doll."

She smiled viciously as the young leader of the band stood at the edge of the stage.

"Here's the rules! Couples Charleston only. No singles. Everyone starts dancing when the music starts. There are three judges who will be on the floor looking for form, coordination, and enthusiasm."

Caleb winked at Arianna. "We've got this in the bag."

"If you are asked to leave, please do so quickly without disturbing the other couples. The music will start over if there are any couples left on the floor and continue until there is only one and we have our winner."

Claire leaned over to Gordon. "They did this for five hours one time. I hope it doesn't go on all night."

"I heard it was going to be limited to two songs to avoid that. They'll start eliminating people pretty quick," Jonathan said.

All eyes were on the dance floor as the piano began playing. There weren't a lot of couples. Seven, Arianna counted. They started safe and simple, the way they always start, coming together with his hand on her waist, her hand on his shoulder, hands clasped in the front. With a steady rock, they scissored opposite legs, keeping perfect time. Step back, step forward, kick back, kick forward. Arianna broke away, kicking in a circle and Caleb caught her on the return. They repeated forward and back, and then Caleb broke away. She was right where she should be, held on to him again, and they worked backward and forward, picking up the pace. Then they both broke away, kicked in a fast circle, joined and really started to put some flair into their steps as two couples were eliminated for not keeping time.

After repeating the back and forth a few more times, they turned toward each other and kicked high—Caleb's leg over hers and people started to cheer. Two more couples gone for being out of sync with each other. Having even more room, they bumped it up another notch. Caleb moved behind her, and they threw their legs out in opposite directions, pumping their hands in the air with big smiles. Arianna stepped aside, keeping the basic movements and Caleb threw a wide circle with his leg, and then threw them open wide. Arianna jumped in front of him, and he snapped back up. She hiked her already short skirt higher, showing her expert crisscross legwork. The crowd really grew loud as yet another couple was asked to leave.

They were down to two as they started the whole thing over again. Looking over and seeing Donatella and Marvin as the only remaining competition, Arianna threw a heavy twist in her hips as her feet scissored back and forth. They were fast as lightning, and she and Caleb moved as if they were one. Radiant and energetic, the judge walked past them and gave Donatella and Marvin the thumb.

Arianna threw her hands up with a shriek, grabbing Caleb in a stranglehold.

"I told you, baby. We always win," he said with a wide grin.

Arianna and Caleb sat down to the whole table clapping and cheering.

"Was there any doubt?" Caleb asked sarcastically, holding his hands out.

He sat down and wiped his brow. Arianna was beaming.

This was so much more delicious than the dance victories she had grown accustomed to. This brought her tickled joy to the depths of her soul, and she made sure to give Donatella her brightest smile.

She didn't have long to revel in her victory before they spotted Donatella making her way across the room. Caleb tapped her shoulder and pointed.

"No one look at her," Arianna said to everyone at the table. They all looked down, up or away. She smiled and enjoyed every one of the ten seconds Donatella stood by her, waiting to be acknowledged.

"Oh, sorry, didn't see you there." Arianna smiled.

"I just wanted to congratulate you on winning."

"Why, thank you." She kept her claws on her lap, folded neatly.

"Of course, how could anyone not win with a partner like Caleb? He's a natural. He could lead any woman to victory." She smiled at him with a feminine eye flutter. He did well and ignored it, sparking random conversation with Jonathan.

"I must say, it was a shock for us to not win. We *always* win, Marvin and I. You see, I was gardening a few days ago and got the most wretched wrench in my back. If not for that, I'm positive it would be *you* walking to my table to congratulate *us*."

Arianna smiled tightly. "I doubt it." She began to strain under the weight of politeness.

Donatella made another futile attempt to flirt with Caleb, growing frustrated at her inability to get a reaction. Two women walked by with a watchful eye on the situation. Donatella jumped on the opportunity and called them over by name. They came hesitantly as if they had no idea who she was. Or at least wish they didn't.

"This is the girl I told you about."

Arianna recoiled at the touch on her shoulder. The women moved closer.

Donatella turned to face Arianna. "Maybe you could share with them the cream you used to cure that terrible bald spot you had. Looks like it filled in." She craned her neck, inspecting. "Mostly."

Arianna threw her chair back and stood up.

Patrick quickly lay a quarter on the table. "I'll put this on Arianna." He glanced around excitedly. "Anyone else?"

Jonathan rolled his eyes. "Patrick, really." After digging in his pocket, he tossed two singles on the table. "Have some faith in our girl and pony up a real bet."

"Are they really going to fight?" Gordon asked, horrified.

Patrick leaned over to Maura. "If they forfeit, we all get our money back, right?"

"They might," Claire said. "Why don't you put one on Donatella and I'll wager on Ahna. That way no matter what, we win," Claire said.

"Are you serious?" Gordon asked, gawking.

"Well, I can't bet against my friend," she said with a shrug. "And there's no stopping her."

Marvin walked up and stood near Donatella but made no move to stop her.

"No one is going to win if the bets are one-sided." Maura leaned over the table and tossed fifty cents in a separate pile. "I'll take the Italian. Just because I warned Miss Arianna."

Caleb stood up and touched Arianna's arm. She jerked away, staring at Donatella with her nostrils flaring. All the activity and music in the hall had ground to a halt. It was nearly silent as everyone looked on, waiting for someone to make the first move.

"Don't forget what you told me on New Year's Day," Caleb said quietly.

In the heat of the moment, she had consciously forgotten that she was pregnant. Had anyone else at the table known, they would have never let it get to this point. But they didn't. They all waited with the rest of the hall for a catfight.

Caleb saw the struggle in her eyes, and he knew she didn't have it in her to back down. He stepped close to Marvin.

"Call your wife off, now," he ordered.

Marvin grinned. "Are you sure you don't want to let them work it out? This has been a long time coming."

Caleb didn't stop to think or care that Marvin was a sheriff's deputy beneath the fancy clothes he wore as he balled his fist and warned him one more time.

When Marvin laughed him off again, Caleb punched him, sending him sprawling onto his back, looking quite shocked. Everyone in the hall gave a collective 'Oh!' and stepped back.

"Oh, shit," Jonathan said, jumping up. Caleb dropped down and grabbed Marvin by the shirt and gave him a shake. "Call your wife off. If she touches Arianna, or if you take a swing at me, it's a deal breaker, Marvin."

Marvin knew exactly what he was referring to, and it wasn't worth losing the safe spot in Caleb's barn just to let Donatella have her fun.

"Donna! Go back to your seat," Marvin yelled from the floor. She looked at him with her mouth agape in furious horror. "Now," he finished.

Slowly, reluctantly, and angrily, she took a step back, her threatening eyes still pinned on Arianna. Caleb let Marvin get up only after giving Arianna the satisfaction of the whole hall watching Donatella slink away to her table.

Marvin said nothing as he stood up and dusted himself off. He went back to his table whispering furiously to Donatella, and they quickly got up and left. The hall erupted in whispers, and even though everyone had witnessed what had happened, they all asked each other if they had just seen Caleb punch the deputy and, more astonishingly, how the deputy backed down afterward and could they believe it?!

The music started again as Arianna sat down. She leaned over and put her hand on Caleb's thigh.

"Thank you," she whispered.

"Is it always like this when you guys go out together?" Gordon asked.

"It's always interesting," Jonathan said with a smile.

Arianna stared at the two piles of money on the table, and one eyebrow went up. "Who the hell bet against me?"

Gordon finished his route early and stopped to buy flowers before heading over to Claire's house. He had the ring in his pocket but gave his leg a pat, checking for the tenth time that it was still there. It was a simple silver band, but one day, he hoped to have a diamond put on it for her.

He knocked on her door feeling more nervous than the first time he came calling on her. They both knew it was coming. It wouldn't be a surprise. But it was still nerve-wracking. He cleared his throat, adjusted his shirt, and straightened his posture as he heard someone on the other side of the door. Maura opened it with a smile.

"Hello, Gordon. How are ye today?"

"Good. I'm well. Is Claire here?"

"Of course. Close as she is, I'm not letting her wander. She's just upstairs."

"That's good. Can I see her, please?" His stiff posture and darting eyes gave away the intent of his visit. Maura grinned as she turned away, leaning into the stairwell to call Claire.

She came downstairs a moment later. She walked with a slow and awkward wobble.

"Hi," she said with a smile. "Were you coming over for dinner tonight?" Claire asked with a look to Maura.

"No, I just came to see you." He remembered the flowers and held them out. "And to give you these."

Maura's lips were pursed up in excitement. "I'll just step out now," she said quietly.

"No, Maura. Stay. I'd like you to. After all, you're responsible."

"She's responsible for what?" Claire asked.

"I wanted to do this earlier. Last Saturday night, actually, at the dance. I had it all planned out but, well, things got...interesting, as Jon put it, and the right time never came."

"The right time for what?" Claire asked.

"It would have been so much better last Saturday. The mood and the music, the atmosphere and all your friends there, it just didn't work out that way."

"What didn't?"

He pulled the ring out of his pocket, took a step toward her, and smiled, bashful and terrified.

Claire's eyes widened. Though she had been expecting it eventually, she wasn't prepared for the fact that it was happening *right now*.

He lowered to one knee. "Will you marry me?" he asked, and held his breath.

She nodded with a modest smile. She felt the sting of tears, not for the emotion of this moment, but because she vividly remembered the last time she was asked to be someone's wife. This paled in comparison to the intensity of that moment, and she had to push the memory away.

He stood, put the ring on her finger, and smiled. An awkward moment lingered, and Maura offered to make drinks to celebrate.

Ian congratulated Maura on a job well done as he joined them at the table. Claire and Gordon set a date and began to make plans for a spring wedding.

It was then that something began to bother Maura. This had been her life's work recently, seeing Gordon and Claire to this moment, making sure Claire and her babe would be cared for, and she could find her way to a happy life. It had all worked according to plan, and she should have been overjoyed with herself and the situation. She gazed out the kitchen window, tuning out the others, trying to figure out exactly what it was that nagged at her.

FEBRUARY 20, 1931

awn barely broke for all the black clouds in the sky. They'd been warning of it for days—the old timers, that is—a storm to beat all storms was heading their way. They could feel it in their bones, see it in the odd way their animals acted and could smell it in the icy air. The wise ones closed shutters and kept the candles close by.

Jonathan rose early, hoping they were wrong. He hadn't slept well, between the winds starting to pick up and the bed, crowded as it was. Ava slept with Amy nestled in the crook of her arm, and Jean snuggled in close on the other side. Jonathan had clung to the edge of the mattress all night. He dressed quietly, and as he passed his parent's empty room, he felt the stab of missing them.

He set a pot of coffee to percolate on the stove and pulled back the curtain above the kitchen sink. It was nearly black as night, and the wind had started to pick up. He sighed. There would be no work today.

They had what they needed to get through a storm—a long one, even —and though he was disappointed at not being able to work, he looked forward to spending the day with his little family. He heard footsteps overhead and knew them to be from Jean. Quiet as the child tried to be, he walked like a giant and could be heard coming for blocks. He poked his messy dark hair around the corner.

"Morning, Dadee."

"Morning, son."

"Are we having a storm?"

"Looks like."

"Will it be bad?"

Jonathan shrugged. "Might be. But we'll be fine."

Jean sat down at the table while Jonathan poured him a glass of milk, watered down to conserve.

"Cricket sure cries a lot."

"Babies do that. You can sleep in your room, you know. If her crying bothers you."

His face popped in surprise. "I couldn't do that! What if she needs me?"

Jonathan laughed. "Well, Ava and I are right there if she needs anything."

"No, I should be near," he said firmly. Jonathan wondered if he could talk him into sleeping on a pallet next to the bed to make a little room. Doubtful. Jean loved babies, and Amy was extra special. He hadn't been back to school since Amy was born. Ava had seen nothing wrong with him starting the following year and pulled him out, despite the fit the teacher threw.

A wind gust slammed into the house, and the lights flickered.

"I'd better start breakfast before we lose them," Jonathan said.

"Should I get the lamps and candles?" Jean asked.

"Might not be a bad idea." Jonathan watched the wicked weather and took a deep breath.

CLAIRE WOKE UP WITH A MOAN. She rolled to her side and breathed in quick, hard bursts. The practice pains had been going on all night, and she was growing tired of them. So tired, in fact, that she wished it would all just get started and be over with. She sat up and pushed the hair, wet with perspiration, out of her face.

She took a bath, dressed in comfortable clothes and went downstairs, catching the eye of the ever-observant Maura.

"Have a seat, Miss Claire." She pulled out a chair and motioned for Tarin to get her some water. "How long's it been now?"

"Off and on all night. Started with the storm." She grimaced and stretched her back.

"Here's some water." Tarin set down a glass and looked to Maura. "Should I go get Gordon?"

"No," Claire said. "No one is going to get Gordon."

"So you don't think it's time?" Maura asked.

She twisted in her seat and stood, leaning on the table with her head hanging down, taking deep breaths. Maura glanced at the clock. When the pain stopped, she raised her head. "Oh, I wouldn't say that. I think it is. But he won't know about it until it's over."

"Miss Claire, he's going to want to be here!"

"No. He thinks he does, but he doesn't."

"You're not thinking clearly, dear."

"I'm thinking perfectly clear," she barked as she sat back down. "His wife died in childbirth. The last thing I want is him sitting down here, wringing his hands while I'm up there screaming."

"You don't think he'll be upset at being left out?" Tarin asked.

"Frankly, I don't care if he is. It's for his own good. He's done nothing but think of my feelings, and I intend to think of his. Someone can run over there after it's over."

"Miss Claire, come now. Don't you think he should be with you? At least waiting downstairs? He's going to be your husband."

"Then he can start doing what I say now!" she yelled, growing more uncomfortable by the minute.

"Are you hungry?" Tarin asked. "I can make you a bite to eat."

"No, thank you." She drained the glass of water and held it out to her. "I'm very thirsty, though."

Maura nodded for Tarin to keep an eye on Claire and left the room. Upstairs, she prepared Claire's bed, bringing in towels and cloths, a basin, scissors and twine, everything she thought the midwife might need. She took all the oil lamps in the house, filled them, and clustered them on the dresser as the lights flickered over her head.

"What a day to be born," she said, glancing out at the wind-driven sleet.

IT WAS late afternoon when Maura finally made the decision to send Tarin to fetch the midwife. It wasn't that Claire had progressed much during the day, but the storm had progressed significantly in the last few hours. If she didn't send for help now, she might not be able to later. Tarin put on as many layers as she owned and set out. If it had only been a few degrees colder, it would be snow, instead of hard icy pellets, stinging her face. She braced herself against the wind and turned the corner.

JONATHAN SAT on the couch with Amy on his shoulder, Ava's head in his lap. She had fallen asleep. He patted the baby's back with one hand and stroked Ava's hair with the other. Jean played on the floor with two wooden cars in the lamplight. Jon had lit them and turned off the lights ahead of losing power. He knew it would happen eventually with a storm like this, and he didn't want Jean to be scared when they cut. He laid his head back, trying to catch a nap of his own. The last thing he expected was a knock at the door.

Jean turned and looked at him with fearful eyes. He nudged Ava gently, and she sat up, rubbing her eyes and taking Amy.

Jonathan peeked out the window and flew to the door.

"Tarin! What are you doing out in this?" He pulled her inside. Her teeth were chattering wildly as she unwrapped her scarf.

"Auntie sent me to get the midwife for Claire. I tried, but I couldn't make it. It's so cold, and it's still so far away. Could I trouble you to give me a ride, Jon?"

"Of course, Tarin. Let me get my coat."

Ava smiled. "When did it start?"

"This mornin'. She's not close yet, we don't think. It's just the storm is gettin' so bad."

"I'm surprised Maura sent you out in it," Jonathan said, wishing they could afford to have telephones installed.

"Send us news as soon as you can," Ava said.

"You'll be okay here?" Jonathan asked.

"Of course. I have Jean to protect us," Ava said, smiling at him. "Drive safely in this."

"I will." He kissed her and stepped out with Tarin, bending his head against the wind.

IT WAS ONLY a short while later they returned, shivering and soaked to the bone.

"What's wrong?"

"We can't get through. The sleet is driving so hard I can't see more than five feet ahead of me. Tarin's trying to give directions, but we can't see a thing."

"What are you going to do? You can't leave Maura there alone with Claire delivering!"

"I'm going to Caleb's. I could get there blindfolded. I think he knows exactly where the midwife lives, and we can use his truck. It's better in this weather than our old beast."

It was clear they had only stopped to update Ava, and they set out again.

∽

THE OLD FARMHOUSE had lost power. The windows were dimly lit by candlelight from within.

Jonathan explained what had happened.

"We can use the truck, but I don't know where she lives, I'm sorry."

Jonathan turned to Tarin, growing frustrated. "You don't remember the address?"

"No, sorry. I only knew it from walking there with Claire a few times. Maura might know if we can go back for a moment."

"We'll have to. Thanks anyway, Caleb."

Caleb held the keys but didn't toss them to Jonathan. "I'm going with you."

"Are you sure? You don't have to."

"Yes, I do. This is Aryl's baby. I need to be there."

Jonathan stood stock-still. He'd realized, in a distant way, the significance of this birth, but until this moment, he hadn't consciously thought about it. This was a chance to see the part of Aryl that would live on. "We both need to be there," he corrected. "We need to... for him."

"I SEND you for the midwife, and you come back with two men!" Maura wasn't serious in her scolding, just masking intense worry. They all stepped inside, huddling together. The door stood open, letting in the wind and freezing rain.

"I'm so sorry, Auntie. I couldn't get to the midwife. It's so bad out there!"

"Aye, I can see that. Is there any chance one of you can get to her?"

"If you tell us exactly where it is. We can't see a thing so you'll need to give us precise directions," Jonathan said.

She raised her hand to point and started to speak just as an old growth tree came crashing down with a thunderous splintering. The trunk lay down the middle of the road, the branches blocking both lanes.

"Well, directions are a moot point now, aren't they," she said, staring angrily at the fallen tree. She turned to the dripping trio, who all stood stunned. "Looks like it's up to us."

IT WAS CALM, all things considered, as Maura returned downstairs from checking on Claire. The lights had gone out hours ago. The dinner hour came and went, and though Tarin made a simple stew, no one was hungry. Caleb and Jonathan sat on the couch, listening to the storm by lamplight, waiting to be useful.

"If she hadn't been through so much, I'd be tempted to slap her for having such an easy time at this."

It was true. They had heard barely a peep from the bedroom where Claire labored.

"Is everything okay?" Caleb asked. "Usually, they're loud. Real loud. I know Arianna was."

Jonathan grinned. "So were you." Caleb threw his book at him, hitting him in the shoulder.

"Everyone's different," Maura said with a shrug. "But she'll be loud when it gets down to it, I'm sure. Right now, she's sleeping through half the pains."

"I'm glad for her," Caleb said.

"I am, too. It's merciful after all the girl's been through," Maura said, sitting down in a chair. "Tarin, would you get me a cup of coffee, dear?" Tarin scurried away into the kitchen.

"So it'll be awhile?" Caleb settled back on the couch and closed his eyes.

"An hour, maybe two. It's hard to say. I've never done this on my own before." She looked away, and Jonathan could read the insecurity in her voice.

WHEN IT CAME time to push, Maura had to wake Claire up.

"Never in my life have I heard of a woman sleepin' through a birthing!" she said, bewildered and slightly envious. She propped pillows behind her back, brought a towel of supplies to the foot of her bed, and lit every lamp in the room.

"Is it time?" Claire asked, blinking like an owl.

"You tell me, dear. It's your body, not mine." She felt gingerly under the sheets. "If I had to guess, though, I'd say it's time. Sit up a little and try giving a push."

As she did, the mercy of a painless labor was revoked. Lightning flashed as she let out a grunting scream with the next contraction. "My back!"

Maura peeked under the sheet. "Your back?" she asked with a quizzical grin. "It's yer *back* that's hurtin'?"

Claire nodded, grimacing. She flopped back down on the bed, pushed the pillows away, and tried to roll on her side.

"No, now, dear. I need ye to sit up. Sit up and push."

"I can't. I have to get off my back!" She kicked awkwardly at Maura and began a fifty-point turn, trying to get to her side. Another quick peek showed the baby was not going to wait until she got finished. Maura dashed to the door.

"Jon! Caleb! Can I get a hand?"

They moved quickly up the stairs and into the room as Maura tried in vain to keep Claire covered as she flopped.

"She's having back pains and can't sit up. I need you to—"

Before she could finish, they were each to Claire's side, coaxing her to lie on her back. She tried to fight them, but they lifted and turned her anyway. They sat down on the edge of the bed facing her and hooking their arms through hers, pulling her up.

"Perfect," Maura said, smiling.

It relieved some, but not all of the grinding in her back, and when the next pain hit, she pulled against them to lie down. They held on to her, keeping her from falling back as she grunted, sweat, and cried for the next ten minutes.

Mercy returned, and the baby was born. Maura held it, slippery in her hands and for a moment, seemed in shock. Jonathan and Caleb eased Claire down to rest and looked back, seeing only small, purple feet and the umbilical cord.

"Clear the mouth," Caleb said softly.

Maura nodded quickly, coming back to the moment.

"Turn it over and tilt it downward." She did and a small amount of fluid drained from the baby's mouth. It took its first breath—a short, shocked inhale and let out a cry.

"Now, tie off the cord and cut it." She worked quickly as Caleb looked on. Jonathan stared at his steadiness in awe.

The baby was starting to work up to a good cry. Maura's instinct was to cradle him, but Caleb stopped her.

"Let him get going."

"Him?" Claire asked weakly, raising her head.

Maura swaddled the baby. "Aye, dear. Tis a boy. And he's beautiful." She walked around the bed and handed the baby to Caleb, who took a good long look before giving him to Claire.

Jonathan watched as she studied him. His hair was on the darker side. His eyes, too early to tell. Most likely they'd be brown, Jonathan thought. He wanted to say he looked like Aryl. He wanted to see Aryl, but his rational mind knew that it was impossible to distinguish features yet in the small, wrinkled face. *In time,* Jonathan thought, with a smile for the future.

"Have you thought of a name?" he asked.

Claire smiled at each of them in turn. "His name is Jac. One letter for each of you," she said, knowing Aryl was there with them, looking on.

THE STORM BEGAN to wane in the late hours of the night. The clouds parted sharply allowing enough moonlight for them to break back limbs of the fallen tree and get the truck out. It was near dawn when they finally started making their way home.

"You were pretty amazing in there," Jonathan said. "Never in my life did I think I'd see someone else walking Maura through something, but you really got her through those first few moments."

He shrugged, brushing off the compliment. "We owe him, you know?" Before he could get too emotional, he grinned. "The steps are the same. It's no different when a cow gives birth."

Jonathan laughed. "I won't tell Claire you said that."

MARCH 10, 1931

"T he Ides of March," Jonathan grumbled as he carried Jean back to his bed. He'd been terribly sick, vomiting through the night.

He was pale and feverish as Jonathan laid him in his bed.

"How is he?" Ava asked from the darkness of the hall.

"No better. He's burning up. Can't hold anything down." Jonathan sighed and scrubbed his face. Jean whimpered, and Jonathan turned down the oil lamp beside his bed.

"I don't know what to do." He sat back, helpless and weary, looking to Ava for answers.

"Maybe we could—"

"Don't come in here," Jonathan said. "Stay there. I don't want you to get sick. We can't let Amy get it either."

He'd spent the last two days in Jean's room, only traveling to the bathroom and back, in an attempt to not spread the sickness. He cleaned up behind himself and Jean meticulously and prayed it was enough. It wasn't.

Ava stepped into the dim light of the room. "I think I'm getting it anyway, Jon." She was pasty white and beginning to sweat. "I'm sorry. I know how hard you tried to keep it from us."

"What about Amy?"

"So far she seems fine."

Jonathan dropped his head and rocked for a moment. "You've been taking care of her all this time. If she's going to get it, there's no stopping it now."

"We can get some ice from Gordon for Jean's fever," Ava suggested.

"Good idea. I'll go now. Will you be okay here for a bit?"

She nodded.

He walked over to her and felt her head. "You're warm. Try not to handle Amy too much, although it's probably too late. Why don't you get to bed and rest?"

"No, I'll sit with Jean."

Jonathan put on a jacket and stepped out, bracing against the wind. He thought to stop at Caleb's but didn't want to make them sick if they weren't already. The streets were unnaturally empty as he drove. He knew much of the town had fallen ill, and it worried him.

GORDON GAVE him as much ice as he could spare.

"I haven't been to visit Claire and the baby for three days, though I've been making deliveries."

"Are they ill?"

"Ian and Scottie. So far, the rest are fine. Maura has Claire and Jac in her room, hoping they'll avoid it."

"Caleb and his family?"

"No one yet that I've heard."

"That's good."

"Damn near half the town has come down with it."

"Half the town?"

"Seems like it. But then, a lot of folks are holing up at home, trying to wait it out. Seems to ease off after three days."

"Jean's nearly there then."

"Go on," Gordon said. "See to your boy. If you need more ice, I'll see what I can do."

. . .

BACK AT JONATHAN'S HOUSE, he broke the ice up with a hammer, wrapping chunks in towels and sheets. He and Ava striped Jean down to his underwear and packed the ice around him.

"Am I doing it right?" Jonathan asked.

"I think so," Ava said, sitting down to catch her breath.

"You should be in bed," he said, frowning at her.

"No, I want to be here." A wave of nausea rolled over her, and she held her aching head.

"Gordon said no one at Caleb's has it. Maybe we could have Amy stay there until this passes."

"She might bring it to their house. And like you said, if she's going to get it, there's no stopping it now."

He nodded with worry for Jean. He touched his head. He was on fire. Jonathan arranged the ice around him. It had already begun to melt around his body, soaking the sheets and bed. With her eyes closed, Ava leaned over in the chair. Jonathan added more ice until Jean was fully packed and only his face could be seen.

Amy began crying and Ava tried to stand.

"No, I'll get her. I'm not sick," Jonathan said. She sat down wearily and watched Jean. His whole body had begun to vibrate, shivering against the ice.

Jonathan lifted Amy and inspected her carefully.

"How are you feeling, my princess?"

Her blue eyes were bright. She stopped crying when she saw Jonathan and smiled. Her nose was clean and her lungs were clear. Changing her diaper, he found nothing out of the ordinary. Relieved, he kissed her cheek, and she squealed, grabbing handfuls of his hair. Nestling her in the crook of his arm, he took her downstairs and made a bottle. She babbled and waved her fists around, trying to grab everything Jonathan touched.

After feeding her and laying her back down in the cradle, he checked on Jean and Ava. She was sleeping, pale and sweating, over the arm of the chair next to his bed. Most of the ice surrounding Jean had melted.

Jonathan could almost see the heat radiating, and he knew his little body couldn't take much more. He woke Ava gently.

"I'm going to get Maura and more ice. She might know what else to do."

She touched her aching head. "Hurry back," she whispered.

Jonathan left in a rush, and Ava reached out to touch Jean. She knew his fever was high, but his skin was so hot, she pulled her hand back in shock. Vivid and terrifying memories of her parents flashed through her mind.

"God, no. Please, no." Helplessly watching someone die—slowly cooked alive from fever—wasn't something she thought she could stand to do again. Something deep in her mind told her that she'd better prepare herself, just in case. She pushed the thought away, refusing to accept it. This was bigger than she was. Big enough to make healthy adults succumb—let alone a young child.

They had done everything there was to do, which included only aspirin and ice and Jean still lay so sick. She wanted to have faith that Maura would have a magical answer. Pull an old world cure from her bag and save the day. But this was bigger than Maura, too. She could think of nothing else to do, as she knelt by his bed, except pray.

She stayed there a long time. Might have even fallen asleep a few times, poorly as she felt. She raised her head when she felt the bed move. Her weak smile dropped when she realized he wasn't waking up, he was violently shaking. It started quickly. His back arched and the most horrible gurgling noise came from his throat. His eyes were white, having rolled far up into their sockets. Ava screamed. She tried to hold his shoulders, but his body was rigid, twisting, and contorting under her hands. She took a step back, mouth agape in horror, having no idea what to do. She could only watch as powerful currents exploded through his body for what felt like a very long time. And then he was still. She covered her eyes and screamed. And screamed again. Falling to the floor with one last desperate wail, Jonathan burst into the room, Maura close behind him. He took one look at his son and yelled his name. Maura pushed past him and threw herself on the wet bed. She felt his head and moved her hand to his throat.

275

"He's still alive," she whispered. She turned to make sure they heard her and saw Jonathan pulling Ava up.

"What happened?"

"He was shaking…so bad, Jon, his whole body was shaking…I couldn't make it stop."

Maura motioned for Jonathan to move closer. "Feel him, Jon. Is he as hot as when you left?"

After putting Ava in the chair, he touched Jean. "No. He was hotter than this when I left."

"Sometimes a body gets so hot, it'll seize. It's awful to look at, but it serves a purpose."

Ava was still gasping and sniffling. She couldn't take her eyes off Jean.

"Let's pack him with more ice. Take advantage of this small break and see if we can bring it down even more."

Jonathan, who was so very tired, carried large blocks of ice up the stairs. He broke it up and handed the chunks to Maura. And they waited.

Maura left after nightfall to tend to her own. Jonathan slept on a blanket on the floor. Ava insisted on sitting in the chair where she stayed on the edge of sleep, waiting for the horrible gurgling noise again. Amy's cradle was placed in the hallway, close enough to hear, but hopefully, not close enough to catch the illness. For the first time, she slept through the night.

AVA WATCHED JEAN WITH SWOLLEN, tired eyes. The first rays of light were streaming through the window. The birds were attempting to rouse the world, flitting about the windows.

She hadn't noticed him wake up. It was only when he whispered her name, and she nearly jumped out of her chair, did she look at him and see his blue eyes looking back at her.

She was at his bedside in a flash. He was still pale. His eyes still ringed in dark, but his skin was cool and dry. With a ragged breath of relief, she took his little hand in hers and kissed it.

"I'm okay," he said.

"I know." She smiled through her tears. "I'm so glad, Jean. We were so worried about you."

"She said you would be."

"Who said, sweetie? Maura?"

"No, my mother."

"Your...mother?"

He nodded weakly. "I saw her."

Ava stared at him, unsure of what to say. Was it possible to dream with such a fever?

"I saw her," he repeated. "I tried to leave my bed, but she came and said I had to stay. She said I couldn't go with her, that you were very worried about me and would be sad if I left."

Ava's face rippled as she nodded. "I would be. I'm so glad you stayed," she said in a whisper.

"She told me something else. She said she didn't know if you knew, and I should tell you." He looked down at his bare stomach, lacking the energy to do much more than that. "She said that you were my mommy now. And that it was okay." His eyes moved up with hesitation. "Is that true?"

"Yes, Jean. It's true." She broke down in tears, lifted him up, and hugged him.

APRIL 10, 1931

"We can have the wedding here," Arianna said. "We can do it down in the side yard. There's plenty of room."

"That would be nice," Claire said. Jac lay on her lap. She watched his every move and delighted in the twitchy movements of his limbs, as he grew accustomed to his new world.

"Isn't he the most beautiful thing?" she asked, letting him grip her finger. He strained to bring it to his mouth.

"He is," Arianna said, looking down on him. His eyes were deep brown with little flecks of green sprinkled in. His hair, while still thin, was the color of Aryl's, and starting to curl in the same places. He'd plumped up in the last two months, and Arianna giggled as she touched the little roll of fat on his wrist.

"So much like Aryl," Claire whispered. "It's amazing."

Arianna didn't ask if it was hard. She knew it had to be. Her Samuel looked remarkably like Caleb and to have him gone with a walking reminder of him toddling about would be a comforting heartache.

"I don't know if I can bear to leave him," Claire said.

"I'll take good care of him. In fact, I probably won't put him down the whole time you're gone."

Claire hesitated to hand him over. "Promise?"

"I promise. You have a good time with Gordon. And when you get back, we'll talk more about the wedding."

"We're not so much having a good time as we are making plans ourselves. He wants us to move in with him after the wedding."

"Well, you weren't going to continue to live in separate houses, were you?"

Claire turned her eyes to Jac, feeling silly. "I hadn't thought about it, really."

"How could you make plans to marry someone and not think about living with them?" Arianna laughed.

Claire shrugged. "I don't know." She took a deep breath and stroked Jac's head. "You know, sometimes when you look to the future, you can see some things and not others?"

Arianna shook her head, clueless.

"What I mean is, when I think of living with Gordon, I just can't see it. I mean, I know it's going to happen. It's just hard to picture. Being busy with Jac has kept me from thinking on it too much, I guess," she said, seeming to answer her own question.

"Everything will work out, Claire. Now go have a good time. It's such a beautiful day, and you look fantastic. And maybe walking around Gordon's house and making plans with him will help you see it," she said with a shrug

"Maybe," she smiled. Reluctantly, she handed the baby to Arianna and stared at him for a long time.

"Jean's coming over today."

"Is he?" Claire asked.

"Oh, yes. He found out the baby would be here, and wild horses couldn't keep him away. I will have an expert helper."

She smiled as Claire stood, ushering her out the door. She turned several times to look at Jac desperately.

"He'll be fine," Arianna assured. "I've done this before, you know."

～

GORDON MET her on the porch with a kiss. "I'm glad you came."

"It was hard leaving Jac," she said.

"You could have brought him."

"I thought we were going to do some work getting the rooms ready."

"We are. Well, I did already. I wouldn't have you moving furniture." He laughed as if she were silly and held the door for her. His home smelled of cleanser, and she could tell he'd been working hard. All the small breakables had been moved, the bottom half of the bookshelves sat empty, and the knit doilies that had hung over the edge of the end tables were tucked back, away from little fingers that might grab onto them and pull the table over.

"You've been busy. There was time to do all this, you know. He's not getting around just yet."

"I have a room cleared out for him. I just don't have any furniture in it yet." He opened the door to an ordinary bedroom with a big window that let a lot of natural light in. Their voices echoed off the walls and hardwood floors.

"I can bring his cradle," she said. Other than that, all he had was a bag of clothing and diapers. They walked together through the living room and down the hallway.

"I made some other changes, too. I moved my room. Our room." He closed his eyes and corrected. "I hope you don't mind."

"No, I don't." Her heart began to beat a little faster as he opened the door to his bedroom. The four-poster bed was neatly made. The bedside tables each had a lamp, and small rag rugs lay in front of each one. A large chest of drawers against the wall had been cleared of all pictures.

"I started to clean out some of the drawers for you, and that's when I realized that I needed to move everything. I needed a little distance myself. New life, new room."

"I understand," she said. And she did. Nothing else needed to be said.

"I gave you the top three drawers so you don't have to bend over."

She smiled. "That's so sweet." He had a way of doing things for her that, while not grand or gushingly romantic, told her he thought about her and cared. And right now, while her heart had started to mend but wasn't entirely whole, she accepted it as enough. She scanned the room and tried to see it. Changing by the closet, getting into bed with him, waking up next to him. She sighed, unable. Perhaps separating herself from the home she'd shared with Aryl, much in the way that Gordon had separated the bedroom from the one he shared with Marjorie, would help. Even if she couldn't see it right now, it was happening. One month from now, she would be his wife.

He put his hand on the small of her back, leading her out of the room.

He talked a lot as he made their lunch and as they sat across from each other at the table. She got the impression he was a little nervous, and she found it endearing. Music floated in from the next room and filled the empty spaces. The space wasn't so much between them but in the hollow room around them.

"Arianna offered to have the wedding at her place," Claire said, ending his disconnected rambling.

"That's nice." He studied his plate for a moment. "I thought you wanted to have it in a church?"

"Well." She bit her lip, appearing deep in thought.

"Be honest with me, Claire."

"I just...I feel like church weddings are for the first time, you know?" She covered her face with her hand. "I know that sounds horrible."

"No, that's okay if that's how you feel. We can do it at Arianna's. That's fine."

"Are you sure?"

"Positive. We should do something different. Our own thing."

"Thank you."

"I'm sorry I can't take you on a proper honeymoon."

"That's okay. I couldn't bear to leave Jac for long, anyway."

"Well, we'd take him with us," Gordon said, smiling. "I wouldn't expect you to leave him here."

She laughed. "Then it wouldn't be much of a honeymoon, would it? He's up at least twice a night."

"We'd make it work," he said, and his smile faded. "I wish I could take you."

"It's all right. Really. Our honeymoon will be settling into real life here."

281

"You can change whatever you want. If you don't like the curtains or the doilies, feel free to change them. I want you to feel like it's your home now."

She glanced around the kitchen. It didn't feel like hers. The style wasn't hers, and she tried to envision making small changes to make it so.

After finishing her lunch, Gordon took her plate. "Did you want to go into town? Go for a drive maybe?"

She did, but she knew that her time would be better spent here, getting used to the place. She told him no and began to wander from room to room while he followed her quietly.

"Talk to me. Please?" he asked softly. "What's on your mind?"

He didn't flinch or become insecure when she talked of her past or her hesitation with the future. Still, she felt guilty saying the words.

"I just can't see myself living here." She turned to face him. "I don't mean to sound ungrateful, and I'm not backing out. I'm trying to see it. Really, I am. But, I walk around here, and I can't picture Jac playing on the carpet in the living room. I can't imagine cooking your breakfast in that kitchen. I want to see myself bathing in that long bathtub, but I can't."

She appeared helpless in explaining further.

"Look," he said, putting his hands on her shoulders. "I don't expect you to see it. I'm having a hard time with it myself, actually."

"You are?"

"Yes. That's why I had to change the rooms up. The only woman to ever walk around this house was my wife, and trying to pry her memories out and insert you into the picture is hard to see right now. But that doesn't mean it won't happen. We'll make our own memories and start to see ourselves here, together, with time."

As usual, Gordon calmed her nerves. She wished she could feel more for him. Beyond gratitude for his kind words. Beyond caring for him, and though there was the smallest seed of love based on that gratitude and caring, it paled in comparison to the intense love affair she'd had with Aryl. That sense of belonging together that went all the way to her soul. Not just wanting but *needing* to be as close as possible to him, and the feeling that it still wasn't close enough. Having felt that, been a part of something that special was something she could never forget. No matter how much time went by.

The familiar ache was back, and she fought her tears.

Gordon kissed her, trying to pull her back to this moment, but it didn't last long. He watched her, wanting to help, holding her close. She looked apologetic but no longer struggled against the tears that brimmed to the edge. She closed her eyes. Having tapped into that deep well of emotion, wishing with all her might she could have that again, but knowing it was impossible, she folded and did something she swore she would never do.

She summoned Aryl from the depths of her heart and with a deep breath, the room spun around her, and he appeared.

The tears spilled over and rolled down her cheeks as she opened her eyes. He stood before her more beautiful than the last time she saw him. His smile made her heart stop. His messy brown curls were everywhere, and her hands disappeared in them, remembering the feel of it. Drawing her hands down, she felt his face, running her fingers over his lips. They kissed her fingertips gently. She touched his throat, and down further, placing her hand over his heart. It beat strong and steady beneath his shirt. She could smell him, that distinct yet indescribable scent she knew so well. He held her close, kissing her cheek, ear, and neck. She knew it was a mistake, but she couldn't stop herself. For these precious moments, she would allow herself to hold him here with her, to not let the vision fade.

The way he looked at her made her catch her breath as he told her he loved her. And, as she slipped her dress off her shoulders, she had the overwhelming feeling that she couldn't get close enough to him. This one time, she would allow herself to feel him again. And then she would say goodbye.

APRIL 25, 1931

"Pink or white?"

Claire jolted from a distant place.

"What?"

"Do you want to carry pink or white flowers?" Arianna asked.

"Pink, I think."

Flash A thick cluster of white roses...the tips dipped in silver glitter...long tresses of silver ribbon swaying as she walked.

"And you're wearing Maura's dress, right?"

Flash Heavy satin, so smooth against her skin...trimmed in lace and pearls...a wide, full skirt with a train three yards long.

"Yes, she said I could use it."

"It's white?"

"Cream, actually. It's a simple thing. It'll be perfect."

"Okay." Arianna checked a few things off her list and scribbled a few notes.

"And I gave him back the ring so he can put it on during the ceremony," Claire said, glancing down at her naked hand.

Flash A diamond encrusted band of white gold, a delicate inscription inside.

Claire smiled at her. "Thank you for doing this. If it were left to me, we'd just go to the courthouse."

Flash A cathedral with stained glass windows. So large a single breath echoed. Brilliant, blinding light streaming from high above as she walked down the aisle.

Arianna made a face. "Not while I'm alive." She went back to her notes. "Besides, I love this. Now, for the reception, I thought we would keep it simple. Since it's a sunset wedding, we can assume people have already eaten dinner. We can just provide light refreshments and the..." Her mouth dropped open. "The cake. How did I miss that?! You need a cake!" She scoured her notes.

Flash Four elegant tiers with a white and silver topper, his hand over hers and holding the knife.

"I can make it. If you'd like," Tarin said from the doorway. Both women smiled.

"Tarin, you would be a lifesaver. Thank you." Arianna scribbled in her notepad.

"What do ye have in mind, Claire? I'm fair good at decoratin'."

Tarin lacked her usual energy, though she didn't look tired. Normally, bright and chipper, she seemed flat as she stood to wait for Claire's direction.

"Um, I don't know. I haven't really thought about it. I'm sure whatever you come up with will be wonderful."

"All right then," she said and turned to leave.

"What's with her?" Claire asked Arianna.

"Just wanted to help, thankfully. I'm not sure what I would have done."

"No, not that. She seems so down."

Arianna gave a shrug without looking at her. "Now, who's performing the service?"

Claire's turn to shrug. Arianna's hand fell, hitting the paper with a smack.

"Don't tell me you haven't arranged for someone."

"No, I've been busy."

"What about the pastor of the Pigeon Cove Chapel?"

Flash A tall man, standing on the beach, giving Aryl's eulogy...

"No."

"Why not?" As soon as she said it, she felt stupid. "I'm sorry. We'll find someone else. In fact, I'll take care of it. You just show up and look pretty."

"Thank you," she said quietly.

"Speaking of showing up, don't you think you should stay the last night at my house? That way you just have to wake up and get ready."

"I suppose," she said, indifferent.

"And what about a honeymoon? Do I need to arrange anyone to take you to the train station?"

Flash Newlywed suite on a luxury cruise liner, moonlight streaming in the windows, the scent of roses...

Claire's face turned hard. "You're thinking of our old life," she accused Arianna.

"What do you mean?" she asked. Her eyes were owlish and confused.

"We don't have the money for a honeymoon, Arianna. We're just going back to his house. No frills, no fuss. We're just going to start our life."

"At least, tell me he's going to make you breakfast the next morning," she said with a twist of her lips.

Claire smiled. "Probably."

"One more thing. Normally, I wouldn't ask...okay, I *would*, but I'm not just being Arianna here, I'm being your friend. I need to know you're going to be okay. You know. With the wedding night."

Claire blushed fiercely, shaking her head. "Arianna, I swear."

"No, I'm not just being dirty, honest." She held up her right hand. "Have you thought about how hard it might be to be with someone else? Don't you think that's when the memories will be the strongest?"

Claire studied her hands, folded in her lap. "Yes, I've thought about it."

"And you'll be okay?"

"I already have been." She faced Arianna.

"Oh, you...*really*?"

"Yes. Oh, don't look at me like that. You don't understand."

"Then explain it to me." She scooted to the edge of her seat.

"I did it to...to say goodbye. So that after we're married, I knew it would only be Gordon I saw. It worked." She fought tears, and for the moment, was winning. "I said goodbye to Aryl, and I haven't seen his face in my mind since that night." She looked away, and Arianna couldn't tell if she was happy or sad about that.

MAY 1, 1931

"I t's the nice thing to do," Jonathan reminded him.

Caleb scoffed. "He's not the party type, Jon. You saw him at the Valentine's dance. Gordon looked like he wanted to crawl out of his skin the way we were."

"This isn't a party. Not like the kind we're used to. It's a small guy's night—a pathetic excuse for a bachelor party—just drinks and cards, but he'll appreciate it. We should do this for him. Help him feel welcome and all that. Besides, it's too late now." He glanced at his watch. "He'll be here in twenty minutes."

Caleb slogged across the kitchen and pulled out a bottle from under the counter.

"Where'd you get that?" Jonathan asked.

"When I stopped grief drinking, I stashed some away. Figured we'd need it for something or other, eventually."

"Way to have willpower, buddy. And way to plan ahead."

Caleb wasn't willing to accept a compliment for a lie. He brushed it off with a grunt, digging through a drawer for the playing cards.

~

GORDON SHOWED up in his uniform. All white with a black tie. Even wore his little hat. He looked too formal, and Jonathan had the amusing thought that he and Caleb should make it their mission to loosen this guy up a bit.

The twins were fussy, and Arianna doted like it was ladies tea time, so they moved to the barn.

A rickety old table with hay bales for seats served as the central spot for the bachelor party. Caleb had finished the collages and hung them above the desk.

"Why do you keep these out here?" Gordon asked.

"I don't want to look at them all the time. Just sometimes," Caleb said.

Gordon studied them, seeking out the ones with Claire. In all the pictures of her, Aryl stood close by. He was taller than she was and handsome. He had a look in his eyes that hinted of a mischievous spirit. In every photo, he was touching her. Always with his arm around her, holding her hand or clutching her close. And they all looked so damned happy. There was radiance in those pictures where they all stood together. One that wasn't there when it was just the women, just the men, or half the group. There was something about all of them being together as a whole, and though Gordon couldn't put his finger on exactly what it was—why it was—he marveled at it. He wished he had ever, *could* ever be a part of something that special. He turned toward Caleb and Jonathan. Perhaps that's what this night was all about. Trying to place him in the group. He wasn't excited about the prospect. Throwing a last glance at the pictures, he knew those were shoes he could never fill.

MAY 2, 1931

C laire sat at the small vanity table, her long gown gathering in soft piles of cream-colored satin at her feet. She stared at her reflection for a long time. She didn't recognize the bride staring back at her. She closed her eyes and took a deep breath. *This is normal,* she reminded herself. *Maura told me this is normal.* The feeling of betrayal was bone deep.

"He's gone," she repeated softly, as she had hundreds of times since Gordon's proposal. "And he would want you to be happy." Her eyes misted at the thought of Aryl.

"You'll ruin your makeup, Miss Claire," Maura said softly from the doorway. Claire nodded quickly with tightly closed eyes, willing the tears and the memories away.

"I know. I'm sorry." She dabbed at the corners of her eyes carefully, trying not to disturb the makeup Arianna had carefully applied that morning. Claire normally wore little makeup. She needn't bother with a sweet round face and envious ivory complexion, smooth as porcelain.

"Don't be sorry, love," Maura said as she stood behind her, arranging bits and pieces of blonde hair and sprigs of baby's breath that threatened to fall.

"It's normal," they both said in unison, and laughed.

"I'm awfully proud of ye, Miss Claire. You've come a long way, so ye have."

"Thanks to you." Claire met her eyes in the mirror and held them there for a long moment. Maura broke the stare and turned away before her own eyes misted.

"I do believe your family is a wee bit upset with me," Maura mentioned casually with a hint of amusement in her voice. She went about tidying the room, which had been left a fair mess after the flurry of activity as the bridal party prepared for the ceremony.

"Why is that?" Claire asked, hardly surprised. Since Maura had moved to Rockport, there had been no shortage of ruffled feathers and stirred emotions. However, Claire knew there was always a good reason for it.

"I told 'em they couldn't see ye 'fore the wedding."

"Ah." Claire smiled at her thoughtfulness. "I would have been okay, you know."

"Well, I'm not takin' the chance, Miss Claire. I'll not have one of them mentionin' anythin' that might make you upset on yer weddin' day." She puffed up protectively, like a mother hen.

Claire smiled again. She could hardly believe sometimes that Maura was only a few years older than herself, but she was wise beyond her years. She had the wisdom to counsel the brokenhearted, instinct to know when she was needed, and somehow, always knew what to say. Those deep green eyes could see deep into a soul. If you were lost, and Maura's eyes found you, it wouldn't be long before you found yourself. She'd see to it, with a hard love people came to depend on. Claire smiled as she thought of the other side of Maura, too. The one that could, and eagerly would rain hell down upon anyone who threatened those she loved.

It was a bittersweet day.

Claire moved slowly to the window and pulled back the curtain. The softest of breezes pulled earthy smells from the garden and an odd assortment of food for a small reception set out on long tables. The side yard of Caleb and Arianna's farm was decorated modestly, though Claire was amazed at how Arianna had transformed it into a lovely and

291

romantic spot, with a small arch covered in wildflowers where she would soon stand and begin a new life.

She turned as Jac stirred in his cradle with the soft coos and grunts a little one makes as they wake from a long doze. She watched as Maura quickly moved and scooped the baby up, murmuring loving sayings in Gaelic. Claire stepped toward them, but Maura held up a hand.

"No, I've got him, now. The last thing ye want is to have him spit up on yer dress." She smiled.

Claire ran her hands over the lovely silk of the cream-colored dress. "Thank you for letting me borrow it."

"It's no trouble." She bounced Jac on her shoulder lightly, his brown curls moved airily. "You remember what I said now?" she asked.

"I do." Claire nodded, pausing until the lump in her throat subsided. "Leave the past behind, except to tell Jac of his father." She paused again and cleared her throat. "And don't compare."

"Aye. You'll never be happy if you let a ghost stand between you and Gordon."

Claire nodded, tears threatening again. Maura smiled a mischievous grin as she moved to the door, patting Jac on the back.

"Did I tell you I ran into Gordon earlier this afternoon? While he was readying himself for the wedding, I mean."

"No, you didn't," Claire said, grateful to move off the topic of Aryl's ghost.

"Aye. He was in the bathroom, and being in a fluster and flurry such as I was, I burst right in." She glanced back at Claire over her shoulder. "I think you'll be quite pleased, Miss Claire," she said with a wry grin. Claire's mouth dropped open and hot blood flooded her cheeks in ruddy patches.

"Maura!"

Maura giggled as she stepped out of the room. She poked her head back in. "*Quite* pleased."

Claire held her smile for several moments after Maura left. Turning back to the window, she watched the small crowd as they mingled and made last minute arrangements. Her eyes settled on Caleb, who for the first time looked happy as he greeted guests. She couldn't help but think this was ending a painful chapter for him as well. Maybe now he could put down the guilt of surviving and move on with his life, with her and Jac cared for.

Arianna bustled around, fussing over details, playing the perfect overbearing party organizer. Claire smiled, watching her walk over to Savrene and Samuel, and hand them a cookie. In the chaos of the day, Caleb had driven a stake in the ground and tied the newly walking toddlers by a length of twine around the waist, so they had about twenty feet of freedom, but they couldn't get lost in the commotion. Arianna had thrown a fit, yelling at Caleb for tying her babies up like dogs, but she soon saw the wisdom in it after he silently released them, and she was overwhelmed trying to keep track of both of them, organize the wedding and reception details, all while largely pregnant with their third child.

Her eyes rested on her bridegroom standing in a circle of men as they gave congratulatory handshakes and backslaps. He was a good man and would make a good husband. She was sure Aryl would approve of someone as kind and gentle as Gordon raising their son in his absence.

And he is handsome, she thought with a grin. He was dashing in his borrowed tuxedo. She had always been grateful that he looked so opposite of Aryl.

She watched Arianna's babies with a smile. Savrene pushed a wobbly Samuel over on his side and yanked his cookie from his chubby fist. Samuel came up screaming and swinging and took it back. Caleb skipped over to quell the fight. He bent over and picked up Savrene, moving her away from Samuel, who was nibbling his cookie with tear stained cheeks, scowling at his sister. Savrene howled in protest, and the whole crowd hushed suddenly.

It was an eerie silence, the toddlers piercing cry filling the side yard. Claire watched Caleb as he tried to soothe Savrene. He started to stand, and something caught his eye and demanded his attention. His face was that of shock, and he sat back down hard next to his daughter, staring.

Aunt Mildred, Claire thought as she closed her eyes.

Aunt Mildred was slightly touched in the head and always doing things that shocked and appalled. Like the time she wore her undergarments *over* her clothes. She also liked to make dyes out of berries to dye her blond hair colors God never intended to grace the tops of human heads. The last time Claire had seen her, it was as purple as a grape. As it was, she missed her train twice, and Jonathan had been dispatched to fetch her from the train station at the last minute. She could see the corner of his Model T from the window.

They would be coming for her soon to begin. It was nearly sunset, the overbearing summer heat of the day waning. Scanning the crowd, all faced toward Jonathan's truck, she saw Gordon take two steps back with a very unreadable expression. Maura crossed herself.

Gracious. Aunt Mildred must be quite the sight today. She thought with a shake of the head. She sat herself back down in front of the mirror to make last minute adjustments.

It won't be as hard as I thought, she thought with gratitude, *between Maura's distracting comment and Aunt Mildred's wild antics, I'll be through it in no time.*

"COME IN," Claire called to the soft knock at the door. The door creaked open slowly, and Jonathan stood in the doorway.

"Claire, I'm sorry." His voice broke, and he cleared his throat.

"Jon, I'm used to it. Aunt Mildred is...special. It's okay." She smiled.

"Not that," he said. His eyes were brimming to the edge with tears, and Claire tried to read his face, beginning to become concerned.

"I'm sorry it took me so long."

"It's not even sunset." She smiled. "It's fine."

Jonathan shook his head and could no longer see her, only a blurred cream-colored image, the blonde hair piled on her head looked fuzzy, resembling a halo.

"I'm sorry it took me so long to find him," he whispered again and stepped aside.

Aryl, shaggy, disheveled, and desperately thin, stood at the threshold of her door.

Claire's face froze, instantly drained of blood. Then she gasped, and fainted dead away.

"Grab her!" Jonathan yelled as Aryl lunged forward. Catching her head just before it struck the floor. He sat down quickly, cradling it in his lap. He stayed silent for a long time, just staring.

"I can't imagine what a shock that must have been." He pushed the hair off her forehead.

"She'll be okay."

"I wasn't counting on this. I didn't think she'd faint."

"You didn't exactly have a whole lot of time to think about it."

Jonathan quickly wiped at his eyes.

"She's going to want to know where I've been."

"We all do, Aryl. But there's time for that. You're home now." He bent down and put a hand on his shoulder, nearly laughing at the touch. "You're skinny as hell, but I can't tell you how glad I am to see you."

Aryl looked up. "I'm glad to see you, too. Where's Caleb?"

"Right here," Caleb whispered from the door. He had stared for a long moment before he found his voice again. "You have no idea how confused everyone is down there. I came up to see if I was seeing things." He walked closer. "But it's really you."

Aryl nodded with a smile. "You look good, Caleb."

He turned and leaned on the doorjamb. "Jesus Christ," he whispered. "Back from the dead. How in the hell..." He turned to Aryl again, who was concentrating on Claire's face.

"How, Aryl? One minute you were there, and the next you were gone, and now here you are! You drowned! We searched for days! What the hell is going on! Would someone please tell me that?!"

Jonathan stood up and steadied a wild-eyed Caleb.

"There's time for all that, Caleb. And it doesn't matter. He's back now!"

"The hell it doesn't matter!" He shoved Jonathan and stormed out.

Jonathan thought about going after him. Instead, he sat down. "I'm sorry. People are going to react differently. You have to be prepared for that."

"I know how Caleb is." He smiled. "I'll talk to him later. Right now, I'm only concerned with how she reacts." He started picking the sprigs of baby's breath out of her hair. "Looks like she moved on. Ready to get married." He swallowed hard. "Nice guy?"

"Obviously, she's not getting married now, Aryl. She's going to be so happy." He stopped and cleared his throat.

Aryl looked up at the window gleaming with the early rays of a brilliant sunset.

"But she would have. Talk about being just in the nick of time."

"It wouldn't have mattered if you were five minutes late. You're her husband, and you're alive."

With those words, Jonathan sucked in a breath. "Oh, my God. Your parents. Someone has to go get your parents. Your mother's been labeled crazy, you know."

"Was it that hard on her?"

"No. I mean, yes, it was, but she never accepted it. She has been running around telling everyone you're alive for months now."

"How'd she know?"

"A fortune teller in town had her believing it. We all figured she was stringing her along for money. No one would have ever guessed it was true."

Claire took a long breath in through her nose and stirred. Aryl turned to Jonathan. "Will you go get my folks?"

"Are you sure? We don't know how she's going to react."

Aryl looked back down at Claire, excited and nervous. "I'm sure. I want to do this alone."

Reluctantly, Jonathan closed the door softly behind him.

Claire opened her eyes. She didn't scream or weep or even scarcely breathe. She just stared. She'd seen him in dreams like this, where he didn't move, and neither did she. When she did, he disappeared. But this time, he smiled. And stayed. Slowly she lifted her hand toward his face. She stopped.

"If I'm dreaming, I don't want to wake up," she whispered.

He put his hand over hers and pressed it to his face.

"You're not dreaming."

Her eyes filled with tears, her face contorted with emotion, and she reached for him. Hugging him close, she sobbed. So did he.

❧

JONATHAN WAS SWARMED as soon as he stepped outside. Maura stepped up demanding the first question.

"It's him?"

"It is." He smiled.

"How?"

Jonathan waved over a man who had ridden in behind them. He sat in Vincent's car, smoking a cigarette.

"This is Detective Sloan. He was the one who really tracked Aryl down."

A firestorm of questions assaulted the detective as he walked up. He was tall and thin with squinty eyes. He stubbed out his cigarette and smiled, ignoring them all. Then he reached for Jonathan's hand.

"I'm glad this was a happy ending for you," he said. "They aren't always."

"Thank you. But we were hoping you could fill us in on how all this came about? How did you know to look for Aryl when the rest of us thought he was dead? Where did you find him? How did you find him?"

The detective fished in his breast pocket and pulled out a small notebook. "While we were sailing from Paris, I recounted the whole crazy thing. I'd love to stay, but see, I've decided to retire. I'm ending my career on a good note. And I'm gonna take my wife on a vacation. I'd really like to get home and tell her."

Jonathan took the notebook. "This explains it?"

"It explains everything." He smiled. "You folks take care." He tipped his hat and slipped through the crowd back to the car.

Suddenly, everyone surged on Jonathan.

"Whoa! Hold on!" He held the booklet high in the air. "Look, I think we need to hear it from Aryl first. Let's give him a chance to talk, okay? Then we'll read this. There are more important things to deal with. Now, where's Gordon?"

"He's gone," Maura said. "He took one look at Aryl and left." She looked around and nodded, volunteering herself. "I'll go to him."

"Thank you, Maura," Jonathan said.

"Can I go with you, Auntie?" Tarin asked anxiously.

"Yes, you can. Arianna, will you take Jac?"

She had Samuel on one hip, Savrene hugging her leg and took the baby in her left arm. Her stomach bulged in the middle.

"Some women wear jewelry. I wear babies," she huffed.

"I need to go get Aryl's parents," Jonathan said. "Has anyone seen Caleb?" Everyone looked around. No one had. "He was upstairs with me a minute ago. Arianna, have you seen him?"

"No. Last I saw, he was headed inside to see if it really was Aryl." She glanced at the house, and a shadow crossed her face. "Check the barn."

WHEN CLAIRE'S sobs died down to a whimper, she pulled back and pressed her forehead to his.

"I've had dreams that were almost this real," she said, gasping. "I'm so scared if I open my eyes you'll disappear."

"I won't. I promise."

Slowly, she opened them and studied his face.

"I'm sure you have a lot of questions," he said, holding her close.

"Not right now. Not yet," she said and kissed him.

JONATHAN WALKED into the barn and pushed open the door to a stall. "Caleb, what the hell are you doing?"

He had already begun to work his way down a bottle in a short amount of time.

"Leave me alone."

"I need you to go with me to get Aryl's parents."

"And I need you to go to hell!"

Jonathan stared at him for a moment.

"Caleb."

"Shut up, Jon. Just shut up."

"Why the hell are you mad at me? Why are you mad at all? Aryl's back! Aryl's alive and—"

"And nothing else matters, right?"

"Right."

Caleb yelled and hurled the bottle at Jonathan, narrowly missing his head. It exploded on the wall behind him.

"Hey!"

"Nothing else matters! You don't know what I went through! You don't know how badly I wanted to die after he died! I was alone out there, Jonathan. You weren't there. I was all alone in that ocean thinking my best friend just died right in front of me, and I wasn't strong enough to save him! I nearly drank myself to death trying to forget that! And then I get it together and sober up. Start being the family man and going through the motions. And everyone's happy. And I even start to think *I* might be able to be happy again one day. Then he shows up. He shows up alive! No, Jonathan, it *does* matter where he's been. He owes me that! He disappeared right before my eyes, and then shows up, and he needs to explain to me how that happened!" He turned away and reached for another bottle.

"I know you suffered, Caleb. I can't imagine what it was like that night. And I can't imagine what you've had to go through every single day. I know Aryl will explain where he's been. But you've got to give him time to reunite with Claire. He has a son he's never even seen. Give him time to adjust. I promise he'll sit down with us and tell us everything we need to know."

Caleb stared at the bottle in his hand, debate raging inside him. Finally, he nodded reluctantly with a clenched jaw.

~

CLAIRE BROKE SUDDENLY FROM A DESPERATE, greedy kiss. She wanted more—much more—but now that she knew he was real, had felt and tasted him, she had to know.

"Where've you been?" she whispered. "All this time, where've you been?"

"I've been lost."

"Lost? Lost where? Why didn't you try to come home?"

"I did. When I remembered where home was."

"Are you saying you forgot where home was?"

Aryl moved away just enough to sit up. He crossed his legs and leaned his elbows on them, taking a deep breath before speaking.

"Worse than that. I forgot who I was. I remember it all now, but I didn't then. Not until recently. The explosion on the boat. Caleb bobbing around, screaming my name...and then a wave hit me. Knocked me under, and I remember feeling something slam against my head. Debris from the boat, most likely." He looked away and squinted. "It's all really a blur. When I could finally think clearly, I was on a ship and then wandering the streets."

"And you didn't know who you were?"

"I didn't know anything but pain. I was so cut up and bruised, and my head felt like it'd been split open. I didn't care about anything—who I was, where I belonged, or how I ended up on a dirty trading ship. I just wanted the pain to stop."

Claire's brow furrowed. "I hate to think of you in pain." She reached out and touched his face.

"They had medicine and gave me quite a bit of it. I slept most of the journey."

"Journey where?"

There was a knock at the door. Claire debated calling whoever it was in. She wanted this to last forever, this time with him so close.

"It's Arianna. I've got Jac."

Claire's eyes lit up, and she grabbed Aryl's hands. "Do you remember the last trip we took to the lighthouse?"

He smiled. "Yes."

"Do you remember what I told you that you already knew because of your nosy mother?"

"That you were going to have a baby."

"He's right out there. Do you want to meet your son?"

"Son?" he whispered. "Yes, I do."

Claire called Arianna in. Arianna was all smiles as she knelt down beside them and carefully handed Jac to Claire.

"He looks just like you, Aryl."

His eyes followed the baby, staring with wonder. "How old is he?"

"Three months."

"He's so small." He reached out and stroked one finger along his downy head.

"His name is Jack?"

"Jac. There's no K. I named him after Jonathan, you, and Caleb. Since you didn't have any friends whose names started with K, it just stayed Jac."

"I never would have thought to do that," he said.

"Do you like it?"

He smiled. "I do."

"Jonathan and Caleb helped deliver him, you know."

His eyebrows went up. "They did?"

"There was a fierce storm, and no one could get to the midwife, and even if they had, there were four babies born that night. She was very busy. So, Maura was there. Tarin managed to get Jonathan and Caleb, thinking they could get to the midwife. They couldn't and so we had to make do with what we had. I thought it was only right to name him after all of you."

"You did good," he said, looking over the baby. "Can I hold him?"

"Of course." She placed him in his arms and adjusted the blanket to cover his little feet.

"He's so beautiful."

"Wait till he wakes up. His eyes are so much like yours. It was hard to look at them sometimes." She choked up a little and cleared her throat, smiling through misty eyes.

～

IT WAS WELL past dark when Aryl came down the stairs holding Jac, Claire clinging to his side. He also still held his bag, keeping it very close. The whole room went silent. No one breathed.

"It's good to see everyone again," he said quietly.

Maura walked up to him with open arms.

"Do you have any idea how much you were missed?" She pulled back and held his thin face in her hands. "How much you are loved?"

"I think so, Maura. Thank you."

"Come and sit. You look tired. Arianna is making some iced tea, and there's plenty of food that was prepared for the, well, the wedding." She smiled nervously.

Aryl stiffened at the word wedding but followed Maura and sat where she pointed. Claire sat close beside him, taking Jac on her lap. He chewed on his fist and stared curiously at Aryl.

He expected a firestorm of questions, but everyone just stared. It was as if everyone wanted to know but was all afraid to ask. It quickly became awkward, clear that if there were to be a conversation, he was going to have to be the one to start it.

"Maybe someone could fill me in on what I missed. How's everyone been?"

The room started to come to life as the back door burst open and heavy, hurried footsteps rushed to the living room.

Kathleen stood at the threshold, staring. She blinked, shook her head, and stared again. Michael stood behind her grinning, tears brimming to the edge.

"I told you!" she screamed as she ran across the room. Aryl stood up just in time for her to crash into him, hugging him in a stranglehold. "I told you! I told you! I told you!" she continued to yell as she rocked him back and forth.

"My boy!" She took his face in her hands. "You're so thin…so thin. But you're alive!" She threw her head back, cackling and hugged him again, jumping up and down. Michael moved in, anxious for a touch, and it took her a moment to finally step aside. While he embraced his son, Kathleen ran around the room, from one person to the next, yelling. "I told you!" "I told you he was alive!" "You didn't believe me!" "You said I was crazy!"

Everyone couldn't help but laugh at her, animated as she was, her hair flying and her eyes bulging. Tears of laughter and joy flowed again from almost everyone in the room.

When Kathleen finally settled down, Arianna and Maura set the long table with food that had been prepared for the wedding. Arianna set a stack of plates at the end and announced dinner, buffet style. There was no big rush, but people straggled in one and two at a time to fill their plate.

"Have you seen Jean?" Jonathan asked Ava as they sidestepped down the length of the table.

"No, not in the last half hour or so." She looked up at the back door, and through the screen, she could see him sitting on the top step with his chin in his hands. She nudged Jonathan. "He's out there."

Jonathan craned his neck and set his plate down. "I'll go get him. You go ahead and eat."

He sat beside Jean, trying to see what he was seeing. The child stared intently at nothing in particular.

"Penny for your thoughts," Jonathan said.

Jean shook his head. Jonathan dug in his pocket. "Okay, I think I have a nickel."

"No, Dadee. Save it for the bebe. I'll tell you for free. If you promise you won't be angry."

"Why on earth would I be angry?"

Jean shrugged. "Because I was wondering things."

Jonathan laughed. "I wouldn't ever be angry at you for wondering things. That's how you learn."

"Well," he started, drawing up courage and sitting up straight, "Aryl came back when everyone thought he was dead."

"Yes, it's quite a miracle."

"And I got to thinking, what if my mommy comes back, even though everyone thinks *she's* dead."

Jonathan felt a heavy weight of incompetence, and he scrubbed his face with his hand, buying time. He hated moments like this when he had no idea of what to say besides the hurtful truth.

"Jean, I'm so sorry, but your mom is not coming back. That is totally different."

"Why is it different? He came back when no one thought he would."
He looked up with big eyes that begged for a shred of hope.

"Aryl was picked up by another ship and taken away." At least that's
what Claire told him when she stepped out to use the restroom and
Jonathan caught her in the hall. "He never really died."

"And my mommy did?"

"Yes, Jean. She did."

"How do you know?"

"Because...I just know. When she died, her attorney had a trunk
shipped here for you. Attorneys wouldn't lie." He opened his mouth to
correct that but decided to leave well enough alone.

"Will you take me there?"

"Where?"

"To Paris. To see her grave. Then I'll know for sure."

"I wish I could. That's a very expensive trip. Maybe one day," he said
and put his arm around Jean. "Let's go inside and get something to eat,
okay?"

Laughter rang from the house as they stepped inside. Ava turned and
smiled from where she sat, and Jonathan smiled back. Kathleen and
Michael were telling a very manic version of how she nearly drove them
to the poor house with the fortune teller.

Aryl sat and though he appeared to be listening, Jonathan could tell
his thoughts were elsewhere.

When Kathleen stopped talking, she took a deep breath and simply
stared at her son. "It's a miracle," she whispered. "Aryl, you have to tell
us how this happened. Where have you been?"

"Oh, it's a really long story," he said, not looking anyone in the eye.

"Well, we've got all night." Jonathan laughed, and the room grew
quiet, waiting for Aryl to speak. "And I don't think anyone's going
anywhere!"

"I really..." His body and eyes shifted uncomfortably. "I really don't
want to talk about it just yet."

"But, son."

"Mom, please. It's been a really long day, and I'm tired. I'm still...
getting used to this."

"It's just that we care. We all do. And we're so happy you're home. We just want to know what's kept you from us all this time."

"I know!" He rocketed out of the chair, his face angry, his fists clenched at his sides. "I know you want to know, but I don't want to talk about it!"

His sudden explosion silenced the room. The small children looked up at him, frightened. The grown-ups stared, confused. Looking pained, he quietly apologized for yelling.

"I have to use the bathroom," he said as he rushed past his friends.

Jonathan waited outside the bathroom door. He heard Aryl shuffling around on the other side, occasionally muttering to himself. He leaned against the wall and waited until Aryl unlocked the door and stepped out.

He leveled his head and pushed off the wall. "You okay?"

"Yeah." Aryl looked down. "I'm really sorry. I didn't mean to yell."

"It's gotta be hard."

Aryl nodded.

"But you have to understand how happy we are. We care and we're curious."

"I know you are. I just can't talk about it right now."

Jonathan pulled the notebook out from behind his back. "The detective gave me this. Said it explained everything. How he found you and all."

Aryl looked at it for a long moment and put his hand out. Jonathan handed it over.

"Do you mind if I keep this for a while?"

"No. But why? If you don't want to tell us what happened, maybe it would be easier if we read it. Save you the trouble."

Aryl opened it and scanned several pages.

"This isn't the whole story anyway." He flipped it closed and tucked it inside his bag. "I'd like to keep it." He didn't wait for an answer before heading back to join the others.

$\sim$

IT WAS LATE, and Claire was nervous as she readied for bed. She pulled her dress over her head, dropped it on the bathroom floor, and reached for her thin white nightgown. She knew he was changing right now in the bedroom. She could hear the baby fuss downstairs, but he settled quickly. Maura had offered to take care of him for the night to afford them some time to get reacquainted. She found herself wishing she hadn't accepted the offer. Jac's fussing would provide a nice distraction. They could only discover each other again so quickly dealing with a newborn in the room.

She closed her eyes feeling guilty. This was her Aryl, and she was happy beyond words that he was back. She knew every inch of his body, and he knew hers. There was nothing to be afraid of. She'd felt him alive when it defied all logic, connected to him on a level few couples experienced. And yet she felt more nervous than on her wedding night as if she were getting ready to climb into bed with a stranger.

She was surprised to find Aryl standing by the window in their bedroom. He was still fully clothed, staring out into the darkness.

"Are you okay?"

He turned. "Fine."

"Are you tired?"

"Exhausted."

She pointed her thumb toward the door. "I can give you more time if you need to change."

"I'm all right."

They stood in awkward silence for a moment and finally, Claire moved toward the bed, pulling the covers back.

"There's no pressure, Aryl. I mean—" She flustered and blushed fiercely.

"I know what you mean."

"It's not that I don't want you to, it's just—"

"There are things we should talk about first."

"Okay." Not what she was expecting to hear.

"I've been gone, and you've moved on."

"HAD moved on. Past tense. It's not like I've moved on now. Now that you're back, I'm right here. Not...there." She glanced out the window.

"Were you there before?"

"Was I where before?"

"With him."

"We were going to get married."

"So you were."

"I'm going to need you to be a little clearer with your questions, Aryl. What exactly are you asking?"

She crawled into bed and pulled the covers up. He moved away from the window, and she startled at how he looked. More ragged than before, starting to sweat, squinting as if he were in pain or angry.

"Did you sleep with him?"

She stared at him with wide eyes.

"You asked me to be clear."

She took a deep breath and nodded, looking down.

He shoved his hands in his pockets and began to pace the room.

"Aryl, you don't understand." She wanted to say more. To explain what really happened that night with Gordon.

"I understand well enough."

"I thought you were dead. We were going to get married!"

"I'm aware of that. I just figured you hadn't. I was hoping you hadn't. "He stopped and raised his shoulders, holding his hands out. "I figured that's the kind of decent girl you were. Maybe you'd make him wait."

"Aryl!" Her eyes filled with tears.

"Well, why, then? Did you think he wouldn't marry you unless you did?"

"No, that's not why."

"Just felt like it then? A long walk on a moonlit night, all romantic and sweet and you just lost your senses and ended up on your back? Or were you tired of being lonely and since your husband died *so* long ago, might as well drop to the ground and go for it. Nothing better to do. Or it could have been just to seal the deal. So he could feel like Jac was his son, not mine."

"No, that's not how it was! What's wrong with you?" she yelled and covered her face with her hands, crying.

He stopped and looked at her as if seeing her for the first time.

"Oh, God. I'm sorry. Claire, I didn't mean—" He grabbed handfuls of his hair and grimaced. "You don't understand," he said and grabbed his bag on the way out of the room.

Locked in the bathroom, he leaned his head against the door and took several deep breaths. The last thing in the world he wanted to do was hurt her. And yet, when he felt the monster rising up, it was all he *could* do. His battle was with *it*. But the monster was clever when it crept up, needing to be fed. It wouldn't fight him directly. Instead, it made him hurt the ones he was near, ones he cared about; he didn't want to, it *made* him, until he couldn't stand to hurt them anymore and gave it what it wanted.

Feed the monster...feed the monster...feed the monster.

"Fine," he growled and tore open his knapsack. Coming home was supposed to be a new leaf for him. Getting rid of this stuff for good. He didn't want to feed the monster anymore, didn't want to live with it anymore. He hated himself, and he hated the opiates he could never get more than a few hours away from. Always on the search for more, always worried he wouldn't find more, and the monster would get louder and louder and make him do things he really didn't want to do. He shuddered with memories. It was unfair that he'd lost his memory of his happy life, even just for a time, but couldn't lose the ones from the last eleven months.

I can help you forget, for a little while.

He did want to forget. Needed to, even. The only thing the monster promised to do in return was to blur the memories he'd prefer not to have. Sometimes, that alone was worth giving in. He took a long drink.

There. You happy now? Will you leave me alone now?

Yes, I am. You know what will happen if you don't feed me.

Aryl looked at his dark, sunken eyes in the mirror.

Then I become the monster.

That's right.

. . .

CLAIRE CRIED SOFTLY as Aryl sat on the side of the bed.

"I'm so sorry," he whispered. He tried to touch her arm, and she swatted it away. "I didn't mean it, Claire. None of it. I was an ass, and I'm sorry. This isn't easy for me, you know. For all of you, life has continued on, and I know it was hard, but everyone's been in the same life...progress, setbacks, happy times, hard times. But me...I was thrown into another life and had to figure it out pretty quickly and then, just as suddenly, ripped from that life and thrown back into this one. My head's still spinning, Claire."

She pulled her head up from her knees. He looked tired but peaceful. The dark shadows were gone from his face, and he appeared sincere.

"Why did you have to know? About Gordon, I mean. What does it matter?"

"It doesn't."

"It sure did ten minutes ago!"

"I was wrong. I shouldn't have asked."

"Should I not ask as well?"

After a long silence, his eyes begged her not to.

"Don't worry. I don't want to know, Aryl."

"I'll tell you anything." *Quick, take advantage of this minute while the monster is asleep!*

She shook her head.

"Am I still welcome to sleep here?" He tilted his head and smiled. The old Aryl.

She moved far over as he pulled the blankets back.

"Aren't you going to change?" she asked as he climbed into bed.

"I'm sort of used to sleeping in my clothes. If that's okay."

"I guess. If that's what you're used to."

He turned off the light. They lay stiff and awkward beside each other. A few restless moments later, he rose and opened the window. "Seems hot in here."

She watched him silently.

Returning to bed, she could see just enough in the moonlit room. He put an arm out to her in invitation. She hesitated. Lying on her side, she nestled close to his body, his arm around her shoulders. They still fit perfectly together. She tried to shake off the ugliness of the night and stay in this exact moment. She could hear his heart, and every beat sounded like a miracle. A tear slid onto his chest. He didn't seem to notice. In fact, it was only a few moments later she felt his body relax and heard his slow, deep breathing.

She rose on one elbow and watched him. He still had the same long lashes, the same full lips. She tilted her head. His nose was crooked. Was it always like that? No, she decided. It was slightly different. She supposed it would be hard, being thrown into a new life and suddenly ripped back to the old one.

She wondered where he'd been, really, all this time.

"You're home now, my little drifter," she whispered as she gently pushed a brown lock off his forehead.

MAY 5, 1931

C laire's slippers sank down into the sand with every step. Aryl walked beside her, holding her hand.

"We had the memorial service over there." She pointed. "I remember because of that great big piece of driftwood. Jonathan chose this spot so people could come here and sit. And it's opposite of the lighthouse, which he figured I couldn't bear to look at. He was right."

It was hard to talk about, even with him standing right next to her. And it was odd pointing out the details of someone's memorial when they stood alive and well. "There were a lot of people. You should be proud to know how many friends you had. Have," she corrected.

"Everyone gathered on the beach to talk about me? I hope it was good things." He smiled shyly.

"Of course, it was good things, Aryl." She reached up to brush the hair off his forehead. "Some funny things, too, although no one was really in a mood to laugh."

"What happened after everyone was done talking?"

"We buried a box. It was Caleb's idea. He bought a box and everyone put something in it that reminded them of you. Then we all buried it together. I thought we could dig it up today."

"Is that why you brought me here?"

She nodded. "I'd like you to see how much you were loved. Are loved," she corrected again. "And I'd like to get my ring back." She held up her hand. "I put it in there."

He took her hand and studied it. "I hadn't noticed it was gone," he said.

"It's been a whirlwind few days. But I'd really like to have it again."

"Then I'll get it back for you," he said. She made her best guess where it would be based by the driftwood, and he sank to his knees, scooping sand with his hands. Several minutes later, he was elbow deep and still pulling out sand.

"How far down did you guys put this thing?" He smiled at her, the sun glinting off his hair, and she felt lightheaded. It was surreal. Him on his knees, digging up the memorial box, his smile, just his being here, living and breathing, seemed like it was too good to be true. She dropped to her knees beside him. She couldn't help it. Grabbing his face, she kissed him. After what wasn't nearly long enough for her, she sensed others on the beach and released him.

An older couple passed them a moment later, walking slowly and grinning.

"Good to have you back, Aryl," the older gentleman called.

"It's good to be back." He waved. After they had passed, he turned to Claire. "Who the hell was that?"

She giggled. "I have no idea. Word travels fast, though."

He reached back into the hole. "I'm going to have to talk to Jon about the way he buries things."

"How do you know it was him?"

"Because, when we were kids, he had this goldfish. It died, and we buried it. I just dug a few inches down, and Jon kept saying, 'no, go deeper.' I think that goldfish ended up two feet down when it was all said and done. Same thing with his rabbit." He smiled at her again, leaning far over into the hole. "That's how I know this was him." His eyebrows shot up. "I think I feel something." He wrestled with it, pulling hard, and as the wet sand finally released it, he grunted, nearly falling backward. He sat on his knees setting the box on the sand in front of him.

Claire stared at it. She recalled the horrible sadness she'd felt the last time she'd seen it and wiped away a sudden tear.

"You want me to open it?" he asked, brushing the top clean. "We could always wait."

"No, open it."

He did and moved around all the small mementos, searching for the ring. When he found it, he rose up on his knees and held it out to her. She stepped forward and reached for it.

"Wait, you don't think I'm going to let you put your ring back on yourself, do you?"

She smiled and held her hand out, palm down. He put it on the tip of her finger and paused.

"I know the last few days have been—" He frowned searching for the words. "I just want you to know that I *am* glad I'm back. I am glad I remembered, and I'm glad to be putting this ring on your finger again."

"I am, too, Aryl. You have no idea."

"Just don't give up on me."

"What?"

"I know that you thought I was dead and moved on to marry Gordon, but now that I'm back, please don't give up on me."

She went down on her knees to look him in the eyes.

"Why on earth would you ask me that?" She touched his face, searching his eyes.

"I'm a little different now. I'm sure you've noticed that. I'm dealing with a lot of things that I can't talk to you about right now. I just need to know you won't give up on us. No matter what.

"I will never give up on you or us, Aryl. Ever. I promise."

He slipped the ring on her finger as the lighthouse sounded its foghorn behind them. He looked toward the beacon.

"It's barely sunset and not even foggy."

"Maybe it's for us." She smiled and took his hands. "Maybe it's time we go back to our lighthouse."

The joy drained from his face. "Not yet."

She bit her lip. Their first night together had been a disaster. The second, they seemed afraid to touch each other, and the third when they

313

had tried, he was distracted and unable. So far, the romance of her love returning to her stopped at the bedroom door.

"We could go just to go," she suggested. "We don't have to do anything. You told me you need some time, and that's fine."

"Soon. I promise," he said, standing and tucking the box under his arm. "For now, walk with me?"

"Don't you want to see what else is in the box?"

"Later."

Arianna and Ava knocked on Claire's door. They were both light and happy delivering dishes and treats under these circumstances. A completely different feeling than before when they would come to check on Claire, disheveled and depressed.

She opened the door and invited them in. Arianna looked around expectantly.

"Where's Aryl?"

"Oh, he's sleeping."

Ava glanced at the clock. "It's three in the afternoon."

"I know. He seems to be a bit of a night owl."

"He never used to be that way."

Claire took the dish from Ava and tried to brush past the topic.

"You guys really shouldn't have, but thank you."

"Well, we figured this would be something like a honeymoon, you know." Arianna wiggled her eyebrows. "No time to cook."

"Oh, I wouldn't say that, exactly." She took the dish to the kitchen, placed it in the icebox, and hesitated to return to the living room. When she did, Arianna took her arm and pulled her to the couch.

"Sit. Talk," she said.

"There's nothing to tell."

Arianna stared at her.

"Honest. It's wonderful to have him back," she said, smiling.

"You mean to tell me, after the most impossibly romantic reunion I have ever seen, there's nothing to tell? You had to know we'd be over for details."

"Well, you would be," Ava said to Arianna with a teasing smile. "I just want to know it's all going well. Not everyone thinks like her," Ava assured Claire, gesturing to Arianna.

"Yes, they do. They just won't admit it. And don't pretend you're so prudent that you don't want to know all the details, Ava. I mean really, after something like this, they had to have torn each other apart."

Ava laughed, and Claire blushed fiercely again from a different kind of embarrassment.

"No. Not really," she said tentatively. "He's kissed me."

Arianna's face fell flat. "You have to give us more than that."

"There's nothing to give!" she said a little too loudly and glanced at the staircase.

"You mean you haven't?" Arianna asked.

"No," Claire said with a squirming blush. "He needs some time."

"Some...time?"

"Yes, he's having a hard time adjusting to everything."

"O...kay."

"It's just that he's a little different now. And I'm not sure why, exactly."

"Have you gotten it out of him where he's been?" Ava asked.

"No, he won't talk about it. To be honest, I think it—" She stopped and looked down feeling silly.

"It what?" Arianna asked.

"I think, whatever happened, wherever he's been...it haunts him."

Arianna sat back with surprise. "Haunts him?"

"I don't know, but he has nightmares. That's what keeps him up at night. And when we've tried to...you know—"

Arianna leaned forward. "Now we're getting somewhere."

"No," Claire said with her eyes bulged. "We aren't. He can't." Her voice was both disapproving of Arianna's tone and the situation at hand.

"He doesn't eat a lot, and there are times when—" She glanced toward the stairs and lowered her voice. "When he's fine one minute and then he's really nervous, almost fitful and angry. Like the first night when he came back after he had exploded at his mother. He leaves the room, and when he comes back, he's fine. And for a little while, he's like he used to be."

Arianna sat expectantly for more as Claire finished. "I am so glad to have him back." She smiled sincerely. "It's just not what I expected."

"Is it ever?" Arianna said with a disappointed sigh.

MAY 7, 1931

"They told me I could find you here." Aryl walked into the barn as Caleb just finished cleaning a stall. "That was a nice party you had for your kids. I can't believe they're a year old."

"Time has flown," Caleb said, continuing to work.

The goat trotted up to Aryl, sniffing and nuzzling his leg.

"Damn, he's an ugly little guy."

"Hey, that's my goat. He's a good goat. We've been through some hard times together." Caleb set the pitchfork against the wall and clicked his tongue. The goat bounded over to him.

"Well, he can't be any good for conversation," Aryl said with a smile.

"You'd be surprised," Caleb said, scratching the goat's head.

"Is this my replacement? Is this who's been sitting on the bench with you and Jon after I left?" He chuckled.

Caleb stood up. "You didn't leave. You died. Or so we thought."

"You know what I mean."

Aryl sat on a hay bale and held his hand out to the goat, which began sniffing and licking it. "Does he have a name? It is a he, right?"

"It's a he, and I just call him goat."

Aryl bent down to get on eye level with it. "Sorry, lil guy, but I'm back now and fully plan on taking my place on the bench. Hope you don't mind."

"I saw Claire earlier. She looked like she'd been crying."

Aryl sat up straighter and lost most of his smile. "Just still overwhelmed that I'm back, I guess."

"Is it hard? Being back, I mean. Sometimes you look like it's hard."

"A little."

Caleb stopped working and watched him for a moment. "Where were you, Aryl? All this time, we've been crying and grieving and trying like hell to find a way to keep going another day. Where were you?"

Aryl stiffened. What was left of his smile vanished. "I'll tell you, a little anyway, but I don't want you running your mouth."

Caleb agreed.

"England. And France. Mainly England."

"What the hell were you doing there?"

"Working, mostly."

"Working? In England? You just hit your head, a ship dropped you off in England, and you didn't know your name, but you got a job?"

Aryl gave a lopsided smile. "Yeah, pretty much."

"What kind of work did you do there?"

He clenched his jaw and dropped his eyes. "I did all sorts of things."

"Did you meet anyone there?"

"I met lots of people."

"Did you make friends?"

"Sure."

"Do you miss them?"

Aryl stopped to think for a moment. "A few. Others, not so much."

"Did you meet any women there? Or did you spend the whole time a nameless monk?" Caleb had a way of wandering around half tuned into the rest of the world. But with this situation, Aryl's behavior, and Claire's crying, he honed in like a hawk. With the help, of course, from a talkative wife.

"Jonathan said you wanted to talk to me. That's why I came out here." *Not to answer those questions,* his expression said.

319

"I did. I wanted an explanation, is all. Where you've been, how you got there, how you found your way home, all that."

Aryl shoved his hand through his hair. "Maybe I should just call a town meeting and have 'Aryl Explains' hour. Get it over with all at the same time."

"Why is it so hard to talk about?"

"Because I want to forget about it. It's not important. And it's nobody's business."

Caleb did a double take. "Nobody's business?"

Aryl looked pained, and Caleb sighed. "Hey, I have an idea. I'll play you for answers."

"What?"

"We'll play Blackjack. And I'll provide drinks."

"What is this? Caleb's speakeasy?"

He grinned. "If I tell you a secret, you promise not to tell?"

"Of course. If you don't say anything about what I told you."

"Go look in that back stall there. The last one on the right." Aryl got up and lumbered back, swinging the rusty hinges open.

"Whoa! Where'd you get all this?"

"Long story. Doesn't matter. And you can't say a word. I told Jonathan months ago that it was going away. Just grab a few bottles off the top while I get the cards."

"I won't say a word. Hey, if you get busted with this, I've got amnesia again, my friend."

Caleb laughed. "Just grab one and get out here."

Aryl lifted the top crate and froze. He squinted and tilted his head, taking a moment to be sure he was seeing what he thought he was seeing.

"All this is what? Brandy? Gin?" he called.

"Little bit of everything."

"So it seems," Aryl whispered as he bent down and reached into the center of the pile. He pulled the cork out of a bottle and smelled. He closed his eyes. His body washed over with relaxation. Hunger pains growled from somewhere deep in his soul.

"What's taking you so long?" Caleb yelled. "I can't shuffle forever."

"I know you, Caleb, and you're probably setting the deck."

"If you don't hurry, I will."

"Just deciding between gin and brandy."

Caleb stopped suddenly, and his eyes flashed. He dropped the cards and walked to the back of the barn just in time to see Aryl coming out, holding a bottle of cherry brandy.

"Will this do?"

"Yeah," Caleb said, eying the stack over his shoulder. Everything seemed to be in order. He breathed a sigh of relief and closed the stall door.

"You didn't have to be a baby and throw the cards down," Aryl said, grinning.

"Well, if you didn't move as slow as an old lady, I wouldn't have."

Aryl opened the bottle while Caleb picked up the cards.

"So, Blackjack for answers, huh?"

"Sure. Why not."

"We should get Jon."

Caleb shook his head. "Let's keep it just us for now."

Aryl's eyes were wide and excited. "No, I'm gonna go get him. That way I won't have to repeat myself later."

"How am I going to explain the brandy? He doesn't know I have it."

"I'll say it's mine." He held up a finger. "I'll be right back." He grinned and jogged to the door.

Caleb sighed and slammed the cards on the table. He eyed the bottle and shook his head. *Only for fun times*, he reminded himself of his promise to Arianna. He bounced his leg, waiting impatiently. Something bigger nagged at him.

He rose with a start and opened the door to the stall. He put his hands on the top crate but then stopped. Deep down, he really didn't want to know. But, deeper down, he knew it would explain a good many things about Aryl's behavior since he'd returned home. And if any opiates were missing, he'd have his own explaining to do to Marvin. He lifted the crate quickly, jerking it off to the side with closed eyes. He opened them, and his shoulders dropped.

"Oh, no."

Three bottles from the top were missing. He knew Aryl wouldn't be back today.

His first instinct was to run to Jonathan and tell him, get his help. But he couldn't. Jonathan thought the stuff had been moved. He felt trapped and picked up a bottle of gin, very much wanting to indulge—to forget the mess he'd gotten himself into.

Claire knew she was doing the right thing as she set out for Gordon's, even if it was going to be hard on both of them. Gordon had been good to her. And even though she wasn't in love with him, she did care about him a lot. She was even sure that with time, she would have loved him. He had helped her through the worst time in her life, and she couldn't simply *never* speak to him again after getting ousted from his own wedding. She owed him more than that.

She knocked on the door and took a deep breath, suddenly not wanting to do this. She fought the urge to run away.

He peeked through the curtain, and there was a delay in opening the door. When he did, he tried to smile.

"Hello, Claire."

"Hi, Gordon."

They simply stared at each other. Finally, Gordon spoke. "I'm happy for you, Claire. Really, I am. It's a miracle."

"I want to apologize, but that feels wrong. I'm not sorry he came back. I am sorry that you might be hurting."

"Might be?" He gave a gruff laugh. "I think it's safe to say that."

"I never wanted to see you hurt."

"I know that, Claire. This whole thing, it's a happy ending for you, a one in a million happy ending at that, and tough luck for me." He shrugged. "But, if it had been Marjorie that showed up right before we said our vows, I can't say that I wouldn't have run right into her arms. Maura talked to me for a bit after I left that day."

"So you don't hate me then?"

"No, I don't hate you."

"I'll never forget what you did for me," she said, beginning to get choked up. "How much you helped me to feel alive again. How much you cared. I'll always be grateful."

He nodded, his face beginning to reveal stinging emotion.

"You're welcome," he managed. Clearing his throat, he stepped back. "I've got something in the oven if you don't mind. Best of luck, Claire." And he closed the door.

She stood for a moment not feeling ready to leave. Not sure what she had wanted to accomplish by coming here, but she didn't feel like she'd done anything but further upset his day.

MAY 16, 1931

Caleb knocked on the door, worried that Aryl would be the one to open it. Thankfully, Claire did. She looked tired, her hair a bit unkempt and she seemed thinner. She held Jac around the belly, facing out. He stared, as he did with every visitor.

"Oh, hey, Caleb. Come in."

He stepped inside and looked around. "If you're here for Aryl, he's still sleeping."

Caleb glanced at his watch. "It's almost noon."

She averted his eyes and focused on the baby. "Well, he had a rough night. Trouble sleeping. And it's Saturday, so..." She shrugged her shoulders.

"That's okay. I'm here to talk to you anyway."

"Me? Why?" Jac began to fuss, and she turned him around against her shoulder, patting his back.

Caleb spoke quietly. "I know I'm not the only one that notices Aryl is different."

Her eyes avoided him. "No. They say it's to be expected after what he's been through. That he'll be back to his old self in time." She nodded firmly and patted Jac's back harder.

"Have you noticed the mood swings? One minute, he's almost like the old Aryl. And the next he's, well, he's an ass."

She glanced at Caleb and back to the baby.

"He's been moody, yes."

"And have you noticed that when he really gets on an angry streak, he walks away, and when he comes back, he's merry old Aryl again?" He knew she did. But would she admit it?

She stopped patting. "Yes," she said cautiously.

"I think I know why he's like that."

"Because of the accident, that's why."

"No. No, Claire, there's more to it than that. I think he's using opiates. Hooked on them, even. He can't live without them."

After a second, she broke out in a smile. "Now, that's ridiculous, Caleb. Really." She took the baby to the couch and laid him down, checking his diaper.

"Claire, I'm serious."

"Look, I'm having a hard time with the way Aryl has been since he came back. But that's quite an assumption to make. Opiates. Honestly, Aryl would never touch the stuff!"

"Shh! Lower your voice, please." He stole a peek at the stairs and moved closer to Claire.

"It's hard to think about, I know. But I have proof."

She stopped, wet diaper held mid-air. "What proof?"

"I can't explain, exactly. I'm not supposed to say anything to anyone, and this particular secret is proving to be a lot harder for me to keep than any other."

"You've never been good at secrets, Caleb."

"Well, I have to try with this one. Please, take my word for it. I know he's using it."

With a dismissive shake of her head, she went back to changing the baby.

"I have another question for you. Have you wondered at all how Aryl's mother knew he was alive all this time?"

"She said something about the gypsy lady in town."

"And how did she know?"

Claire scoffed. "Dumb luck. Of all the wives and mother's she's been feeding that line to, she got lucky with this one. I've heard her business has tripled since Aryl got back."

"What if it wasn't luck? What if she is gifted and she really knew."

"I don't know, Caleb," she said with a sigh. "What are you getting at?"

"Another question."

"I do have work to do, you know." She stood, shifting Jac and walked the soiled diaper through the kitchen out into the mudroom, tossing it into the wash bucket.

"Do you ever wonder where he's been? He hasn't told you, has he? Keeps it all secretive and dodges the subject. Aren't you curious?"

She stopped and turned slowly. "I do wonder, Caleb. But he'll tell me in his own time."

"I don't think he will." He put his hands on his hips and stood tall. "I don't think he has any intention of telling us, and I think it has to do with the opiates." He saw the frown cross her face and quickly corrected. "Mood swings, then."

"Well, what do you suppose we do?"

"We could go to the gypsy that knew he was alive. If she knew that, she might know where he has been."

"You're putting a lot of stock in this woman. Smoke and mirrors, I'm telling you."

"Just go with me into town to see her."

"I couldn't afford it anyway, Caleb." She cast her eyes down. "Since I won't let Aryl go back out on the boats, and he hasn't found any other work, we're living on charity."

"I've got payment covered. It's in booze, but I'm sure she'll take it." He held out his hand. "Please? I know you might be content to wait patiently, but I need to know. Besides, it'll do Jac good to get some fresh air."

She flipped her hand in the air. "Fine. Let me get a blanket for Jac and leave Aryl a note," she said as she walked away.

CLAIRE SMILED DOWN at Jac as she pushed the old stroller toward Main

Street. She'd found it in the attic of their rental house, and it had cleaned up well.

Caleb was deep in thought as they walked, and when they got close to the storefront taunting fortunes and spells, he picked up his pace.

With his hand on the doorknob, Claire stopped.

"You go. I'll wait out here."

"No, I thought you wanted to know."

"There's nothing saying this woman knows what she's talking about. I don't believe in all this garbage, and even if I did, I respect Aryl enough to wait until he's ready to tell me himself."

"I don't think you want to know."

"Yes, I do!"

"Then let's find out."

With pursed lips, she looked up, defiant and said, "I will. From him."

"Fine," he said and threw open the door. Claire pushed the stroller to a bench and waited, watching people as they went about their day.

AFTER WHAT SEEMED LIKE FOREVER, but in reality, had only been twenty minutes, Caleb returned, white-faced and shaken.

"Did you find out what you needed to?"

"Yes and no."

"I'm telling you, Caleb. She got lucky with this one."

She watched him as they walked down Main Street. "Whatever she told must have been important. You look like you've seen a ghost."

"She had some to say about Aryl, but then she went off and started telling me things about myself."

"Like what?"

"Things I'm not sure I wanted to know," he said quietly.

"You can't put too much stock in whatever she said, Caleb. Did you find out where Aryl has been?"

"Well, no."

"See. She didn't tell you what you came to know because *she* didn't know. But she did get you worried about yourself. She's probably pretty confident you'll come back to find out more." She shook her head slowly. "It's a scam."

As they passed a small office with a rickety shingle, something in the window caught Claire's eye. She only had to think for a moment before handing the stroller off to Caleb.

"Your turn to sit and wait. I'll be right back."

She pushed open the door and stepped inside a small, sparsely furnished office. A young woman looked up from an old, discolored wooden desk.

"Can I help you?" She had full, dark brown hair, messily piled on her head beneath a fedora hat. She smiled, her teeth slightly crooked and coffee stained.

"I saw your sign in the window. Are you still looking for an artist?"

Her eyes lit up as she stood and extended her hand. "I am. My name is Muzzy Brown."

Claire smiled. "Muzzy?"

She waved her hand, scrunching up her nose. "It's an old nickname that just stuck. Can you draw?"

"Well, I paint, mainly. But I can draw as well. What exactly are you looking for?"

"Someone to do a satire piece twice a week."

"I think I could do that."

Muzzy sat back down. "Do you mind if I see some of your work?" she asked, trying to look official.

"Oh, I didn't bring any." Claire pointed toward the door. "I can go get some of my paintings if you'd like."

Muzzy handed her a tablet and a pencil. "Maybe you could just show me here?"

Claire took the tablet, crossed her legs, and placed it on her knee. "What would you like me to draw?"

"Whatever comes to mind." Muzzy smiled.

She went to work, sketching, tilting her head this way and that, turning the tablet, and after giving it a nod of approval, handed it over.

Muzzy laughed. It was a drawing of her, as she appeared to Claire, sitting at her desk. Only she had a bubble above her head holding the words, "You're hired!"

"This is good." She nodded. "But can you do satire?" She leaned forward eagerly. "That's big in New York and Boston right now. That's what I need. Outrageous, thought-provoking, defiantly political, and funny. "

"Hmm." She held out her hand for the tablet, and Muzzy passed it to her. Claire thought for a moment before setting her pencil to work.

"You want some coffee?" Muzzy asked.

"Love some, thanks," Claire said without looking up.

"Cream and sugar?"

"Black is fine."

"I'll be right back." The door behind Muzzy's desk was labeled, "Mr. Brown, Owner." She opened it a crack and slipped through sideways. A few moments later, she emerged with two cups of coffee.

"Here ya go." She tried to steal a peek as she set the mug on the far side of the desk. Claire stopped drawing, but kept her eyes on the tablet and reached for the mug.

She took a sip and her eyes went wide. "Wow, that's strong!" She looked up at Muzzy, who was smiling back at her. It explained her frazzled, wired appearance.

"Newspaper business is demanding. That stuff keeps me going."

"For days, I'm sure."

Claire went back to work, and Muzzy began reading over copy for the next edition of The Rockport Review.

"There. How's this?" She handed it over and cringed slightly, waiting for Muzzy's critique.

She slammed her open hand on the desk and let out a laugh. "This is perfect! I love it! Wall Street fat cat strolling down Main Street screaming, "Recovery! Recovery! Tomorrow is looking brighter than ever!" and there's change falling from his pockets. You've got these peasants ignoring what he's saying and dashing for the pennies falling to the ground." She sat, staring with an open smile. "It's perfect. Just what I need." Looking up at Claire she said, "You're hired."

Claire beamed and did a little wiggle in her seat. "Really?"

"Yes, really. But before you accept, you should know a few things. This is a small paper. A start up, really." She cast her eyes down. "A newsletter, if I'm being perfectly honest."

"That's okay, everyone has to start somewhere. Even the New York Times started with that first paper."

"And a hell of a lot more money than I have. Er, than the owner has." Her face went serious as she pointed over her shoulder at Mr. Brown's office.

"But I'm looking to expand. I've got big ideas. Big dreams. I'm gonna build this paper up and expand it, and it's gonna be huge. You'll see."

"I'm sure you will, Muzzy."

"The other thing, it doesn't pay much."

"That's fine."

"No, it *really* doesn't pay much." Her eyes went wide with a smile. "But you get a free subscription!"

Claire laughed. "Sounds good."

"I need two of these a week. Paper comes out Tuesday and Saturday, so I'll need the copy the day before each printing. Early in the morning. Even the night before is fine. I don't have a large print run right now, but, as I get bigger, I'm going to need it..." She paused, looking up at the ceiling. "Two days before the run."

"I can do that," Claire said, wondering how much coffee Muzzy had already this morning.

"And I'd like to have a staff meeting once a week for everyone to plan and come up with ideas. The first one is tonight. Can you make it?"

Claire bit her lip, wondering if Aryl was ready to watch the baby for a few hours. Ready or not, he was going to have to. After all, she had a paying job now, despite how little it paid, and he didn't. He needed to support her in this.

"I'll be here. What time?"

"Seven o'clock. Right here, and I'll have coffee ready."

"Sounds good. Who all will be at the staff meeting?"

Muzzy looked off to the side, pretending to count. Then she grinned, and her eye twitched. "Me and you."

~

ARYL WAS AWAKE, sitting at the table with a cup of coffee when Claire walked in. Jonathan and Ian were sitting with him. None of them appeared very happy.

"Where've you been?" he asked.

"I've been in town. I left a note." She nodded a hello at Jonathan and Ian before continuing. With a big smile, she announced, "I got a job!"

Aryl's face fell into shock, and she held her hands up. "I know what you're thinking, but it isn't full time. I'm working as a cartoon artist for that little newspaper. I can do all the work here, and I only have to go in for one meeting a week." She beamed with excitement. "It's not much money, but everything helps, right?"

Aryl stretched his torso in his seat and readjusted. "Jon and Ian here were just talking to me about that. Going back to work." He shot an angry look at them that Claire didn't understand.

"Aryl, be fair. We've tried to be. You've had a little time to get used to being home again. We just don't think it's fair to keep splitting the money we make on the boat four ways when only three of us are working."

"We thought you'd be appreciative," Ian said. "We set that up for Claire and Jac, so they'd have your share of the income for as long as they needed it, even though you were gone."

Aryl looked down, temporarily shamed. "I am."

"But now that you're back..." Jonathan trailed off, waiting for Aryl to finish the sentence.

"Yeah, I get it. What time do you guys shove off? I'll be there." He crossed his arms with a creased brow.

"Now hold on a minute!" Claire yelled. "He's not going back out there, Jon. Not ever."

"Claire, I understand your hesitation. But we can't keep going like this. The other families are nearly starving."

"Then cut us off! But he's not going back."

"We don't want to cut you off. That's not why we're here."

"Claire, I'll handle this, okay," Aryl said with a hint of irritation.

"Excuse me?" she asked, putting her weight to one side with her hand on her hip. "You'll handle this? Well, Aryl, you better handle it the right way. Because I will not have you go back out on that boat again! You won't be so lucky next time."

He looked up, his tired eyes circled in dark. "Lucky?" he asked. "You have no idea what you're talking about." He swung his head back around to Jonathan. "What time Monday morning?"

"Dawn."

"I'll be there."

Claire waited until they left before she started yelling. "Aryl! Have you lost your mind? How can you do this?"

"I have to do this. I don't know if you've noticed, but there aren't a hell of a lot of jobs out there. You should consider me lucky to be able to simply go back to work when I want to."

"Well, I don't. Not doing that. Not back on that boat."

Aryl squinted, rubbing his aching head. "Claire, just relax, okay? It's fine."

"Aren't you afraid?"

"No."

"How can you not be?!" she screamed, stamping her foot.

He jumped up and stood very close, looking down on her, and whispered angrily. "Because I've learned there are a lot worse things to be afraid of than dying."

"What are you talking about?" she asked, shrinking back.

"People. And the things they can do. The things they are capable of. You have no idea."

She reached out to put a hand on his arm. He brushed it away at first but let it rest when she persisted. "Are you talking about the life you had while you were gone? You know that whatever happened, whatever you went through, I will still love you, Aryl. Nothing can change that."

I can change that, the monster whispered. Aryl closed his eyes, willing it away. It had only been a few hours since he fed it. It had been growing hungrier over the last few days, developing a voracious appetite.

"I don't want to hurt you, Claire," he whispered.

"Where did that come from?"

333

When she looked into his eyes, she could see a soul in pain.

"I'm so worried about you. Tell me what happened. Please?"

"I can't." He shook his head and turned.

She grabbed his arm. "Wait."

The monster roared up, shook her off, and yelled something unintelligible. She recoiled, frightened.

He looked horrified for a second, whispered, "I'm sorry." And ran to the bathroom. From under the sink, he pulled out his bag. Doing it now to keep her safe.

AS HE SAT on the bathroom floor with his head in one hand, an empty bottle in the other, the idea came to him. He dug through the bag finding the remaining two bottles. He wanted to feel guilty for taking them from Caleb, but he had no business with them anyway. A stash like that could get a man locked away for a long time. He was protecting him. Yeah, that's it. Protecting his best friend. It was the least he could do after all he'd been through. And, if he took a little more, that wouldn't hurt anybody. Aryl stuffed the bag back into its hiding place and bent over the sink to wash his face, working it all out in his head.

CLAIRE WAS SITTING on the couch with Jac. She wiped at her eyes angrily and tried to smile whenever the baby looked up at her.

"All right, I won't go," he said quietly from the doorway.

She looked up, shocked. "Really?"

"Really."

"What are you going to do?"

"I'm going to go out and find a job."

"But you said—"

He sat down beside her, took her hand, and touched the baby's curly brown hair. "I know what I said. Don't worry about it. I'll find one. I won't let you and Jac go without."

"I never thought you would, Aryl. I just can't have you go back out to sea. I'd rather starve. I can't do that again," she said, her eyes brimming with tears.

"Well, put it out of your head. I'll go tell Jon to keep his money, and I'll start looking for work, okay?"

He smiled, and his eyes crinkled at the edges. Pulling her over to him, he kissed the top of her head and then Jac's. "I'll be back in a few hours."

MAY 18, 1931

Marvin's fist hit Caleb's gut like a hammer. It knocked the wind out of him, and he sank to the ground, grimacing.

"Where is the rest of the stuff, Caleb?"

"How the hell should I know?" he grunted. "I stopped drinking months ago."

"Not the gin, you idiot. The *other* stuff. The stuff in the middle."

"I don't know what you're talking about."

"The hell you don't!" Marvin roared as he yanked him off the ground by the shirt and threw him across the room. "I know that Irish bastard told you all about it. I knew he couldn't be trusted. I should have taken him out when I had the chance."

Caleb rolled to his hands and knees, trying to catch his breath and trying to figure out what *the hell* had just happened. Two minutes ago, Marvin had walked in, chipper as ever, joking and smiling. He went to the back stall and came out raging. Next thing Caleb knew, his guts were getting kicked in. Marvin moved next to him and delivered another to his ribs.

"That's for the fundraiser dance," he grunted and began pacing. "This is the thanks I get for saving your friend from Victor? You steal from me?"

"I didn't steal anything." He rolled and started crawling toward the stall. Marvin yanked him up to his feet, and Caleb had the detached thought that Marvin sure was a strong bastard for someone so small. He shoved Caleb along into the stall. The top boxes were removed, and the center was empty.

"You know how much was in there?" he asked.

Caleb shook his head.

"About ten thousand dollars' worth. More money than you'll ever make in your pathetic life." He gave him another shove. "You had better know where it went so I can get it back."

"I don't know." Though he had a good idea, and that idea made him sick.

Marvin raised his fist and then stopped. "Maybe I'll just go ask Patrick. He knew about it." He turned to leave, and Caleb grabbed his arm.

"It wasn't Patrick. I don't know who it was, but I know it wasn't him," he panted.

Marvin put his hands on his hips and dropped his head, taking several deep breaths. When he looked up, he was smiling.

"What it comes down to is this. We have one hell of a problem here."

"No shit," Caleb muttered, sitting down, holding his ribs.

"What I'd like to know is, after Patrick told you I was storing cocaine and opiates here, why didn't you ask me about it?"

Caleb shrugged. "I thought about it. Seemed better not to. I figured you'd get rid of it eventually. What the hell were you doing with it, anyway? You can't tell me that we have that much cocaine running through Rockport."

Marvin paced, and Caleb could read the deliberation on his face. Finally, he spoke. "Not through, Caleb. In."

It took a minute, as most things did with Caleb, but he figured it out quick enough.

"So, you are crooked." He didn't sound surprised, just stating a fact.

He just stood, letting his smile answer the question.

Marvin laughed. "I wear many hats. Some are more profitable than others."

337

"Well, you need to get this damn hat out of my barn. It's caused enough trouble."

"It's not that easy, Caleb. You owe me now. Not only do you owe me for saving your friend's life, you owe me for ten thousand dollars' worth of precious cargo. I have people to answer to, you know. And I don't mean Vincent." He pointed a finger, his smile gone. "Either you get it back, or you pay me personally."

On the way to his car, he saw Patrick heading down the hill toward the barn. He raised his hand in the shape of a gun and whispered, "*Pow.*"

THAT NIGHT, as they slept, the cabin caught fire and quickly burned to the ground. Patrick, Shannon, and the children barely escaped with their lives. All their hard work, gone.

MAY 21, 1931

Vincent pulled into Jonathan's drive. He was quick to show him a big smile and a casual wave. Being the usual bringer of bad news, and this time, he didn't have any, he didn't want to alarm Jonathan.

"Beautiful day," he said, taking off his hat, squinting up at the clouds.

"It is. What brings you out?" Jonathan asked.

"Just wanted to talk a minute."

"I told you, Vincent, I'm done. I don't care what's going on with the rest of the world. I've got my plate full here and—"

Vincent raised his hands in an effort to settle him.

"I respect how you feel, and I'm not here to inform you of developments or give you any news."

"Oh," Jonathan said, visibly relaxing. "Then you just came by to tell me it's a beautiful day?"

"I just had a couple questions, totally unrelated to recent events in your life," Vincent said quickly. "Wanted your opinion on something."

"Okay."

"You know, Jon, this is a small town with small doings. And while I'm a little older and a little slower, I'm still sharp enough to know when something's amiss. When something just doesn't add up."

"And what is it that doesn't add up that has nothing to do with recent events in my life?" Jonathan asked warily.

"Trust me, nothing to do with you. But in this business, you learn who you can trust and who you can't. I can trust you. I value your opinion."

Jonathan's expression was frozen with anticipation.

"What do you think about Marvin?" he asked. He'd been staring at the dirt, but squinted up at Jonathan, waiting for his answer.

"I think...he's your deputy. He's never come across to me the wrong way, but he seems real private. We went to dinner once at his house. He killed Victor. Other than that, I don't know a lot about him." Jonathan crafted his answer carefully, wanting to avoid getting involved in any dramatics.

Vincent nodded. "Has he ever poked around about the boat sinking and the thing with you and Victor?"

"Once, right after he came to town, but I figured he was just trying to get a handle on the town and what had happened recently."

"Okay," Vincent said.

"Is there anything in particular you want to know that I haven't answered?"

"I don't think so." Vincent looked up and smiled. "Thanks anyway." He moved toward his car.

Jonathan put his hands on his hips and dropped his head. "Trying to put the pieces together, huh?"

Vincent turned and nodded. Jonathan growled and shook his head. He didn't want to know. He didn't want to get involved. But something inside urged him to press Vincent for more.

"All right, Vincent, I'll bite. What are you trying to put together."

"Well, seems like the running of alcohol through Rockport has all but dried up."

"That's a good thing, right?" Jonathan asked, quickly adding, "Legally speaking, that is."

Vincent grinned. "It's unusual. All the small suppliers have turned tail and run. Moved away, and while I haven't caught any runners in months, the whole town is drowning in it. And worse. Opiate use has skyrocketed. It's everywhere, yet I can't find a source."

"And how would any of that involve Marvin?" Jonathan asked.

"Looking back, it seems like it all started changing shortly after he showed up."

"Maybe it's his formidable presence," Jonathan said, and Vincent laughed.

Jonathan wrestled and debated with himself. Finally, he said, "If I tell you something, do you swear on your badge that you won't ever use my name?"

"Of course."

"Check with Caleb."

"What would Caleb know?"

Jonathan shook his head. "I'm not saying any more than that. Just check with him. Ask him the same questions you asked me, but *do not* tell him you were here."

"All right, thanks, Jon." He looked as though he were trying to be casual about the way he left, but Jonathan could sense the urgency in his steps.

IT WAS A WARM AFTERNOON. After lunch, Arianna put the twins down for a nap, made lemonade, and brought a glass out to Caleb, who sat on the porch swing. She made him kiss her before she'd hand it over, and then went back inside to knit with Shannon by the open window until the twins woke up. He sipped it looking out over his land, pondering problems he could share with no one. Marvin had begun restocking, sneaking in through the back hatch, but insisted on moving it to the loft, deep in the corner and out of sight.

Whether he was responsible for it or not, a massive debt hung over his head and threatened to destroy everything he'd fought to keep together. Everything Arianna had boasted as all they could provide their children with. He'd wanted to broach the subject with Marvin but couldn't find the right words. He sighed heavily and ran his hand through his hair. He watched Vincent turn up the long drive to the farmhouse and pull up next to the barn. Caleb moved off the porch and met him as he was getting out. Caleb moved to stand in between Vincent and the barn door.

"Afternoon, Caleb."

"Afternoon, Sheriff. How can I help you?"

"Oh, I was just in the neighborhood and thought I'd stop by and see how things were going."

"Going fine. Got another little one on the way. Twins are getting big. Vegetables are good this year." Caleb looked over his shoulder at the field behind the house. "Can't complain."

"Good to hear. I can't help but notice you're looking real good these days."

"Quit drinking," Caleb said. "So much, anyway. I still have one with Jon every now and then."

"That's good. I've seen that stuff destroy some homes."

"That's no lie."

"Have you seen much of Marvin, by chance?"

Caleb stiffened, putting on as blank an expression as possible.

"No, not recently. He stops by every once in a while."

"Oh, does he? Why?"

He decided to use the same story he'd given to Arianna. "I think to check on me. Make sure I don't fall back into a bottle."

"Sounds like something a good friend would do."

"Oh, I wouldn't say we're good friends," Caleb said.

"What are you then?"

"Oh, I don't know. Friends, I guess. Not a real close one. Not like Jon."

"No, he isn't like Jon, is he?" Vincent twisted his mustache, taking his time with his next question. "Tell me, Caleb, even though you aren't real good friends, what's your impression of Marvin?"

"He's..." Caleb's mind scrambled, his eyes darted, and he shrugged. It was better to say nothing at all. "What's there to think?"

"Just thought you might have an opinion. Has he ever talked to you about the trouble with Victor?"

"Yes," Caleb said, instantly wishing he could take it back.

"Tell me about that," Vincent said, his ears perking up.

"He was just trying to help, is all, to help me, not help the case."

Vincent took note of his skittish movements and halted speech and knew he was onto something.

"When was this?"

"Um..." Caleb glanced at the clouds, trying to think. "Last September, I think."

"Okay. Has he talked to you about anything else?"

"No."

"He's never mentioned anything about alcohol or opiates running through here?"

"No, why would he talk to me about that?" Caleb strained to remain calm and unreadable.

"Well, you and Jon run some boats. We've had a lot come in that way lately. Thought he might have mentioned it." He stared at Caleb expectantly.

"No, sorry. Nothing like that."

"Okay. Well, if you remember anything or if he does mention it, do me a favor and stop by the office."

"Sure."

Vincent got back in his car and slammed the door. "And you don't need to mention this visit to him if it's all the same."

"No problem," Caleb said and held his hand up as Vincent backed up and drove away.

He could sense he was being watched and checked the windows of the house. They were empty. He walked back to the porch preparing something to tell Arianna explaining Vincent's visit.

MARVIN PULLED his eye from the knothole inside the barn.

"Dammit, Vincent. You couldn't leave well enough alone," he said as he replaced his deputy's hat and left the barn through the back hatch.

MAY 25, 1931

Aryl came home with flowers, meat, cake, and a toy for Jac. He set the bag he always carried on the couch and called for Claire.

"Where did you get all this?" Claire asked, amazed. She hadn't seen a cut of beef this nice for the better part of a year.

"Work," he said, smiling. "I told you I'd take care of you."

"Where did you find a job?"

"That's not important. Where's Jac? I want to show him what I bought him."

"He's sleeping." She held her hand out, and Aryl handed her a beautiful silver rattle. "How on earth can we afford this?"

"Let me worry about that. Why don't you get started on dinner? I know you'll make that roast divine."

She took it and moved slowly to the kitchen with Aryl following her. "Did you get on at the quarry or another boat?" she asked, knowing a week's wages at either place wouldn't buy all this.

"Did you see your flowers?" he asked.

"I did. Thank you, Aryl." Looking back, she saw he had left, and she put the flowers in a mason jar with water before seasoning the beef. She worked quickly, lit the oven, and tossed it in, and she returned to the living room where Aryl was turning on the radio. "I'd just like to know where you'll be all day. What if something happens and I need to send for you?"

"Claire, I told you I was going to take care of you and Jac, and that is exactly what I'm trying to do. Please trust me."

"It's not a matter of trust, Aryl." *What a lie*, she thought to herself. She moved to the window and stared, feeling his hands rest on her shoulders. He was quiet, and it was so easy at that moment for her to forget the rest. To just feel him near her and ignore everything else. She wanted to so badly.

"I've missed you," he said. "I've missed you so much." His voice was soft, sincere. It was only the old Aryl speaking, and she closed her eyes, hoping he'd stay.

"The last few times it didn't work out so well." He ran his hands down her arms and kissed the back of her neck. "But I think I'm ready. If you are."

She turned around and stood very close to him. He seemed tentative, and she found it endearing.

"I am, Aryl."

He kissed her, and she forgot everything else. The kind of slow, blissful kiss she'd remembered and dreamed about. It awakened a carnal urge in her that she had long suppressed, and she held him tighter.

Then something changed. He stiffened in her arms, his lips morphed into desperate, greedy things.

Suddenly, Aryl kissed her so hard she tasted blood. She broke away and gave him a hard shove. Touching her lips, she realized the blood wasn't hers.

"What's wrong with you, Aryl?"

"Nothing." He held his hands out. "I was just trying to kiss you."

"Your lip is bleeding," she said.

He touched the spot of blood, looked at it, and then wiped it on his pant leg, unconcerned. "You said you were ready. That you wanted to be close to me again."

"Yes, to be close to you, not eaten alive by you."

He sat on the sofa, let out a frustrated sigh, and shoved a hand through his hair. Claire opened her mouth, closed it, and then opened it again to speak. Claire's cheeks and ears grew hot, and she crossed her arms across her chest.

"Don't try to kiss me again unless you can do it the way you used to."

"There's nothing different about how I kiss you. Maybe you've changed. Did you think about *that*, Claire? While I was gone, and you were gallivanting around with Gordon, maybe you got used to the way he kissed you."

She recoiled. "That's not true."

"Well, explain to me then, what I'm supposed to do. Because ever since I came back, I can't seem to do anything right. How am I supposed to be kissing you?"

"I don't know, Aryl, just not . . . rough."

He quieted his restless leg by standing and walking over to her. He put his hands on her shoulders and looked her in the eyes. "I don't want to fight over kissing. Let me try again."

She nodded but didn't uncross her arms.

He leaned in slowly and at first, it was exactly how he'd started the last time. After brushing her lips with his, his mouth was demanding but gentle, leading the kiss with confident passion. Untangling her folded arms without breaking the kiss, he brought them up to his neck. He could feel her slowly relax and melt into him, his need for her making itself obvious. His grip on her lower back and neck gradually tightened, his lips grew more demanding. His heart pounded in his ears.

She stiffened under his hold. He ignored it, pressing her closer, kissing her harder. His short grunting breaths became desperate as he grabbed at her hips and bottom. Her ardor was snuffed out quickly, and she pushed against him. She knew if she didn't stop him soon, he wouldn't be stopped. She tasted blood again as the seam of her dress split at the waist. When he moved his hand to clutch a breast, she took her moment and broke away from him.

"What the hell is wrong with you, Aryl?" she yelled as she stumbled back, touching her swollen lips and holding the seam to her dress closed.

With his hands on his waist, he looked at the floor between them, breathing roughly.

Say it, the monster told him. *Say it or I'll say worse.*

"There's nothing wrong with me," he panted. "I think something's wrong with you."

Her mouth gaped in surprise.

"Aryl—"

He scrubbed his face with his hand and sighed heavily. She expected him to soften and apologize. Instead, he looked at her with a hard glare, his eyes not willing to concede.

Something forced its way to the front of her mind and refused to be ignored any longer. She'd suspected, but now she knew.

"Someone else liked it rough." Claire's statement shocked them both and demanded an answer. He didn't flinch or drop his eyes from hers.

"She made me earn it."

Her breath caught, and she held it tight. Of everything he had ever said, hearing him utter the word *she* was enough to light her blood on fire. Furious tears stung her eyes as she took a few steps toward him, her lips and hands trembling.

"Did you like it, too?" she asked.

His eyes remained cold and distant. "Yes."

Without warning, she brought her knee up sharply, crushing his groin. He collapsed in a grimacing, grunting heap.

"Did you like that, Aryl?" she asked, standing over him. "Because if you did, I'd be happy to do it again!"

He ignored her for the moment, writhing on the floor holding himself, cursing loudly.

Suddenly, his arm shot out and grabbed her ankle, fingers digging into the bone. She yelped, yanked herself free, and jumped over his body before running to her room and slamming the door.

He crawled to standing, and when he rose, he met the hard glare of Maura.

"Sit yer arse back down."

He did, out of obedience or excruciating pain, Maura didn't know.

"Explain yourself."

"I don't have to explain anything to you." He held himself with both hands, staring at the floor.

"You will."

He raised his head and glared.

"Go to hell."

Her hand met his cheek with a loud pop, and after he had righted his head, he stared at her, dumbfounded.

Maura held herself up stoutly, brow knitted and lips set; only her eyes hinted at her true heartache over the situation.

"It's the medicine," she said. "I've been watching you, and whenever you're late for yer medicine, ye turn into the most awful bastard."

He scoffed and sat further back on the couch to afford a little space between them. "It helps me. My lungs were damaged when I almost drowned."

"My arse. Yer mind was damaged by that bottle, and ye know it."

He looked away.

"Do ye have any idea how Miss Claire suffered when we thought you'd died?"

"Well, based on what I saw when I came back, she got over me easy enough."

His head flew to the side again with a sharp jerk from Maura's stinging hand.

"Ye have no idea what yer talking about, ye stupid bastard," she seethed. "But yer in no mind to hear me right now, are ye? Not when ye want the medicine so badly ye forget yourself and those that love ye."

She pulled a small bottle from her dress pocket and tossed it into his lap. He swept it up in his hand and looked up at her. "You had it?"

"I found yer stash under the sink. I wanted to see how bad this craving was, and it's worse than I thought." She paused looking him over as if he were a repulsive insect. "Go ahead. Take it. Then maybe you'll be of a mind to hear what I have to say."

He took a long drink, and Maura waited, sitting on the other end of the sofa, fists balled up on her knees.

After a few moments, his posture relaxed and his breathing eased.

He leaned forward, reveling in relief and leaned his elbows on his knees, hanging his head. "I'm sorry," he whispered moments later.

"I don't want yer damn apology. Ye should be apologizing to that woman in there that nearly died of grief over ye. But you've apologized a dozen times over, haven't ye? Did ye know she didn't eat or talk for days, and it took months for her to return to a decent state of living."

His head stayed low in shame. "I know it must have been hard for her. I didn't mean it when I said she'd gotten over me easily," he said quietly.

"No, ye didn't, ye feckin idiot. How could ye even think such a thing? I've a good mind to slap ye a third time for good measure!" Maura's anger bubbled fiercely. Aryl scooted over closer to the arm of the sofa.

"No one's really told ye, have they. What it was like for her."

He shook his head. "I don't think I want to know."

"Well, isn't that grand. Miss Claire can know of yer vicious romps with some nameless woman, but ye want to spare yourself the details of her misery? Well I won't let ye. I've stood by long enough and been silent. Let me fill ye in, Mr. Aryl, on exactly what yer wife suffered while you were gone."

He shook his head and started to stand.

"Sit!" Maura bellowed. He obeyed.

"When I got word you'd died I was on the next train out. I walked into Miss Claire starin' in shock. The others told me of the night they found out. Did ye know they had to wait fer several hours to find out which one of ye lived?"

Aryl shook his head silently.

"When Caleb got out of the deputy's car, Miss Claire fell to her knees screaming in grief. Mr. Jonathan was there and held her while she cried. She turned on him, beatin' him on the chest, orderin' him to go find ye. She didn't stop screaming for someone to go after ye until the doctor sedated her. When I got to her, it was all I could do to get her to eat a bite, and we could only pray she wouldn't lose the baby."

Maura watched him take a ragged breath as a tear fell on his knee.

"Did ye know that she went to yer lighthouse near every day to talk to ye for six months? That she would walk the beach and stare out over

349

the open ocean, rock herself, and just cry. There was the time she went missing, and we found her sleepin' in the berth of yer boat. I do believe had she not been carryin' yer child she'd have thrown herself into the ocean just to be closer to ye."

Aryl swallowed hard and held his head.

"When Gordon started courtin' her is when she started to show a little life in her. You'll never know the guilt she felt over havin' feelings fer someone else. She asked me a hundred times did I think you'd approve of him. Him being a widower, he understood her sadness and let her have it. They couldn't bear to celebrate holidays for the hard memories, so they set their own. He was good for her, Aryl. Ye need to know that."

He visibly tensed.

"You need to make a decision, and soon. I can see where this road is leading, and it's leading your Claire right back into Gordon's arms. If ye choose the medicine over her, she'll choose him over *you*. I promise ye that."

He sat for several moments quiet, deep in thought. Finally, he spoke. "I've tried to stop," he said. "A few times. I can't."

"Yes, ye can. It's going to be harder than hell, harder than anything you've ever done. But ye can."

"You don't understand. I feel like I'm going to die. My whole body hurts, and my head feels like it's going to explode. I hate myself and everyone around me, and I feel so violent it scares me." He looked at her pitifully. "I don't know how to stop."

Her posture softened, though her face still held a determined hardness.

"We'll help ye. Yer friends and yer family...love of God, I don't know how." She sighed. "But we will." She took his hand and gave it a squeeze. "Ye have to let us, Aryl. Will ye do that?"

He sniffled, giving a quick nod without looking up at her.

Claire found herself on Gordon's doorstep not entirely remembering how she'd gotten there. She shifted Jac to her hip as he made small noises, curiously surveying his surroundings.

She knocked, and a ripple of emotion tore across her face. She hoisted the baby closer and waited. There was a shuffling inside, and the door opened a crack.

"Claire." Gordon's eyes softened as they landed on Jac.

"I'm sorry to show up like this. I needed to talk to you."

He looked uncomfortable, deliberating what to say for a moment.

"Can I come in?"

He moved aside after a quick glance over his shoulder and held the door.

She sat down, arranging Jac on her lap and taking a deep breath.

"I don't know what to do, Gordon," she said and began to cry. "It's horrible. He's not the same person."

When he sat down, he made sure to keep a good distance between them. But he couldn't help reaching out to touch Jac, who smiled at him.

"He has a temper now, and I never know when it's going to flare up. The least little thing sets him off."

"Has he hurt you?" Gordon asked.

She shook her head as he handed her a handkerchief. "But it's getting bad. Maura had to step in yesterday."

"Well, if Maura's involved it'll get straightened out soon enough."

"No. She talked to me after." She threw her hands up. "She doesn't know how to help him. Caleb talked to me about it last week, but I didn't want to believe him. But he's hooked on...something. Caleb says opiates. Might be morphine. Whatever they gave him after the accident." She held her head in her hand. "I didn't believe any of them until last night."

"What happened last night?" he asked not certain he wanted to know.

"He wasn't alone while he was gone. I don't know the extent of the relationship, but I got a pretty good idea about the nature of it."

"To be fair, you weren't either, Claire."

"This was different. There's something sick and wrong about this...*woman*."

She felt violently nauseous as she said the word.

"He won't talk about it. And I don't even know if I want to know. And yet, I *have* to know."

She broke down and sobbed, "I don't even know if I'm glad he's back. Lately, I feel like it would have been better if he had just stayed gone instead of returning angry and broken. Do you have any idea how guilty that makes me feel?" Her tear stained face, wrought with emotion begged him to say something.

Gordon took his time with a response. He focused on the baby. He missed the little guy.

"Have you talked to Jon? All your other friends?"

She felt him placing a gentle wedge between them. This—more specifically, she—wasn't his problem anymore. Wasn't his to care for and look after anymore. That ended the moment Aryl stepped out of the car. Even if he wanted to help, it would be awkward and out of line. Feeling a sudden wave of regret for ever having come, she nodded and began drying her eyes. "I have. They are trying to think of something. No one knows what to do."

She began to gather herself and the baby, signaling the visit was over.

"Claire, I have to be honest with you. It isn't that I don't care. I wish there were something I could do."

"But you can't."

"No, I can't. I don't know how to help either. Even if I did, it wouldn't be proper...it's not proper for you to be here right now—"

From the direction of the kitchen, they heard something fall and hit the ground, followed by a distinctly feminine, "Oh!"

"You have company. I wish you would have said something."

"You looked so sad. I didn't want to turn you away."

"Well, I wish you would have told me, regardless. Who is it that heard our conversation?"

She stood ready to leave but waited for an answer.

"T'was just me, Claire." Tarin stepped into the living room.

"What are you doing here?" Claire asked, shocked.

"I was just visiting, is all," she said softly.

The way he refused to look at her, the way Tarin appeared apologetic, she put the pieces together fast enough. Having no right to be angry, she felt it anyway.

"You realize she's only seventeen?"

He nodded.

"Does Maura know you're here? Because when she finds out!"

"She knows, Claire. And she approves. We didn't want to say anything to ye for fear of hurtin' yer feelings, tender as they are right now. We didn't keep it from ye for meanness. And we didn't mean it to happen, Gordon and I. Not so soon, anyway."

Claire closed her eyes hoping the room would stop spinning, and something would make sense.

"We were going to be married not even a month ago," she said.

Gordon nodded. "Maybe you should sit down, and I can explain."

"Am I that easy to get over?" She looked up at the ceiling, batting her eyes and mouthed the word, *Wow*, in disbelief.

"Please let us explain," Tarin begged.

"Why don't you give me the quick version? I need to get home." Her tone was suddenly hard and short.

"I've loved him since the minute I saw him, Claire. When Jonathan dragged him into the house the first time. He noticed me, too, and thought Auntie was trying to make a match with us. Then he found out it was *you* she wanted to match him with and dismissed his feelings, thinking me too young. When he showed an interest in ye, I backed off. I tried to do the decent thing by ye, seeing how ye needed him more. But then Aryl came back. Auntie and I came over to console him, and I kept coming back after that. Auntie loves Gordon and knows how decent he is. That's why she trusts me here."

"I guess I should be happy for the two of you." She looked them each in the eyes before continuing. "I got my husband back, and you two found true love. Hoorah for happily ever after's," she said, her face rippling again as she turned to the door and left.

ARYL WASN'T HOME when she arrived. While Jac slept on their bed upstairs, she paced the living room floor, desperate for him to walk through the door. When he did, she planned on throwing her arms around him, kissing him, and demanding he tell her everything.

Confront him on his addiction and tell him it wouldn't change anything. She knew, and she still loved him, and they would find a way to help him, and one day, everything would be just how it was before.

She wanted to know everything about the yet undefined, *She*. Claire had to know everything. What this woman smelled like, tasted like, what was her favorite food—everything down to the pitch of her voice. Every detail of her that was like and unlike Claire's own personality. She felt sick at the thought, but it had to be done. Until she knew, she would always wonder, and where there was wonder, there was insecurity. She couldn't handle another shred of insecurity or she might break in two. She had to know everything. It was better to know everything, and she had to know it all, right here, right now. As soon as he got home.

Aryl exploded through the front door.

"Where've you been?" he demanded. Before she could answer, he began searching the house.

She panicked—worried he knew exactly where she'd been. He

looked furious enough. And if he didn't know, it wasn't exactly the right moment to tell him. Instead, she asked, "What are you looking for?"

He didn't answer but grumbled as he pulled a few boxes from the bottom of the coat closet. Finding them empty, he tossed them over his shoulder.

"Aryl?"

"What?!" he yelled, whirling around, glaring at her. He ran his hand through his hair and slapped it on his thigh. "*What*, Claire?"

"I—I was going to offer to help you look for whatever it is you're looking for."

"I don't need your help." He dropped another empty box and threw the door open.

"Where are you going?"

"Out."

She couldn't let him leave. If he did, she wouldn't find the courage later to ask the questions she needed to ask.

"I was at Gordon's earlier," she blurted out.

He stopped and looked at her. "What?"

"You asked where I was. I was at Gordon's." She didn't care if it angered him. She had to get him talking. "Where were you?"

"I was trying to work." He didn't seem concerned with where she'd been but was overly preoccupied with other worries. Jittery and unfocused.

"Where do you go all day and half the night? Where is *work*, Aryl?"

"I don't know now, thanks to Caleb," he grumbled as he walked out.

MAY 30, 1931

Patrick walked around the charred remains of the cabin with an aching heart. Seemed like every time he got close to achieving something, it was torn from him, forcing him to start over. He bent down and pulled some blackened spoons out of the ash. A pot here, a half burned shoe there. Not enough salvageable to matter. And the real kicker was that since Aryl had come back, that's about all the whole lot of them cared about. It's certainly all everyone talked about. Not much fuss had been made about the loss of his home.

Arianna and Caleb opened their home to him and his family again. But it wouldn't do in the long run. The spoon landed back in the middle of the blackened pit. Not worth saving. He was determined to start over. He didn't know how to quit. But not here. There were things going on here that no one would admit to or acknowledge. Bad things that he didn't want to be anywhere near when it all reared its ugly head. He watched Marvin get out of his car and walk towards the barn.

Speak of the devil...

Earlier in the day, he'd asked Caleb for a refund of the money he'd paid him towards the land. He didn't expect him to give it, but Caleb did, and Patrick tore up the contract. When Caleb asked where he was going, he wouldn't say. When would he leave? He wasn't sure. His plans were secret, even to Shannon. After all, she'd tell Arianna, who would, of course, talk to Caleb. And with Marvin being a regular in Caleb's barn...well, it all necessarily had to remain a secret. He'd miss this place a little, he thought. It was the closest he'd ever gotten to having land. And the friends that had grown to be like family? He'd miss them, too, stubborn and blind as they were being right now. Standing up and looking over the farm and its peaceful pasture and large garden, it seemed as if it had been almost untouched by the financial blight that had scarred the rest of the country. Regardless, he would pray for them. He watched Marvin carry a box into Caleb's barn. They were all going to need it. Of this, he was sure.

~

"PATRICK, WILL YOU TELL ME NOW?"

"Not yet. I just need to make a stop at Jon's, and we'll be on our way."

They had left just after dawn on foot. Patrick carried two carpet bags, Shannon carried Roan, and Aislin followed behind. Tired and grumpy, she complained about walking, about leaving and asked if she would go to school wherever they were going.

At Jonathan's, Ava answered the door still in her robe. He asked for Jonathan and she told him that he had already gone to the marina. She invited them in, but Patrick declined.

"We have to be on our way."

Ava spotted the carpet bags, and her mouth dropped open.

"Are you leaving?"

Shannon turned her face, fighting tears.

"Why?" Ava asked, reaching to hug Shannon.

"I can't say. I need you to give this to Jon, please."

She took the letter. "I will, Pat. But I wish you'd tell me why."

"It's in the letter."

She looked helplessly at Shannon again as Jean stepped around her.

"Bye, Aislin."

She ran past Patrick and gave him a crushing hug. "When I learn to write, I'll send you a note." He nodded against her shoulder.

"And I'll send one back. When I learn how."

Aislin broke away with a quivering lip and ran to her mother, hiding her face in her skirts.

Ava didn't know what else to say. She hugged Shannon one more time, kissed Roan, and watched them walk down the street toward the train station.

"She was my first friend," Jean said, struggling not to cry.

"You'll see her again, Jean. I'm sure of it. Patrick and Shannon are like family." She bent down and lifted his chin. "I'm sure they'll at least visit." He nodded with a pout. She set the letter on the side table next to the door. "Let's go get you some breakfast, okay?"

I T WASN'T until they had boarded another train in New York, a west-bound train when Patrick told Shannon of his plans.

"There's some cheap land in Oklahoma. Not a lot of it, but some. That's where we're headed. I have enough to get us there and get a few acres with a little left to get by on. Caleb was good enough to give me back every cent I had paid him."

"But, Patrick, that's so far away!"

"Aye. But the area of land worked has tripled in the last five years! I don't know why I didn't think of it before. We should have headed out there, instead of Rockport, like everyone else that wants to farm. We'd be planting our second season by now." He shook his head in regret.

"Are you sure, Pat? Oklahoma?" Her voice was unsure.

He nodded, his jaw set as he looked out the window. The train jerked forward. "I'm sure." He put his arm around her and settled back with Roan on his chest.

AVA BENT TO lay Amy in her cradle, moving gently to not wake her up. She had begun to teethe, or so Maura had said and was difficult to console lately. She looked down at her with more love than she thought her heart could hold. Still so small and delicate, it seemed like she'd remain a tiny baby forever.

Jean bounded into the room, providing living proof that children grew and changed rapidly, and when no one was looking.

She turned and put her finger to her lips. "She's sleeping," she whispered. She was tempted to lie down and nap herself, tired as she was.

"Oh, I just wanted to let you know the mailman is here."

"Okay, thank you."

"Can I check the box with you?"

"Yes." She took his hand, closing the bedroom door softly. They then walked down the cobbled path to the street. He reached in and took out a small stack of letters, dropped one and bent to pick it up. When he stood, he bumped his head on the metal door and let out a yell. He dropped all of the mail and held his head, fighting tears.

"Oh, let me see," Ava said, bending down and pulling his hand away. There was a red spot on his forehead rising into a lump.

"I know that hurts, honey, let's go inside and put a cool cloth on it."

She scooped up the mail as he continued to make grunts and whimpers in a desperate attempt to be a big boy and not cry.

She smiled down at him as they walked and flipped through the letters. Stepping into the house, Jean closed the door and walked off to the kitchen. Ava stood staring at a letter addressed to her. Her hands were shaking as she tore the seal and opened it. She began to read, and some of the color drained from her face. Feeling lightheaded, she reached back for the side table but leaned a little too hard. It fell backward, spilling the lamp and small stack of books everywhere. Patrick's letter to Jon slipped under the couch as Jean ran into the room to see what had fallen.

"I'm all right," Ava said, struggling to smile. "Everything's fine. I just bumped it, is all." She held the letter behind her back, slowly crushing it into a ball.

~

AVA WAS DISTRACTED and clumsy making dinner. Jonathan tried to talk to her about his day, and most of it went unheard.

She set plates of food in front of them and turned away, ignoring Jonathan, who turned his face up in an attempt to steal a kiss.

He leaned over to Jean and whispered, "Did anything happen today?"

"I hit my head when we checked the mail."

"Ouch. Are you okay?"

"I'm fine."

"Did anything happen with Ava?"

"No." He sucked a long strand of spaghetti through his lips; the end flipped up and smacked his nose.

"Use your manners," Jonathan reminded.

He gave a little pout and picked up his fork.

"Ava, do you want to get away for a little bit tonight?"

"Where am I going to go?" she asked. She hadn't any appetite and stood washing dishes while Jon and Jean ate.

"I meant the two of us. Caleb and Arianna could watch the kids."

"Oh, I don't know, Jon. It's awfully short notice. I don't want to impose."

"Impose? They're our best friends. They won't mind. We'll offer to return the favor whenever they want."

"Where are we going to go? I look a mess, and we don't have any money."

"We don't need money. And you look fine."

"It's getting late."

"It's ten after five. Look, if you don't want to go, just say so."

"It's not that, Jon, I'm just..." She dropped a pot in the sink with a loud crash.

"Preoccupied?"

"Yes."

"Well, let's drop Jean and the baby off at Caleb's and you can tell me about what's bothering you. You'll have my undivided attention."

"I don't know if I want to talk about it just yet."

360

"Then I can have the pleasure of your company."

"I'm sorry, Jon. I just don't feel like going anywhere."

"Are you sure?" He watched her carefully with worry.

"Yes. I'm sure." She wiped her hands dry and left the room.

LATER THAT NIGHT, long after everyone had fallen asleep, Ava crept downstairs. She turned on the light and as quietly as she could, looked through the drawers to find her stationery.

Sitting down at the table after taking one last look up the stairwell, she began to write.

STANLEY,

I received your letter today. In it, you said you might make a trip to Rockport in the near future and call on me. I'm sorry, but that would not be a good idea. I am married now and would have a hard time explaining your sudden appearance to my husband, as I have never spoken of you. I have left the past in the past, and I ask that you do the same. Please don't contact me again.

Ava

HER HANDWRITING WAS SLOPPY; her hands shook. She read over the letter twice, still not happy with the wording, but she lacked the courage to say what she really wanted to say.

"Everything okay?"

Ava jumped, dropping the pen. Jonathan stood in the doorway in his muslin shorts, his tired eyes suspicious as he looked her over.

"Yes," she said and folded the letter quickly.

"Why are you up so late?" he asked with his eyes on the letter.

"I, ah...just had some things I needed to write down. So I wouldn't forget."

"What things?"

"Just...things. Nothing important."

361

"Okay," he still regarded her with a lingering question.

"I'll be along in a few minutes."

He had taken a minute before he turned. "Are you sure everything's all right?" he asked.

"Fine," she said and began to gather up her things. "I'll be to bed shortly." She forced a smile.

JUNE 1, 1931

Jonathan walked through the door yawning. It was well after dinner. The dishes had been washed and put away. Peeking in the icebox, he found a plate Ava left for him as she always did when he worked late. The season was always a busy one, but lower prices meant even longer hours. He was thoroughly sick of seafood but, being something he could bring home frequently that cost nothing, they ate what was available. His stomach growled as he picked at the fish on his plate, not caring that his palate craved something different and exciting.

He heard Jean's laugh from the backyard followed by Ava's flat, quiet voice. His furrowed brow lifted quickly as they came in the back door.

"Dadee, you're home."

"I'm home," Jonathan said with a full mouth.

"Remember your manners," Jean said with a teasing grin.

Ava walked by him holding Amy, and he lifted his head up as she passed.

"Honey, I'm home," he said.

"How was your day?" she asked as she walked out of the room.

"Fine." Jonathan turned his attention on Jean. "What did you guys do today?"

He shrugged. "Not much. I played with Amy, and we took her out to the backyard and let her get some sunshine. She likes birds. I tried to find some crickets to show her, but they are all hiding."

"Try later at sunset. They're easier to find."

"Ava cried today."

Jonathan looked up. "Why?"

He shrugged again. "She told me not to worry about it."

The frown returned as Jonathan went back to eating. "I think I might know why."

"When you find out, will you tell me?"

"That depends."

"On what?"

"If it's adult business or not."

"But I worry."

"I know you do, Jean. I'll let you know if there's anything to worry about, okay? Now go turn on the radio," Jonathan said as Ava entered the kitchen without Amy.

"She's been cranky all day," she said as she filled a glass with water. "She's napping now."

After Jean had left, Jonathan motioned for her to sit down. She seemed reluctant but did.

"Jean said you cried today."

She blew her breath out in frustration. "I told him not to worry you with that."

"Do you want to tell me why?"

"No."

He nodded slowly and took another bite.

"Does it have anything to do with Patrick and Shannon leaving town so suddenly?"

She stared at him, still as stone and said, "Yes, that's it. It was so sudden, wasn't it?"

"You didn't mention it last night when I asked you what was wrong. Don't you think I might have wanted to know that they'd gone? I had to find out from Caleb today."

"I wasn't feeling well and...oh, he did leave a letter for you. It's on the table by the door."

Jonathan rose and walked through the living room, stepping over Jean, who lay on the floor listening to the radio. "Where? I don't see anything."

"It's right there," she said and walked over impatiently. "It was, anyway. It was right here, I swear. Jean, did you move that letter Patrick left?"

"No," he said.

They searched around and under the table, opened the door and looked over the porch, finally moving the search to the kitchen.

"Maybe you put it with the stationery," Jonathan said.

"NO!" she said, slapping her hand on the table.

He stopped, staring at her.

"I didn't. I would remember if I had," she said, trying to regain composure. "I'm sorry, I'm tired, and it's really warm. I'll keep looking for it, okay? Why don't you finish your dinner?"

She managed a nervous smile, keeping her distance from him.

JUNE 7, 1931

Caleb pulled up to the house and checked the address. It was an old neglected place on the edge of town. The yard was over-grown with weeds, a few windows were busted out, and the paint was peeling badly. He didn't know who owned it, and Marvin didn't care to share. Only told him that in order to begin to repay the massive debt for the missing elixir, he was going to have to start doing some jobs for him. Deliveries and pick-ups, mainly. *Monkey work*, as Marvin had insultingly worded it, and during the last week in between fishing, farming, and appeasing Arianna, he'd been traveling to the worst parts of the county, dealing with the lowest dregs of society. This was his fourth 'job' for Marvin.

He took the box from the passenger seat and walked it up the broken front steps. He didn't need to knock as they'd been watching him from the window. A man who looked much older than he probably was opened the door when Caleb reached the last stair.

"You Marvin's man?" he asked. Caleb noticed the bulge under his shirt. Obviously a pistol.

"Yeah."

"You got the stuff?"

Caleb lifted the box he carried. "Right here."

"Bring it in then. Don't stand out here 'case someone comes by."

Caleb stepped inside but not far enough to allow them to close the door behind him. It stunk of mildew and urine. Blankets covered windows. A few people lay passed out over chairs and a tattered chaise lounge. Caleb felt dirty just being here.

"You're a quiet one," the man said. "But that's good. You stay outta my business, and I'll stay out of yours." He grinned. What teeth that weren't busted or missing were horribly stained. He handed over some cash.

"Count it if you want but Marvin trusts me. We go way back."

"That's fine," Caleb said and handed over the box.

"Hey, Johnny boy, come get this and put it in the back room, would ya?"

After a moment, he turned and yelled again. "Johnny!"

Caleb turned to leave, stuffing the money in his pants pocket. He nearly sprinted back to the truck, hating what he'd gotten himself into.

The man watched him slam his door and speed off, leaving a plume of dust. He narrowed his eyes, unsure if he trusted him. Marvin wasn't known for being sloppy, nor was he known for enlisting anyone who was. But there was something about this guy that the man didn't like, something in the way he carried himself. He felt like a fraud.

"Hey, Johnny boy. Didn't you hear me calling you!" the man yelled again.

"Yeah. I was busy," a voice called from the back of the place. "You alone?"

"Yeah, did you see the guy that was just here?"

Aryl stepped around the corner. "No, I heard him, though."

"You recognize his voice, Johnny boy? You know who he is?"

Aryl looked him right in the eyes. "Nope."

JUNE 10, 1931

The whole town was buzzing as Claire made her way to the newspaper office. Not only was everyone moving about a little faster than normal, but they all also regarded each other with awkward, skittish glances. Those who walked closely were whispering. Claire almost smiled wondering what the latest scandal might be and glad that something, anything had taken the town's talk off Aryl returning. The temptation to smile fizzled with the thought of him. He had gotten home very late the night before with no explanation for her, though she'd begged and cried for one. He'd been hard to rouse this morning and not enthusiastic about watching Jac for the bit of time she needed to check in with Muzzy.

There had been moments when she'd caught him watching the baby with wonder. Found him rocking Jac to sleep by the window. Other times, he seemed irritated with the baby's crying and didn't want anything to do with him. This morning he had been somewhere in the middle. Distracted by his own thoughts enough that Claire had to repeat her instructions several times on when to feed Jac.

She stepped into Muzzy's office. It smelled like ink and coffee, and she liked it. She pulled two drawings from her bag as Muzzy looked up.

"Oh, hi! I'm glad you're here. I was starting to get worried."

"Well, here I am." She glanced at the calendar. "It's the day before the print, sorry. I know I said I'd try to get it here two days before, but I've been busy."

Muzzy was especially electrified as she worked frantically, and her fingers continued to fly over the typewriter keys, even as she looked up and talked.

"Doing a special run today with what's happened. If I try, I might could beat Boston in getting this out." She whirled around to grab a pad of notes, tossing a few unneeded sheets over her shoulder and resumed typing.

"What's big enough that would cause a special run?"

The typewriter went silent. "You haven't heard?"

"No, what?"

"What are you—living under a rock?"

She laughed. "I told you, I've been busy."

"The sheriff was found dead in his office this morning. Shot in the back of the head. His secretary found him. There's a murderer in Rockport."

Jonathan sat in Elle's living room. He, like everyone else, was stunned and frightened at Vincent's death. He was growing so tired of death. Tired of black, tired of mourning. Elle walked in, and Jonathan stood up.

"I'm sorry to keep you waiting, Jon. I had to finalize some arrangements."

"That's all right. Is there anything I can do?"

"No. Vincent spoke highly of you." Her voice broke, and her shoulders shook as she suppressed a sob.

"Well, I thought highly of him, too. He'll be missed by a lot of people."

With a weak smile, she sat down.

"Can I help with any of the arrangements?"

"No, I'm having his body taken to Montana."

Jonathan didn't hide his surprise.

"I don't plan on staying here, and I don't want to leave him here. So we're going to leave together." Her tears broke, and she took a moment to gather herself. "I should have let him go years ago. It's where he wanted to be. I was selfish. And now this is all I can do to make it right. Bury him there."

"I'm sure he'd appreciate it. Will you have a service here at least?"

"No. I can't. He's going to be taken on the next train out, so, there's not much to do but pack."

"I know there are a lot of folks in town who would like to say goodbye."

"Then they are going to have to do it privately. I can't bear it." She raised her head, and Jonathan could tell she wouldn't be swayed. "I'm not having one there, just so you know. A service, I mean."

"Are they any closer to finding out who did it?"

"I know the town's in an uproar about it. I might as well tell you since I'm sure it'll be in the papers tomorrow. They are chalking it up to the mafia. My Vincent did such a good job cleaning up this town that they were losing money. They had to do something about it." She drew herself up tall, mustering courage. "I always knew it was a possibility. Part of the job of a sheriff's wife is to be prepared for something like this." Her gaze landed on the window focused on something in the distance. "You're never quite ready, though," she whispered. Her eyes snapped back. "So, you can rest assured there isn't a murderer running around Rockport. No one is in any danger, so long as they aren't involved in running whiskey and opiates."

"No. Do you know who will...who could take his...?" He struggled with a way to put it delicately.

"Marvin is being sworn in as sheriff this morning," she said. "Until elections, anyway."

Jonathan nodded slowly, remembering the last time he saw Vincent. He was asking about Marvin. He didn't trust him. He brushed off the absurd thought. Marvin had already been cleared. Had a rock solid alibi. And though he didn't trust him any further than Vincent did, there was no proof he was crooked. Lawmen had to deal with confiscation and destroying of opiates. And he had gotten the sheriff's supply out of Caleb's barn. Thank God. The last thing he wanted was Caleb caught up in a Mafia drug war.

"We never come to the beach anymore to relax," Jonathan said. "Why is that?"

"It's a good place to think. To talk and plan. That's why we come here." Maura walked slowly, keeping her eyes on the horizon. It was windy, waves crashed in one after the other, and flocks of seagulls called overhead. "I do love the smell," she said.

"The last time we met on the beach to talk it was about Caleb. This isn't about him, is it?"

"No," Maura said, the peaceful look faded. "It's about Mr. Aryl."

"I'm sorry, Maura. I know he's having a hard time adjusting. I don't know what else I can do."

"Well, that's what we're here for. To plot and plan a way to help him." Jonathan was mute.

"I see yer brimming with ideas," she said, giving him a teasing glance.

"I wish I knew."

"Ye don't know, and maybe that's the problem of it. You don't know the extent of the problem. It's much more than having a hard time adjusting. He takes medicine. He says it's for his lungs. But I've not heard him cough or sound in need of it. When he doesn't take it, he gets angry. Mean. There have been a few incidents at the house that Claire forbade me to tell you about."

"Like what?"

"Him not getting his medicine when he needs it. He isn't himself I can tell you that. And what he turns into is ugly. And frightening."

"Why didn't someone tell me about this sooner?"

"I told you. Claire. She had the hardest time accepting anything was wrong in the first place. Made every excuse for him there is. T'was only when I walked in on a terrible fight and confronted Aryl directly that she finally came to accept that he was..."

"Hooked?"

"Aye. Nearly broke her heart, poor thing. She tried so long to deny it. But there's no denying it with how he gets."

"What did Aryl say when you confronted him?"

"He said he would try to let us help. But that was just over two weeks ago. I've tried to talk him into taking less, letting more time pass between doses. Ian's tried too. Aryl gets awful angry. To be honest, he scares me. I don't stand in his way long. He takes it, and he's fine again. For a few hours. Coddling him isn't working. I was stupid to think it would."

"You aren't stupid, Maura. You've never dealt with this before." He sighed. "Neither have I for that matter."

"So you have no ideas?"

"Well, actually, I have one. You said no one really knows about this?"

"Those under our roof. Mr. Caleb is suspicious, at least. If he doesn't know the whole of it."

"What if it came out to everyone? What if we could get him to act like this in front of all his friends, his parents, everyone? I'm sure everyone would be shocked, but he'd have to be so embarrassed he'd see there was a problem. If we all gave him that advice, to start backing down off the medicine, he'd have to listen."

"It could work." She didn't sound convinced.

"Say, where's he getting it, anyway?"

"He told Claire he has a doctor in Boston that's treating him for his *damaged lungs.* I'd like to find that doctor and give him a piece of my mind."

"Do you know who it is?"

"No."

"Maybe we could get it out of him. Let's have a party. A 'thank God Aryl came home' party and get as much information out of him as we can. Speaking of which, has he talked about the last eleven months at all?"

"No. Not to any of us."

"Let's try to get him to open up about that, too. And if he ends up acting like an ass, he'll suddenly be accountable to all of us."

"To be honest, Mr. Jonathan, I don't know if we can get him to leave the house."

"Drag him if you have to."

"I might get in a kick for good measure. The daft arse that he is." Maura bit her lip and growled.

"You love him, Maura. We all do. Let's try this. Who knows, it might work."

"Aye, it might."

He put his arm around her shoulders and squeezed.

JUNE 17, 1931

"Here's to the impossible!" Jonathan raised his glass, quickly surrounded by a dozen others, and the cheers of friends as they huddled around Aryl.

"Thanks, everyone, for coming." He smiled at Aryl. "I can't think of a better reason for a party."

Aryl squirmed, uncomfortable with all the attention paid to him and found excuses to move around often. Claire stayed near him as he moved around the room, holding Jac. Her smile wasn't insincere; it was strained.

Aryl stood near Caleb, who sat on a stool in Jonathan's living room pouring drinks.

"You'd never know there was such a thing as Prohibition with this bunch," Maura said with a wink and held her glass out for a refill. "And that's just fine wi' me!"

Jonathan sidled up to Aryl. The three men stood together unaware of the eyes on them, happy for the sight. Maura went about the room gathering purses and things people were leaving about placing them in a basket by the stairs. Among them, Aryl's bag.

"They won't wait much longer, you know."

"For what?"

"For you to say something."

"Like a speech?" He shook his head. "I'm not good at speeches."

"Unless you're lecturing me," Caleb reminded with a smile.

Aryl remained defensive.

"Not a speech, just a little about where you were. How you got there. You've got to give them something. It's been six weeks. They're dying of curiosity."

Aryl looked at Jonathan, the celebratory mood gone. "No. I don't want to."

He started to say something and Aryl simply walked away. He found a relatively quiet corner and put his back to it, watching the crowd. Everything about his face and body screamed 'leave me alone" and for a little while, that's what everyone did. They chatted amongst themselves, straining to be heard over the radio, gushing over babies and making plans for campouts and beach picnics that summer.

"What the hell, Caleb?" Jonathan asked.

He jerked his head over. "What'd I do?"

"Not you." He nodded toward Aryl. "Him. He looks so hostile. If I were a little more drunk, I'd say he's not even happy to be back."

"I don't know. Maybe he needs to relax a little. That's why we're doing this, right?"

He handed him the bottle and gave him a nudge.

"Oh great, send me." Jonathan grinned.

"I'm right here if you need me," Caleb said with a hiccup. "I've got your back."

"You've barely got your ass in that seat. How long ago did you get started?" he asked with a critical eye.

Caleb gave a sloppy shrug. "Doesn't matter. Aryl's back. We're celebrating."

"You're supposed to be helping me with this."

Jonathan turned, and Caleb grabbed his shirt, nearly falling off the stool.

"What?"

He motioned him closer.

"If he doesn't want to talk, push him gently. It'll come out eventually.

Just be nice. You need to try to *understand* that he's been through a lot." He finished with a slur and an exaggerated blink.

"I can handle it, Caleb." Jonathan rolled his eyes. "Can you handle staying on that stool?"

Caleb laughed and called for Arianna. "Just in case," he said with something that was supposed to be a wink.

"Mind if I join you?"

Aryl's tightly folded arms said no, but he whispered, "Sure."

"You okay?"

"What if I said I wasn't?"

"Then I'd ask how I could help."

His steely gaze remained on the floor in front of him.

"You can't."

"Whatever you tell me, I won't tell anyone. I swear."

His eyes debated, barely breathing. "Outside."

Jonathan opened the front door, and they slipped out. It was dark and other than the noise from the house, quiet. They walked slowly to the street. Finally, Aryl took a deep breath.

"I'm so sick of hearing it. Aryl's alive. Where've you been? What were you doing there?"

"They're curious."

"I know." He kicked a few pebbles down the road.

"I'm all ears. And I'll take it to my grave if you want to tell me."

Aryl walked slowly with his head down, hands shoved in his pockets. "Believe me, I wish I could unload it all."

"Then do it. It might be hard at first, but it'll get easier."

"Judgment."

"Excuse me?"

"It's not that I can't talk about it. I just don't want to deal with every-one's judgment, what they might think."

Jonathan held his arms out, the bottle still clutched in his right hand. "I won't judge. But you won't know that until you give me a try."

"Where I've been...what I've been doing...it's not good, Jon."

Jonathan walked beside him with a clean expression that Aryl checked frequently.

377

"I lived a life over there that I'm not proud of. I'm glad to be home. I'm glad that I remembered who I was, and I don't have to live like that anymore."

"Live like what, Aryl?"

"A constant state of survival. Looking over my shoulder all the time. Worrying about who I could trust. Trying to save people that couldn't be saved."

"Who'd you try to save?"

He took a few seconds to answer, and when he did, he lowered his voice. "This girl named Gina."

It took great effort, but Jonathan kept a neutral expression.

"A friend?" he asked, hoping his voice didn't sound too insinuating.

Aryl's silence was a partial answer.

"How am I supposed to tell Claire about that?" he asked and kicked the dirt.

"That depends on the nature of...*that*."

"I got mad at her the first night I was back. For Gordon."

Jonathan opened his mouth as Aryl continued. "It's not fair, I know. And I have no business being angry at her."

"She thought you were dead. You didn't know who you were. You remember when all that came out at the tenement about Elyse. You got it all out in the open and worked through it."

"I was a one sided ass then, too. When she told me about Steven."

"Now that..." He paused a moment to think. "Aryl, if that didn't tear you apart, this won't. The circumstances are totally different. Have you thought about just telling Claire?"

"She sort of knows this part."

"Sort of?"

He grew increasingly uncomfortable. "She knows there was someone. She hasn't asked for details."

"I'll bet my last dollar she wants to know, though."

He shook his head. "No more than I want to know details about Gordon."

"If that's how you guys need to deal with it." Jonathan shrugged, remembering that he needed to lend a neutral ear, not try to fix the situation. For now.

"I started to treat her like I treated Gina. Or rather..." He grew increasingly uncomfortable. "How Gina wanted to be treated. I wasn't thinking. I got so used to the way she was...the way that whole screwed up relationship was, and I have to constantly remind myself that Claire isn't like that. And that's good," he added quickly. "Claire is the love of my life. The last thing I want to do is hurt her. But it seems to be all I'm doing lately." He looked away, mustering courage. "For some reason, I can't respond to the way Claire is if you know what I mean."

"Why do you suppose that is?"

He shrugged.

Finally, Jonathan felt like he had an opportunity.

"Why don't you sit down with her and get it all out, Aryl. Spill every detail, every ugly detail about the last year and get it out of your system. You can practice on me first if you want."

"No." Aryl turned back toward the house.

"Look, I'm not going to lie to you. Everyone notices you're different. Everyone wants to know why." Jonathan took a deep breath, knowing this was where things could get nasty if Maura were right. "A few of us know, but we haven't said anything."

Aryl slowed down, and his eyes shifted to the side. "Some of you know what?"

"About the medicine."

"That's for my lungs. They were damaged in the accident."

Jonathan stopped and stared at him.

"Bullshit."

For a split second, Aryl looked like a scared rabbit needing a place to run.

"Not once have I heard you cough or wheeze. And you forget, I've been through this whole thing with Caleb."

"Did Maura talk to you?"

Jonathan nodded.

His face showed a flash of anger and then mellowed. "Well, that was a few weeks ago. I'm fine now. I don't hardly need it anymore."

He tried to continue walking casually, but Jonathan didn't follow.

"Aryl."

"What?"

"Let us help."

He turned slowly. His voice was no longer Aryl's. "You can't. Leave me alone."

Just before he reached the porch, Jonathan said, "Come sit on the bench with us and have a drink. For old time's sake and I promise I'll drop it. It's your business."

"Promise?"

Jonathan waved him around the side of the house.

"Sit here. I'll go get Caleb." He handed Aryl the bottle of whiskey and disappeared.

HE GRABBED Caleb by the scruff of the neck. "Get sober, now."

"Whoa, what's going on?"

Jonathan darted over to Maura. "Make some coffee for Caleb, please. I'm getting close to getting through to him."

Maura nodded and went to work.

"Meet me out there as soon as you can and..." He pulled Caleb's face over to look him in the eyes. "Go along with whatever I say, not matter how crazy it sounds."

"Got it," he said with a wobbly nod.

Jonathan returned looking as casual as he could, with two small glasses.

"Where's Caleb?"

"He'll be along. He's way ahead of us, anyway. Here, let's catch up."

Aryl threw his glass back with barely a grimace.

"That's sipping whiskey, you know."

"Well, I'll sip the next one."

"To old times," Jonathan said. "Our old times. This bench was mighty lonely without you."

Aryl adjusted in his seat.

"Sorry, I know you're sick of hearing it," Jonathan said as he poured again.

"It's okay." Again, Aryl downed the drink.

"Can you hold that okay?" Jonathan asked.

"Better than most," he said with a cocky grin.

"Oh, that sounds like a challenge."

He refilled the glasses. Aryl drank, and Jonathan made the motion but let the whiskey fall back in the glass, discreetly dumping it by his leg. For the next several drinks he did this and thinking Aryl was sufficiently drunk enough to get some real information out of him, turned to speak. Aryl beat him to it.

"What the hell are you doing?" he asked. His eyes were cold and accusatory.

"Just relaxing." Jonathan followed his eyes. He was staring past his leg, where he'd been dumping his whiskey. He knew he'd been caught.

Aryl had grown accustomed to being leery of everyone, all the time. He'd learned to read people well. Jonathan was trying to paint this as a long overdue reunion, but he smelled something else.

"Relax, Aryl." Jonathan was trying not to tip his hand. He failed.

"I'm done."

"No, Aryl, wait…come on, we haven't even gotten started! Caleb's not here."

"Were you going to start drinking after he got here?" He looked pointedly at the puddle by Jonathan's shoe.

"I just didn't want to miss anything you said."

Gotcha.

"I'm done." He made a move toward the house and Jonathan bolted up.

"Wait, please."

It wasn't that Jonathan was lying to him. It wasn't that he had a feeling Jonathan was up to something or that Caleb was taking forever to join them. It was the monster rising up, waking from its slumber, and demanding Aryl's attention. The alcohol had delayed it only by minutes. Like drinking water when you're starving. It only did so much.

"Aryl." Jonathan grabbed his shirt.

Aryl shoved him, seeing him now as an obstacle standing between him and his bag. The last time someone stood between them...well, it wasn't pretty. Bloody memories flashed through his mind, and he nearly cried remembering what the monster made him do, needing to get to the medicine so it could take it all away.

"Move, Jon."

"No, I want to talk."

Aryl barreled through him, knocking him into the screen door. One hinge broke, and Jonathan went sprawling in the dirt.

He stomped through the kitchen, into the living room and began to search.

Claire whirled around and clutched the baby closer with a look of terrified knowing.

"Where's my bag," he grumbled.

The chatter started to die down as one by one people noticed him.

"Where's my bag!" he screamed and began pulling furniture out, looking in obscure places, throwing cushions, not thinking clearly in his desperation.

The room fell silent.

"Stop staring at me!"

Maura stepped away from the basket. She'd buried it deep enough. He wouldn't see it walking by. It was part of the plan. To get him worked up to a state without the medicine and to let him show his ass. Through the embarrassment, maybe he'd admit he had a problem. They had arrived at the embarrassing part.

It didn't seem to be working as he raged about the room. Jonathan stumbled in, his leg and side dusted with dirt.

"Get out of the way," he said to anyone listening as he moved closer to Aryl. The women grabbed their children and scrambled toward the door. Only Kathleen stayed, maintaining a distance. Caleb stood up, and Ian moved in to close the triangle, moving toward Aryl slowly—as if he were a wild animal that they were trying to coral.

"Where's my bag?" he screamed.

Kathleen watched with tears in her eyes. She glanced at him and then to the bag in the basket that was poisoning her boy. She'd been told, but she hadn't wanted to believe it. And now she knew. There was something terrible about knowing. Still, she reached out to him.

"Son, just calm down," she said as she moved closer. She made the mistake of touching his arm, and the monster growled, pushing her away. She lost her balance and fell. Ian had caught her before she hit the ground and that gave Aryl a moment. He darted to the basket and dumped it out. Jonathan tried to tackle him, but Aryl slithered out of his grip and dashed for the bathroom. With a slam of the door, Jonathan realized not only had they failed, but it was also worse than any of them had imagined.

LATER, Ian took Aryl home. They made no further attempts to keep him from his bag, and he didn't bother to apologize. He couldn't even look his mother in the eyes as he walked out. Embarrassed he was. Admitting he wasn't. The rest of their household, Claire, Jac, Maura, Tarin, and Scottie stayed at Jonathan's.

"Give him the night to cool off," Jonathan said. Though he would be the first to admit, he had no idea what to do after that.

JONATHAN AND CALEB sat on the bench behind the house. The sobering reality that their friend was in trouble was more effective than coffee, and Caleb sat deep in thought.

"He's here and yet he's not."

"He's addicted, Caleb. He's using it for more than medicine."

Long pause. Deep sigh. Uncomfortable shifting.

Finally, Caleb said, "Remember when our parents used to take us out to the woodshed when we got in trouble?"

"Oh, yeah. Me and you, anyway. I don't think Aryl's parents did that. They just gave him a stern talking to."

After a long silence, Caleb slowly turned toward Jonathan. "Maybe we should take him to the woodshed."

Jonathan grinned. "Who's gonna beat his ass, you or me?"

"Okay, well, maybe not the woodshed, but the woods. We could take him out like we're camping and keep him there until he's off the stuff."

Jonathan nodded slowly. "Not a half bad idea. Might take a while, though. It only takes a few days for that junk to get out of your system but a lot longer for your mind to get away from it."

"We'll keep him out there for as long as we have to. We could take turns, even," Caleb said. "I know the others would help out running supplies and sitting with him."

"They would. The thing is, how are we going to keep him out there?"

Caleb thought for a moment. "We could tie him to a tree."

Jonathan gave a lopsided grin. "Wouldn't that piss him right off."

"How else would we keep him?"

"That would be about the only way."

"I don't care if I have to stay out there the whole time myself, Jon. I couldn't save him before. I won't let that happen again. He needs to be here with us." He gave a hard glance at the space between them on the bench. "And he's not. He's lost, and we have to help him find his way back."

Jonathan stared into the dark yard, thinking. The moon was nearly full, illuminating the clouds, casting the faintest of shadows. He liked Caleb's idea. Besides admitting him into the asylum for feeble minds and lunatics, there wasn't much else to do—and they couldn't do that. People left there worse than when they walked in. If they left at all.

"It's just crazy enough to work. We could tell him that we're just going out on an overnight for old time's sake. Like we used to when we were kids," Jonathan suggested.

"But we'll have to tell everyone else what we're really doing."

"Oh, absolutely."

"I think Maura will like it."

"She'll love it. This sort of thing is right up her alley. I'm surprised she didn't think of it. When should we do it?" Jonathan looked over at him, liking how he'd started to behave lately. A man of decision and action.

"The sooner, the better," Caleb said, sitting up straight, resting his palms on his knees. "How about tomorrow night?"

"Sounds good."

Before Jonathan could stand, Caleb did, shoving his hands in his pockets, looking at the ground.

"I gotta be honest with you about something."

"Oh?"

"Marvin never moved the stash." Jonathan just stared at him. "I asked him to, and he said he tried and couldn't find another place. He offered to pay me a storage fee every month." Caleb shrugged. "I don't have to tell you how hard times are. I couldn't turn down the money."

"I just don't want to see you get in trouble, Caleb."

With a sarcastic smirk, he looked up at the night sky. He wanted to tell him everything. The fact that Aryl stole from the barn and now he was up to his eyeballs in debt to Marvin, the jobs he'd had to do to begin to repay him, deliveries, handling, transporting, and dealing with the ugliest side of society. His shoulders were so heavy as he stood, desperately wanting to lighten their burden. But he couldn't. He could feel Jonathan's disappointment in what little he'd already told him.

Instead, Caleb said, "I'm the one that paid Ava's hospital bill, Jon. I don't want thanks." He held his hands up to shield any gratitude that might come his way. "The only reason I'm telling you is so you know I'm trying to make some good come out of the whole situation. It's true, I didn't have the guts to run him and his stuff off my property, and I know the money Marvin pays me is dirty. But it does good things once it crosses my hands."

Jonathan took a moment. "You don't want thanks, but I'll thank you anyway. That was a huge burden lifted off us."

Caleb shifted uncomfortably.

"You have a big heart, Caleb. But are you sure you—"

"I just needed to tell you the truth. So you'd know. I don't have a big heart. I'm just trying to get through like everyone else. I'd really like to go back to planning how we're going to help Aryl now." He sat back down. "Please."

Jonathan opened his mouth to speak, and Caleb sprang back up. "Dammit!" he yelled as he jumped to his feet.

Jonathan's eyes widened. "What the hell, Caleb?"

"There's more. Aryl knows it's in the barn. Or was. Marvin hid it in the loft, and he can't get to it now. Doesn't know where it is. Before that, I know some of the stuff he's been on came from my barn." He sat down again with a thud. "That's all I'm saying."

Jonathan leaned forward and sighed. "A lot of bad things have been happening lately revolving around that stuff. Like with Vincent."

"I know."

Jonathan opened his mouth to speak but stopped, turning is head toward Caleb. "Is that all you want to tell me?" he asked.

The debt he was in, the jobs he did for Marvin...those he had to keep to himself. That wasn't information that would help Aryl.

Caleb nodded. "Yeah, that's it."

"Okay." Jonathan paused, glancing at Caleb, just in case. "We'll deal with getting that stuff out of your barn for good as soon as we can. For the time being, we need to help Aryl. And we can use that to our advantage."

Caleb narrowed his eyes. "How so?"

MAURA, Ian, Claire, and Ava listened intently as Jonathan explained the plan the next morning in his living room. They would show up that afternoon at Aryl's for a spontaneous overnight trip. Caleb would be sure to mention that Marvin had just delivered, which would be too hard for Aryl to resist. They would stop by and pick some up before heading out into the woods behind the farm. After they had left, Claire would gather up a few days' worth of his clothes and have them ready when Caleb or Jonathan came to check in with her. Ian would go ahead of them and scout out a good area. He was to choose a good open spot with a solid tree. Jonathan handed him a length of rope to leave under some brush nearby. Maura was in charge of informing his parents and arranging who would bring what food and when. Her most important job was to make sure no one ventured out there for the first three days. Only Ian would know where they were during that time. Caleb would run in for anything they needed and after that, Jonathan would schedule visitors. There would be no work for a few days, but after they got Aryl past the worst of it, Jonathan and Caleb would take turns going out with Ian.

Claire crossed her arms tightly, daring not to get too hopeful.

"Do you think it will work?"

Jonathan raised his shoulders. "I don't know. But we have to try. We'll be over at your place later this afternoon. Go home and act normal." Jonathan held his hand up. "Don't act too surprised to see us. If he smells anything isn't right, he might not go."

Maura gave an indignant huff. "Then we pick his arse up and carry him out there kickin' and screamin'!"

Caleb shuffled with a muted snicker. "It's important to act like last night didn't even happen."

"I will need your help, Maura. Later, after Caleb and I grow tired. Are you strong enough? Tell me honestly because this is going to be nothing short of an exorcism."

She drew herself up tall. "Aye. I'm strong enough. You just let me know when I'm needed."

~

AVA WATCHED from the doorway as Jonathan packed a bag.

"Can you afford to do this?"

"We don't have a choice. Aryl will end up killing himself or someone else if we don't."

"You don't think he had anything to do with Vincent, do you?"

"No," Jonathan said quickly.

"When will you be back?"

"In a few days. Ian will be making the rounds to check on you and Arianna in the meantime, and if you don't want to be alone, you could take the kids and go over there."

She sat on the edge of the bed, looking lost.

"I'm sorry I have to go."

"We'll be all right."

387

"Will we?" Jonathan asked her with a pointed look. He stopped packing and waited for her to answer.

She looked away.

"I don't like having to go away when things aren't right with us."

"What are you talking about, Jon? Things are fine." She picked at the fabric of her skirt.

"No, something's happened. You haven't been the same since the day Patrick left." He sat down on the bed beside her.

"There's nothing to tell." She moved away. Just an inch, but he noticed.

"Look me in the eyes and say that."

She stood up, growing angry. "I really wish you'd just drop it, Jon. This is all your imagination. There's nothing wrong with me." She tried to smile and laugh him off as silly.

He watched her walk out, picked up his bag, and followed her.

"I have to go do this because things are getting out of control with Aryl. If it could wait, I'd put it off and stay here with you."

"I know," she said, facing away and trying to appear busy.

"But when I get back, we're going to talk, and I'm going to find out what's wrong with you."

She squeezed her eyes shut, wishing he'd just leave it alone. "When you get back, you'll see that there is nothing wrong, Jon." Her attempt to hide her irritation failed miserably. They were at an impasse.

"Can I get a kiss goodbye?"

She put on a smile and turned around. "Be safe," she said and brushed her lips over his.

"That's it?"

He leaned in for a real kiss, noticed how she stiffened and stopped. He looked at her for a long moment—so long that she began to squirm. "I love you," he said. "Don't ever forget that." She nodded and took a step back.

"We'll talk when I get home, okay?"

She knew it was the only way to get him to stop so she said okay, and then stepped aside to allow him room to leave.

~

THE SUN HAD WANED but not quite set. Aryl slung his bag over his shoulder. Inside it was a pillow, blanket, a change of clothes, and enough opiates to get through the night.

"Just like when we were kids, huh?" Aryl asked.

"Yeah," Jonathan said with a forced smile. "The good old days."

"Just decided to take a camping trip on a Thursday?" He didn't look suspicious. They caught him at a good moment. The monster had just been fed.

"Life is too short not to be spontaneous," Caleb said. "I looked at Jonathan today and said, 'Let's go camping' and here we are. Marvin dropped off some stuff," he said casually. "We can stop and pick up a few bottles on our way out."

Suddenly, Aryl smiled and slapped him on the back. "Why the hell not. Let's get going then."

"Be careful," Claire said, smoothing out the wrinkles in his shirt. He looked at her with distant, glassy eyes.

"We're just going to build a fire and have some drinks. Sleep under the stars. What's there to worry about?"

"Oh, snakes, spiders, that kind of thing." She brushed off her comment with a shrug and put her hands on his shoulders. "I just want to make sure you come home to me safe. Can you do that, Aryl?"

She couldn't help it, and her lip quivered. She gave him a quick hug, squeezing her eyes shut against the tears.

She watched from the window as Jonathan and Caleb led him away.

"Please come home, Aryl," she whispered as they disappeared around the corner.

JUNE 19, 1931

Aryl stirred at the base of the tree. Shreds of nut casings rained down on him as a pair of squirrels perched on a low branch worked studiously on their breakfast. He brushed them off his forehead clumsily and held it with a long moan. Slowly, he rolled to his side, letting his throbbing head rest on the cool ground.

"I think you drank too much," Jonathan said, eyeing him from his squatting position near the campfire. He sniffed the percolator of fresh coffee and smiled, pouring himself a cup. Aryl's eyes opened a crack, and the light was like razors to his eyes.

He grunted an unintelligible response and slowly pushed himself up to a sitting position, his back resting against the tree. With fine sweat appearing on his brow and the slightest green hue to his face, he waited with closed eyes for the nausea to pass.

"Coffee?" Jonathan asked invitingly, holding up a tin mug.

"No. Not now," Aryl whispered. He could see every beat of his heart like a white throb behind his eyelids.

Jonathan laughed, and it was a little too loud for Aryl's liking.

"What's so damn funny," he grumbled. A few more shards of nutshells fell atop his head as the squirrels peered down curiously as they munched.

"You," Jonathan said. Aryl could hear the smile in his voice, and it irritated him. "You remind me of Caleb."

"How's that?" Aryl asked flatly.

"Well," Jonathan let out a light grunt as he settled himself against a tree, opposite Aryl. "When you died—when we thought you had died, it hit us all hard, but it really did a number on Caleb. It had to have been three solid months he drank himself to sleep in the barn. Either Arianna or I would wake him up damn near every morning with a bucket of cold water."

Aryl opened one eye a tiny slit. "Don't even think about it."

Jonathan smiled. "He woke up many a morning looking like hell." He held his mug out in front of him. "Just like you do now."

Again, the smile in his voice grated on Aryl's nerves. "Where's Caleb?" He opened one eye experimentally, and then the other, just a crack.

"He went for a walk." Jonathan sat with his legs crossed as he watched Aryl. Taking a few deep breaths and stretching his neck slowly to each side, he opened his eyes and surveyed the campsite. It was tidied up and food and cooking gear that wasn't there the night before was arranged on a large tree stump near the campfire. Fire licked at the bottom of a metal pot set over the center of the fire.

"What are you making?" Aryl asked.

"Oatmeal."

"You hate oatmeal."

Jonathan shrugged. "It's what we have."

"I gotta piss. Then I want some of that coffee," Aryl said with a wave of his hand.

Jonathan nodded and waited.

Aryl stood, and in the process of brushing woodland debris from his pants and shirt, he found the thick rope tied around his waist, taut but not constricting, but tethered him to the base of the tree he had passed out under.

"What the hell is this?" he asked, eyebrows raised.

"It would appear to be a rope."

"That much I know, you ass. Why am I tied up?"

"We're gonna get you off that stuff, Aryl," Jonathan said and stretched his legs in front of him, crossing them at the ankles. He leaned his head back to rest on the bark of the tree. "You're destroying yourself, and you're taking Claire with you. We're not gonna let it happen."

He glared at Jonathan, not needing any further clarification. "Untie me," he demanded.

Jonathan shook his head slowly. "Not until you're right."

Aryl burst into a flurry of frustration, jerking at the rope. Losing his balance, he went sprawling into the dirt.

"This isn't funny, Jon. Untie me."

"It isn't meant to be funny." Jonathan stared blankly.

"Look," Aryl held up his hands. "If this is because of what I said last night about Gina, you took it the wrong way."

"There was only one way to take that, Aryl. But no. This isn't for any of the ridiculous shit you said last night."

"What are you going to do then? Keep me tied to a tree like a dog forever? You have to let me go sometime." His face hardened. "Soon as you do, I'll go find more. It's everywhere."

"We're not letting you go until you don't want it anymore."

Aryl stood and bolted toward Jonathan. He folded in half and hit the ground inches from Jonathan's feet.

"I measured that distance before I cut the rope." Jonathan smiled. Aryl growled and cursed, pulling at the rope. He reached behind his back to work at the knot.

"You'll never get that knot undone," Jonathan said and sipped his coffee. "You taught Caleb that knot. It has to be cut."

"You better let me go, Jon," he seethed.

"Or what?"

Aryl didn't have an answer as he stumbled to his feet and glared.

"I found some canvas and poles we can make a shelter for him with," Caleb said stepping into the clearing. "Oh, you're awake."

Aryl glared as he passed by. "No, there's not going to be any shelter. This camping trip is over," Aryl said.

"Not by a long shot," Jonathan said and signaled Caleb to keep working. Aryl growled and yanked on the rope. He walked around the tree and tried unsuccessfully to untie it, and then beat it with growling fury.

Jonathan bent to pour more coffee. "I told you, Aryl. That rope is going to have to be cut. And I'm not cutting it until you're right."

Aryl walked slowly around the base of the tree, watching Caleb. Just as he hammered the first stake in the ground, Aryl yanked it out and threw it far into the woods. He stared at Caleb in defiance. Caleb rose, brushed off his knees, and lumbered after it.

"If you do that again, you'll sleep under the stars," Jonathan warned. Aryl just stared at him, breathing angrily through his nose. Caleb set to work again, and again, Aryl pulled the stake and threw it. As Caleb rose with a sigh, Jonathan raised a hand. "No. I warned him."

Caleb and Jonathan went to work on their tent. It was a sturdy canvas, with enough room for the two to make camp for the duration of what was to come.

"I still have to piss," Aryl said.

Jonathan pointed without looking up. "Behind the tree."

He grumbled, and they heard the rustling of clothing a moment later, but not the telltale sound of relieving oneself.

"I took it, Aryl," Jonathan said intuitively. "And I dumped it out."

"You what?" Aryl shot from around the tree, grabbing Jonathan by the back of the shirt. Jonathan swung around, and his fist met Aryl's jaw. He fell back onto his backside as Caleb watched uncomfortably. Aryl scrambled to his feet and lunged, grabbing Jonathan around the waist, growling into his stomach as Jonathan spun around, sending him into the dirt.

Jonathan stepped away, picking up his end of the canvas to secure to the poles.

"When I get free, I'm gonna kill you," Aryl seethed.

"No, you won't," Jonathan said as he secured his edge of the tent into the ground. "You'll thank me."

"Like hell." He noticed Caleb's furrowed brow and deep-set frown. "Caleb. You know this is wrong."

"No." He looked to Jonathan for reassurance. "It's not wrong. We're trying to help you."

"By tying me up like an animal?"

Jonathan smirked. "That was Caleb's idea."

"Some friend you are," Aryl said, glaring at him.

Caleb stopped working. "I am your friend. I couldn't save you before. I'll be damned if I'm gonna lose you now."

Aryl grabbed his bag and tore out the contents, hoping Jonathan didn't find the bottle he kept for emergencies, deep in a side pocket. Digging in the bottom, he didn't find his bottle.

Instead, he found Maura's heirloom straw cross.

"What the hell is this?" he asked.

"That has gotten a good many people through some really hard times. It's your turn to hold it, Aryl."

He tossed it in the dirt and Jonathan had to resist the urge to punch him. Instead, he picked it up and dusted it off. He gave Aryl a hard shove to the side and wedged the corner of the cross in the tree bark high above Aryl's head.

"This is for your own good," Jonathan said, sitting down and crossing his legs at the ankle. "You might want to get comfortable. We're going to be here awhile."

MLG

Next in the Series:
Drifter – Book Four

ABOUT THE AUTHOR

M. L. Gardner is the bestselling author of the 1929 series. Gardner is frugal to a fault, preserving the old ways of living by canning, cooking from scratch, and woodworking. Nostalgic stories from her grand-mother's life during the Great Depression inspired Gardner to write the 1929 series—as well as her own research into the Roarin' Twenties. She has authored seven books, three novellas, three serials, one book of short stories, and one cookbook. Gardner is married with three kids and three cats.

f

Made in the USA
Las Vegas, NV
30 September 2021